To Ben, as always.
And for my grandma Doris Garland Shukert
(no relation to Judy).

PROLOGUE

February 12, 1938

It was one of those nights in Hollywood, the kind that made gossip columnists and newspapermen and the announcers on newsreels say, "It was one of those nights in Hollywood."

Searchlights swept the starlit sky. Flashbulbs popped, littering the ground with shattered glass like piles of diamonds. Down on Hollywood Boulevard, the marquee of Grauman's Chinese Theater was ablaze with light, its copper roof and red lacquer columns emitting an otherworldly glow that gave it the aura of an ancient sacred temple.

And up the crimson carpet came the deities themselves, wrapped in pale satin and shining furs, striking poses for the photographers, pausing now and then to bestow a ruby-lipped smile or extend a slim gloved hand to one lucky supplicant among the teeming throng of frantic fans.

Deep within the crush of people shouting and begging and brandishing autograph books, two teenage girls held on to each other for dear life.

"Margaret!" the smaller one shrieked. "Somebody just pinched me!"

"Never mind, Doris," the one called Margaret shouted, expertly twisting her slim body this way and that through the crush. "Just keep hold of my hand. If we get separated we'll never find each other again."

Together, they wended their way toward the front, until at last they had a clear view of the blazing marquee.

OLYMPUS STUDIOS PRESENTS
DIANA CHESTERFIELD
IN
MANHATTAN MEMORIES

"Look, Doris," Margaret said excitedly, despite the fact that her head was being wedged beneath the less than fragrant armpit of a tall man in a damp tweed jacket. "Look at that marquee. Isn't it beautiful?"

Squashed behind a very fat woman in a flowered dress, Doris jumped as a flashbulb popped right next to her face. "It's awfully *bright*."

"Well, if you're a star, you get used to that," Margaret said. "Diana Chesterfield told *Picture Palace* that when she was just starting out, she used to practice posing by shining a triple-watt flashlight in her eyes every night in front of the mirror."

Turning her face toward the glare of the flashbulbs, Margaret demonstrated her idol's technique. She had practiced it herself for hours back home in Pasadena.

"Do you think Mickey Rooney will be here?" Doris asked hopefully.

"Doris." Margaret rolled her eyes. "This is an *Olympus* picture."

"So?"

"So Mickey Rooney is under contract at MGM. At Olympus, instead of Mickey Rooney, they have—"

"Jimmy Molloy!" Doris's shrieks of ecstasy pierced the din as Olympus's biggest musical star cavorted down the aisle, his famously dazzling grin calibrated to a blinding level. Eyes bright below his swooping quiff of ginger-colored hair, he clapped a hand over his mouth and blew a big kiss in the girls' direction. The photographers snapped away.

"Oh my Lord!" Doris cried. "I'm going to faint, Margaret. I am positively going to faint! But who's that *girl* with him?" Her eyes narrowed jealously.

Margaret squinted through the lights to where a petite brunette in virginal white lace was signing autographs at the edge of the carpet, just a few feet away from Jimmy. "Oh! That's Gabby Preston."

"Who?"

"Gabby *Preston*. Honestly, Doris, sometimes, I think you don't even read *Picture Palace*. She's that singer that Olympus just signed to a seven-year deal. We heard her on the *Royal Gelatin Hour* on the radio the other day, singing 'My Baby Just Cares for Me,' don't you remember? You thought she was swell?"

3

Doris glowered as Jimmy Molloy put his arms around the girl, playfully kissing her cheek for the photographers. "Well, I don't anymore."

"Oh, it's just for show. They're starring in the new Tully Toynbee picture together. Actors always go out with their co-stars for publicity," Margaret said knowingly.

"Jimmy wouldn't do that. After all, he told *Picture Palace* that his greatest ambition was 'finding true love.'" Doris closed her eyes in a halfway swoon. "Isn't that the most romantic thing you ever heard?"

Margaret laughed at her friend. "Really, Doris, there's no need to be so starstruck. They're just people."

Jimmy and Gabby were halfway up the red carpet when a fresh chorus of screams erupted from the crowd. A gleaming black Duesenberg pulled up, and Dane Forrest, Olympus Studios' most famous leading man, emerged. Standing at the edge of the red carpet, he cast a moody gaze out at the cheering fans, not even bothering to smile for the photographers suddenly swarming around him.

Back home in Pasadena, pictures of Diana Chesterfield might cover Margaret's bedroom walls, but Dane Forrest, in all his brooding, black-haired glory, occupied the otherwise bare place of honor above her bed so he could be the last thing she saw before she went to sleep at night and the first thing she saw when she woke up in the morning. And now here he was, standing ten feet away from her, in the flesh. She didn't know whether to cry or to scream or to be sick. She felt as if she had just swallowed a hummingbird and it was beating its wings against her chest and throat, frantically trying to get out.

"Oooh," Doris murmured teasingly beside her. "Who's star-struck now?"

But Margaret was hardly the only one. Next to the girls, the fat woman in the flowered dress was so overwhelmed it seemed she was about to collapse in a fit. "Mr. Forrest!" she screeched, her face as red as a strawberry. "Over here! Mr. Forrest! *Mr. Forrest! I love you!*"

Yet Dane Forrest seemed to take no notice. Having completed his minute or two of perfunctory posing, he strode purposefully up the red carpet with nary a wave, although he did pass by so close that Margaret thought she caught a musky hint of his cologne wafting from the collar of his immaculately tailored tuxedo. The odor suffused her with such desperate longing that she had to clutch Doris's hand, willing herself not to faint.

Doris was less impressed. "What's his problem? He looks like such a grouch."

"Dane Forrest is *not* a grouch," Margaret insisted. "He's brooding and sensitive and he hates crowds, like all real artists."

"Well, why isn't he with Diana, then?" Dane Forrest and Diana Chesterfield were widely recognized as Hollywood's most beautiful couple, both on- and off-screen. There were regular photographs of them in *Picture Palace* and *Photoplay* and all the magazines dining and dancing and looking terribly glamorous and in love. For him not to escort her to such an important premiere was unthinkable. Doris grinned. "Maybe they broke up, Margie. Maybe there's hope for you yet."

"No." Margaret shook her head. "She's just making a grand entrance. Look. Here she comes now."

At least three spans longer than any of the rest, the approaching limousine was painted the palest, most delicate of eggshell blues. It was a trademark of Diana Chesterfield's that her cars matched her gowns: a coral-pink Rolls-Royce had echoed the spectacular pink tulle (and even more spectacular pink diamonds) she'd worn to the premiere of *Glissando*; a butter-yellow Duesenberg had perfectly complemented the confection of golden taffeta and the blonde mink she had donned for the opening night of *It Happened in Algiers.*

The photographers held their cameras poised in anticipation. Dane Forrest stood at the doors of the theater like a groom at the altar awaiting his bride. The crowd maintained a reverent hush in breathless anticipation of the descent of its idol from her gorgeous conveyance. Margaret gripped Doris's hand, her heart swelling with buoyant adoration and furious envy, her knees spontaneously half bending in a kind of reflexive curtsey.

The car door swung smoothly open.

And a short, balding man with a pencil mustache climbed out of the car and walked sheepishly to the bank of microphones beneath the marquee.

In Glendale and Burbank and Santa Monica and Encino and Tarzana and Hancock Park, the folks listening intently on the radio clearly heard the man's flat voice reading the following statement:

"On behalf of Olympus Studios, I regret to inform you that Diana Chesterfield is sadly unable to be with us tonight. Miss Chesterfield sends her sincerest good wishes and humblest thanks to all her fans, for whose support and admiration she is eternally grateful. She hopes all of you will enjoy her latest picture, *Manhattan Memories.*"

But there in the crowd at Grauman's Chinese Theater that night, all Margaret Frobisher of Pasadena could hear was the question buzzing on everyone's lips, as clearly as if the assembled fans had cried out in unison:

Where is Diana Chesterfield?

And why would she stand up a man like Dane Forrest?

ONE

"Hey, sweetheart, you gonna pay for that?"

The rough voice startled Margaret out of her skin. She tipped forward off the vinyl-covered stool, just managing to grab her glass of chocolate ice cream soda before it deposited its half-melted contents all over the freshly mopped floor of Schwab's Pharmacy.

"I—I'm sorry?" she stammered. "Pay for . . . what?"

The soda jerk tipped his peaked paper cap a few inches back from the expanse of his sweaty forehead. "That rag you got there," he said, angling his bristled chin toward the open copy of *Picture Palace* in front of Margaret on the white Formica lunch counter, where the Technicolor visage of Diana Chesterfield gazed serenely from its glossy pages. "I ain't running no lending library around here, see? You read, you buy. Store policy."

He leaned over the counter for a better look at the magazine, so close that Margaret could smell the sour milk and stale whiskey on his breath. Her hand flew to the gold circle pin fastened to the collar of her sweater. A family heirloom, her parents had presented it to her for her sixteenth birthday the year before, and Margaret soon found herself worrying its little cluster of pearls whenever she got nervous. Somehow the feeling of their smooth, cool surface under the tips of her fingers always seemed to calm her down. "Who you got there? Diana Chesterfield?"

"Yes, sir."

"Always liked her." The man gave an approving nod. "Nice girl."

Margaret gasped. Getting into a conversation with the soda jerk was the last thing she wanted to do; still, she couldn't keep herself from asking. "You don't . . . you don't actually *know* her, do you?"

"Sure do. She'd come in for an egg salad sandwich with french fries every other Tuesday, strict as clockwork. Used to make up her order myself, right here at the counter." His sharp face took on a dreamy look. "She liked my egg salad, Miss Chesterfield. Perfect ratio of mustard to mayonnaise. That's the key, see. You gotta get the proportions right."

"She told you that herself?"

"Well, not exactly. She's one of the quiet ones, you know. Keeps to herself, like. Most of the time she'd send her driver in while she sat pretty in one of them fancy cars of hers. But every so often she'd come in herself with her sunglasses on and sit right on that stool where you're sitting now."

Margaret couldn't suppress the excited shiver that ran down her spine, despite the soda jerk's too-appreciative gaze. When she'd decided that morning to play hooky from her afternoon classes to have a sandwich at Schwab's, she'd hardly supposed she'd be receiving intimate information about the sandwich preferences of her favorite movie star.

Although Margaret had to admit that after the events—or lack thereof—of the premiere at Grauman's, it was decidedly unnerving to hear Diana referred to in the past tense.

"I take it you're a fan of hers?" the man prompted.

A *fan?* Margaret knew practically everything about Diana Chesterfield. She knew her middle name (Constance), her birthday (December 10) and her birthplace (Hampshire, England). She knew her favorite color (lilac); her favorite meal (steak Diane—*bien sûr*—with potatoes dauphinoise); and obviously, her romantic status. Before Margaret had started high school and thus become far too mature for such things, she'd even been the president of the Official Bellefontaine Street Diana Chesterfield Fan Club. True, the only other member was Doris, who had served as a kind of vice president/secretary hybrid, but she had sent away to Olympus Studios for a special Diana Chesterfield Fan Club President badge, which she kept tucked away in her top dresser drawer, along with her film star scrapbook, the dried corsage from the Christmas dance last year when she'd kissed Phipps McKendrick, and Florence the rag doll, whom she hadn't slept with since grade school but couldn't bear to give away. But none of this was anything the soda jerk needed to know about. After all, this was *Schwab's,* the unofficial canteen of the Hollywood colony. He might be a working stiff who dished out french fries and strawberry phosphates for a living, but he was serving them to some of the biggest legends in the movie business.

Margaret decided to play it cool. "Yeah, I guess," she said. "I mean, I've seen all her pictures." *And studied her voice, her walk, her wardrobe, her makeup, and her hairstyle, and can recite every single one of her famous movie moments from memory . . .*

"The latest one too? *Manhattan Mammary* or whatever?" He leered.

Margaret ignored the soda jerk's crudeness, as she imagined the famously genteel Diana Chesterfield herself did on her infrequent sojourns among the little people. "*Manhattan Memories*. Yes, I have." *Three times.* "Actually, my good friend and I even attended the premiere."

"Oh, pardon me." The soda jerk held up his hands. "I didn't realize I was speechifying in front of a . . . whaddyacallit . . . a *premiere attendee.* Don't tell me you're an Oscar winner too."

Margaret blushed. "No. I mean, we weren't guests, exactly. We were just standing in the crowd on Hollywood Boulevard."

"I heard about that." The soda jerk smirked. "Nice of her to show up, wasn't it?"

"Well, like you said, she's known for being *private,*" Margaret said defensively. Plenty of fans grumbled about Diana's legendary reclusiveness, which the tabloids claimed had grown even more pronounced of late, but not Margaret. In fact, the star's lack of accessibility was one of the main reasons Margaret admired her. Diana's mystery made her so glamorous. "Still," Margaret continued, "it is unusual to miss a premiere like that. I suppose she must have been terribly ill."

"That's one way to put it."

12

"Whatever do you mean?"

"*Whatever do you mean?*" With a thrust of his nose in the air and an exaggerated flutter of his eyelashes, he mimicked Margaret's prim private school elocution. "I don't mean to be coarse, but let me put it this way, sister: I ain't expecting Diana Chesterfield to nibble on my egg salad again anytime soon, see?"

"No. I'm afraid I don't," Margaret told him.

"Look. A job like this, you hear things. Someone's getting hitched, I hear about it. Someone's headed for Splitsville, I hear about it. Someone's cracked up or stepping out or headed for the big house—"

"You hear about it."

"You bet. And what I heard, girlie, is that Diana Chesterfield, Our Lady of the Weepies, went missing the day of that premiere."

"That's not fair. She makes comedies too."

"You dumb or something, girlie? I said, Diana Chesterfield is *missing*, and has been ever since that runner she pulled at the premiere of *Manhattan Melodies*."

"*Memories*," Margaret corrected him stubbornly, although she had to admit it *was* an awfully generic title. "But that was *weeks* ago."

"Yup, and I'm telling you she ain't been seen since. Not here, not at the studio, not nowhere. Think about it, sugar. A dame like Chesterfield, sure, she ain't exactly a social animal. But with a new picture out, it's a different story. She's out dancing, dining, you know, living it up. Believe you me, she gets around plenty when she needs the press. But the past six weeks, zip. *Nada*. A feature in *Picture Palace*, sure. They probably put that to bed months ago. But not so much as a mention in the comings and goings. You're such a big fan, you musta noticed. And if you don't think something smells fishy about that, then I got a piece of the Pacific Ocean to sell you. It smells plenty fishy too."

He's right, Margaret thought with a start, her hand flying back up to the comforting smoothness of her little pearl pin. *Diana has been awfully absent from the gossip columns lately.* That was one of the more infuriating things about the picture rags. You'd blow your allowance in anticipation of an exciting new cover story about one of your favorite stars and then realize it was exactly the same article you'd read three months ago, just with the name of the old movie swapped out for the new one. "You don't . . . you don't think something's happened to her?" Margaret asked.

"I don't think," the soda jerk said. "I listen. And there ain't been a word from the studio to listen to, which, let me tell you, says a whole hell of a lot."

"Such as?"

"Such as Leo Karp himself don't have a clue where on God's green earth she is. . . ."

"Anything else?" Margaret was starting to worry.

"Or they're hiding something so bad even the very best liars in the business ain't got a matchstick's chance in hell of figuring out how to cover it up. And if they can't cover it up, it's because that something . . ." Looking around, he leaned in closer. Margaret, steeling herself against the rotten-milk breath and the pale eyeballs all but burning a hole in the front of her sweater, edged toward him. "That something is *irreversible.* Something like . . ."

Gravely, the soda jerk drew a chocolate-flecked index finger across his Adam's apple.

"All right, Wally, I think you've scared the poor girl enough."

In her terror—when she glanced down, she noticed that her knuckles had turned white from clutching her pearls—Margaret had failed to notice the man sitting at the other end of the counter, calmly smoking a cigarette behind the latest *Variety*, so crisp and fresh you could probably still smell the sharpness of the ink wafting from the pages.

"Mr. Julius!" Wally the soda jerk's face turned as white as his apron. "I . . . I didn't even see you there."

"So I gathered. I was wondering what a fella had to do to get a cup of coffee around here. I was beginning to worry I'd have to turn myself into a beautiful blonde. And I'm afraid peroxide wouldn't do a thing for my complexion." The man grinned, a diamond pinky ring flashing as he brought a hand up to his swarthy cheek. Margaret suddenly had the feeling she'd seen him somewhere before. She was sure he wasn't an actor, and with his heavy features, pencil-thin mustache, and wide-shouldered double-breasted suit, he hardly looked like the kind of fellow she'd see having after-tennis cocktails with her parents at the Pasadena Country Club. But judging from Wally's panicked reaction, the man was clearly a "somebody." The only question was which "somebody" he was.

"I'm sorry, sir," Wally gasped. "One coffee, right away, sir. Only . . ." Pressing his thin lips together, he stole a last desperate glance at Margaret. "Only she has to pay for that magazine, see! I ain't running no—"

"Lending library. So I heard." With a chuckle, the man dug a handful of change from the pocket of his gray silk suit pants

15

and deposited it on the counter with a dull thud. The pile of silver was so bright and sparkling new Margaret suspected you could almost see your face in it. She reflexively averted her eyes, as her mother had taught her to do in the "most unlady-like" presence of cold hard cash. But she'd counted at least five silver dollars.

Poor Wally, she thought, watching from the corner of her eye as the soda jerk frantically scooped up the coins before the high roller could change his mind. *That's probably more than he makes in a whole week.*

Before she could utter so much as a thank-you, the man put down his paper and moved a couple of seats over until he was sitting next to her. "You mustn't mind Wally. He's harmless enough. Just looking to pitch some woo your way." His tone was pleasant, but his eyes were hard. Not cruel, exactly, but something about the unsentimental shrewdness of his expression made him seem as though he'd be tough to shock. Or, for that matter, to impress.

"Pitch some . . . *woo?*" she repeated, bewildered.

"Sure, kiddo. You know. Float you some sweet talk. Hit you with the big come-on." The man cast a nonplussed glance over at the defeated Wally, who was desultorily flicking a wet rag against the malt machine at the other end of the counter. "But look, I can't say I blame the poor sap for trying. You're quite an eyeful. A real knockout, if you know what I mean."

"I'm not sure I do."

"Oh, you don't need to put on that modesty song and dance for me. You may be young, duchess, but I can't believe you don't get that sort of thing all the time."

Twisting her pearl pin, Margaret blushed furiously. Unlike

most of the other girls she knew, she wasn't particularly vain. She had never asked for charge accounts at I. Magnin or Saks Fifth Avenue, and according to the inimitable Miss Schoonmaker, in whose odious Poise and Presence class at the Orange Grove Academy for Young Ladies she would be prancing around with a stack of books balanced on her head right now if she weren't playing hooky at Schwab's, she usually went around looking as though she "wouldn't know a curling iron from a five iron." Yet to plead ignorance of the simple fact of her beauty—the buttery hair that fell sleekly to her shoulders; her wide, silvery-blue eyes; the sculptural cast of her sloping cheekbones—was disingenuous at best. *She* might deny she was beautiful, but there would still be the stares to deal with: the knowing winks from boys whose tongues would turn to wood when she tried to talk to them; the guilty leers from her father's stodgy friends and the subsequent chilly smiles of their disapproving wives. But this flashy, fast-talking stranger sitting uninvited beside her, casually lighting another cigarette from the still-burning end of his last, talked about her looks in the same tone he might use to talk about the weather. His disinterest was strangely comforting; it made her feel she could trust him.

"Well, he's got a pretty morbid way of doing it," Margaret said.

"You'll get no arguments from me. But at least now I get to be a hero."

Is this a come-on after all? The soda jerk was one thing, but this man was old enough to be her father. "What's that supposed to mean?"

"What I mean, duchess, is that I'm delighted to inform you

that good old Wally, the Mata Hari of the Malt Machine, is one hundred percent wrong as usual. Your Miss Chesterfield's not been bumped off or knocked off or shuffled off or any other off. Aren't you relieved? Now go on. Smile. I bet a smile from you would be something to see."

"But if no one's seen her in weeks . . . ," Margaret began, "I mean, how can you be sure?"

"Perhaps I ought to be a gentleman and introduce myself," the man said, putting out his hand. "Larry Julius. Director of the publicity department at Olympus Studios."

"You!" Margaret suddenly realized where she'd seen the man before. "From the premiere! You made the announcement about Diana."

"Don't hold that against me. I'm not much of an orator."

"But . . . you must know where she is! You do, don't you?"

"Maybe." Larry Julius looked thoughtful. "If you were Diana Chesterfield, where would you be?"

"In New York, rehearsing a glamorous new play on Broadway," Margaret replied dreamily. "Or in Paris, shopping for all the latest couture fashions. Or in England, at the stately home of a handsome and fabulously rich duke who wants to marry me but I'm not sure I want to give up my career."

Larry Julius laughed. "That all sounds lovely. I'm sure she's doing one or all of those things." *He knows, but he's not telling me,* Margaret thought, but something sharp in his tone warned her not to press any further. Stubbing out his cigarette, Larry gazed pensively at Diana's photo in the still open copy of *Picture Palace* for a moment before looking back at Margaret.

"You an actress, kid?"

18

"No," Margaret said, eyes wide with surprise. "I'm from Pasadena."

Larry Julius's hoot of laughter was so loud and startling that Margaret almost knocked over her chocolate soda again. "'I'm not an actress, I'm from Pasadena!' That's good. I'm going to have to remember that one." Still chuckling, he reached into the inside pocket of his suit jacket, extracting an engraved gold case, which he opened with a smooth click. "I'll tell you what, kiddo. I like you. You got something, some fire under all that finishing-school class. Maybe this is crazy, but if you ever get a yen to see how that little mug of yours would hold up in front of a camera, you let me know."

If nothing else, a childhood of interminable Rotarian dinners and country club dances had taught Margaret how to tell when a business card actually meant business, and the one Larry Julius pressed into her hand was about as business as it got. Cream-colored, almost too thick to bend. The name embossed richly in swooping black Aviator typeface. And at the very top, engraved as deeply as if it had been carved by the finger of God himself, a picture of a lightning bolt crowned with a wreath of laurel. The same one that swooped grandly across the screen, accompanied by a majestic fanfare of trumpets, every time the lights came down for a picture starring Diana Chesterfield or Dane Forrest or Jimmy Molloy.

The logo of Olympus Studios.

"You think I could be in the pictures?" Margaret squeaked. "Me?"

"Well, let's not get carried away." Larry Julius held up his hands. "All I'm talking about is a test. You call up my office, say, 'Hello, this is . . .'"

"Margaret. Margaret Frobisher."

"Frobisher?" Larry Julius made a face. "We can fix that. You call that number and we'll take it from there. I'm not making any promises. But from the looks of you, unless the camera magically reveals you've got a set of antlers and no arms or legs, I think you'll be all right, kid."

Margaret suddenly felt dizzy. This was the sixth time so far this school year she'd worked up the courage to skip out on her afternoon classes and make the long journey by streetcar from Pasadena to Hollywood. She'd get off at the Hollywood Boulevard stop and find a ladies' room somewhere to change clothes. She'd go in looking like a schoolgirl in the navy boiled wool uniform of Orange Grove (which was based on those of its sister academy in Scotland and which no one had ever thought to adapt to the Southern California heat) and emerge a sophisticated starlet in the outfit she'd stashed that morning in her schoolbag: a snug cashmere sweater, a slim pencil skirt, a healthy pucker of the Helena Rubenstein Chinese Red lipstick her mother had strictly forbidden her to wear. She wouldn't do anything special, just sit around at the soda fountain at the Formosa or Schwab's or John's Cafe drinking Cokes and reading magazines until she ran out of money, or walk up and down Highland looking at the palm trees. Sometimes she'd even spot a movie star in the flesh: George Brent working his way through the tuna salad platter at Schwab's, Jackie Coogan reading comic books off the rack, Ann Sheridan combing her famous red hair in the backseat of a car.

But the whole time, in a deep, dark corner of herself she scarcely dared visit, Margaret was hoping that someone would notice *her*. That someone important would see that she was more than just some silly teenage fan, staring and squealing and trying to get up the nerve to ask for an autograph in the little yellow leather album Doris had given her for Christmas. That just like Ann Sheridan or Joan Crawford or Diana Chesterfield, Margaret Frobisher could be a star.

"Do me one favor, huh, kid?" Larry Julius was saying, draining the last of his coffee. "Now I've put the idea in your head, don't go waltzing off to Paramount or MGM, seeing if they've got an eye out. You're a lady, aren't you?"

"I hope so."

"Good. Because every girl we got at Olympus is a lady, and if she isn't, we turn her into one. And we've got a saying: 'A lady leaves the dance with the one that brung her.' You got me?" He peered at her intently. "Say, duchess, you look pale. You feel okay?"

"Yes. I mean . . . it's just . . ."

"Spit it out, kid. You ain't cracking up on me, are you?"

Margaret squeezed her eyes shut tight for a moment, trying to collect her thoughts. "It's just . . . it can't happen like this, can it?"

"Like what?"

"Like this." Margaret gestured toward the counter. "I mean, you can't be a schoolgirl drinking a chocolate soda one minute and a star the next. Things like that don't happen in real life. Things like that only happen in the movies."

Larry Julius put on his hat. "This is Hollywood, kid. Who the hell knows the difference?"

TWO

Amanda Farraday looked like trouble. That was what folks had been saying ever since she was a little girl back in Oklahoma.

She was Norma then, Norma Mae Gustafson, the redheaded daughter of the town drunk. By the age of twelve she already had the kind of body that made the matrons in the front pews of the clapboard church cluck their tongues in disapproval. By the time she was thirteen they'd put that clucking to words.

"Watch out for the Gustafson girl," they'd say to their sons and brothers. Even their husbands. Even their *fathers*, if the old coots looked like they were getting any ideas. "That Gustafson girl looks like trouble."

They were still saying it, for all she knew, but she wasn't around to hear them. She'd gotten so tired of hearing it that she'd run off at fourteen, with no more than the dress on her back and a pickling jar filled with cash from doing things she'd rather not recall, and by doing more of the same, and with no more in her belly most nights than grit and fear, she'd made her way west to Hollywood. But even in the movie colony, where bodies and faces like hers were scarcely in short supply, she knew folks were saying it still.

Harry Gordon had said it, the first time they met, in the casting office in the Olympus lot. It had been just a few weeks ago, but it seemed like a year. Her skin was as soft as silk now, her copper hair sleek, her tapering fingers perfectly manicured. The body, a touch more fashionably slender than in the Oklahoma days, had been encased in a black silk dress that cost a hundred dollars. There was no trace of the rough farm girl who had drawn stares and hisses when she walked down the main road in town every day, and who had cowered on her straw-stuffed mattress every night, hoping her stepfather would come home too drunk to bother her instead of hollering about how the Bible said that since her mother had gone and died, it was Norma's duty to take her place. She knew what he meant by that, and even now it made her shudder to think of it. She had a new name, a new identity, a new life.

And still, Harry Gordon, the young writer once called "the fiercest and freshest voice of our age" by no less an authority than Brooks Atkinson of the *New York Times*, had raked his eyes from the tip of her expensively shod toe to the crown of her shining hair, and murmured, "Here comes trouble."

She was reading for a bit role in a gangster picture he'd done some rewrites on; he—in one of the series of degrading errands he was forced to run in his role as a glorified, and gloriously overpaid, script assistant in Hollywood—was delivering the pages. She didn't get the part, not that day.

But she got something better. She got Harry.

"Oh boy," Harry had said again, after their chaste first kiss outside the Top Hat Café that night. "I'm in trouble now."

Funny, Amanda had thought at the time. Because in all of her eighteen years of life, the only person her astonishing looks had ever brought trouble upon was herself.

Well, not anymore, thought Amanda as she pulled her pearl-gray Packard convertible into Olive Moore's pink gravel drive for what she hoped would be the very last time. *From now on, things are going* my *way.*

It wasn't dark yet, but the party inside Olive's house looked as though it had been going for hours. As she entered the parlor, Amanda heard the pop of a fresh champagne cork, sharp as a gunshot, followed by a chorus of raucous cheers. A plump man in a tailcoat was sprawled across the red velvet love seat as three girls coiled around him, like serpents in satin. Another drunken customer—a small-time producer, Amanda thought— was passed out on the floor, snoring fiercely beneath a pile of feather boas. A washed-up crooner pounded out a popular tune at the white lacquered piano. He seemed to be having a little trouble keeping focused with Dot, a brassy blonde in a lurid violet gown, warbling along at the top of her lungs, although to be fair, the problem wasn't so much with Dot's singing as the fact that she was lying directly across the keyboard.

"*I can't give you anything but love, baby,*" Dot bellowed. "*That's the only thing I've plenty of, BAAAAAAABY!*"

She kicked her leg up in the air, sending an unbuckled evening slipper flying across the room, where it narrowly missed Amanda's head.

Amanda sighed as she ducked. She could hardly pretend to

be shocked at a scene of debauchery. After three years at Olive's house, a girl got used to anything; Lord knew she'd seen worse. But now, with her new life, and Harry, beckoning on the horizon, it all felt so pointless, so embarrassing, so *dirty*. Once, Olive's house had seemed like a refuge. Now it was just another place she had to escape to get where she was going. Just like Hollywood Boulevard, and the dance hall in Nevada, and the orphanage in Denver, an unbroken line reaching all the way back to Oklahoma. Amanda was always on her way somewhere. Sometimes she thought that feeling of moving forward was the only one she trusted. She just wondered whether she'd know when she was *there*.

Carefully stepping around the snoring pile of feathers, Amanda made her way over to Lucy, who was wisely standing as far from the piano as possible and was engaged in an intense conversation with a slender young man in a monocle, who, upon closer inspection, turned out to be a slender young woman. *It takes all kinds*, Amanda thought wearily.

"Ginger!" Lucy exclaimed. It was what all of the girls at Olive's called her. Only Olive knew Amanda's real name, which of course wasn't her real name at all. "Where ya been?"

"Oh, just a little place called *not here*."

Lucy grinned at her companion. "Ginger likes to be mysterious. She thinks it's part of her charm, but the rest of us just find it an awful drag. Ginger, this is Erika. Erika, Ginger. Erika just came here all the way from *Berlin*," Lucy added. "That's in Germany."

"*Gute Nacht, gnädige Fräulein.*" Clicking her heels, the woman in the monocle made a great show of manfully kissing Amanda's hand.

25

"Nice to meet you." Amanda turned to Lucy. "You seen Olive?"

"Sure. She's upstairs, going over figures. Where else? You want a drink or something?"

Amanda smoothed her skirt down the sleek curve of her hips. "I just really have to talk to Olive."

"Suit yourself." Lucy turned back to her companion as Amanda walked away. "A nice girl, that Ginger. I just hope she's not in any *trouble*. . . ."

The office was at the top of the curving staircase, tucked away in a complicated warren of rooms Amanda thought of as Olive's secret hideout. Unlike the rest of the house, which was a riot of feathers and fountains and gilt-covered statues, Olive's private rooms were tastefully furnished: heavy Oriental rugs, moss-green taffeta curtains hung everywhere to muffle the sounds of revelry from below.

But the most tasteful decoration by far was Olive herself, sitting at an antique mahogany desk, her honey-colored head diligently bent over a stack of leather-bound ledgers. "Amanda, dear!" She looked up with a pearly smile. "I didn't expect to see you tonight."

"You got a . . ." Amanda stopped herself. Olive was terribly strict about elocution, insisting that all of her girls speak as correctly as she did. "Do you have a moment?"

"Of course, dear. Come right in." Olive beckoned her with a brisk nod. "Would you like a sherry? I'm having one."

"Sure." *What the hell.* With what she had to say, they were both going to need one.

Olive rose to pour the sherry. Amanda couldn't help smiling at the way the older woman was dressed. Her impeccably tailored black suit and spotless white blouse with the knife-edge pleats at the collar and cuffs had almost certainly come straight from Madame Chanel in Paris. The creamy pearls at her ears and throat were undoubtedly the South Sea's finest, as was the little gold-and-pearl pin she always wore fastened to the shoulder of her jacket. Olive had far more lavish jewels, but Amanda had always loved that pin. It was so sweet, so understated, so *classy*. If she ever had enough money to spare, she was going to buy one just like it.

There was only one conspicuous flaw in Olive's appearance: the thin red scar running down the right side of her face. She always kept it carefully powdered and camouflaged beneath the neatly marcelled waves of her hair. It was the only part of Olive's appearance that hinted at a life more colorful than that of your average society matron, let alone a woman of Olive's profession.

But Olive's views on her "profession" were hardly typical. For one thing, she hated the word *madam*, preferring instead the far more genteel term of *concierge*. When a traditional concierge's client required flowers, the concierge contacted a florist. When the client wanted to go to the theater, the concierge procured tickets. Olive's clients required beautiful girls to go out with them, keep them company, and not ask for much in return, so that was what she provided. Anything that might happen next was solely at the girl's own discretion. Naturally, some of the girl's were a bit more . . . *eager* than others, but the ones who had been around for a while knew you didn't have to try too hard to make a man happy. Amanda had become particularly adept at doing the bare minimum. For the vast majority of Olive's clients, just being seen in public with a girl as gorgeous as "Ginger" was enough. Her beloved Packard convertible hadn't cost her more than a few kisses and a caress or two in the back of a limousine. It was just as Olive had told her the night they'd met, three years ago, when she'd found the fifteen-year-old Amanda begging in the rain on Hollywood Boulevard, hoping to get enough for a flea-infested room and a hot bowl of soup: *It doesn't matter who you are or what you do. If you want to get anywhere in life, you always leave them wanting more.*

"Well?" Olive handed Amanda a tiny crystal glass filled with amber liquid. "What do you need to speak with me about?"

Courage, Amanda thought, swallowing her sherry in one gulp. "I've been offered another job," she said quietly.

"Oh?" Amanda detected a slight tightening around Olive's mouth, but otherwise, her face was as blankly friendly as usual. "And what might that be?"

Amanda took a deep breath. "At Olympus Studios. As a contract player."

Olive allowed herself the daintiest sip of sherry. Her hair fell back as she drank, revealing an extra inch or so of pink scar, and Amanda suddenly thought of Olive's other scar. She'd seen it by accident, when she'd walked into Olive's changing room to borrow a pair of stockings, not realizing Olive was inside. It was a pink line running about five inches along Olive's belly. Amanda had seen a scar like that only once before, when she was a little girl. It was on Mrs. Anderson, the wife of the hired man on her father's farm. When she'd asked her brother Jacob how somebody got a scar like that, he said it was what happened when they had to cut a baby out of your belly. After that, Amanda had tried not to think about Mrs. Anderson's, or Olive's, scar ever again. "I never realized that was something you wanted," Olive was saying.

"Of course I do," Amanda snapped. "I told you the first time we met."

"That's funny. Because the way I remember it, all you wanted at the time was a bed to sleep in and a meal that didn't come out of a garbage can."

She's hurt, Amanda thought suddenly. *She thinks she's given me everything and I'm letting her down.* "Olive, look," she said urgently, leaning over the desk to look directly into the woman's unblinking eyes, "I will always be grateful to you. You took me in when I had nothing, and I will never forget that. But let us also not forget that you've made out pretty damn well too." Amanda let her eyes wander to the huge diamond ring sparkling on Olive's right hand as it fluttered nervously to adjust her collar. *Wonder how much of that rock I paid for.* "Any debt I had to you was settled long ago," she continued firmly. "Now I have a chance to make a fresh start."

Olive drank the last of her sherry and delicately poured herself another glass. "Do the other girls know about this?"

"No. Lucy knows I've been going to the casting office. But she doesn't know I had a screen test or that they offered me a contract. And she won't tell anyone anyway."

"And when they see you in the pictures? Provided things make it that far?"

Amanda understood the implication. She knew very well how the studio system worked. The kind of contract she'd been offered, as a short-term featured player, was no guarantee that she'd even make it into a movie, let alone become a star. It was really nothing more than a holding contract, a small stipend for remaining at the studio's exclusive beck and call until she became successful or they got tired of her, whichever came first. Almost like being somebody's mistress, although as a mistress, Amanda thought, she'd never be so underpaid. But you had to start somewhere, she reasoned. Even Diana Chesterfield had begun her career as a contract player, although given the stories she'd heard lately, perhaps it was better not to think about Diana. Or Dane Forrest, for that matter . . . but Amanda was an expert in not thinking about him. She shrugged. "To the girls, I'm just Ginger. No last name, no real first name. The studio invents new backgrounds for all their players anyway."

"And the press?" Olive asked.

"It'll just be a rumor, and the studio can take care of those," Amanda said. On one of their first dates, Harry had told Amanda all about the various tactics the Olympus publicity department, led by a man named Larry Julius, used to strong-arm the press, bribing or blackmailing editors into running items that flattered its stars and killing stories that did not. There was a story of which he was particularly fond about the treatment received by a reporter who had a scoop about an Olympus star with a major drug problem. "Larry Julius flew out one of Al Capone's goons from Chicago," Harry had told her as excitedly as if he were laying out a grand new idea for a screenplay. "The goon shows up at the newspaper office and the whole time this reporter is typing his column, the guy stands behind his desk with a gun to his back. Then the editor comes over, looks at the goon, says, 'Who the hell are you?' The goon says, 'I'm his brother.' The reporter is too scared to say a word, he just nods, and then the editor invites them both down to the bar for a round on him! So the goon says yes, he'd love to, and the whole time they're drinking in this bar, laughing and joking, this poor reporter's got a snub-nosed Smith and Wesson pressed against his back, not knowing if he's going to live or die. Can you believe it? That's the Olympus publicity department!" Amanda had pretended to be appalled at the story; it was what Harry seemed to expect. But secretly, she was relieved. If any cub reporter someday put two and two together about where he'd seen her before, she sure as hell hoped Larry Julius wouldn't hesitate to pull out the big guns. Literally. "The publicity department will keep it out of the papers," Amanda added, with more confidence than she felt. "May I have another sherry?"

"Help yourself." Olive sat back in her chair, caressing her pearls with her finger. "May I ask the terms of this contract?"

Amanda turned back toward the desk, sherry in hand. "What do you mean, terms?"

"Money, dear. I know what you're worth to me; I want to see if they agree."

"Fifty dollars a week," Amanda mumbled.

"Fifty dollars a week." Olive's perfectly made-up mouth broke into a wide smile. "So I'll keep you on the roster, then."

"No," Amanda said, struggling to keep her voice down. There were few things guaranteed to enrage Olive more than a woman with a raised voice. "You don't understand. This is it for me. I'm done."

"Amanda dear, be sensible." Olive sighed. "Fifty dollars a week might make you a Rockefeller back in Hayseed, Oklahoma, but out here, it's hardly going to keep a girl like you in lipstick and stockings, let alone in Lanvin and Mainbocher. You aren't going to get anywhere in the pictures without looking like a queen, and believe me, my dear, you're not going to do it on fifty dollars a week. Even you aren't that pretty."

"Maybe I'm talented."

Olive pursed her lips. "Amanda, please be practical. There's nothing wrong with supplementing your income with a few carefully chosen patrons. You'd hardly be the first girl on the Olympus lot to do it. Unless there's something holding you back." Olive narrowed her eyes, searching Amanda's face. "Or some*one*."

"I don't know what you mean."

"There's a man. Isn't there." It wasn't a question, so Amanda didn't answer. She didn't have to. "Well, I declare." Olive brought her hands up to her mouth in mock amazement. "I do believe love has finally found Andy Hardy."

"Stop."

"Who is he? He'd have to be rich. A producer? No, that's too obvious. A press agent, maybe? Very useful at the beginning, what he lacks in money he makes up for in connections, but I can't think of one that would turn that copper head. Wait, I know! A moneyman. One of those serious types who come in from New York with a suitcase full of cash and a wife they're wishing away."

"He's a writer, actually," Amanda said quietly.

"A writer." Olive shook her head sadly. "How the mighty have fallen."

"He's brilliant," Amanda insisted. She had hoped to keep Harry out of all this. Even having him be a topic of discussion in this setting seemed disrespectful somehow. But she was damned if she wasn't going to defend him. "He was a playwright in New York before he came to Hollywood. The

New York Times called him the fiercest and freshest voice of our age!"

"Ah." Olive swept a hand around the room, the pleated cuff of her sleeve fluttering like a ghost in its wake. "And tell me, dear, does the fiercest and freshest voice of our age know about any of this?"

Amanda dropped her gaze into her lap, willing away the tears. Leave it to Olive to plunge an arrow into the Achilles' heel of the whole enterprise. Larry Julius might be able to protect her from the newspapers if it suited him, but even he couldn't save her from a broken heart.

"I see," Olive said softly. "And who exactly does he think you are?"

"He thinks I'm a nice, wholesome girl who caught a break." Amanda looked up defiantly. "Nothing that isn't true."

"Oh, Amanda," Olive sighed. "You sweet, brave fool." Smoothing her hair back over her scar, Olive rose to her feet. "Come. I want to show you something."

Olive walked to the far corner of the room, where she swept aside the heavy taffeta curtain to reveal a hidden door. From the cuff of her blouse, she produced a tiny gold key, which she slid into the lock. Behind the door was a small, closetlike room. Amanda could just make out the long shelves lining the walls. Olive flicked a switch, and one by one, the shelves were illuminated, revealing row after row of photographs in gorgeous mirrored frames. As Amanda's eyes adjusted to the sudden burst of refracted light, she saw that all the photographs, every single one, were of a young and beautiful Olive.

Olive, dressed in a Victorian-style gown, with curls cascading winsomely down her back. Olive as Cleopatra, her kohl-lined eyes gazing enigmatically toward the camera. Olive at a movie premiere, diamonds dripping from her wrist as she waved regally to a crowd of adoring fans below a marquee that read in lights:

JOHN GILBERT & OLIVE MOORE
IN
THE EMPRESS OF EL DORADO

"You were . . . in the pictures?" Amanda asked incredulously. "You were a star?"

"I was an *actress*," Olive corrected her. Smiling wistfully, she picked up another photograph and handed it to Amanda. It was a close-up of Olive, young and lovely and unscarred. She wore an old-fashioned nurse's uniform, her hair covered by a starched white cap, her eyes dark and sad over a Cupid's bow mouth. "This was my big hit. *He Never Came Back*. I played a young British nurse who fell in love with a doomed French soldier during the Great War." She picked up another frame, this one holding a yellowing clipping from *Picture Palace* magazine, dated May 14, 1922. It showed a smiling Olive, dressed like a flapper and wearing a feathered headband, under a caption reading *The Next Lillian Gish?*

"So what happened?"

Olive shrugged, but her hand flew up to her scar. "It was the twenties. Short skirts, short hair, short memories. Sound came to pictures, and great stars, far greater than me, came crashing to the ground. A lisp, an accent, a high-pitched voice, and suddenly, you were a nobody."

"But the scar?" The words were out of Amanda's mouth before she could stop them.

"Never mind," Olive said shortly. She put the framed clipping back on the shelf. "The point is, my time in the spotlight was through. Still, I thought I'd be all right. Early retirement wasn't what I had in mind, but I'd made a fair amount of money and invested wisely. Or so I thought."

Amanda felt a sudden lurch of dread. "And then . . ."

"That's right." Olive nodded. "And then 1929. The crash. Oh, I kept myself afloat for a while, selling off my jewelry, piece by piece. When that was gone . . ." A shadow crossed her face, and Amanda thought it was the only time she'd truly seen Olive look old. "Well, I made a living selling the only thing I had left."

"Wasn't there anyone who could help you?"

"Who?" Olive barked out a short laugh. "There was no Olive Moore in those days to pick lost young things off the street."

Amanda blushed. "I mean, your family, or—"

"My family disowned me when I went into the pictures. In their minds, being an actress was no better than being a whore. Ironic, isn't it? As for friends from the old days, well, that's the thing about this town. Picture people are superstitious. They think failure—and success, for that matter—is contagious. When you're on top, everyone wants to be your friend. They'd give you their firstborn child if you asked. But when the chips are down, in this town, there's no such thing as friendship."

"And love?"

"Believe me, there's even less of that."

"Why are you showing me this?" Amanda asked. She was

suddenly furious. How dare Olive mock her one shot at happiness? "Are you trying to make some point? A cautionary tale about not trusting too much in the stock market? Because if that's the case, lesson learned."

"You could certainly do worse than to take financial advice from me." Olive smiled her Cheshire cat smile. "But no, dear, I'm simply reminding you that everyone has a past. And we have no way of knowing when—or how—it might intersect with the present. Or the future."

"Is that a threat?"

"There's no need to be so *unimaginative*. I'm simply advising you to look out for yourself. When you're walking through a nest of vipers, it behooves you to tread carefully. That is to say, give the people what they want."

"I won't keep working for you." Amanda fought to keep calm. "I can't."

"No, I think not," Olive said reflectively. "At least, not for some time. Believe it or not, dear, I'm very fond of you. I've no desire at present to stand in your way. But from time to time I may need to ask a favor of you, and I certainly hope that given our previous *relationship*, you'll find that it's in your best interest to oblige me. After all, why burn bridges with old friends?"

Amanda felt her eyes sting with unshed tears. Desperately, she looked back to the photo of the young Olive waving to her fans from beneath the blazing marquee. She looked truly radiant, glowing with promise and hope and happiness, and suddenly, Amanda saw for the first time that the young Olive's hand was tucked into the crook of a tuxedoed elbow. *A man's elbow.*

The man himself had been carefully folded, or maybe cut, out.

In spite of herself, Amanda felt a flood of compassion for

Olive. *Her heart was broken!* No wonder she was so cynical about friendship, about love. Perhaps the man had been her husband. Perhaps he had left her when her career petered out. It all made sense now. "I understand, Olive," she said, and impulsively seized the older woman's hand. "I understand everything. But it's going to be different for me. Harry loves me. He does. And I love him. We're going to be happy. I'm going to get everything I want out of life, you'll see."

"Amanda, dear," Olive said, gently pulling her hand away, "who are you trying to convince?"

Honestly, Olive Moore thought as she watched the girl walk down the steps, her copper hair glinting in the low lamplight, *I should have been expecting something like this.*

Amanda was too beautiful a girl to stay put forever. It was inevitable that she would want more, but Olive had always expected her to be a bit more *sensible.* She had never been fully apprised of the details of Amanda's former life—the past was not something you talked about at Olive Moore's house—but it was hardly an unfamiliar story: the Oklahoma Dust Bowl, the drunk stepfather who couldn't leave her alone. After all that, she'd figured Amanda would want safety, security, the white picket fence. All the hallmarks of respectability.

And yet here she was, just another starstruck eighteen-year-old girl. A girl in love with a boy and the starry vision of herself she saw in his eyes. A girl in love with her dreams, who thought she was willing to give up anything to make them come true.

Well, Olive had been that girl herself once, and she'd learned

37

that giving things up at the beginning was the easy part. Afterward, when you realized you'd sacrificed all you hadn't even known you wanted until it was too late: that was what was hard.

Sighing, she switched off the closet light and returned to her ledger, to the list of her girls and how much money each of them had brought in that week. *Lucy: $200; Dot: $205; Claudie: $315.*

These are my children, she thought. Not the girls: the numbers. The money. Money was the only thing you could count on, the only thing that mattered. Money kept you safe. It could bring people to you, but it could also keep them away. Sure, you could lose it, but unlike a lover, you could always win it back. And when it came back to you, it came back strong. It came back as if it had never left.

Olive allowed herself a small smile as she ran her finger down the neat list of names, until she came to the one she was looking for.

Ginger: $750.

Olive picked up her heavy fountain pen to strike out the name. She'd be sorry to see her go. The girl was a good earner, no doubt about that. Olive Moore was not a sentimental woman, but she'd meant it when she said she was fond of the girl. Not the way she'd felt about Diana, and not exactly as she might about a daughter, but . . . still . . . there was a kind of protectiveness there. . . .

Olive put down the pen and gulped the rest of her sherry.

She'd leave the roster as it was for now. Just in case Amanda came back.

In Olive Moore's considerable experience, they always came back.

THREE

"Margie! You're going to be famous!"

For such a small person, Doris Winthrop had a screech that could wake the dead. Her round gray eyes bulged with amazement as her mouth hung open, revealing a clump of Margaret's Chinese Red lipstick on her top row of teeth. "I can't believe it! My best friend is going to be a movie star!"

"It's just a screen test," Margaret tried to protest, but she found herself flushing with pleasure nonetheless. Doris's ability to get completely overexcited about things was one of her best qualities. She was exactly the person you wanted to tell first when great things happened, because you knew she would react in the most endearing way. "And I still have to get my parents to agree."

"Ugh." Doris wrinkled her nose. Even in Pasadena, which its denizens liked to say was as stuffy as a head cold, Margaret's parents were notoriously strict. "I see what you mean."

"And even if by some miracle they do let me," Margaret continued, "that doesn't mean I'll pass it. After all, I've never acted before."

"What are you talking about? You played Mercutio in *Romeo and Juliet* and Judith Bliss in *Hay Fever* last year at school and you were swell. Everybody said so."

"That was onstage, though," Margaret said. "The camera is entirely different. I mean, look at all those great Broadway stars who can't make a go of it in Hollywood."

"Can't make a go of it because they're uglies up close, and that, Margie, is one thing you're not. You want to see an ugly? Look at me." Doris excavated a crumpled handkerchief from the detritus of makeup and movie magazines strewn across the carpet of Margaret's bedroom and began to rub her stained teeth furiously in the dressing-table mirror. "I can't so much as get a boy to invite me to *watch* the pictures, let alone be *in* them."

"Doris, you know that's not—"

"No, don't go buttering me up," Doris interrupted. "I'm actually awfully sore at you. Sneaking off to Hollywood all those times without asking me to come along. What, did you think I'd embarrass you or something?"

"Of course not," Margaret murmured, although neither of them had forgotten the time Doris had screamed so loudly when she saw Carole Lombard riding on the beach in Santa Monica that the terrified horse had nearly trampled three small children building sand castles nearby. "I just thought you probably shouldn't miss class, that's all."

Doris rolled her eyes. "Don't remind me. If Mother and Dad

find out I'm failing French, I honestly think they'll cancel my coming-out ball. And then it's goodbye to life."

The coming-out ball. For Margaret, Doris, and practically every last one of their classmates, the upcoming debutante season was supposed to be the highlight of their lives. In just a few short months, it would begin. A debutante was expected to attend the entire whirlwind of parties and teas and dances, but the personal coming-out ball, in which a girl was officially presented to polite society as an eligible young lady suitable for courting, marrying, and replenishing the ranks of Pasadena's better families, was the most important night of all. It was a night that could decide the course of a girl's entire life. True, things had been scaled back in some ways since the Gilded Nineties, when solid gold cutlery and precious gems presented as party favors were the norm. That kind of thing might still fly among the new money crowd in New York, but in ossified Pasadena, whose lofty inhabitants had perhaps been hit slightly harder by the Depression than they cared to admit, such a display would be considered the height of bad taste. Yet to forgo the ritual entirely was unthinkable. After all, if you didn't have a coming-out party, you'd never get a decent man to propose to you, and—as mothers, teachers, and virtually every other adult with whom an Orange Grove girl came into contact expressed repeatedly in manners both implicit and explicit— if you couldn't get a man to propose to you, you might as well be dead.

"I told you I'd help you," Margaret said. "You just need to spend some time on it, that's all."

"Oh, it's no use. It might be French, but it's all Greek to me.

41

The whole class is positively idiotic, anyway. I mean, who are we supposed to speak French to in Pasadena? The gardener?"

"You're good at math," Margaret said, eager to pull her friend out of this familiar rut. "Great, in fact."

"Yes, but math isn't an 'accomplishment' for young ladies, is it?" Doris tossed the scarlet-smeared handkerchief back down to the floor. "Oh, and speaking of young ladies and their dubious accomplishments, Evelyn Gamble was going around telling everyone today that you were absent because you had 'female trouble.'"

"She said *what?*" Margaret blanched. Evelyn Gamble was the privileged daughter of Pasadena's wealthiest family. She was also a six-foot-tall psychopath with the body of a Valkyrie, the brain of a giraffe, and the personality of Vlad the Impaler who never missed a chance to humiliate anyone outside of her tiny clique of appointed lackeys. If Evelyn had started to notice Margaret's absences and saw an opportunity, it could mean big trouble indeed. "When? *Where?*"

"Oh, in Poise and Presence, mostly." Doris hooted. "You should have seen the look on Schoonmaker's face! She went positively white as a sheet." Thrusting her chin in the air, Doris peered cross-eyed down the bridge of her nose in a frighteningly accurate imitation of their teacher. "'Miss Gamble, I have no females in my classroom, only ladies. And a lady never discusses such matters in the presence of other ladies. Therefore, the only *female* present is you.' That told her! The whole class was positively in hysterics."

"Still. I don't know why she has to be so nasty."

"Because she's jealous," Doris said simply. "She may be rich, but you're prettier. And you're the one Phipps McKendrick kept

42

asking for all the slow dances at the Christmas dance, and that's not even counting what happened outside on the golf course after. *Which* no one knows about but me," Doris added hastily. "And Phipps, of course."

"Well, I'm sick to death of it. And the next time I see her I'm going to give her what for."

"You'd better start practicing, then. I mean, just think how jealous she's going to be when she finds you're going to have a screen test in Hollywood! Imagine all the stars you're going to see! You might meet Diana Chesterfield!"

"Doris—" Margaret bit her lip. Should she tell Doris what the soda jerk had said about Diana being missing? Doris would never forgive her if she kept something juicy to herself, but then again, Doris had an awfully big mouth, and the whole Diana thing seemed like awfully sensitive information. . . .

"Or Dane Forrest!" Doris shrieked, before Margaret could make up her mind. "Maybe you'll get to meet Dane Forrest!" Scrambling onto the bed, Doris gazed in mock adoration at the framed photo of the handsome star that hung on the wall above. "Do you think you'll be in a movie where you get to kiss him on the mouth?"

"Doris! Don't be ridiculous."

"Oh, *Dane!*" Doris shrieked, peppering the photo with slurping mock kisses. "I love you! I want to kiss you until our faces melt together and we have only one face!"

"Doris, *stop it!* You'll get lipstick all over him!"

Shrieking with laughter, Doris expertly dodged Margaret's volley of pillows. "Just remember," she shouted, "when you're a big famous star with the world falling at your feet: you leave Jimmy Molloy alone. Jimmy Molloy is *mine!*"

"Just what in the name of heaven is going on in here?"

Looming in the doorway was the well-upholstered figure of Emmeline, looking like someone had set her girdle on fire—while she was still in it. Both girls froze.

"Well?" The housekeeper crossed her arms over her chest. "Would you like to tell me what you're doing up here, screaming your heads off like a couple of banshees?"

"Oh, Emmeline—"

"Don't you 'oh, Emmeline' me, Miss Margaret! Never in all my born days have I heard such hooting and hollering from a pair of young ladies! I don't like to think what the missus must have thought."

"Mother?" Margaret's stomach lurched. "She's home?"

Emmeline's eyes glittered. "And the mister."

"B-but I thought they were dining at the club tonight!" Margaret sputtered.

"There's been a change of plans. They're having their cocktails in the library now. And I hope you don't mind me saying it, Miss Margaret, but you're mighty lucky it was me up here in the next room and not her."

Margaret gasped. Emmeline must have heard everything. This was a catastrophe. She'd counted on time to plan, to figure out the best way to broach the subject with her parents. Now she would have to tell them tonight, before Emmeline could.

"Dinner at home," Emmeline muttered furiously. Clearly, she was in one of her moods. "And me without so much as a joint or a bird for the table. But the missus wants what the missus wants. Young Miss Doris better hightail it on out of here. She'll eat better at her own table tonight than at this one, to be sure. And you, Miss Margaret." The housekeeper rounded on Margaret, her red round face like a thundercloud. "You'd best be downstairs at seven on the dot, scrubbed and dressed something proper, or you'll have hell to catch from the missus." She cast a long look around Margaret's ruined bedroom. "And best clear up this mess or you'll have hell to catch from *me*. I'm a housekeeper, not a chambermaid."

"Jeepers." Doris watched Emmeline's plump form retreat down the carpeted hallway. "What a grouch."

Margaret sighed. "Believe me, if you had to spend all day trapped in this house with my mother, you'd be pretty grouchy too."

fOUR

The tall carved chairs lined the long polished table like faceless sentries. Dark velvet curtains, tightly drawn, seemed to mock even the possibility of light. The food, which Mrs. Frobisher summoned wordlessly from the kitchen course by course by means of a little brass bell, was a punishment in and of itself: brown soup, brown vegetables, brown sauce, brown meat so defiant in its dullness that Margaret sometimes imagined she could hear the recently deceased animal speaking from beyond the grave: *Go on, eat me. I promise you won't enjoy it.*

Other families might playfully tease one another over dinner, sharing stories of their day or raucous jokes, but at the Frobisher table, children were encouraged to be silent, and women ornamental. This left just her father to hold forth, through course after course, on the pressing social issues of the day. If it weren't for the specific targets of his rants, Margaret thought with increasing despair, a casual observer could be forgiven for believing they had somehow time-traveled back to the nineteenth century.

"And as for Roosevelt," Mr. Frobisher was saying, brandishing a forkful of the disconcertingly chewy lamb Emmeline had rustled up from who knew what godforsaken corner of the icebox, "don't even get me started on that traitorous criminal."

He'd gotten started on "that traitorous criminal" during the consommé and hadn't let up since. Franklin Delano Roosevelt, currently in his second term as president, was at the head of a long list of people Lowell Hornsby Frobisher III did not care for, a rogue's gallery that also included (but was hardly limited to) immigrants, Democrats, Communists, Jews, Negroes, Mexicans, Chinese, psychiatrists, interior decorators, hoboes, Catholics, jazz musicians, and so-called warmongers (a term that, in his mind, was generally interchangeable with immigrants, Democrats, Communists, and Jews). Margaret, who was expected to remain dutifully silent throughout her father's oratories, often kept herself sane by running a mental tally of how many times he could mention one of those despised groups in a single sentence.

"As if the blasted New Deal weren't bad enough," her father continued, "with him and his Democrats (*ding!*) giving a bunch of no-good hoboes and immigrants (*ding, ding!*) the rightful property of millions of decent, hardworking Americans like us, now he'll try to drag America into a war with Germany, a war that will benefit absolutely no one except a bunch of warmongering Communists and Jews."

Ding, ding, ding! Margaret thought with satisfaction.

"Never mind the fact that Herr Hitler hasn't given us the

47

slightest indication he has any intention of war." Mr. Frobisher paused to spread a bit of his lamb chop with a dollop of unaccountably olive-colored mint sauce before he continued. "Germany is simply exercising the right of a sovereign nation to arm itself. As for this latest business in Austria, well, the Austrians greeted Herr Hitler with open arms. Two peoples with the same culture, the same language, the same blood; there's no point in keeping them divided."

Mrs. Frobisher nodded vigorously as her husband triumphantly chewed his morsel of meat. "Of course, dear." Her face was as rapt as though she hadn't heard this exact lecture at least a hundred times before. It was an endless source of mystery to Margaret how her mother, capable of striking terror in the stoutest of hearts, could so convincingly play the "little woman" in the presence of her father. It almost gave her a strange kind of hope for her own future as an actress. "Of course, you're perfectly right. Still, there's just something about Mr. Hitler that rubs me the wrong way." Mrs. Frobisher gave a little shake of her head. "I understand he's done *wonderful* things for Germany. But I'm afraid when I see him in the paper, or in the newsreels, I can't help but cringe. With all that shouting, he just seems terribly *uncouth*."

"*Uncouth?*" Mr. Frobisher roared with laughter. "Uncouth indeed! And that, my dear, is precisely why women have no place in politics." He wiped his eyes with the corner of his monogrammed linen napkin. "Herr Hitler is governing a *nation*, Mildred, not presiding over a meeting of the Junior League."

"Oh dear." Mildred Frobisher tittered along gamely. "I suppose I've made myself look rather silly."

"Never mind." Mr. Frobisher patted his stomach. "We'll turn

48

the conversation to something of more interest for you ladies. Let's see . . . Margaret." He turned to his daughter with a start, as though surprised to see she'd been sitting there all this time. "What happened to you today?"

Here it was. The chance she'd been waiting for since she'd come downstairs for dinner. She took a deep breath, struggling to control the butterflies fluttering wildly in her stomach. "Well, Father, actually, my day was rather interesting."

"Oh?" Her mother's tone was superficially friendly, but Margaret could immediately hear the suspicion in her voice, and she knew at once she'd used the wrong word. *Interesting?* The guiding principle of the Frobisher household was to make sure nothing interesting happened, ever. "And just what might you mean by that?"

"Well . . ." Margaret dug her fingernails hard into her palms, steeling herself to continue, and launched into the story she had mentally prepared while dressing. "Ah, you see, after school, some of us girls went to the ice cream parlor."

"Margaret, *really*," her mother scolded. "What have I told you about eating between meals? The beginning of the summer season is just two months away."

"I *know*, Mother," Margaret replied, gritting her teeth. "But I only had a Coke."

"Still. You can't be too careful. With your figure—"

"It was a special occasion!" Margaret blurted out. "It was . . . it was Evelyn Gamble's birthday."

She hadn't planned to say that, but once the lie was out of her mouth, she realized it was the perfect alibi. Her mother was always after her to spend more time with Evelyn Gamble. That the two girls had hated each other virtually their entire lives was irrelevant; in Mildred Frobisher's world, social standing was a much more important reason for being friends with someone than actually enjoying her company. But instead of the expected coo of approval, her mother frowned. "Isn't Evelyn Gamble's birthday in November? As I remember it, the dinner dance the Gambles hosted for her sweet sixteen was just before Thanksgiving."

Rats! Leave it to Mildred Frobisher to remember every party to which the Gambles had reluctantly invited her. "Oh, well, it wasn't her actual birthday! It was her . . . her . . ." Margaret's eyes darted to a crack in the heavy curtains, through which she glimpsed a sliver of purple blossoms from the garden. "It was her . . . jacaranda birthday!"

"Her *what?*"

You want to be an actress, Margie? Start acting. "Her jacaranda birthday. For the . . . the Jacaranda Club. It's kind of a secret . . . a secret society some of us have at school. It's very exclusive, just me and Evelyn and"—she groped for some names of which her mother would approve—"Claire Prince and Mary Ann Nesbit and Jeannie McFarland and Eleanor Gump. And Doris, of course." Even if it was an imaginary club, she didn't want Doris to be left out. "The day you join, that's called your birthday. So today was Evelyn's birthday."

Her mother looked horrified. "You've a secret club you've only just invited Evelyn Gamble to join?"

"Oh no! It's um . . . the one-year anniversary of her joining." Better to get back to the original story, and fast. "Anyway, there we were at the ice cream place, having a swell time . . ." Margaret stopped herself again; *swell*, along with *bucks*, *nuts*, and *dump*, headed the long list of words Mrs.

50

Frobisher deemed unseemly for a proper young lady to use. ". . . I mean, a marvelous time, when a man came up to speak to me."

"A man?" Mr. Frobisher looked up from his mashed potatoes for the first time since he had magnanimously extended his daughter her invitation to speak. "What the devil did he want?"

"Oh, he wasn't being fresh or anything like that. Honest, Father. He was very polite. He just said that he'd noticed me and"—the words came out in a tumble—"and would I want to be an actress and if so then he'd like to give me a screen test."

Her parents stared at her blankly.

Margaret forged on. "You know. It's like a tryout for the pictures. First you have to take a test, to see how you photograph. They have you come in and you play a scene and see if you're any good, and if you pass the test they offer you a contract."

Her father gave her a long, disbelieving look. He opened his mouth as if to say something.

And then, to Margaret's horror, he burst out *laughing*.

"You were right, Margaret," he hooted. "That certainly was very interesting. Very interesting indeed. Mildred, I think you can have Emmeline serve the dessert now."

"*Wait!*" Margaret had not raised her voice to her father since she was an infant mewling in her crib, but desperate times called for desperate measures. "This is real! He's the real McCoy! Just look!" Frantically, she pulled Larry Julius's creamy business card from her satin sash, where she had tucked it for just this moment, and thrust it into her astonished father's hand.

"Julius," her father grunted, examining the card as though it

51

were a square of soiled toilet paper. "What kind of name is that, Roman? He must be a Catholic."

"For Pete's sake, Dad! He's probably a Jew, but who cares about that? This is Olympus Studios!" Margaret was yelling now. It didn't matter anymore. All that mattered was that she got through to them, made them understand how important this was. "I know what you think about actors, but you're wrong. Katharine Hepburn is from a society family. So is Franchot Tone. Diana Chesterfield—well, *Picture Palace* said that Diana Chesterfield happens to be a cousin of the king of England himself! There's no reason a nice girl can't go into the pictures if she wants to! And I want to. I want it more than anything I've ever wanted in my whole life!"

"*ENOUGH!* That is enough!"

Margaret had never heard her mother shout before. It stunned her into silence.

"You are a *lady*, do you understand me?" Mrs. Frobisher hissed. "A *lady*. You are not going into the pictures. You are not even going to think of it. The only thing you are going to do is make a successful debut and find a suitable husband. That is your duty, to your father, to your family, and to me. Anything else, any other course, is unacceptable. Do I make myself clear?" Her face was as white as the china on the table.

"But I—"

"*Do I make myself clear?*"

Briskly, her mother snatched the business card from her father's fingertips, ripped it to pieces, and dropped them into the congealing puddle of sauce and fat on her still full plate. She patted her hair and took a sip of water. Then she reached for her little brass bell.

"Emmeline, see that this goes in the incinerator." Mrs. Frobisher smiled serenely as the quaking housekeeper materialized by her side. "And then you may bring in the dessert."

With her flowered pillow packed tightly around her head to muffle her sobs, Margaret almost didn't hear the first gentle rap of knuckles on her bedroom door.

"Who is it?"

"It's Emmeline. Can I come in?" The housekeeper seemed to take her silence for a yes. "I brought you up some pie. Thought you might be a mite hungry, seeing as you barely touched your supper."

Pushing aside a stack of movie magazines, Emmeline set a domed plate on the desk, lifting the lid to reveal a huge wedge of lemon meringue.

"Take it away. I mustn't eat between meals, after all."

"Aw, now, Miss Margo," Emmeline said, calling her by her childhood nickname. "You mustn't be too hard on your mama. She only wants what's best for you."

"She's got a funny way of showing it."

"Maybe. But she's just doing what she thinks she has to. Now you go on and eat up that pie, 'cause the kitchen's closed for the rest of the night."

Margaret stuck her face partway out from under the pillow. The sticky-sweet aroma of the perfectly browned meringue was too much for her to resist. Resignedly, she reached for the fork, and then she saw it.

Tucked under the folded linen napkin. Each piece had been carefully wiped and dried, then joined to the others with a layer of cellophane tape. The card was smudged and rumpled and still a little greasy to the touch, but it was legible.

Larry Julius. Olympus Studios.

"Emmeline." Margaret's eyes filled with tears. "I . . . How did you . . . How can I ever thank you?"

Emmeline made a harrumphing noise as she gathered up the tray. "Miss Margo, I'm sure I don't know what you're talking about." She paused at the door, looking over her shoulder. "But I'll tell you what: you get me Clark Gable's autograph, we'll call it even."

FIVE

"And step-ball-change, step-ball-change, fan kick, pivot, fan kick, pivot, pirouette . . ."

Suddenly, Gabby Preston felt the scuffed soles of her tap shoes slide out from under her. She let out a little cry of pain as her ankle buckled and she crashed to the ground with a dull thud.

"No! No, no, no, *no!*" Tully Toynbee, Olympus Studios' legendary director and choreographer, brought his bamboo cane down with a smack so savage Gabby jumped, as though the polished floorboards of rehearsal studio #3 were her own skin. "You don't stagger drunkenly into the pirouette like a wino chasing a pigeon. How many times do I have to tell you, Ethel? You have to—"

"Pivot. I know." Gabby hissed through the pain. "And stop calling me Ethel."

"What else am I supposed to call you?"

"Gabby, for a start."

Tully shook his head. "Gabby Preston is the name that was given to an Olympus star. A doctor isn't called a doctor until he's licensed to practice medicine. If you want to be called by the name of a star, you have to earn it. Right now, the only Olympus star I see in this room is Jimmy Molloy."

"Aw, jeez, Tully," Jimmy said. Having naturally pivoted perfectly into *his* pirouette, Jimmy was leaning against the ballet barre at the mirror, his feet splayed in a perfect fourth position. "Give the kid a break, will ya? She's doing the best she can."

"That's unfortunate," Tully sneered. "Because if falling on her ass every five minutes is the best she can do, we're in even bigger trouble than I thought."

Gabby looked anxiously toward her mother, who was perched on her usual folding chair in the corner next to the battered piano. She wasn't going to get any help from that quarter. Viola was wearing what Gabby's older sister Frankie used to call her "thousand-yard vaudeville stare." Gabby had seen it a million times, starting back when she and Frankie were still a double act. "I don't care if you're tired, or sick, or scared," Viola would say, with that stare that peeled paint from the walls of rehearsal halls and dressing rooms and flea-infested vaudeville theaters from Secaucus to San Diego. "You better go out there and sparkle or there's not going to be any dinner tonight, and most likely no breakfast either." So Frankie and Gabby—which was what everyone had called little Ethel ever since she could remember, supposedly because she could never stop talking, she would just gab, gab, gab away—would go on and sparkle, and everything would be all right again.

56

But three years ago, Frankie had run off with Martini the Magnificent, the magician who'd been opening for them in Grand Rapids, and after that, nothing had really been all right again. Gabby had been thirteen, maybe fourteen; she wasn't sure. Viola had always been a little vague about ages—if a theater booker wanted her girls younger, they were younger; if he wanted them older, they were older; and as for birthdays, they just celebrated them all together on Christmas. "If it's good enough for the Baby Jesus," Viola would say, "it's good enough for the Preston girls."

It had been Christmas Day when Frankie eloped with Martini. Gabby had stood in their hotel room in Detroit, in front of the pine branch she and Frankie had stuck in a coffee can and decorated with popcorn strings, watching Viola tear Frankie's goodbye note into little pieces before Gabby even had a chance to see it.

"Good riddance," Viola had said, stuffing the shreds of the note into the little blue velvet pouch where she kept her well-worn rosary and an old pipe that Gabby's father, "that no-good hobo," had left behind. "The act's better off without her anyway. You're the real talent, baby." As much as she missed Frankie, Gabby had to admit it was true. She'd spent ten years trooping around the vaudeville circuit with Frankie in a kiddie sister act, getting nowhere fast; now, after three years on her own, here she was in Hollywood, living in her own little house off Fountain Avenue with a Cadillac in the driveway and Viola in mink, rehearsing a number at Olympus Studios for the newest musical extravaganza by the great genius Tully Toynbee.

In the days when he'd been just a whimsical name at the

end of the opening credits, Gabby had imagined Tully Toynbee as a twinkly, benevolent figure with spectacles and a big white beard: a Santa Claus who made movies instead of toys. Like most things in Hollywood, the fantasy couldn't have been further from the truth. The real Tully Toynbee was a stern, unsmiling taskmaster, knife-edge thin in his skintight pants and India silk scarves, who whacked the backs of her legs with his Japanese bamboo cane whenever she missed a dance step.

Singing was a different story. All she needed was to hear the opening notes of her music, and suddenly it didn't matter that she was barely five feet tall, with stumpy legs and unruly curls the color of mud; when she sang she was beautiful. But Leo Karp, the president of the studio, had told her before she signed her contract that there was no place in the pictures for a singer who didn't dance. So Gabby was in the rehearsal room at dawn and stayed there until nine, ten, eleven o'clock at night, learning everything the studio had to offer: tap, ballet, jazz, ballroom, flamenco, even that newfangled "modern dance" stuff, for which they'd brought in a special teacher, a coat hanger of a woman who'd been flown out from New York City at ten times her usual salary. Gabby had thrown her back out twice. She had a torn muscle in her groin and tendonitis in her right ankle. Her knees ached when it rained—thankfully, not often in Southern California—and her bleeding toes had ruined the inside of every single pair of shoes she owned.

And I'm still a lousy dancer, Gabby thought bitterly. Gingerly, she prodded her throbbing ankle, trying to determine the extent of the damage. *No tears*, she commanded herself, gritting her teeth against the pain. *Sparkle.*

"We'll take it again," Tully said carelessly. "The kick into the pirouette. And try to stay upright this time."

"Just hold on a minute, Tully." Jimmy Molloy, his rosy skin even pinker than usual under its slick sheen of sweat, knelt at Gabby's side. "Are you sure you're all right, Gabs?"

Viola stood up. "Of course she is!"

"I was asking *Gabby*."

"I'm fine," Gabby said quickly. "I'm a trouper, you know that." Even through the pain, she managed to turn the corners of her mouth up in her best sparkling grin, sucking her cheeks in slightly to show her dimples off to their best advantage, the way Viola had taught her. The last thing she wanted was to look like a wimp in front of Jimmy Molloy, who had performed the famous barnyard number in *Donny Daley Had a Farm*, involving a somersault off the top of the corn silo onto the back of a waiting Holstein to a hot jazz arrangement of "Old McDonald," with his ankle fractured in two places.

Jimmy shook his head. "I don't think so." His ginger forelock dangled down his forehead as he prodded the top of Gabby's sore foot with expert fingers. "The tissue here is awfully swollen; the tendon could have snapped. Honestly, I think you'd better see the doctor."

Jimmy pursed his wet rosebud mouth in gentle concern, and Gabby wondered, not for the first time, what it would be like to kiss him. Not a movie kiss, with the klieg lights and microphones all around, and of course, the camera, big as a golf cart and noisy too, practically pressed against their faces. A real kiss. All alone, someplace dark and private. The beach, maybe, walking along the wet sand in their bare feet, the pounding surf ringing in their ears. They'd stop to look up at the full moon, and then Jimmy would turn to her, his beautiful cherub face all glowing and grave, and he'd brush a dark curl away from her cheek, and press his body to hers, and . . .

"The doctor!" Tully brought his cane down with another smack that made even Viola jump. "Why didn't I think of that? That's an excellent idea! By all means, take her to the doctor—"

"Tully—"

"And tell him the only way to save this movie is to amputate both her feet. Then she'll be out of the picture and they'll let me borrow Judy Garland from MGM like I wanted in the first place."

"Mr. Toynbee, *please!*" Viola was already on her feet, her dark eyes large, a hand fluttering beseechingly over the director's chest. "There's no need to talk like that. Gabby is just *fine*. She'll work harder. We'll bring in more private instructors. She'll go from dawn to midnight, if that's what it takes. Won't you, Gabs?"

"Sure," Gabby said weakly.

Tully sighed. "I appreciate your commitment, Mrs. Preston. But I'm afraid all the training in the world would do nothing to address the underlying problem."

"What's that? Tell us and we'll fix it. Cross my heart and hope to die."

Soundlessly, Tully pivoted on the heel of his soft-soled oxford to glare in the mirror at Gabby's body, still crumpled in an undignified heap on the floor. "Observe," he said, pointing his cane at her as though she were a cadaver on the dissection table, "the short neck, the barrel chest. An excellent build for a singer—or indeed, a longshoreman—but for a dancer?" He shook his head. "There's no flexibility, no grace. A dancer's

neck should resemble that of a swan, her carriage, a gazelle's."
He cleared his throat. "The height, or lack thereof, is not ideal,
but since Jimmy is rather . . . *abbreviated* himself, in this case, it's
not a problem. But then there's this." The bamboo cane moved
swiftly down the mirror to point accusingly at Gabby's thigh,
exposed almost in its entirety by the brief rehearsal romper the
studio required her to wear. She knew she should have worn
ballet tights or even stockings, but she'd torn the ones from the
day before, and she'd woken up too late that morning to bother
digging through her laundry pile for an undamaged pair. "No
wonder she can't make the quick turn into the second kick sequence," Tully continued, "with this *thing* quivering, wobbling
about like a jellied ham. You see, Mrs. Preston, the problem
with Gabby isn't that she's a lousy dancer." He brought his cane
down to the wooden floor with a sickening crack. "The problem is that she's just . . . too . . . *fat*."

Going over this scene later in her mind, Gabby would
come up with all kinds of stinging comebacks for Tully Toynbee. Something along the lines of *"The problem with Tully
Toynbee isn't that he's a derivative egomaniac whose pictures
haven't made a dime for at least five years, the problem is that he
has an asshole where his mouth should be."*

All those days and nights slaving at the ballet barre, pushing
through the pain, all that worrying that no matter what she did
she was never going to be good enough? None of it mattered.
Not a damn bit. God, it was almost a relief.

Gabby hauled herself to her feet, pushed open the door, and
ran outside into the dazzling California day. The sun felt deliciously warm and golden on her bare skin. *How long has it been
since I've been in the sun?* she thought.

"Just what the hell do you think you're doing?" Viola ran after Gabby as fast as her short legs could carry her. "Come back here this instant!"

"Leave me alone."

Viola seized her by the arm. "And let you run out of a rehearsal? Over my dead body! You might not care about your professional reputation, but I'll be damned if I got you all the way to Hollywood so you can throw it all away."

I got me to Hollywood, Gabby thought fiercely. *Me and my talent.* "Let me go."

"Where? Where the hell do you think you're going?"

"To the doctor."

"Gabby, listen." Viola's expression softened. "The space is only booked for another hour and a half. You said yourself it was nothing."

"You're right. I did."

"Then come on. Before Tully gets so mad we can use him to cook hot dogs over."

"No, *Mother.* You see, I'm not going to the doctor for my ankle." Dimples sparkling, Gabby let out a terrible joyless cackle. "I'm going so he can make me *thin.*"

SIX

"Frobie! Hey, *Froooobiieee!*"

Evelyn Gamble came sauntering across the Orange Grove Academy hockey field. She was accompanied by Claire Prince and Mary Ann Nesbit, her two dimwitted henchmen: Claire, dainty as a doll, exactly three steps behind Evelyn to the right; Mary Ann, whose enormous, shelflike buttocks would have been her most salient feature if not for the competing gigantism of her chin, three steps back to the left. Their formation was so precise and unchanging that Margaret sometimes wondered if they employed a protractor to assemble a perfect isosceles triangle every time they made a move.

"Where you going, Frooobiiieee?" Evelyn brayed. "We just wanna talk to you!"

"Yeah, Frobie," echoed Claire. "We just wanna talk!"

"Frooobiiieee," added Mary Ann, apparently too uninspired to form a complete sentence.

Margaret felt Doris stiffen. It was difficult to face Evelyn with dignity at the best of times, but doing so while wearing the regulation Orange Grove gym uniform was especially hard. Consisting of an orange blouse paired with deeply unflattering Kelly green bloomers that reached the knee, the gym suits were supposed to be a tribute to the school's namesake, and in one regard they were perfectly successful: in the right breeze, the billowy cut of the bloomers *did* make you look like you had on a diaper full of oranges.

"Hello, Evelyn," Margaret said, drawing her spine into as regal a posture as she could muster. *Think of it as acting*, she told herself. *You are a queen, and they are*—her mind drifted to the lecture Mr. Hawthorne had given earlier that week in European history—*they are but three disfigured peasant women come to beg you to cure their scrofula.* Evelyn quickly fell into step beside her, drawing her wide mouth back in a horrible grin. Her teeth were remarkably long and sharp. "What can I do for you?"

"Well, we heard a rumor about you, and we want to know if it's true," Evelyn said coyly.

Margaret steeled herself for the worst. *Scrofula*, she reminded herself sternly. *They have it.* "What rumor?"

"Well . . ." Evelyn had a rare talent for making innocuous statements while sounding as though she were telling you a pigeon had just gone to the bathroom on your head. "We heard you'd been discovered. By *Hollywood*."

"Oh?" Margaret felt a sudden stab of cold terror shoot through her throat, as though someone had injected a syringe full of ice

64

water into her carotid artery. It had to have been Emmeline. She must have said something to the Gambles' maid at some kind of Pasadena maids' symposium, where all the disgruntled neighborhood domestics gathered together to share cleaning tips and humiliating secrets about the personal lives of their employers. "How on earth did you hear that?"

"Oh, a little bird told me." Evelyn winked at Doris.

Margaret turned toward her friend, whose flush was rapidly spreading to every part of her face, including her quivering—and very beaklike—nose. *"How could you?"*

"I'm sorry," Doris whispered back, her eyes wide with fright. "But I was *defending* you, Margie, honest I was. This morning in Hygiene when we were learning about what not to do with boys, she started going on and on about how the reason you kept missing Schoonmaker's class was because you were sneaking over to St. Paul's and letting the football team do . . ."

"Do what?"

"I don't know. The things we were talking about in Hygiene class. You know. Things only married people are supposed to do."

Margaret closed her eyes. "What happened to 'female trouble'?"

"That was last week. Anyway, I told her to shut her big fat mouth, because the reason was that you'd been chosen by Hollywood and she was going to be sorry when you were a big star." Trembling with fury and fear, Doris bravely stepped forward to address their tormentor directly. "And anyway, it's true! Margie *has* been discovered by Hollywood! And you're just jealous because Phipps McKendrick would never do any of the things Miss Rumplemeyer tells us we're not supposed to do with boys with you. Not if you begged him! Not even"—Doris paused to take a deep breath, urging herself to deliver the knockout blow—"not even if you *paid* him."

"Aw, Frobie. Look how your little woodland creature stands up for you." Evelyn kept smiling her carnivorous smile. "It would almost be sweet if it weren't so unnatural. You do understand what I mean by *unnatural*, don't you, Frobie?"

On the other side of the hockey field, Miss Cumberland, the Orange Grove Academy gym teacher, a stout woman in her midfifties with a leg brace and severe male-pattern baldness, gave a piercing blast on the silver whistle that hung on a cord around her fat neck. A signal that the girls were now supposed to pick up their pace from an amble to a trot, it was universally ignored.

"Does it make you uncomfortable that your so-called best friend is an invert who is unnaturally in love with you, or is that just the way you two are together?" Evelyn asked while Claire and Mary Ann laughed.

Margaret didn't bother to question the logic that had her doing unspeakable things with Phipps McKendrick under the St. Paul's bleachers on the one hand, and on the other, embroiled in the Love That Dared Not Speak Its Name (to quote the title of one of the smutty books her father kept tucked away in his cigar humidor). Reasoning with Evelyn Gamble was like teaching a mountain lion how to crochet: you could try as hard as you pleased, but sooner or later they were both going to get impatient and rip your throat out. "Evelyn, what do you want?"

"I want to know about Hollywood. Is it true?"

"As a matter of fact," Margaret said haughtily, "it is. I happen to have been offered a Hollywood screen test."

Evelyn's long face went white. Whatever she'd been expecting Margaret to say, it hadn't been that. "By whom?"

"Why, Olympus Studios." Margaret was beginning to enjoy herself. It was fun to see Evelyn squirm. "Perhaps you've heard of them? They boast such stars as Diana Chesterfield and Dane Forrest. . . ."

"And Jimmy Molloy," Doris piped up.

"Shut up, dwarfis," Evelyn said.

"A man called Larry Julius spotted me," Margaret continued, in the same studiedly blasé tone of voice that Diana Chesterfield had used in *The HMS Cupid,* when she'd played a daffy countess pretending to be a stowaway in order to win the heart of the devastatingly handsome midshipman. "Obviously, I wouldn't expect anyone outside the industry to recognize the name, but he's the head of the publicity department over at Olympus. *Fearfully* important, you understand, a great friend of *practically* everyone who's anyone, and he thought I'd be a natural. Of course, I haven't decided to accept just yet, but it is terribly *flattering,* if I do say so myself."

Evelyn was practically purple with rage. "I don't believe you."

Margaret stepped forward. "Are you calling me a liar?"

"That's right, Frobie."

"Nobody calls me a liar."

Evelyn smiled her horrible crocodile smile. "Then prove it."

Orange Grove's only working phone box had been a gift from the outgoing senior class of 1934. A glass booth with a sparkling paintwork border of mimosa flowers, it was easy enough to access from the hockey field unseen.

Squeezing five people, two of them rather large, into a booth designed to accommodate one fashionably petite young lady of Orange Grove posed a more significant challenge. Margaret and Evelyn crowded around the receiver, so close they were practically locked in an embrace. Doris was wedged in a ball under the phone itself, like a walnut in its shell; Claire was flattened against the glass like a fly that had caught the wrong end of a swatter. Mary Ann, unable to fit, had to stand outside to keep watch.

Fingers shaking, Margaret maneuvered her arm up the front of Evelyn's blouse to deposit the nickel, still warm from when it had been fished from the depths of the pocket of Mary Ann's capacious bloomers. In her other sweaty palm, she clutched the greasy reconstituted remnants of Larry Julius's card.

"This is the operator. How may I direct your call?"

"Burbank 4716, please."

"Just a moment, please."

The phone seemed to ring for an eternity. Margaret could feel Evelyn's hot breath on her neck. Her own gathered in droplets on the lip of the receiver. Finally, a woman answered. "Olympus Studios. How may I direct your call?"

"Larry Julius's office, please."

"One moment."

Another ring that felt like it lasted a lifetime. From the floor of the booth, Doris let out a little whimper of pain, which Evelyn silenced with a swift kick.

"Ow!" Doris shrieked.

"Larry Julius's office."

"What'd she do that for?"

"Doris, shhh! Hello? Owww!" A set of sharp teeth had just sunk into the flesh of Margaret's ankle.

"Sorry, Margie," Doris whispered. "I was aiming for Evelyn."

"*Be quiet!* Um, is this—"

"May I help you?" The woman sounded annoyed.

"Yes!" Margaret practically shouted. "I mean, hello! I mean, um, who is this?"

"This is Gladys, Mr. Julius's secretary."

"Is Mr. Julius available?"

There was a long, deliberative pause on the part of Gladys. Margaret couldn't blame her. It must have sounded as though she'd just gotten a call from a cage at the zoo. "Who may I say is calling?"

"Frobie! Tell him it's Frooobiiieee!"

"Evelyn, shut *up!*"

"I beg your pardon?"

"There must be something wrong with this connection," Margaret said desperately. *Isn't that the truth.* "Please tell him it's Margaret Frobisher calling."

"Very well, Miss Frobisher. Please hold." There was a brief pause before the woman came back on. "I'm afraid Mr. Julius doesn't know anyone by that name."

Anxiously, Margaret glanced toward Evelyn, but this close, all she could see was teeth. Huge, curving, predatory teeth. "Tell him it's the girl he met at Schwab's last week," she said. "The girl he rescued from Wally the jerky soda jerk. Tell him."

"I really don't think—"

"*Tell him!*"

Gladys sighed. "One moment, please."

"Duchess!" Larry Julius's voice came bubbling down the line, brighter and brasher than she remembered it, but Margaret didn't care. She could have cried with relief. "Ain't this a treat! I figured you chickened out."

"No, of course not," Margaret said. "I just had to . . ." *What? Be threatened by a playground maniac? Risk being grounded forever by my terrifying parents?* "I just had to think things over, that's all."

"Well, your caution speaks very well of you." Larry Julius sounded amused. "Wait . . . hang on just a second, will ya?" Larry put his hand over the receiver. Margaret could hear talking in the background. The voices were muffled, but she made out a few clear words: "meeting" and "Chesterfield." Margaret gasped. *Diana Chesterfield.* There was some kind of meeting about Diana Chesterfield! Perhaps she'd been around all this time after all? Or perhaps . . .

"What is it?" Doris whispered. "What's he saying?"

"Margaret, you still there?" Larry's voice came back clearly on the line.

"Yes," Margaret said shakily. "Yes, sir."

"Listen, honey, something's come up and I've got to run. But you just give your particulars to Gladys and we'll be in touch."

"M-my . . . particulars?" Margaret stammered. "Couldn't we arrange everything now?"

"Now?" Larry sounded annoyed. "Look, honey, I'm a busy man. You got me on the phone once, but I'm not exactly a social secretary, you get me?"

"No, of course not, I'm sorry—"

With a hollow click, the original operator got on the line. "Please deposit five cents for an additional three minutes."

70

Oh God. Frantically, Margaret searched her pockets for change. Larry Julius's laughter echoed down the line. "Duchess, are you calling me from a pay phone?"

A trickle of sweat raced down Margaret's face from her hairline and fell directly into her eye. "I . . . I guess so."

Larry Julius was still laughing. "And the Great Depression has finally reached the hallowed streets of Pasadena. All right, you win. Gladys?"

"Yes, sir?" *Has his secretary been listening all this time?* Margaret wondered.

"See if there's a soundstage available a week from Thursday. Tell Kurtzman we'll need him to direct. Margaret, you call to confirm. That is, if you can come up with another nickel."

"Oh, Mr. Julius—" Margaret began, but she was interrupted by Mary Ann Nesbit, banging furiously on the side of the phone box.

For on the horizon loomed the unmistakable receding hairline of Miss Cumberland the gym teacher. Mary Ann was already running down the hill to safety, Claire Prince in hot pursuit.

"Margaret!" Doris screamed. "Run! Run!"

Margaret ran. She jumped over the gate and under the box hedge; she ran the length of the hedgerows and down the hillock. She ran all the thoughts of Hollywood and Larry Julius and Diana Chesterfield clear out of her head. She ran so fast and so furiously she didn't even notice Evelyn Gamble crouching on the floor of the phone box, quietly pocketing a small square of crumpled card.

SEVEN

Olympus Studios was like another world.

Set on the side of a hill, it was partially hidden by fat clouds, like some artist's rendering of the mythological home of the Greek gods that was its namesake. Rows of fragrant eucalyptus trees flanked the winding path that led to a tall outer wall of glittering pink stone. Metro-Goldwyn-Mayer, Olympus's chief rival studio, had a famous slogan: "More Stars Than There Are in Heaven." Maybe MGM had more stars, Margaret thought, gazing up at the enormous wrought iron gate, worked in an Art Deco motif of moons and shooting stars. But what did it matter, when entering the gates of Olympus was like entering the gates of heaven itself?

Margaret had awoken that morning at the crack of dawn. Her parents were still snoring away in their separate bedrooms just down the hall when she crept out of bed, quiet as a mouse.

She scrubbed her face and neck with cold water from the porcelain washbowl on her dressing table—she couldn't risk the noise of the running water from the bath—and carefully undid the big hot rollers she'd put in all around the bottom of her hair and covered tightly with a piece of pink netting the night before.

From her dresser drawer, she took out the apricot silk slip with lace insets that she'd secreted from her mother's drawer a few days earlier. The latest issue of *Picture Palace* had run an interview with Joan Crawford in which the star waxed rhapsodic for several paragraphs about the importance of beautiful lingerie. "For me," Joan had said, "it is the most important thing I put on. A modern American woman knows her most impenetrable armor is an exquisite foundation." Joan Crawford wasn't Margaret's favorite actress, not by a long shot. When Margaret was a child, her mother used to say she would always catch her being naughty because "I have eyes in the back of my head." For some reason, Margaret had pictured Joan Crawford's eyes staring out from just above Mrs. Frobisher's smooth marcelled chignon, a deeply unsettling image she'd never quite been able to shake. Still, Joan Crawford always seemed confident. Terrifying, but confident. And today of all days, confidence was what Margaret needed most.

Over the slip, she put on the brand-new suit her mother had bought her at Bullocks on Wilshire Boulevard: a gorgeous cerulean crepe with a diamond-shaped velveteen panel down the front of the jacket. She was supposed to be saving it for her debutante wardrobe, but it made her waist look about ten inches around. Her little pearl pin went on the jacket, of course. Then a swipe of Scarlet Crush, a spritz of Evening in Paris perfume—

73

contraband and, like the lipstick, surreptitiously paid for with weeks of unused milk money—and finally, she dared to look at her finished reflection in the mirror. Not bad, not bad at all. But a movie star?

Well, Margaret thought, *that's what I'm going to find out.*

There was a little security hut off to the side of the main gate. She was nervously whispering her name to the noticeably sleepy guard when an extremely thin young man with an undone bow tie flapping around his scrawny neck leapt toward her. "Miss Frobisher?"

"Yes?"

"Welcome! I'm Stanley, one of Mr. Julius's assistants. I'm here to see that you get where you need to go."

"Thank you, Mr. Stanley. That's very kind."

"Oh, no, Miss Frobisher. Stanley's my first name."

"It is?" Margaret blushed. She was hardly accustomed to being on a first-name basis with strange men. "And you don't mind my calling you that?"

"Unless you can pronounce Cimenoczolowski."

"I guess Stanley it is."

Stanley guffawed, a bit more loudly, Margaret felt, than her feeble joke deserved, even locating a skinny knee inside his loose tweed slacks to theatrically slap. "You're a keen one, Miss Frobisher, that's for darn sure. Mr. Julius sure knows how to pick 'em."

'Em? Margaret wanted to ask. *Which 'em? How many of 'em?* But she held her tongue. After all, a true star—a Diana Chesterfield sort of star—wouldn't ask such questions. *Confidence,* she thought. *Just think of your underwear and you can do anything.*

"Do you have an automobile?" Stanley asked.

Margaret shook her head. "I took the streetcar."

Stanley nodded approvingly. "That's good. Mr. Karp will like to hear that. He likes a practical girl."

Margaret suddenly felt dizzy. The idea of Leo Karp, the president of Olympus Studios, being even remotely aware of her existence made her stomach flip dangerously. "We're not going to see Mr. Karp now, are we?"

"Oh gosh, no, Miss Frobisher! Hardly anyone gets in to see Mr. Karp. I haven't even met him, and I've been working here for more than three years. I did get to wash his car once." Stanley's eyes took on a dreamy cast. "A '36 Duesenberg. Absolutely gorgeous. Cream exterior, leather seats the color of butter. I rubbed it with a cloth diaper after and it gleamed like a South Sea pearl." Abruptly, he cleared his throat, shaking himself out of his reverie. "But that's Leo Karp for you. Likes to have the best of everything, no matter what. That kind of attention to detail is an ethos you'll see repeated, ah, repeatedly throughout the Olympus grounds." Straightening his bow tie, he tentatively proffered an arm. "Now, Miss Frobisher. Please allow me to welcome you to the Dream Factory."

The Dream Factory.

Margaret had heard that phrase a thousand times; she'd always thought it was one of those hazy terms, like Tinseltown or La-La Land, that movie magazines and gossip rags like to toss around to make it seem as if Hollywood were a land apart, a through-the-looking-glass kind of place where the rules of the real world did not apply. She'd never considered that it might have something to do with the fact that being on the studio lot felt a lot like stepping into a dream.

Yet that was exactly how it felt. For example, here they were walking down a broad paved street lined with stucco bungalows and neatly kept flower beds. It was a scene that would not have been out of place in any middle-class Southern California suburb . . . until a man in full cowboy regalia appeared on the sidewalk, swinging his lasso absentmindedly behind him like a tail. The clattering pickup truck that came driving by couldn't have been more prosaic, except for the gaggle of Marie Antoinette–style courtesans piled in the back, cigarettes dangling from their rouged lips as they held their towering powdered wigs in place. On an ordinary park bench, a very large man dressed as a pirate sat calmly sharing a sandwich from a paper bag with his companion, who was dressed in blue maintenance coveralls and holding a large broom. Olympus was like a fantastical dream, but it was real.

"The main grounds of Olympus—what we on the lot call the Village—are laid out to resemble the prototypical American small town," Stanley was saying. He gestured toward a row of cheerful-looking white stone storefronts punctuated by old-fashioned lampposts and a red and blue striped barber's pole. "We are now walking down Main Street, where one can find the studio's own full-time barber shop, dentist's office, doctor's office, a general store, an all-access branch of the First National Bank, and a post office. We even have our own zip code."

"My goodness!"

"That's right. Everything one needs for a healthy civic life. Olympus is primarily a place of business, but it's also a thriving community. And that, of course, includes all types of fun and games. Outside the Village, we have a year-round ice-skating rink, three Olympic-sized pools, tennis facilities, and extensive

76

horse stables. These are all open to Olympus employees, providing they aren't being used for filming. Our world-famous studio commissary serves gourmet breakfasts, lunches, and dinners from five a.m. until midnight. To your right you'll see the Olympus movie theater, which features five showings a day of beloved pictures from the Olympus vaults for anyone who needs an hour or two of happy relaxation, or perhaps a reminder of why we're all here, doing what we do."

Margaret's gloved hand flew to her mouth. "You mean you can just watch movies again and again?" How often had she longed to see a favorite movie one more time after it had left the theater for good? The idea was positively magical.

"Sure thing. It's a different picture every day. And it only costs a dollar."

"A *dollar?*" The movie theater in Pasadena cost twenty-five cents, and that bought you a double feature with the newsreel and the cartoon. On Thursday nights, they even threw in a small box of popcorn. Margaret shook her head. "I knew it was too good to be true."

Stanley grinned. "Not a *real* dollar. An Olympus dollar. The only currency accepted by any establishment on the Olympus lot."

Taking out a worn leather wallet from his pocket, he handed Margaret a small, rose-colored bill. It was smaller and printed on more delicate paper than regular money, and trimmed all around with silver foil. One side was printed with the Olympus logo of a lightning bolt surrounded by a crown of laurel leaves, beneath which was the Olympus motto: *Like Heaven Itself.* On the other side was a miniature portrait of Diana Chesterfield in a diamond tiara. Her image, limpidly beautiful as always, was encircled by a narrow ribbon upon which was engraved in elaborate cursive so minuscule it could have been written by a fairy: *Diana Chesterfield, Box Office Queen 1937.*

God, Margaret thought, *she's even on the money. If only she were here in real life.*

"You get issued a certain sum every payday, along with your paycheck," Stanley continued. "The props department prints up a new batch every January first, with the faces of the stars who did the biggest box office the previous year. Mr. Karp started it up ten years ago, when the silents went out. Everyone was awful blue back then, and he thought it would help morale. You know, incentive. Your pictures make money, you get your face on it." He took in Margaret's rapt expression. "I'm guessing you're a fan of Miss Chesterfield's?"

"Oh yes." Margaret nodded fervently. "She's my absolute favorite actress of all time."

"You don't say. Well, in that case, you can keep that one. I can never spend 'em all anyway."

"You don't think we'll *see* Miss Chesterfield, do you?" Margaret asked hopefully.

Stanley's eyes darted sharply to the side. "What do you mean by that?"

Margaret's heart leapt in her chest. It had slipped her mind in all the excitement. *Wally the soda jerk was right,* she thought. *There is something fishy going on with Diana.* "N-nothing," she stammered. "Just that I'm a huge fan, and it would be such a thrill to meet her."

"Well, perhaps we can arrange something. In the future, of course." Stanley gave her a tight smile. "But look at the time!

We've got to get you into wardrobe or there's going to be trouble. Hey, watch it!"

There was a loud skidding noise, and a golf cart pulled up beside them, nearly plowing Margaret over. A round-faced man in a flat cap hung out the side.

"Jesus, Al!" Stanley exclaimed. "Watch where you're driving that thing!"

"Whatever you say, Chimney," said Al. He looked Margaret up and down with his beady eyes. "Who's the twist?"

"Tryout. Stage fourteen. I'm the walker."

"Ditch her. I'm on orders. Julius needs you in publicity stat. We got a major SOS regarding the Ice Princess, and the boss says there's no time to lose."

SOS? Margaret glanced down at the bill she still clutched in her hand. Diana's crowned image was drained of color, but you could still somehow feel the clear ice blue of her eyes. *The Ice Princess?* Were they talking about Diana?

Stanley turned to her, a newly tense expression on his bony face. "It's soundstage fourteen. All the way down this road, then make a left. You think you can find it?"

"Chimney! *Tempus fugit!*"

"You go ahead," Margaret assured him. "I'll be fine."

But as soon as they sped away, the well-ordered streets of Olympus seemed to bleed into chaos. Swarms of funny little carts, identical to the one that had carried off Stanley, sped by, laden with racks of costumes or camera equipment. Script assistants on bicycles whizzed by with piles of paper balanced precariously on the handlebars, sometimes stacked so high she wondered how they could see where they were going. A gleaming

79

white limousine made its stately progress up the street, perhaps bearing a star deemed too important to be seen traveling—at least, not before the hair and makeup department had worked its magic. Margaret tried to peer through its darkened windows for a better look. Could that be Diana? Had that been Diana? And would that be Margaret herself someday?

Stop it, Margaret, she said to herself, shaking her head. *You've got Diana Chesterfield on the brain.*

"Look out below!"

Before she could figure out where the shout was coming from, a heavy black telephone came flying out a second-story window, narrowly missing her head as it shattered on the pavement with a deafening crash. On the balcony, just above the silver lettering over the doorway that spelled out *Writers' Building,* stood a young man, his arm still poised in midair. "Notes, Howard?" the young man shouted, with a mixture of equal parts fury and glee, down at the broken phone. "That's what I think of your goddamn notes, you *prick!*"

Even if he hadn't nearly killed her with a flying telephone, Margaret would have thought he was an extraordinarily curious-looking fellow. His frayed sweater, thick and navy blue, like the kind that sailors wore, hung loosely on his slight frame. Behind his horn-rimmed glasses, Margaret thought his eyes were an inky, bottomless black.

Running his hands through his unruly stack of black hair, he flashed a malevolent grin in Margaret's direction. "Hang that up for me, will ya, sweetheart?"

Still in shock, Margaret half lunged toward the splintered receiver when she heard a breathy coo from behind her. "Harry, darling, you *really* must learn to assert yourself if you want to get *anywhere* in Hollywood."

The young man, Harry, grinned in response. Margaret couldn't catch a glimpse of the girl's face as she slipped past her and up the stairs toward the young man; she saw only a curtain of gleaming red hair sweeping her shoulders and, clad in a tight-fitting black skirt, a backside that Margaret could tell was rather spectacular, even from her limited experience. No sooner had the girl reached the young man than he swept her into a passionate embrace, pressing his body against hers and gazing into her still-hidden face as though she were the only woman in the world.

Then he swept her into his waiting office and shut the door.

Now, that, Margaret thought, *is Hollywood.*

EIGHT

"What was *that* all about?" Amanda giggled, when they came up for air.

Harry Gordon raked his hands down her back, his lips still pressed warmly against the soft skin of her neck. "Oh, that. I think you know."

Amanda giggled. "Not *us*, silly. I mean, I don't know if you noticed, but you just hurled a phone off a balcony. You almost killed that poor terrified blond girl."

"Oh, *that*." Harry pulled away from her, frowning. As he put his thick glasses back on, Amanda studied his face. It wasn't that Harry was exactly handsome. With his too-crooked nose and too-wild hair, nobody would ever confuse him with a matinee idol. But every time Amanda saw him, she thought she noticed something she'd never seen before. How the third finger on his right hand had a permanently ink-stained callus from long hours with the fountain pen. How the tiny mole under his left eye seemed to make it sparkle more brightly than the right. She could look at him forever. "That was just my troglodyte producer." Harry scowled. "If only we'd done a face-to-face. I could have given him the old defenestration, otherwise known as the Coney Island Special. Solve all my problems in one fell swoop."

"What's he giving you grief about this time?"

"The Chesterfield picture," Harry groaned. "*The Nine Days' Queen*. He's read the latest draft, and he thinks it's too depressing when Lady Jane Grey is beheaded for treason. Wants to know if I can have her and the husband make a run for it in the end, or better yet, figure out some way she gets to be Queen of England after all. You know, slap a happy ending on it. Make it peppy." Harry shook his head in disbelief. "'Can you make it peppier?' He actually *said* that."

"Well . . . can you?"

"No, Amanda, I can't," Harry replied testily. "You see, *The Nine Days' Queen* happens to be based on actual historical events, events that I have been researching in *detail* ever since the studio brought me out to this *farkakte* place. Not to mention the fact that the entire thing is an allegory for how totalitarian governments force their citizens into complicity with evil, which you'd think might have *some* resonance given what's happening in Europe right now, but I'm not even going to *talk* about that, lest I scare the sniveling cowards in the production department off completely."

"Harry—"

"I mean, God forbid we try to *say* something with our pictures, right? And of course, I have to pretend I don't know that all these sudden 'issues' with the script isn't them just stalling for time because no one knows where the hell Diana Chesterfield is."

Amanda frowned. Like everyone around the studio lot, she'd heard things about Diana being missing, but picture people were highly prone to exaggeration, and anyway, it seemed so impossible. A major star like Diana was more than a person. She was a vast moneymaking enterprise, practically a whole corporation. For her to simply vanish from the Olympus lot without a trace was like Wall Street suddenly forgetting where it had put U.S. Steel. "Really? I thought that was just a rumor."

"Funny thing about rumors," Harry said bitterly, "they sometimes turn out to be true. Isn't that just my luck? Months out here, I finally get a script out of the starting gate with these clowns and the star disappears. Damn these Hollywood bastards!" Harry slammed his fist down on the desk. An untidy stack of books fell to the already litter-covered floor with a crash. "I never should have left New York."

Amanda looked down at the ground, consciously hiding the hurt in her face. "If you'd never left New York, you'd never have met me," she said in a small voice.

Harry's face softened. "You're right." He ran his finger tenderly down the curve of her cheek, his mouth set in a solemn line. *Promise you won't go back to New York*, Amanda yearned to say. *Promise you'll never leave me.* "Look," Harry said. "Let's forget all about this. It's payday, I've got money in my pocket. We'll go to the Polo Club."

Amanda laughed. "You mean the Polo Lounge?"

"Sure." Harry grinned, unembarrassed by his mistake. "See how the other half lives, have white wine en flambé and

84

all that jazz. I'll even ring down to wardrobe and see if they can send up some moth-eaten penguin suit in my size. Whaddya say?"

Amanda bit her lip. "Oh, Harry, that sounds like heaven . . ."

Harry's face fell. "But?"

Don't look at me like that, Amanda thought desperately. *I can't stand it.* "I . . . already have plans for dinner."

"So cancel."

Amanda shook her head sadly. "I can't. It's with a producer over in Max Wineman's division."

"I see." Pushing her away, Harry turned toward his desk. "I see. Well, I'd better get back to work."

"Harry, no! You don't understand—"

"I *do* understand. You've got a date with a bigger fish than me. Well, I hope you hook him. I hope you reel him in real good."

"It's not like that! Come on, the guy is probably old enough to be my father."

"Do you honestly think that makes it *better?*"

"Harry, it's just business, honest!" Amanda pleaded, desperate to make him see. "The guy is looking for a fresh face to put in the new detective picture he's making with Spencer Tracy over at Metro. Larry Julius's office set it up, for chrissake."

Harry's voice was dangerously soft. "I always knew Larry Julius was a thug. I didn't realize he was also a pimp."

"Harry, please . . . ," Amanda croaked. She felt as if she had just been punched in the gut with a fist made of ice. "You don't know what you're saying. . . ."

"Oh, come on, Amanda! You think I don't know how it works? 'Oh, *Harry,*'" he simpered, imitating Amanda's breathy coo, "'*he might give me a part in his new picture.*' Well, I can't

85

stand it! I can't stand the thought of him touching you, looking at you, *leering* at you, thinking about all the things he'd like to do to you, if you only give him the chance." Harry was shouting now. "You're supposed to be my girl, Amanda!"

"But I am!" Amanda cried out. "I am your girl!"

Harry suddenly lunged for her, catching her in a crushing embrace, his lips devouring her, his breath burning her neck as they tumbled to the floor. Urgently, his warm hands undid the buttons of her jacket. *He thinks I'm a nice girl,* Amanda thought wildly. *Do nice girls let their boyfriends touch them this way?*

"Harry—wait. . . ."

"You're right. You're right." Harry pulled away. "I don't know what got into me. Well, I mean, I *know* . . . but I shouldn't have let myself get carried away like that. I'm sorry."

"That's . . . that's okay," Amanda stammered in bewilderment. This was all so new to her, these rules of courtship that Harry seemed to know automatically and to obey effortlessly.

"You're a special girl, Amanda. A *rare* girl." Harry stroked her cheek, as gently as if she were made of glass. "And your first time should be special too."

"My first time?" Quickly, she dipped her head, praying that Harry wouldn't see the panic in her eyes. The memories came unbidden: the dull thud of her stepfather's heavy tread in the hall, the click of the doorknob as it turned. *No,* she told herself firmly. *That happened to someone else.* But the other times, the years at Olive's house, well . . . maybe if she just tried, if she could just forget hard enough, a year from now they would have happened to someone else too.

"It's nothing to be ashamed of," Harry was saying, although he was blushing. "With the right person, it can be beautiful.

Being with someone who"—he hesitated—"who really *knows* you. Who knows everything about you. And loves you, for everything that you are."

Everything? Amanda thought ruefully.

"I want to give that to you, Amanda," Harry was saying. His open, hopeful face shone with love. "When you're ready. I want to be your first."

Leave it to Harry Gordon to want the one thing she couldn't give him.

NINE

The Olympus soundstage was a huge, windowless barn big enough to hold an airplane, or maybe two. Painted black all over. Lights dangled from the ceiling; wires were taped haphazardly across the floor. Men swarmed all around, tools strapped to their belts, fussing and cursing over towering pieces of odd machinery the likes of which Margaret had never seen before. *This is the place,* she thought with a shiver of terrified excitement. *The place that will decide my fate.*

A stagehand directed her to the makeshift wardrobe department, a corner sectioned off with some curtains and a sheet of plywood. In a folding chair beside a single full-length mirror sat a middle-aged woman with a cigarette between her lips, a tape measure draped around her neck, and a red scarf tied around her head, its ends pointing upward like the ears of an alarmed terrier.

"Yummrrtsst?" the woman said as Margaret tiptoed inside.

"I'm sorry?"

With great reluctance, the woman removed the cigarette from her mouth and set it carefully on the edge of an ashtray already overflowing with lipstick-smeared butts. "You the test?" She raked her eyes over Margaret yet managed to betray not the barest flicker of interest.

"Yes. I'm—"

"You're late."

"I'm sorry. The gentleman who was showing me around was called away, and I'm afraid I got a little bit lost." *And a little bit almost killed by a projectile telephone,* she thought, but it seemed wiser not to mention that.

"You shouldn't be late. They don't like it."

"No, but . . ." Margaret felt her cheeks begin to color. "It's not too . . . I mean, they haven't called off the test, have they?"

The woman shrugged. "As far as I know, I put you in a dress, I send you out there, I go to lunch. Next time, don't be late."

"I won't be, I promise. I'm Margaret, by the way." Margaret extended her hand. "Margaret Frobisher."

"Good for you. My name's Sadie. Sadie the Wardrobe Lady. It rhymes, so you can remember it." With a grunt of effort, the woman heaved herself from her chair and over to a clothes rack. Unzipping a large garment bag, she pulled out a floor-length yellow sprigged muslin with enormous leg-of-mutton sleeves and a stiff collar, the kind of dress that was in fashion when Margaret's grandmother—or maybe her great-grandmother—was young. "Here you go. They wanted you in something period, so I pulled period."

"This?" Gingerly fingering the bright yellow fabric, she

89

looked down at her chic fitted suit. "Are you sure I can't just wear what I have on?"

Sadie grinned, exposing a set of magnificent gold molars. "Not unless you don't mind looking like your armpits just went to the bathroom."

Margaret crossed her hands defensively over her chest, hiding the damp patches of nervous sweat she could suddenly feel under her arms. "It's hot today."

"Honey, I don't judge. The things I see in this place? Please. You could walk in here with a lizard's tail, I wouldn't blink an eye. Besides, what is it they say? Horses sweat, men perspire . . ."

"Ladies only glow," Margaret finished. It was something her mother said. *Oh God. Mother.* How was she ever supposed to have her suit cleaned without her mother finding out? She poked at the yellow dress again. "Are you sure it'll fit?"

"Eh, you girls are all the same size." Expertly, she hustled Margaret out of her blue suit and hat and into the dress. Margaret looked at herself miserably in the mirror. The lacy collar was dangerously tight. She was nervous enough without worrying about being strangled to death by her costume. And the sleeves . . . well, the sleeves were something else. The sleeves looked like zeppelins ready to take flight. If she could somehow manage to set them on fire, she could go on Halloween as the *Hindenburg* disaster.

"She is almost ready?" Without bothering to knock— although to be fair, Margaret thought, on what door?—a little old man stuck his head through the dressing room curtains.

"Just about," Sadie replied.

"Good. Get her out here, please. We have very little time."

"Sure thing, Mr. Kurtzman."

90

Tell Kurtzman you need him to direct. Margaret suddenly remembered what Larry Julius had said on the phone that day. "You're Raoul Kurtzman? The director?"

"Quite so. At your service." He gave her a short bow, punctuated by a smile that did not quite reach his eyes. Margaret had always imagined a movie director as an imperious figure, the sort to crack a riding crop against his polished boots as he strode around the set, haughtily barking orders at his cowed underlings. But the small bespectacled figure standing before her, his remaining strands of white hair plastered against his skull, spoke softly in a thick foreign accent that made him difficult to understand.

"I'm so sorry about being late—" Margaret began.

The director silenced her with a hand. "This is not what she is wearing, surely?"

"Yep. She really looks like her, don't she? More than any of the others." *Like who?* Margaret thought. *What others?*

"My dear woman, she looks like a banana."

Sadie put her hands on her hips. "Look, Mr. Kurtzman, I ain't no Edith Head. You said period, I gave you period. Period."

"Surely we have something more appropriate. One of the original Chesterfield costumes, perhaps."

"Chesterfield? You mean Diana?" The words were out before Margaret could stop them, but neither Sadie nor Kurtzman seemed to be paying the slightest attention.

"Mr. Mandalay doesn't want those used for tests," Sadie said.

"Something else, then. Something more . . . how do you say it? Sedate." He shuddered. "I just can't bear the abomination of this yellow on the screen."

"Then I guess you're in luck," Sadie replied testily, "because

91

the last time I checked, in *America,* the pictures is still in black-and-white."

Mr. Kurtzman let out a truly majestic sigh. "Very well, Sadie. I've no wish to waste any more time on these trivialities. You, Fräulein . . ."

"Frobisher," Margaret said quickly. "Margaret Frobisher."

Again, he seemed not to register the fact that she had spoken. "Anyway. Here is the scene you must play." He held up a packet of pink carbon-copied pages. "You are in the role of Lady . . . what's she called . . . Lady Olivia." He gazed at Margaret impassively over his half-moon glasses. "A most tragic character. At this moment in the scene she is making her eternal goodbye to Lord Gregory, who is her lover, with whom she shares a great passion. You know what I mean by this passion? You have felt this before?"

Margaret frowned, remembering those few minutes on the golf course with Phipps McKendrick. She'd been awfully excited—even passionate—about the idea of kissing him before it happened, but once it did, it had been sort of horrible, really. Having to sit there pushing his hands back from places they didn't belong while his tongue just lay there against the top of her mouth like a slab of wet sponge. "I don't know. Maybe."

"Hmm." Raoul Kurtzman looked unconvinced. "Well, Lady Olivia has a great passion for her lover, but her evil guardian has falsely accused him of murder."

"Oh no!"

"Oh yes. He says if you go through with the wedding, your lover goes free; if not, he will die. But they have deceived you, and even after your marriage your lover still rots in jail. You are thinking this is the last time you will ever see him, for tomorrow he must meet the executioner and bravely die."

"And in the end? Is he saved?"

Raoul Kurtzman shrugged again. "At the last moment, the king pardons him, the evildoers are punished, and the lovers sail off together to the New World."

Margaret shivered with delight. What a romantic story! Exactly the kind of picture she and Doris would blow their weekly allowance seeing three times in the theater. "It sounds wonderful."

"It's garbage," Raoul Kurtzman said. "But you must make me believe it. And then you will be a big star." He dropped the papers in her lap. "We roll in fifteen minutes. Find a way to break my heart."

Two hours later, Margaret had come to the sad realization that if she was breaking Raoul Kurtzman's heart, it was for all the wrong reasons.

Not that she wasn't trying. But every time he called action, it seemed she was looking into the wrong camera, or looking too directly at the right one. It was as though she'd been thrown headfirst into the deep end of a pool. Sink or swim. And Margaret was definitely not swimming.

"Chin down!" Through his director's megaphone, Raoul Kurtzman's soft voice had transformed into a menacing bellow. "Now turn your head to the right. Your *other* right! And don't forget to hit your mark."

The lights were blinding. In the glare, she could barely make out the short flight of steps she was supposed to walk down, let alone her "mark," the tiny cross of red tape on the floor she was supposed to stand on to make sure she was correctly framed in the shot. The soundstage was boiling hot. She could feel the sweat pouring down her forehead.

"No squinting! What is this with your hand over your eyes?" Kurtzman shouted through his microphone. "I assure you, Fräulein, there are no Indians coming over the horizon! Oh, cut. I said, *cut!*"

And so the huge camera would have to shudder to stop, and start again with a labored whir, and the kid with the slate board would storm out to announce another take while glaring at Margaret as though she'd just murdered his dog.

The last thing anyone seemed concerned with was her actual acting. The director himself offered her little guidance in that capacity except to point out where the cue cards were and ask her, somewhat disconcertingly, if she could read.

"You'd be surprised," he had muttered darkly, in response to her puzzled nod. "And remember, you must speak softly. This is not the theater, you understand? You must take care not to overpower this mike."

"Mike?" she asked innocently. "Is he the actor who I'll be playing the scene with?"

That had given them all a nice, cruel laugh. But in fact, the person with whom she was playing her ludicrously romantic scene was not an actor at all. Instead, reading the role of Lord Gregory was a morbidly obese man named Elmer, who sat in a severely overtaxed folding chair just off camera, haltingly speaking Lord Gregory's florid lines in a kind of high-pitched whine, like a mortally wounded Mickey Mouse.

"Oh, Lord Gregory," she intoned, trying desperately to ignore the fact that her scene partner was picking his nose as industriously as if he were digging for diamonds. "How I loved you. How I still—"

"Your eyes are unfocused!" Kurtzman shouted. "It is ruining the shot. Look at Elmer. Speak to Elmer."

Dane Forrest, Margaret thought with every fiber of her being. *Pretend Elmer is Dane Forrest.* But it was to no avail. After eighteen takes, it seemed as if Elmer were everywhere. His voice was stuck in her ear like the refrain of some horrible song. She was beginning to forget that she had ever seen a man besides Elmer in her entire life.

"One more take," Kurtzman said. "Then we are out of time."

The sullen boy with the slate came forward. "Frobisher screen test, take nineteen," he said to the camera.

"Lights," Kurtzman called. "Camera."

"Rolling," came the response.

Margaret took a hoarse breath and pressed her hands against her tight bodice, hoping to massage away the butterflies. *Come on,* she thought. *Make this one count.*

"And . . . action."

"Gregory!" She rushed down the stairs, nailing her mark. *Triumph!* "Oh, my darling, what have they done to you?"

There was a horrible popping sound as a shower of sparks fell to the stage, and the room went black.

"*Cut!* Damn!" Kurtzman shouted. "Damn, damn, damn!"

"Blown fuse," came an irritated voice from somewhere high in the rafters. "We've got to fix it before we keep shooting."

Kurtzman groaned. "How long?"

"Ten minutes, maybe fifteen."

"All right." Sighing, Kurtzman raised the megaphone to his lips. "Fifteen, everyone. *Strict* fifteen. Then we come back and put this thing out of its misery."

There was a fresh burst of activity as the crewmen descended ladders, lit cigarettes, wound and unwound great coils of snaking cord. In the bustle, no one seemed to notice the small forlorn figure in yellow quietly making her way to the door.

She knew she should go back to the dressing room. Go over her lines, walk through her blocking, touch up her makeup, anything that might help keep her most cherished ambition from slipping forever from her grasp.

But all Margaret wanted was to take a last long look at Olympus before she lost her chance to be a part of it.

I'll be like a camera, she thought as she walked outside, breathing deeply in the orange-scented air. She would make a memory of the towering stages and mysterious equipment and the people moving swiftly and purposefully, each with an indispensible part to play, and remember how she'd almost been one of them. Her own private movie she could watch in her mind's eye when she was back in Pasadena, feeling her soul wither from the inside out, slowly and fragrantly, like fruit left too long on the vine. She could close her eyes and see Olympus, and the image would last her the rest of her life. Then the tears came thick and fast, and she couldn't see anything at all.

"And they say it never rains in Southern California."

The man's voice was so strangely familiar that Margaret opened her eyes.

And her jaw dropped.

96

It was Dane Forrest.

Dane Forrest, the movie star.

Dane Forrest, whose glossy eight-by-ten photo hung above her bed at home.

Dane Forrest, who had featured in practically every daydream she'd ever had to do with getting married—and more than a few that had been a lot less ladylike.

Dane Forrest, the lover and rumored fiancé of the mysterious Diana Chesterfield.

And here he was, talking to *her*.

"You . . . you're . . ."

"Too much of a gentleman to walk past a lady in distress without offering some form of assistance. Or maybe just an irredeemable busybody you should tell to get lost. But either way"—he pulled a large white handkerchief from his pocket and held it out to her—"I thought you could use this."

Margaret accepted the handkerchief and held it against her face. *Limes,* she thought. *It smells like limes.* And pine needles. And something else, something dark and manly that she couldn't quite identify and wasn't sure she ought to. "Thank you. That's very kind."

"You mind?" He sat down on the empty spot on the bench next to her.

She had only seen him once before in color, that night outside Grauman's Chinese Theater, when he'd looked as if he'd rather be anywhere else in the world. *The night Diana went missing,* she thought. Close up, his dark hair looked lighter and softer, falling over his forehead in a boyish wave. Without the heavy makeup of the screen, his skin was rosy and deeply tanned. Margaret had always thought his eyes were blue, but as the light fell over his face she could see that they were green, shot through with a golden hazel.

"Not going great, huh?" Dane said.

"What?"

"The screen test."

She gasped. "How did you know?"

"Well, I know what going great looks like, and believe me, this isn't it. Unless you're one of those Method actors from New York and you're just gearing yourself up for the big waterworks by reliving the day your beloved goldfish died."

"Not that." Margaret smiled in spite of herself. "I meant the screen test."

"Well, you're on stage fourteen, aren't you?" Dane gave her one of his famous grins and gestured toward the number on the wall of the soundstage. "Screen tests are about the only time they get this old ruin up and running. And the dress, well . . ." He grinned again. "Let's just say that's a very screen test dress."

"It's awful, isn't it?" Margaret looked at the soaking hand-kerchief, streaked with sooty smudges of mascara. "I must look awful."

"You think I would have stopped if you did?"

"You're teasing me."

"Would that I were so clever. But actually, it's just dumb luck my handkerchief and I managed to happen by. I drove in this morning from Malibu, clearheaded, lines learned, only to find out the shooting schedule on my latest desert epic has run into a bit of a sandstorm, if you will."

"Not *The Pharaoh's Serpent*?" Margaret had read all about

Dane's new movie in *Picture Palace*. He was supposed to play an archaeologist who uncovered a jeweled serpent that sent him back to the time of the ancient Egyptians.

"That's right. Please don't tell me you're some kind of Hollywood insider."

"I just read the trades, that's all," Margaret said proudly.

"And you seemed like such a nice girl." Dane shook his head. The soft forelock of hair fell into his eyes, and Margaret had to fight the urge to smooth it back with her fingers. "Well, what the trades won't tell you," Dane continued, "is that von Steinbach decided to hold up the next three days of production on account of the slave girl costumes weren't up to snuff. Although if you ask me, I think the problem was the slave girls themselves. No prospects for old Steinbach there."

"You mean they were . . . unattractive?"

Dane grinned. "Oh, much worse. Married."

Margaret flushed. "You're not serious."

"Aren't I? Anyway, you can imagine how relieved I was to run into you and think that all that gasoline might not have burned in vain. It's not every day a fellow gets to play Good Samaritan, especially when the Samaritee is as pretty as you. Say, who've they got running the show for you, anyway?"

"Mr. Kurtzman."

Dane raised his eyebrows. "Raoul Kurtzman?"

"Don't tell me he's 'very screen test' too."

"No." Dane's tone was suddenly grave. "Quite the opposite, actually. What scene are they having you play?"

"Oh, Lady Olivia, and, um—"

"Lord Gregory? And you're visiting him in his cell, just moments before his unjust execution?"

"You know it?"

"Know it? I *played* Lord Gregory."

"But that's impossible!" Margaret exclaimed, before she had time to think better of it. "I'd never seen it before, and I've seen every single one of your films."

Dane rolled his eyes. "What a disappointment. From the looks of you, I should have hoped you'd have better taste. But you haven't seen this one. *Love's Last Song*. Boy, was it. The screenwriter had a nervous breakdown; the director was so sozzled he had to check himself into a sanatorium halfway through shooting."

"And nobody ever saw the finished film?" Margaret was fascinated.

"There never *was* a finished film. Some of the battle scenes were recut and turned up in *Field of Honor*, I think. The rest?" He made a scissors-like gesture with his fingers. "On the scrap heap."

"Does that really happen?"

Dane shrugged. "All the time. They try to make the best of it, but in this business, you win some, you lose some."

"I was so excited when I came in." Margaret looked down at her lap, twisting Dane's handkerchief in her hands. "But then I get the scene, and with all the lights around, and Elmer . . ."

"You got Elmer?" Dane let out a low whistle. "That is a tough break. But you'll be all right. You just need an idea, that's all."

"An idea? What do you mean?"

"See, the thing about acting is you've got to make it seem like something that's happened to you."

Margaret frowned. "But I've never had a lover beheaded before."

Dane laughed. "Of course not, dimwit. That doesn't matter.

The point is Lady Olivia wants Lord Gregory to live, more than she wants anything in the world. And that's what you've got to identify with. Surely there must be something *you* want. Something you want terribly. Your truest heart's desire."

His face suddenly felt very close to hers. She could almost feel the heat radiating from his lips on her own. "Yes," Margaret breathed. "Yes, of course."

"And so you can imagine how it might feel to have it suddenly taken away." His clear green eyes were clouded with pain. He looked very far away. She felt an impulse to reach out for him.

Instead, she blurted out abruptly, "I wish you could play the scene with me."

Dane's eyes snapped back into focus. "Me?"

Oh God. Margaret flushed. *What have I just done?* "I'm so sorry. Of course not. I was just being silly—"

"You know what?" Dane looked at her for a long moment. She felt herself twisting in the intensity of his gaze. "Come on."

"Oh no!" Flooded with horror, Margaret dashed after him as he strode across the lawn toward the soundstage. "Really, it isn't necessary! Please! Mr. Forrest . . . *Mr. Forrest!*"

Raoul Kurtzman was bent over a camera lens muttering something to the operator when he saw Dane. "Forrest! Who invited you onto my set? Kindly get lost at once."

Dane clapped the older man fondly on the back. "Always good to see you too, Raoul."

"What the hell are you doing here? I thought you were over making some sort of desert abomination with the Hun."

"You mean the *other* Hun? He's running behind."

Kurtzman scoffed. "Disgraceful. And he calls himself a German."

"Well, God bless him, he unexpectedly left me with the morning free. So when I happened upon my good friend, Miss . . ."

"Margaret," Margaret whispered in terror. *This is crazy*, she thought.

". . . Margo here, I thought I'd see if I might be permitted to put my admittedly limited talents at her disposal."

"Interesting. Very interesting." Kurtzman gave Margaret a penetrating stare, as though he were only now seeing her properly.

"So whaddya say?" Dane asked. "Feel like taking a chance on an unknown kid?"

For the first time all day, the shadow of a smile seemed to touch the corners of Kurtzman's narrow mouth. "You want to play the scene, Forrest? Okay. You play the scene." He pointed at Margaret. "You. It seems I have underestimated you. We shoot." He raised his megaphone. "Places, everyone!"

"It's Margaret," she whispered to Dane as the guy with the slate ducked in front of them to announce the final take for the camera. "My name is Margaret."

"Lights!" Kurtzman bellowed.

Dane shook his head. "Margo's better. More unusual. People will remember it better."

"Margo." *Like when I was a little girl.*

"Camera!"

"Oh! Just one question," Margaret put in hurriedly, whispering over the fresh whirr of the camera.

"Shoot."

"Who was Lady Olivia? When you played Lord Gregory, I mean."

"Oh." Dane looked straight ahead into the camera, his expression unreadable. "Diana, of course." *Of course.*

"And . . . *action!*"

"Gregory! My darling!" Lady Olivia rushed down the steps and into her lover's open arms. A delicious surge of electric warmth pulsed through her body as he embraced her, pressing his cheek against hers.

"Olivia, angel! What in heaven's name are you doing here?"

"My own love," Lady Olivia intoned, "my dearest own. As long as there is breath in my body, I will always come to you."

"But it's far too dangerous, my love. Your father's guards surround the castle. If they should catch you . . ."

"Run away with me, Gregory." He was still holding her, and his breath on her neck made her shiver. "I've a horse downstairs and gold enough to bribe the warden. We'll away to Bournemouth, and then across the channel to France, and freedom."

"Olivia, Olivia," Lord Gregory moaned. "And does your father not have eyes in Bournemouth and even ears in France? His spies are everywhere. It's impossible, my darling one. I must go tomorrow to my death."

"Then there is nothing left to hope for." A perfect glistening tear trickled down Lady Olivia's pale cheek. "There is nothing left to hope for. Nothing left to live for."

"No, my darling." Lord Gregory brushed away the tear of his beloved with tender fingers. "There is one place where they'll never find us. Where our love will always be free."

"Where, my darling? Tell me?"

103

The tiny part of Lady Olivia that was not, in fact, Lady Olivia knew that Lord Gregory's next line was laughably over-wrought, but the intensity of his green gaze made her feel as though he could see all the way into the darkest recesses of her soul. "Here, my love." Tenderly, he placed his hand over her breastbone. "Carry me in your heart. And know that my own, for as long as it beat, beat for you."

The tears were falling again. "My love . . . is there nothing more I can do?"

"Kiss me," Lord Gregory murmured. "Kiss me for the last time."

He searched her face for an endless moment. Then he brought his mouth to hers, and . . .

"*Cut!*" Raoul Kurtzman's megaphone boomed through the soundstage. "And print! That's a wrap!"

TEN

The famous commissary on the Olympus lot was more than just a place to eat. As any of its patrons would tell you, from the great star holding court to the lowly second electrician grabbing a quick bite between takes, it was the heart and soul of the studio lot.

The leather booths were so cozy and deep you could practically sleep in them. A team of chefs stood by, prepared to whip up nearly anything that happened to catch your fancy. Elaborate decorations changed with every season, and throughout the month of December, carolers in Dickensian costume roamed the tables serenading the diners, artificial snow fell from the ceiling on the hour, and every meal was accompanied by a small wrapped surprise, which might be anything from a ten-cent yoyo to a hundred-dollar bill folded meticulously into an origami rose. On Christmas Day, the commissary was the scene of a lavish party attended by interested members of the press—which naturally was all of them—and virtually all of Olympus's major stars, several of whom would inevitably take their turn performing at the garland-festooned piano placed for maximum photogenic effect beneath the twinkling thirty-foot-tall Norwegian pine. The yuletide festivities were presided over by none other than Leo F. Karp himself, who one year furnished *Picture Palace* with one of his extremely rare on-the-record remarks when an impudent reporter asked him why his employees weren't at home with their families. "They *are* with their family," he had said imperiously. "Olympus is their family."

Yet for all the "one big happy family" talk, the commissary was also a place of intrigue. If Schwab's Pharmacy was the unofficial headquarters of Hollywood's chronically overhopeful and underemployed, this was the nerve center of the insiders. Somewhere in the ambient din, deals were made, confidences shared, illicit liaisons formed, and secret assignations arranged. The fates of countless men and women were decided within its walls by tables of suited executives as they jovially slurped down jiggers of Scotch and plates of Yankee bean soup. Stars were made—and destroyed—in the protective shelter of those high-backed booths. The commissary was a hearth, but it was also a hideout, a courtroom, and, on very bad days, a gallows.

To Margaret, it felt like a hostile school cafeteria. She was the new girl, and no one wanted to sit with her.

With Dane Forrest/Lord Gregory's kiss still buzzing warmly on her lips, she had been changing back into her street clothes—which had miraculously been sponged and pressed and returned to her, the gold-and-pearl pin fastened a bit higher on the collar, where Sadie claimed it would cast a more flattering glow on her face when it caught the light—when a bespectacled assistant burst into the dressing room and offered to either validate her parking or give her a voucher for lunch, whichever she preferred. Considering she didn't have a car, it wasn't much of a choice. Besides, she was dying to see the inside of Olympus's famous commissary. She'd do a little stargazing, have a quick bite, and catch the 2:25 streetcar back to Pasadena before anyone had time to miss her.

Besides, she thought with a little shiver of excitement, *maybe Dane will be in the commissary.* They'd hustled her into the dressing room so fast she hadn't had a chance to say goodbye. Perhaps she'd see him sitting at a table, smoking one of his cigarettes and drinking . . . coffee? No, Scotch. He'd be drinking a Scotch, like a sophisticated gentleman, while he read the newspaper. In her chic blue suit with the newly light-reflecting brooch, she'd slowly slink up to his table, his eyes on her all the way, like when Diana Chesterfield slunk across the ballroom to him in *That Kensington Woman.* And in her throatiest, sexiest voice, Margaret would say: "Dane Forrest. Fancy meeting you here." Then he'd laugh and rise to his feet and invite her to sit down and tell her how beautiful she looked when she wasn't dressed like a nineteenth-century banana. They'd get to talking and he'd tell her how he and Diana, whatever the rumors, had only ever been just good friends, and in fact, Diana was getting married to someone else, someone impossibly glamorous . . . who would it be? Clark Gable. Diana was getting married to Clark Gable and the wedding was top-secret, naturally, and that was the reason she hadn't been seen in public for almost two months. Perfectly reasonable, when you thought about it; nothing unsavory about it, and certainly nothing that

107

had to do with Dane. But now that he'd met Margaret, he knew that she and Diana would be just the best of friends and that she absolutely had to be his guest at their lavish star-studded wedding, which would be in . . . New York? No, Paris. And she'd say, "Of course, but only if you'll consider being my escort to my coming-out party." And he'd say the same thing he'd said to Diana in that same ballroom scene, when she asked him if he waltzed: "My dear, now that I know you exist, I couldn't possibly think of doing anything else."

God! Wouldn't that be something! Entering her debutante ball dressed all in white silk, on Dane Forrest's arm, practically like a bride—which, obviously, would be the next step. Her parents would be terribly against it, of course (not only was Dane an actor, but Margaret remembered reading something a couple of years ago about him giving a speech at a rally for FDR), but when they saw how charming and well bred and wonderful he was, they'd soon come around. And Doris and Diana Chesterfield would be her two maids of honor in lilac dresses, and Evelyn Gamble would be . . . well, what was greener than a pea? Broccoli. Evelyn Gamble would positively turn into a great big stalk of broccoli.

Speaking of green, it was nearly St. Patrick's Day, and the Olympus commissary was absolutely swathed in it: green tablecloths, green flowers, green bunting. *Picture Palace was right,* Margaret thought delightedly. *They really do decorate for everything.* At the entrance, a child dressed as a leprechaun offered her a shamrock corsage.

"Oh, thank you!" Margaret cooed. "Aren't you adorable!"

"Cut the crap, lady," said the leprechaun, in a surprisingly deep voice. On closer inspection, she could see a distinct tinge of five o'clock shadow beginning to sprout beneath his heavily rouged cheeks. "You think I'm thrilled about this? I know I'm practically the only little person within a hundred-mile radius not working on the MGM lot for *The Wizard of Oz*, so just put a sock in it, will ya?"

"Oh! I'm terribly sorry," Margaret began, but the leprechaun had already returned to the cigar butt he had left smoldering in the ashtray behind the cash register.

Margaret blushed for what felt like the millionth time that day. *Maybe this was a mistake*, she thought. What did she think she was going to do? Sit alone in her too-fancy suit, as if she were playing hooky at Schwab's? Besides, Dane Forrest was nowhere in sight. She didn't know anyone and they didn't know her. *I don't belong here*, Margaret thought gloomily. *I should just catch the Red Car back to Pasadena before anyone notices I'm gone.*

"Hey!" Just as she was about to slink away, she noticed a small but unmistakably familiar figure waving frantically in her direction.

"Hey! Hey there! You, in the blue!" With the bottom of her hair in curlers and wrapped in a pink flannel bathrobe to pro-tect her dress, Gabby Preston looked like the world's youngest housewife finally settling down to breakfast after her brood had left for the day.

"Me?" Shyly, she took a small step toward Gabby's table.

"Yes, you! I know you! Hannah, right? You were in the chorus line at the Palace Theater in Newark, isn't that right? *Pretty Babies of 1936*? You remember, when that Polish girl, Gertrude or whatever her name was, caught bedbugs from that stage-door Johnny with the limp and passed them on to the whole rotten dressing room."

"I . . . I think you must have me confused with some-one else."

"Oh." Gabby shrugged. "Well, never mind. Come and sit with me anyway."

"I wouldn't . . . I wouldn't want to impose."

"You're not meeting anyone, are you?"

"No . . ."

"Then sit."

"Well . . . if you're sure you don't mind." Margaret sat, hoping Gabby wouldn't notice her obvious relief.

"Don't be ridiculous. There's positively no one amusing in here today, and I simply detest having lunch alone, don't you?" Gabby didn't wait for an answer. "Normally, I lunch with Jimmy, but he's gone off to the Derby with some agent or other, Selznick, I think, promising him the moon and the stars if he only gives him ten percent for life."

Jimmy Molloy at the Brown Derby with Myron Selznick, Margaret thought, with a shiver of delight. It felt deliciously insider-y to know that right at this very moment, Olympus's biggest box-office star was eating Cobb salad at Hollywood's swankest eatery with the most powerful talent agent in town.

"Anyway, he's left me here high and dry with positively no one to talk to," Gabby continued, "and once you've been *seen* in the Olympus commissary, it simply doesn't do to leave it. So I'm quite glad you turned up unclaimed or I'd have had to sit here chattering to myself and everyone would think I'd properly gone crackers for good. Oh! My name is Gabby, by the way."

"I know who you are." It probably wasn't a very sophisticated thing to say, but Margaret couldn't help herself. "I saw you in *No Time but Swing Time.*"

Gabby waved her hand dismissively, but Margaret could tell she was pleased. "Oh, that. That was just a short."

"Well, I thought you were swell. Although I wish they'd had you sing a ballad. I heard you doing 'But Not for Me' the other day on *Gussie Gilmore's Radio Spectacular* and it was absolutely beautiful."

"Gershwin." Gabby smacked her lips. "I guess you've got taste, then. What's your name, anyway?"

"Mar . . . go," Margaret said. *Why not?* The new name made her feel deliciously undercover, as if she were Mata Hari. "Margo."

"Margo? That's pretty. And you're contract?"

"Excuse me?"

"Are you under contract to the studio? As an actress?"

"Oh." Margaret shook her head. "No."

"You're not a writer. I haven't seen many writers who look like you."

"Oh, no, no."

"Don't tell me you're an extra. Well, don't worry. You'll get noticed soon enough. Just show a little leg when the casting guys come around, but don't believe a word they say if they promise you anything. It's like Viola always says, why buy the cow when you can get the milk for free?"

"I don't know," Margaret said, startled by Gabby's frank implication. "Maybe so you can slaughter it and turn it into steaks and handbags?"

Gabby laughed with wide-eyed surprise. "Hey, that's funny. Maybe you should be a writer after all."

"Actually"—Margaret leaned forward shyly—"I've just finished filming a screen test."

"What? Now? Your first one?"

Margaret nodded. "I've only just come from the soundstage."

Gabby let out a little shriek. Her huge chocolate-colored eyes, wide with excitement, seemed to take up half of her small face. "Congratulations! That's marvelous!"

"I don't know." Margaret shook her head. "I wouldn't congratulate me just yet."

"Trust me, doll, if you can still stand being around this when it's over, it went just fine. Who'd they get to direct it?"

"Mr. Kurtzman."

Gabby's eyebrows shot up about three inches, which, in a face as small as hers, meant they practically touched the top of her head. "Raoul Kurtzman?"

"Yes. Is that good?"

"It's interesting," Gabby said. "Let's just say usually the kind of guy they get for that sort of thing is some no-name hanging around reading comic books at Schwab's, desperate to be picked as a runt when they're choosing up sides for football. Not someone like Raoul Kurtzman."

"Well, I'd never heard of him."

"That's because he's only been out here for about a year. But before that he was one of the most famous film directors in Germany. A real *artiste*, so to speak."

"Why'd he leave, then?"

Gabby looked at her as if she were crazy. "Why do they all leave? Hitler." She shrugged her small shoulders. "Although I can't for the life of me understand why so many people are so afraid of some crazy guy who looks like Charlie Chaplin. But I don't know anything about politics. Studio politics, yes. And politically, for Raoul Kurtzman to direct a screen test, well, that's very interesting. Very interesting indeed."

"Well, whatever they're looking for, it started out horribly," Margaret said. "The lights were so hot, and I couldn't find my 'mark' or whatever it's called . . ."

"And they put you in some horrific dress and kept shouting through that ghastly megaphone," Gabby finished. "Believe me, I know. I've been here six months now, but I'm still practically in the same boat as you. I mean, I've gotten used to the camera and the lights and all that, but still, the famous directors, the Kurtzmans and the Toynbees, they're the worst. You miss a dance step or a music cue, or you're so much as five minutes late for morning call because you were rehearsing until three in the morning the night before, and they look at you like you're something they just stepped in. Because they're the artist, you see, and you're the one ruining their artistic perfection." She gave a rueful giggle. "And that's not even counting all the gorgeous glamour girls swanning all over the place, making you feel about four feet tall. Of course, I *am* only about four feet tall." Gabby nodded in the direction of the scowling leprechaun at the door, swigging liberally from a flask of something before he welcomed the next party. "If I were any smaller, they'd have me dressed up like Barty. Of course," she continued, "that won't be a problem for you. You're not an ugly duckling like me. You know what they say about ugly ducklings in Hollywood?"

"What's that?"

Gabby grinned. "They turn into even uglier ducks."

"Oh come on," Margaret said. "You're hardly an ugly duckling." It was true that Gabby was certainly no classical beauty, but with her huge sparkling eyes and bouncing dark curls, she was undeniably adorable. The first time Margaret had seen her picture, she'd thought Gabby looked exactly like Esmeralda Annabel, who had been Margaret's favorite childhood porcelain doll until Emmeline knocked her off the shelf when she was cleaning and cracked her face in two.

"Oh, I wasn't fishing," Gabby said matter-of-factly. "I'm cute as a bug's ear, or so everyone keeps telling me, but around here I sometimes feel like something they dredged up from the pond. If I couldn't sing, the closest I'd get to this place would be working as a washerwoman. Or a script girl, I suppose, although then I'd have to be able to read."

"You mean . . . you can't . . ." Margaret tried not to look shocked, but she was unaccustomed to anyone revealing such personal information so early in an acquaintance.

"Oh, I'm exaggerating. Of course I can, a little. But everything I know my sister Frankie taught me. You see, there just wasn't any time for proper school. Traipsing all over creation doing vaudeville from the time you can walk doesn't exactly turn you into a scholar." She slumped her head dramatically down on the table and sprang back up with a start. "Ow! I forgot I was wearing these stupid curlers! My poor head."

A green-jacketed waiter, of normal height but with an enormous shamrock in his buttonhole, approached the table. "Are you ladies ready to order?"

"I . . . I haven't even seen a menu," Margaret said.

"There isn't one," Gabby said. "And if there were, no one would order off it. Everyone in Hollywood is always on some crazy diet. Just order whatever you want to eat, and they'll make it. This is the Dream Factory, after all."

"Oh, I see. Um . . . do you have egg salad?"

Gabby rolled her eyes. "Margo, I told you, they have everything. Just go ahead and order. Be as big a pain as you can be."

Margaret took a deep breath. Her mother had always told her it was unladylike for a lady to be too particular about her food in public; actually, in public, a lady was scarcely meant to eat at all. But as long as they were offering, why not go for it? "In that case, I'll have an egg salad sandwich on rye toast. Don't make the toast too dark, please. Iceberg lettuce on the sandwich, no tomato. The tomato I want on the side, with just a sprinkle of salt and pepper. And to drink, I'll have a Coca-Cola . . . no, wait, a seltzer water, with lime. But the lime cut crosswise, not lengthwise. If you don't mind."

Gabby nodded approvingly. "You're a natural. The crosswise-cut lime is an especially nice touch." She turned to the waiter. "For me, Tony, I'd like a cheeseburger, please. And a dish of french fries, with lots of ketchup. And two—no, make it three pieces of fried chicken, and some mashed potatoes with gravy. Give me a pork chop too, if you have one, with applesauce. Oh, and a hot fudge sundae, with chopped nuts and two cherries on top, please. You can bring it all out at once."

It was an outlandish lunch order for a girl who had just given a long interview in *Picture Palace* about her latest slimming regime, Margaret thought, but it would obviously be the height of rudeness to point it out. She changed the subject. "My friend Doris bought the recording of you singing 'Zing Went the Strings of My Heart.' We listened to it again and again. We couldn't believe how it sounded *exactly* like it did in *No Time but Swing Time.*"

115

Gabby laughed. "That's because it was exactly the same recording."

"You mean—that wasn't . . ."

"Me singing live? God, no. You go in and record the song in a booth, with the orchestra, and then they play it back when they shoot the scene and you just mouth along. Otherwise, you'd have to pay the musicians a fortune to sit there while they fuss around with the lights and the set and powdering all the actors every five seconds like we're babies with diaper rash. Honestly, isn't making pictures just the absolute dullest? Give me a live audience any day. But vaudeville's dead, and Viola doesn't fancy me doing eight shows a week for pin money and Broadway, and anyway, she says the cold bothers her sciatica."

"Who is Viola?" Margaret asked.

"My old lady. The old ball and chain."

"Your . . . your *wife*?" Margaret asked, confused.

Gabby hooted. "My mother."

"You call your mother by her first name?"

"What else am I supposed to call her? Darling Mama? She's not exactly the type. Although she turns it on for Karp. We both do."

"Leo Karp? You mean the head of the studio?"

"The very same. He's a hard-nosed businessman, but there are two things that get him right in the gut: patriotism and motherhood. Listen, kid, you ever run afoul of old Karp, you just get a tear in your eye and talk about how much you love your mother and your country, and he'll turn to mush so fast you can eat him with a spoon. But I'll tell you what, Viola doesn't exactly inspire sonnets. Ugh. Mothers. Am I right or am I right?" The arrival of Tony the waiter with her egg salad and seltzer, prepared exactly as requested, saved Margaret from having to respond. In front of Gabby, he unceremoniously plunked down a bowl of unadorned chicken broth. Not a French fry or an ice cream sundae in sight.

"She's developing expensive tastes out here too," Gabby continued rapidly, seemingly oblivious to the food. "Just the other day, she shows up at my dance rehearsal wearing yet another new mink stole she bought for three hundred dollars. Three hundred dollars! For her trip to Palm Springs, she says, also undoubtedly paid for by the sweat of my little brow. You look shocked. You should be shocked! Who the hell wears fur in the desert?"

"No . . . ," Margaret began, although the truth was she was shocked by so many things about Gabby that she hardly knew how to separate them. "I think they brought you the wrong meal."

Gabby finally glanced down at her soup. "Oh, that!" She laughed. "Don't mind that. You see, Tully Toynbee—you know, the director?—got Mr. Karp to tell the commissary to serve me nothing—and I mean nothing—but chicken soup until I lose twenty pounds."

"*Twenty pounds?*" Margaret's mouth fell open. Even with the bulk added by her oversized bathrobe, Gabby looked like the kind of delicate fairy you'd see tiptoeing over the petals of a flower in a Victorian picture book, with a snail shell for a hat and a needle for a sword. "From where? Are you supposed to cut off your head?"

"Spoken like one of the naturally slender," Gabby muttered. "I know it sounds like a lot, but it isn't really. The cameras put on at least ten, and I was at least ten too big to begin with. Anyway, it's fun to order the most outrageous things I can think of, just to get a rise out of the waiters. Yesterday, I asked the fellow for an entire roast beef, two dozen scrambled eggs, and a New York cheesecake with strawberry sauce on top. And then I asked him if he would bring me the bucket of fat drippings out of the kitchen to wash it all down with."

"And they don't say anything?"

Gabby's eyes twinkled. "Not a word. It's company policy. They're not supposed to ask any questions, or even so much as crack a smile. I heard that Garbo got a waiter fired for asking if she wanted him to leave the dressing off her salad, and frankly, I think he got off easy. I mean, really, offending Greta Garbo? At MGM? Mayer could have had him executed for that. No, go ahead, don't wait for me! Eat! You must be starving."

Reluctantly, Margaret picked up her sandwich. "Don't you get hungry?"

"Not a bit. Not with these marvelous little pills Dr. Lipkin gave me."

"Dr. Lipkin?"

"The studio doctor. Absolutely the nicest, cleverest man in the whole wide world. All you do is go into his office and tell him you need to lose some weight. First he gives you a shot, just to kick-start the process, and then he gives you these darling little pills. You swallow one down whenever you get the teensiest bit hungry, and presto, not hungry anymore! I've lost six pounds already and it's only been a week."

Margaret frowned. It sounded awfully dangerous. "What does your mother think?"

"Did you not listen to anything I told you about Viola? She's thrilled. She says her only regret is that I didn't start taking them three months ago, when I lost that big part at MGM to Deanna Durbin." Gabby snorted. "They said they were 'going in a different musical direction,' but really it's because they thought I was a big fat pig. Now Viola's practically shoving the pills down my throat. And the best part about them is not only are you not hungry, you've suddenly got gobs of energy, like you could practically take on the world. The only teensy tiny problem is that sometimes they make it a little hard to sleep, but Dr. Lipkin has some pills for that too, not that I have much time for sleeping. Honestly, it all works a treat. Dr. Lipkin told me that Diana Chesterfield was practically the size of a garage when she first came to him. . . ."

"And now she's disappeared altogether." The words were out before Margaret could stop them.

Gabby's eyes flew open as she lunged across the table "Why! What have you heard? Did Kurtzman say something?"

"Oh, no!" Margaret backpedaled furiously. She couldn't help feeling as though she'd spoken out of turn. "Nothing like that. It's just that—"

"Because he's supposed to be directing her new picture, you know. *The Nine Days' Queen.* Big costume drama. It was supposed to be his first big project since Europe. The studio spent a fortune on it, and now it's on hold, and nobody . . . *Oh God.*" Gabby's gaze drifted suddenly across the room. "Not her. Just look at her."

"Who?"

"*Her.*" Gabby pointed a finger toward the entrance. Snaking a path through the commissary floor, leaving in her wake a trail of tables full of awestruck men with half-chewed food visible in their open mouths, was the most extravagantly beautiful girl Margaret had ever seen. Her hair was a radiant shade of red, like that of a nymph in a Pre-Raphaelite painting, and cascaded luxuriously down her shoulders in glossy, sensuous waves. Even from across the room, her large hazel eyes emitted a vivid glow. Her magnificent figure was encased in a tight black bombazine suit that hugged her in all the right places and set off her pale skin and fiery hair to glorious effect. Only when she had finally reached her table—the absolute farthest from the commissary door, clearly selected solely for its ability to afford her the longest possible procession—where she was partially hidden by an enormous bunch of emerald balloons, did the hush lift from the room and the diners return to their previously scheduled activities of eating, gossiping, and complaining.

Gabby shook her head in disgust. "Honestly. Who the hell does she think she is?"

"I don't know. Who *is* she?"

"She calls herself Amanda Farraday," Gabby sneered. "I suppose she's some kind of *actress*, although I've yet to see her do much acting—that is, in the traditional sense. All I know is that no one had ever heard of her, and then all of a sudden she shows up on the lot with a private dressing room and an umpteen-dollar Packard convertible and a bunch of clothes straight from Paris. All black, for some ridiculous reason."

"Maybe she's in mourning."

"Yeah, for her virtue."

"Gabby!" Margaret was startled by the visible change in her new friend. The bubbly, mischievous Gabby of just a few minutes earlier had transformed into a hard-eyed girl with an unnerving edge of bitterness in her voice.

"Oh, come on. Not a single credit to her belt, and she waltzes in with all that?"

It hit Margaret like a flash. "I've seen her before. I mean, I *saw* her. Early this morning. Going into the office of a young man, a writer, I think. I only saw her from the back, but I'm sure it was her."

Gabby nodded smugly. "There you go. Covering all the bases. It takes an awful lot of guys to keep a girl like that."

"You mean there are others?" Margaret whispered.

"I'd bet my bottom dollar on it. Agents, producers. Maybe Mr. Karp; wouldn't surprise me. Sure, he puts on that whole kindly grandpa act, but he's a man, just like any of them. Maybe even Hunter Payne."

"Hunter Payne?"

"The big moneyman in New York," Gabby said. "He runs the corporation that owns Olympus. Put it this way, if Karp's the king, Payne's the Pope. They say the only thing he cares about is the box office, but believe me, he has other interests. And I guarantee you that Amanda Farraday knows all about 'em."

She held up her tiny hand before Margaret could interrupt. "Listen, Margo, there's no point in defending her. Girls like that just make things harder for the rest of us. You think it doesn't happen? Listen, when I was ten years old, playing the Palace Theater, some pervert producer told my mother he'd make me the headliner if she'd let him have a couple of hours alone in a room with me. To my continuing surprise, Viola was actually horrified. Even she has her limits, I guess. But the next thing I know, I'm off the bill, and another girl, even younger than me, is at the top of the marquee. I guess her mother wasn't so easily shocked."

Margaret suddenly felt desperate to change the subject. She didn't want to hear about this. Hollywood was supposed to be a fairyland. The Dream Factory. Gabby made it sound more like a nightmare. "Tell me more about 'Zing Went the Strings of My Heart.'"

Gabby looked at her incredulously. "What do you want to know?"

"Well . . ." Margaret thought frantically. "What do you think made it . . . so . . . so good?"

"Well," Gabby said, sitting back in her chair with a satisfied look, "with a song like that, you have to act it. You have to think about how it relates to your life and put that emotion behind the words." *Just like Dane said about Lady Olivia,* Margaret thought. "You've got to think about the person your heart goes 'zing' for." She leaned forward mischievously. "So I thought about Jimmy."

"You? And Jimmy?" For a moment, Margaret forgot all about Amanda Farraday. Wait till Doris heard about this. "Are the two of you . . . going together?"

Gabby smiled mysteriously. "Not technically. But I imagine it's only a matter of time until we're allowed to announce."

"Announce?"

Gabby laughed. "Well, it's not as though Jimmy and I are just ordinary kids. These things have to be considered. But we're starring in the new Tully Toynbee picture together, for Pete's sake. And we're the same age, same image, same kind of properties. It makes perfect sense."

"It doesn't sound very romantic."

Gabby giggled. "Don't be silly. I couldn't dream of falling in love with someone who wasn't in everyone's best business interest. But as it happens, I think Jimmy Molloy is the sweetest, dearest, handsomest, funniest, cleverest, most wonderful boy in the whole world."

But Margaret wasn't listening to Gabby anymore.

Dane Forrest had just entered the commissary.

He'd changed clothes since she'd seen him last, into a gray flannel suit. His dark hair was freshly slicked back from his face. His eyes gleamed with that *look*. The smoldering ballroom look from *That Kensington Woman*.

Gabby grinned. "Hmmm. Ring-a-zing-zing."

Margaret's heart was pounding. As he drew nearer, she thought it would leap right out of her chest and land in Gabby's untouched soup.

But without so much as a nod in Margaret's direction, he passed her completely and walked straight over to Amanda Farraday. Grabbing the beautiful redhead's hand, he leaned in close to whisper something urgently in her ear. She whispered something back, through glistening parted lips. He gave her the tiniest of nods as she took her hand from his and slipped out the back door. He stood at the table for a moment, looking around anxiously, before he stealthily followed her out.

"Covering all the bases," Gabby snorted. "Diana Chesterfield, how quickly we forget." And with that, she picked up her spoon and helped herself to an enormous mouthful of chicken soup.

ELEVEN

She was exactly where she said she'd be, in the small, shady orange grove behind the commissary, leaning against a tree studded with bright fruit. The dark green leaves cast a lacy pattern of shadows across her perfect face. Dane started toward her, his arms outstretched. "Ginger. What are you doing here?"

She raised a pale hand, holding him off. "It's Amanda now."

"Is that your real name?"

"Real enough. As for what I'm doing here, it just so happens I'm under contract." A proud smile played across her lovely face.

"As an actress?"

The smile faded from her lips. "Don't look so surprised."

"It's just I never knew that was part of the plan."

"Oh?" She raised her chin defiantly. "What did you think the plan was?"

He struggled for a moment, trying to think what to say.

Dane Forrest was used to beautiful girls, but this one, Ginger, or Amanda, or whatever she wanted to call herself, had always unhinged him somehow, made him feel young and callow and ill-equipped, as if he was always about to say the wrong thing. "I don't know," he said finally. "I guess I figured some man would come along eventually and take you away from all this."

"As it so happens, one has."

"Anyone I know?"

"I imagine so," she said seriously. "His name is Harry Gordon."

"Not the *screenwriter?*" Dane felt as if he were going to choke.

"Again with the shock. You really have to work on that, Dane. It's terribly ungallant."

A writer. And not just any writer. *Harry Gordon.* Dane shook his head. Someone like Harry might be fine in Greenwich Village, but in Hollywood all that radical idealism tended to turn to rot. Either you destroyed it or it destroyed you, and it was too early to tell which way Harry Gordon would go. "I always had you down as a practical sort, Gin. Thought you were more of the type to go for an agent, or a producer—"

"Or an actor?"

His eyes bored into her. She returned his gaze. He knew they were thinking about the same thing. The same night. It had been two years earlier. He'd been a bit player then, of the sort Los Angeles was teeming with. Just another handsome, hungry young man on the make. Hardly the sort to come around Olive Moore's place, but Olive had been awfully good to him over the years. Dane was a sentimental sort.

That evening Olive was out. It was one of those hazy blue nights, the kind where sadness and beauty seem like the same thing. That was how being with Ginger had felt. Very sad, and very beautiful, and all the more so because they both knew it would never last. And they'd been right: Dane became famous, and he couldn't be seen at a place like Olive Moore's anymore, or with a girl like Ginger. Not in a million years.

"How is Diana?" Her voice was ice cold.

"Ginger—"

She stepped toward him for the first time, placing a hand against his chest. "That's not my name, Dane. It never was. That girl *never* existed. And we've never met before. Do you understand?"

"Yes." He laid his hand over hers.

She pulled away. He watched her dart coltishly through the trees in her severe black suit, her bright hair like a bobbing flame through the green leaves of the trees.

He had let her down, he knew that. He had let them all down, all those girls who asked so little and needed so much. He had even failed Diana, in the end.

Well, he wouldn't fail her this time. He hoped she knew that. In a strange way, it was a relief. For the first time, a girl had asked of him something he was capable of doing. All she needed him to do was to keep her secret, and Dane Forrest was an expert at that. After all, he had so many secrets of his own.

There was not the slightest doubt in Evelyn Gamble's mind that she was doing the right thing.

In the first place, she was a Gamble. The Gambles had been dictating what was correct and proper to the gentry of Southern California since the Gold Rush, when Great-Great-

Grandpa Augustus Johannes Gamble had discovered that the real gold was in selling picks and pans to unwittingly hopeless prospectors, thereby earning his many descendants nearly a century of unimpeachable rectitude. A Gamble of Pasadena simply could not be wrong.

And in the second place, and more importantly, *something* had to be done about that Margaret Frobisher. The head on that cocky little upstart was blowing up like a balloon. Someone had to pop it once and for all, and Evelyn Gamble, by the very fact of being a Gamble, knew she might be the only one with a sharp-enough pin.

Evelyn didn't know exactly what had happened between Margaret and Phipps McKendrick on the golf course at the Christmas dance, but the crude mechanics were beside the point. Phipps's father was eyeing a run for the governorship. Phipps would want to follow in his footsteps—Evelyn would see to that. And there was no way he could get anywhere in the California Republican Party without the full support of the Gamble family. A Christmas engagement would be just the thing to let everyone who mattered know exactly where the family's alliance lay.

But Margaret Frobisher, Evelyn had to admit, had thrown a bit of a wrench in the plan. Even with the weight of the entire Gamble dynasty behind her, Evelyn harbored just the teeniest, tiniest doubt that she could compete in the marriageability stakes with a gorgeous society debutante who also happened to be a movie star. She'd been sure that that little nobody Doris had been lying about the whole Hollywood thing, but after the two girls had humiliatingly called her bluff that terrible afternoon—not to mention landed Evelyn a week in detention—she couldn't be totally sure that the hated "Frobie" wouldn't succeed.

Margaret Frobisher. It wasn't just that she was beautiful—if you were into that whole regal blonde thing, and Evelyn wasn't. Claire Prince was beautiful, and Evelyn wasn't the least bit threatened by *her*. But Margaret had something different. Something that made people look at her, even before they knew what her last name was. Even, Evelyn thought bitterly, society people who *really* should have known better.

Well, if Hollywood wanted Margaret Frobisher, they could have her. All Evelyn wanted was to get her the hell out of Pasadena. Thirty other debutantes with their whole lives riding on not being overshadowed during the upcoming season would thank Evelyn. It was her duty, as a future leader of society. It was absolutely the right, *the only*, thing to do.

"May I help you, miss?"

A maid in a blue and white striped kitchen uniform answered the door. *Strike one.* If the Frobishers really thought it was acceptable not to have a butler, the least they could do was have someone dressed properly to answer the door.

"I'm here to see Mrs. Frobisher."

"Who may I say is calling?"

Strike two. Evelyn was hardly a regular visitor at this house, but she would have expected as assiduous a social climber as Mildred Frobisher to make sure her staff knew the living members of Pasadena's most important family by sight.

"Miss Evelyn Gamble," she said meaningfully.

"Oh!" The maid looked startled. "I'm sorry, miss, but Miss Margaret . . . she . . . she's not home from school yet."

Evelyn was beginning to lose her patience. "I *know* that. I go to school with her, don't I? I want to see *Mrs.* Frobisher."

"Oh." The maid eyed her suspiciously. "Well, you'd better come in, then. You can wait right here in the hall." It was so ludicrous Evelyn almost laughed out loud. By rights, she should have been shown into the parlor, even the morning room, although it was technically afternoon. *Strike three, Frobie,* she thought. *Three strikes and you're out.*

"Evelyn! How lovely to see you, dear!" Mildred Frobisher pounced into the hallway, a tense smile plastered across the taut planes of her well-preserved face. "Emmeline, I don't know what you're thinking, keeping Miss Gamble in the hallway. Come into the drawing room, dear, and do sit down. Emmeline, we'll have tea, and some sandwiches, I think. Unless you'd prefer something else, dear? Chocolate, perhaps, or orange juice?"

"Tea is fine."

The maid scurried away. Mrs. Frobisher gave a theatrical sigh. "It's nearly a cliché, but it bears repeating—it is so difficult to get good help these days."

"Our staff is excellent."

Mrs. Frobisher's smile faltered. "Well, I'm sure your mother struggles mightily to keep them so. How is she, your dear mother?"

"She's fine."

"Please do send her my very best." Mrs. Frobisher blinked, as though waiting for Evelyn to say something equally friendly in return. Evelyn decided not to oblige. "Ah! Here's the tea."

The maid set down the tray, and Mrs. Frobisher busied herself for a few long moments, pouring and passing and continuing to

129

pretend that there was nothing odd about having her daughter's classmate, whom she had scarcely met before, drop by in the middle of a school day for a sandwich and a spot of tea. Only when the sandwiches had been repeatedly proffered and declined and the delicate porcelain teacups could not hold so much as another drop of tea or splash of milk did she address the elephant in the room.

"You're out of school quite early today, aren't you, dear?"

"I have last period free," Evelyn lied.

"Isn't that nice. I'm expecting Margaret home any minute now, although lately, she's been a . . . a little . . ."

"A little what?" Evelyn prompted.

"A little *unpredictable,* I suppose. But I understand the two of you have become quite chummy, and frankly, I couldn't be more delighted or relieved. I just know you'll be a good influence on her. You'll help her to see what's really important, won't you, Evelyn, dear?" She reached over and patted Evelyn's hand.

Damn! Evelyn was practically feeling *bad* for this woman. Whatever her feelings about Margaret, when Evelyn had first hatched this plan, she hadn't given much thought to the collateral damage. "Actually, it's Margaret I came to talk to you about." She steeled herself with a deep breath. *It's the right thing to do.* "You see, it's come to my attention that she's been hanging around with some . . . some *Hollywood* types."

The color seemed to drain from Mrs. Frobisher's face, but she kept the smile fixed to her lips. "I beg your pardon?"

"Hollywood." *I just have to say it and get it over with. It's too late now.* "She says they've offered her a screen test. For the pictures."

Mrs. Frobisher let out a silvery chuckle that was terrifying

130

in its utter lack of mirth. "My dear, I hope you're not taking Margaret seriously when she says things like that."

"Well, I didn't think she would go through with it, but then when she didn't turn up at school today . . ."

"She wasn't at school today?" Mrs. Frobisher's face was white.

"No, ma'am."

"Well, her father will certainly give her a talking-to when she gets home. But as for this screen test nonsense, Margaret is a very . . . imaginative girl. Perhaps she was just—"

"We heard her making the appointment over the telephone. I didn't believe her at first, so she said she'd prove it. It was with this man."

And with that, Evelyn played her trump card: the battered, pasted-together business card she had surreptitiously picked up from the floor of the phone box. Mrs. Frobisher gazed at it with a horrible expression of recognition, as though she were identifying the body of a loved one in the city morgue.

"I see," Mrs. Frobisher whispered finally.

"Anyway. I just thought you should know." Putting down her teacup, Evelyn got up to go.

"Evelyn, wait." Mrs. Frobisher grasped her hands. Her eyes were unnaturally bright. *Oh God,* Evelyn thought with horror, *is she about to cry?* "I want to thank you for bringing this to my attention. It's important. And it's also very, very important that this information about Margaret stay between you and me. Please. You must tell no one else about this. Not your friends, not your mother. Do you understand?"

"I already told my mother," Evelyn whispered.

Mrs. Frobisher closed her eyes for a long moment. "What did she say?"

"I don't—"

"Evelyn, what did you mother say?"

On the way over, Evelyn had imagined the triumph of this moment. The final scoop of dirt in Margaret Frobisher's social grave, and she was the one wielding the shovel. "She said that under the circumstances, she couldn't imagine how it would be appropriate for Margaret to socialize with the other debutantes this year. She said you're obviously free to bring her out if you wish, but she would certainly think twice before accepting any of Margaret's invitations, and that she would urge her closest friends to do the same. She said this sort of thing might be acceptable in San Francisco, or even in New York, but not in Pasadena, and that with your family's history, you of all people should understand that." She stared into the woman's ashen face. "I don't know what she meant by that, your family's history. Do you?"

Before Mrs. Frobisher could answer, there was a commotion in the hall, and Margaret Frobisher herself came bursting wild-eyed through the door. Emmeline clung frantically to her wrist, as though trying to hold her back. "What are you doing here?" Margaret cried, her eyes shooting daggers in Evelyn's direction. She was wearing her school uniform, but her flushed, panicked face bore telltale smears of makeup that no Orange Grove girl would think of wearing before nightfall.

"I . . . I came to see you," Evelyn stammered.

"Bullshit!"

"Margaret!" Mrs. Frobisher was on her feet, her face as white as a sheet. "How dare you speak to our guest that way?"

Evelyn was already out the door. She ran through the foyer and down the outside steps. She thought she'd run all the way home, but halfway down the garden path, something made her turn around. Maybe she wanted to witness the havoc she had wreaked. Maybe she wanted to see if things would magically go back to normal. Maybe she was just perversely, incurably curious, but she soon found herself crouching in a bed of nasturtium outside the window, peering into the Frobishers' drawing room through a gap in the taffeta curtains.

She had expected shouting. She had expected crying, and pleading, and begging. But she had never imagined that Mrs. Frobisher would raise her hand and strike Margaret so hard across the face that the girl went reeling. She hadn't thought she would see Margaret Frobisher in a crumpled heap on the floor, sobbing as blood slowly seeped into her golden hair. No, Evelyn hadn't expected that at all.

I did the right thing, she thought as she felt hot tears course silently down her burning cheeks. *The right thing, the right thing, the right thing . . .*

TWELVE

Larry Julius hated Pasadena.

It never failed. Every time he had to come over to this god-forsaken side of the mountain, the snaking boulevards and leaf-canopied drives functioned like a devilish hedge maze before a medieval chateau. No wonder he was hopelessly lost. The whole place was designed to keep people like him out.

Rolling down the car door window, Larry expelled a huge sigh. The resulting cloud of cigarette smoke nearly obscured the returning figure of his chauffeur, Arthur, scurrying out of the gas station and into the safety of the driver's seat. "You got the directions?" Larry asked.

"Yes, sir . . ."

"But?"

Arthur leaned over the seat to look at his boss. His dark face was stricken. "The fellow in there didn't seem too happy to see someone who looked like me."

"I doubt he'd be my biggest fan either, Arthur."

"I mean, he *acted* like he was telling me which way to go, but for all I know he might have directed me right on out of here. Wouldn't be the first time something like that happened somewhere I wasn't wanted."

"I'll tell you what, Arthur." Larry let out another of his great smoky sighs. "If we get lost again it'll be my turn to go into the gas station. Deal?"

"If you say so, Mr. Julius."

"Good. Now let's get going. I want to make it back to Beverly Hills before we're both ignored to death by an angry mob."

Arthur straightened his cap and pulled out onto the street. Larry lit himself a fresh cigarette and settled back against the creamy leather seat of the Rolls-Royce Phantom. Flashier than Larry would normally have preferred, and certainly a mite too conspicuous out here for Arthur's taste, but that was the point. It was a car designed to intimidate. A car that said: "Don't even bother to argue; you already know we've won."

God, it really was ridiculous. A man of his stature, second in command in all but name at the biggest studio in Hollywood, making an evening house call like some country doctor. But something had to be done. It had been almost a week now. A week of phone calls and messages and telegrams, and nobody had heard so much as a peep from this girl. Most of the hopeful young starlets counting on Larry to make all their dreams come true were not nearly so circumspect. Most of them, it was all he could do to keep them from stalking him at restaurants, or shipping themselves to his office in packing crates (which scared poor Gladys to death), or hiding in his shower to jump out unexpectedly the second he dropped his robe.

In a way, he almost welcomed the desperation; at least it showed that they were serious, that Hollywood was what they wanted and they'd do whatever it took to make it there. There was nothing wrong with playing a little hard-to-get, but if you ran from the Big Bad Wolf too long, he just might get tired of the chase and move on. After all, this was Hollywood. If one Little Red Riding Hood slipped out of the wolf's grasp, there was always another one coming down the path, brighter and younger and tastier than the one who came before.

But this girl was different. Kurtzman and Karp and Forrest were all convinced she was the one they'd been looking for so frantically for the last three months. For Kurtzman, she was the key to the film that would allow him to reclaim the career the Nazis had stolen. For Karp, she was a way to keep things on budget, recoup costs, get Hunter Payne and New York off his back and out of his studio. And for Forrest . . . well, Larry was pretty sure he knew what Dane saw in Margaret Frobisher. But they'd cross that bridge when they came to it.

As for Larry, he was just happy to be proven right. He'd known the girl had something special from the moment he'd seen her sitting at that lunch counter. Even with the schoolgirl sweater and the too-red lipstick, there'd been a kind of light around her.

There was a satisfying crunch of pebbled gravel under the wheels of the Rolls. Arthur was pulling into a long, curved drive.

"We here, Arthur?"

"I reckon so."

Larry stuck his head out the window and peered at the house. Standard California Arts and Crafts. Respectable, not palatial. Nothing to keep her down on the farm if she had a mind to leave. "All right, Arthur. I'm going in. Be back in half an hour, tops."

"Oh no. No, you don't."

"I beg your pardon?"

"Respectfully, Mr. Julius, you ain't leaving me here sitting alone in no Rolls-Royce Phantom in a driveway in this neighborhood, you understand me?"

"For God's sake, Arthur, we're not in Mississippi."

"Respectfully, Mr. J., that's easy for you to say."

"Fine. If anyone comes, honk the horn real loud. Loud as you can."

"And if that's not good enough?"

Larry climbed out of the car and narrowed his eyes at the name on the mailbox, half hidden under a spray of wisteria. *Frobisher.* And below that: *Trespassers Beware.*

"If that's not good enough, Arthur, frankly I think we're both screwed."

"Miss Margaret, I'm coming in."

"I wish you wouldn't," Margaret moaned. The housekeeper ignored her, as usual.

How many times over the years has Emmeline found me like this? she wondered. *Sprawled across the bed, face streaked with new tears and swollen with old ones?* They'd developed a standard operating procedure over the years: Emmeline wordlessly

137

bringing up a tray of food, Margaret choking down bites until she was calm again, at which time Emmeline would mouth a couple of meaningless platitudes and put Margaret to bed. But this time the system had failed them. It was as though these latest developments—Evelyn's betrayal, Margaret's mother's sudden lapse into icy violence—had ripped away a decade's worth of bandages to reveal for the first time the unhealable wound that lay beneath it.

"When God closes a door, he always opens a window." That was one of the things Emmeline liked to say. *But not this time,* Margaret thought. This time, when the door had slammed shut, she'd been left out in the cold. Her mother had barely spoken to her since it had happened. Her father had mourned the social ruin of his daughter in his own way: he'd taken off for the beach hut with God knew which of his fake secretaries and had only returned that morning. Emmeline still brought the food, but even she seemed to realize that the despair of Miss Margaret's current purgatory was at last out of her jurisdiction.

"You haven't touched your dinner."

"I told you I wasn't hungry."

Emmeline clucked her tongue. "Three days of meals you turn your nose up at, when there's children starving in Europe."

"Not anymore, there's not."

An image of Gabby Preston looking wide-eyed at her sad little bowl of unadorned chicken broth swam into Margaret's head. She buried her face in a pillow. She didn't want to think about Olympus; she couldn't bear it. "Is that why you came up here, Emmeline? To see if I choked down any of your meat loaf?"

"No, miss. I came to tell you there's a gentleman downstairs wants to see you."

"What kind of a gentleman?" In Margaret's experience, Emmeline's iteration of the term could apply to anyone from a colleague of her father's to Timmy Mulvaney, the six-year-old boy down the street she sometimes babysat.

"He didn't tell me anything, Miss Margaret. Not even his name. But I overheard him say something about the movies."

Fifteen minutes later, Margaret left her bedroom for the first time in a week. The faint shadow of bruising around her eye had been carefully powdered away. Emmeline had fixed her part so that the small bandage over the cut on her temple was masked by the fall of her hair. She had changed out of her dirty pajamas into the simple gray dress with the little white collar that Doris said made her look like a French orphan. The idea was to descend the stairs looking beautiful and somber and un-forgiving. Like Diana Chesterfield in *Vengeance Is a Woman*, when she realized her evil fiancé had secretly embezzled her inheritance while plotting to murder her. *Except this is my own movie*, Margaret thought. She could barely wait to see how it would turn out.

Her father was seated stiffly on his usual horsehair chair, an empty glass of brandy by his side. Her mother hovered near the piano, refusing to meet her eye. And perched on the velvet settee her mother usually occupied, calm as could be, was Larry Julius.

She had not seen him since that day at the lunch counter at Schwab's. After the past few weeks, during which he had assumed almost mythic status in her mind, it was shocking to see him in the flesh, let alone in her house. Yet here he was, serenely blowing smoke rings as casually as though he dropped by all the time.

"Margaret," her father said, his voice tight with unexpressed rage. "This . . ."

"Julius," Larry prompted pleasantly. "Larry Julius."

"This man Julius would like to speak with you."

"Miss Frobisher," Larry said warmly. "What a pleasure it is to see you again." He gestured toward the brocade chair her parents usually offered to guests. "Won't you sit down?"

Her father pressed his mouth into a thin line. "There's no need for pleasantries, Julius. Just say whatever you have to say to the girl." *The girl*, Margaret thought. *It's as if he thinks I'm his servant.*

"I appreciate your bluntness, sir," Larry said, "but where I come from, it wouldn't be right to leave a lady on her feet."

Mr. Frobisher looked incredulous. "And where is that, may I ask?"

"Oh . . ." Larry gestured vaguely. "Somewhere back east."

Her father sniffed. "The tenements, I suppose."

"A bit farther than that." Larry was still smiling, but his voice had a hard edge to it. "But even Attila the Hun was known to offer a chair to a woman from time to time."

"Sit down, Margaret." From halfway across the room, her mother's voice was calm and clear, although she still avoided her daughter's eye. Margaret sat.

"Good girl." Larry lit himself a fresh cigarette. "I have to tell you Miss Frobisher, you're a very hard person to get a hold of."

"I . . . I don't understand."

"We've phoned, dozens of times. We sent telegrams." Larry shrugged. "No reply."

Margaret jerked her head toward her mother, who was look-ing at her at last, her blue eyes cold and defiant. *She knew,* Margaret thought. *And she kept it from me.* Her hand flew up to the small bandage over her eye as images of that horrible after-noon flooded into her mind. The raised hand. The pain of the blow and the wet, warm trickle of blood on her forehead. And worst of all, the terrible look in her mother's eyes. Not anger, not concern, not even sadness: it was at once all of those and greater still, a dawning of the awful knowledge that something between them had been broken and could never be mended. "Oh." It was all she could bring herself to say.

Larry chuckled. "Now, if it was me, I would have just given up on you. 'She's not interested,' I would have said. 'Why try to buy what's not for sale?' But Leo Karp doesn't think that way. He said, 'Larry, I want to hear it from the girl's own mouth.' So here I am. To hear it from you. And then I can go back to Hollywood, and as God is my witness, you'll never see the likes of me darken your beautiful doorstep again."

"Hear what from me? What are you talking about?"

Larry looked surprised. "Why, about the contract, of course."

Her stomach lurched. "What . . . what contract?"

"The one Mr. Karp wants to offer you."

Margaret felt faint. She was suddenly inordinately grateful to Larry for insisting she sit down. "Mr. Karp wants to give me—"

"A contract, yes." Larry nodded. "That's Leo F. Karp, the presi-dent of Olympus Studios," he added, presumably for the Frobishers' benefit. "It's very rare, you understand, for him to take an interest in a young actress, particularly one with no experience. But he was tremendously impressed with the screen test of young Margaret here, and he'd like very much to put her under contract. He's offering our standard one-year exclusive, with an option to renew. She'll have speech lessons, singing lessons, dancing lessons. The wardrobe, hair, and makeup departments will overhaul her image. Deportment coaches will teach her how to walk, how to sit, which fork to use at dinner—not"—he cast an admiring, if sardonic, glance around the lavishly appointed room—"that I expect she'll need much help with that."

"And where is she supposed to live while you people are transforming her into this creature?" Mr. Frobisher interjected. "For it won't be under my roof, I can tell you that."

Really? Is my father really prepared to turn me out? Margaret felt a little short of breath.

"In that case," Larry said quietly, "she'd be given a place at the studio. It's hardly without precedent. Many families in a similar position turn guardianship over to us. She'll be adequately housed and supervised until her eighteenth birthday, which I believe is not so very far away, and then she can live on her own if she likes. She can certainly set up housekeeping on seventy-five dollars a week. That's what we'd be paying her for the first year."

"Seventy-five dollars a week? *Seventy-five dollars a week?*" Mr. Frobisher raged.

"Only to start," Larry said. "By the time her guardianship ends there's every expectation she'll be earning significantly more than that. More than enough for her to keep herself in the manner to which she is accustomed."

"So let me get this straight," Mr. Frobisher sputtered. "You come in here, to my home, uninvited, offering to . . . *buy* Margaret from me for seventy-five dollars a week?"

"No, not quite," Larry said cheerfully. "Obviously, we'll need you to cosign the contract, but Margaret's salary is paid only to Margaret. If she chooses to share it with you, that's up to her."

"Share it? With *me?*" Mr. Frobisher's already florid face turned crimson.

"Lowell, please." Holding up her hand, Mrs. Frobisher strode commandingly to the center of the room, waiting until all eyes were on her before she began to speak. *My God,* Margaret thought, *she thinks she's giving a speech.*

"Mr. Julius," her mother began, "just a few short weeks ago, such an offer would have been unthinkable. Apart from the obscenity of any respectable girl *earning* her own *living,* the idea of flaunting oneself in public, for the delectation of *strangers . . .*" She shuddered. "Let us just say for a girl like Margaret, a girl who has been raised a certain way, with certain expectations, it would be unimaginable."

How is that any different than a coming-out ball? Margaret thought furiously. *How is appearing in the pictures worse than parading down a staircase for a bunch of rich men to stare at, while the women plot to sell me to the highest bidder?*

Her mother barreled on. "Times may change, Mr. Julius, but nice people do not. And something upon which all nice people agree is that a respectable woman's name should appear in the newspaper but three times: when she is born, when she marries, and when she dies. A respectable woman is the soul of discretion. Her life is spent in the sacred service of her husband and her children—if she is lucky enough to have them—and in upholding the standards of her community. That Margaret seems to feel otherwise can only reflect badly on Mr. Frobisher and me. The only excuse I can offer is that she lived with us as an only child for seventeen years and that we indulged her."

Hardly.

"While I have known for some time of Margaret's vanity and . . . shall we say . . . *unbecoming* ambition, I told myself that this was simply a young girl's fancy, and that when the time came she would put such childish, selfish things aside and do her duty to those who gave her a home. Instead, by consorting with you and others of your . . . your *persuasion,* she has severely jeopardized her future, and made a mockery of all that Mr. Frobisher and I have offered her."

"Hear, hear," Mr. Frobisher said.

"Quiet, Lowell." Mrs. Frobisher turned to her daughter. "Margaret, I put it to you. You have heard Mr. Julius's offer. If you want to go with him, we will not stop you, but we will wash our hands of you." For a moment, the icy film over her eyes suddenly seemed to thaw, giving her a vaguely haunted look, as if she were looking at something terrible that only she could see. "You will be on your own, without support or family. Should you wish to return to us or to Pasadena at any time, you will find the door firmly closed."

"Or?" Margaret whispered. Her throat was dry.

"You may stay," Mrs. Frobisher said simply. "We will do whatever we can to repair your damaged reputation. We will bring you out in whatever way is available to us. In return, you will do your duty. You will behave like a respectable young woman. No movie magazines, no truancy, no late-night disappearances from dances with young gentlemen." Margaret blushed. She hadn't realized her mother knew about the Phipps McKendrick episode. "You will obey us unquestioningly," Mrs.

Frobisher continued, "until you are married to an appropriate young man. And you will put all thoughts of *Hollywood*"—her mother almost spat the word—"out of your head forever."

Here it was. The choice that a small part of Margaret had always known she would one day have to make: the choice between who she had always been, and who she had always longed to be.

She thought of her life in Pasadena. Her house. Her friends. She thought of how her father used to push her so high on the rope swing in the backyard she could almost touch the branches of the eucalyptus tree with her toes, how her mother had held her in the water when she taught her how to swim. She imagined herself as the calm, smiling wife of Stephen Van Camp or Frederick Harrington or Phipps McKendrick, living in a beautiful house, arranging flowers in a crystal vase, receiving a chaste kiss from her tired husband as she greeted him at the door with his whiskey and slippers at the end of a long day. She imagined walking in the park with Doris, the two of them pushing their babies in carriages as they gossiped about who was having an affair with his secretary, who was secretly living apart, who was soon to be blacklisted from the next benefit committee or party or ball.

Then she thought of Olympus, of the magical world behind its shining gates. The hushed frenzy of the soundstages, the shady bungalows containing the secrets of the stars. Gabby Preston's big eyes and infectious laugh and mysterious pills, and Raoul Kurtzman's world-weary shrugs, and Sadie the Wardrobe Lady's coral-stained cigarettes. She thought of Amanda Farraday slinking across the commissary floor in her black suit, like a black widow spider hunting her newest prey. She thought of Diana Chesterfield and the mysteries her disappearance held. And she thought of Dane Forrest, the most alluring mystery of all.

"Well, Margaret?" Mrs. Frobisher cleared her throat. "What will it be?"

No tears. Not a single one.

Larry Julius had never seen anything like it. The day he'd left home you could hear his mama's anguished wails all the way to Fourteenth Street. Sure, he knew these fancy-schmancy society types could be pretty cold fish, but disowning an only daughter without so much as a sniffle? As though it were all just an unfortunate inconvenience; as though they were getting rid of a cook who had burned the roast one too many times. And the words that woman used! *Lived with us for seventeen years . . . those who gave her a home.* Not once did she use the word *daughter.* Not once did she so much as mention the word *love.* It was all very upsetting, not to mention suspicious. When it came to smelling a rat, Larry Julius had the best nose in the business. And his nose was telling him that something was very, very rotten in Pasadena. He just didn't know what.

The girl sat beside him in the backseat of the Phantom, perfectly quiet, the glow of headlights and the shimmer of moonlight illuminating her soft yellow hair. Larry had to fight a sudden, wild urge to throw his arms around her and hold her tight. Not in a romantic way; he wasn't a cradle robber, for God's sake. He just felt as if someone should show the poor kid some affection.

But she didn't seem to need any. She stared straight ahead,

clear-eyed and unblinking, like some warrior queen fearlessly surveying the oncoming hordes. Yep, this one had some steel in her spine, all right. *Steel*, Larry thought suddenly. She was going to need a new name for the pictures. What about Steele?

No, that didn't sound right. Too masculine, too unforgiving. This dame needed something classy, something that sounded expensive. They couldn't use Gold—for obvious reasons—or Silver . . .

"Sterling," Larry said aloud.

She turned to him, a marvel with her clear, dry eyes. "What did you say?"

"You need a new name. What about Sterling? Margaret Sterling."

"Margaret Sterling," she said, trying it out.

"Sounds good, right? Like one of those dames you might come across in finishing school."

"Margo," she said suddenly.

"What?"

"Margo. For the first name. It's an old nickname of mine. . . ." She trailed off. "And I think it's better. More unusual. Margo Sterling. People will remember it."

Larry grinned. His whole press team couldn't have come up with anything more perfect. Boy, this kid was something else, all right. "I can already see it in lights."

THIRTEEN

In Olive Moore's day, the movie magazines had been such anemic little things. Printed in black-and-white on cheap newsprint and bound as roughly as though they'd been stapled together in someone's dirty basement. But the fresh new copies of *Picture Palace* and *Modern Screen* and all the others that now littered the surface of her mahogany desk were glossy, and filled with as many full-color glamour shots and painstakingly art-directed photo spreads as an issue of *Vogue*. The first week the houseboy delivered them to her office, she felt almost intimidated by their gleaming, expensive newness. Her Hollywood days were long behind her now; weeks went past when she didn't think about them at all. The magazines seemed to bring it all back: the sting of having been left behind, the pain of seeing the world she had known and loved continuing so swimmingly without her. No wonder she'd never tried to look at them before.

She had steeled herself to continue, and as the weeks receded into the past, the hurt did too. Besides, how else was she supposed to see how Amanda was getting on? If she was making a splash in Hollywood, setting tongues wagging and checkbooks flipping, or if she was likely to come crawling back any day now with her tail between her legs? Either way, Olive figured, she'd rather be prepared.

So far there hadn't been much: just a tiny cheesecake photo of Amanda in a swimsuit in *Photoplay* when Olympus first announced her as a new contract player and a casting roundup in *Picture Palace* that said Amanda would be playing a gangster's moll in some small picture. Every once in a while, there was a blind item in one of the gossip columns mentioning a ravishing redhead in black seen out to dinner at Chasen's or the Brown Derby, usually on the arm of some powerful man or other, which Olive would read with a kind of grim satisfaction. *Good girl. Doing what I taught her.* Still, they were hardly the clippings of a girl who was taking the town by storm.

For so many girls, fame and fortune were only the beginning of the story—first-act stuff, as Amanda's screenwriter might say. They were certainly no guarantee of a happy ending.

Just look at poor Diana. There it was, the lead story in the week's edition of *Picture Palace:*

DIANA CHESTERFIELD OFFICIALLY DECLARED MISSING AFTER LENGTHY ABSENCE. Friends and Family Frantic over Screen Queen's Disappearance. "We'll Do Anything to Bring Her Home," Vows Olympus Studios Chief, Offers Hefty Reward for Star's Safe Return.

Hefty reward. That was a laugh. Olive would have bet a pretty penny that old Leo Karp wouldn't be parting with any of his money soon. The only people with any information on the whereabouts of Diana Chesterfield were the ones busily covering just what those whereabouts might be, and they were undoubtedly on the studio's payroll already. As for anyone else who might have any pertinent information about the vanished star, the only reward they were going to see was a one-way ticket out of town, and maybe a broken leg to go with it. If they were lucky.

Poor Diana. Olive shook her head sadly, drinking in Diana's face, as young and lovely as the day they'd first met. It had been ages since Diana had confided in her. They'd talked about everything in those days. But Diana had left Olive behind. *Just like Amanda,* Olive thought. *Just like everybody in this whole stinking town. Fools.* Trying to outrun themselves. Thinking that if you just forgot about your past, your past would forget about you. And where did it get you? Where had it gotten Diana? She'd heard all the rumors, of course; Olive was always hungry for information where Diana was concerned. An overdose, a crack-up, even foul play: knowing Diana, they were all equally possible. Whatever it was, the fact that a story like this had been allowed to go to press confirmed its seriousness. The studio was in full damage-control mode, trying to turn lemons into lemonade. It was a classic Larry Julius move, perfected back in the twenties, when wild young stars with too much power and too much money were dropping like flies. A stopgap measure until the businessmen moved in with the talkies and realized that if you only paid a star fifty dollars a week, she couldn't spend five hundred on cocaine, and if she

150

did anyway, you could profit from the scandal. You ginned up the mystery for a few weeks, sold a million magazines—with a sizable kickback to the studio. In the meantime, you trotted out a few shiny new stars for the plebes to go gaga over, some young, malleable kids you could underpay and overwork, and in six months—hell, in *three*—no one would even remember the tragic starlet. Eventually, her story might be resolved in a three-line item (or a three-line obit) stuck in the back of a magazine or newspaper, or in a studio press release, but by then, no one would be looking for it.

Still, there was something in the Diana story that gave Olive pause. An ugly little reference at the very end:

In the wake of such fearful uncertainty, we must thank heaven for small mercies: at least Dane Forrest seems to be taking the disappearance of his longtime paramour in stride. As he danced and drank the night away at the Cocoanut Grove last Friday with a bevy of beauteous brunettes, a certain blonde couldn't have seemed further from his mind. . . .

What a dirty trick. Olive couldn't help admiring the malignant smoothness of it all. Not exactly defamatory—in fact, it was probably true—but whoever had written it knew exactly what he was doing. The picture magazines, like the pictures themselves, thrived on the power of suggestion. It was a very short step from suggesting that Dane perhaps wasn't quite as sad and concerned as he should be over Diana's disappearance to insinuating that he might have had something to do with it.

Had he? He'd certainly come a long way from the shy, stammering farm boy Olive had known, but even then he'd had a knack for getting himself in the damnedest heaps of trouble. Clearly, he'd gone and done it again. Somebody, perhaps somebody very powerful, had it in for Dane. She would have warned him to watch his back, but it had been years since Dane Forrest had returned one of Olive Moore's phone calls.

Olive turned the page. Printed in huge curling script that took up nearly half the page, the headline might as well have been accompanied by the fanfare of trumpets and the fluttering of seraphim:

*Is this the most beautiful girl
in the United States of America?*

Olive almost laughed aloud as she read the first paragraph proclaiming the arrival of the Olympus starlet *everybody* in Hollywood was talking about. *Margo Sterling. So this is Diana's replacement.* Quickly, she skimmed the article, written in the Olympus press office's trademark breathless style: how the Sterling girl had been plucked from the debutante doldrums and was destined to dazzle audiences the world over with her beauty and breeding; how she was a natural honey blonde; how she loved horses, chocolate-chip ice cream, and the American way. Boilerplate stuff, really, with scarcely a word changed from the press release, and so *boring*. In Olive's day, the studio had claimed that all the young actresses were lost Russian princesses or the escaped concubines of evil Arabian sheikhs. *Larry Julius is slipping*, she thought with a snort as she turned the page to reveal the girl's photograph.

Her jaw dropped.

Hands shaking, Olive turned frantically back to the article, this time devouring each word with rabid attention. The name meant nothing, of course; Olive herself had been christened after the first tree that fat producer had seen when he'd looked out the window of his office. But the details: *A California native. A dizzy debutante.* They were maddeningly vague and fictional, but then . . . that face. That searching, hopeful, lovely face. A face she somehow felt she knew as well as her own.

Olive closed the magazine. She walked over to the bar, poured herself a giant glassful of sherry from the decanter, and drank it off in one gulp. Her hands were still shaking, so she poured herself another one and drank that too.

Then she walked back to her desk and picked up the telephone. "Burbank 6452, please." She waited as the operator connected her, nervously fiddling with the little gold-and-pearl circle pin she wore pinned to her collar.

"Amanda, dear!" she said, when the girl answered. "How lucky to find you in. This is Olive Moore. . . . Now, there's no need to take that tone, I simply want to see how you are. . . . Good, I'm very glad to hear it. Now, listen, dear, I needed to ask you something. . . . No, not that. . . . You remember I told you that at some point I might need a favor from you? Because I'm afraid that time has come." Olive gave her gold pin a final twist. "I need you to find out everything you can about this Margo Sterling."

FOURTEEN

There was only one thing wrong with the famous Cocoanut Grove nightclub at the Ambassador Hotel in Hollywood: it looked so much like something out of the movies, it was hard to remember it was a real place.

Swaying palm trees strung with thousands of tiny white lights seemed to grow directly out of the floor, forming a sparkling green canopy beneath the graceful Moorish arches. Beside the polished dance floor was a mirrored stage, complete with a twenty-one-piece orchestra and a beautiful singer draped in silver sequins and blue gardenias. The midnight-blue ceiling was painted to look like the night sky, complete with hundreds of twinkling stars. But the real stars, of course, were below, gliding between tables, glittering on the dance floor. Women dripping with diamonds, men in dinner jackets as white as their gleaming toothpaste smiles.

It was a beautiful room filled with beautiful people, and tonight, for the first time, Margo Sterling was one of them. She practically had to pinch herself to make sure she wasn't dreaming. *If only Gabby weren't in such a foul mood,* she thought, *everything would be perfect.*

From the moment Margo had moved into the small bungalow on the studio lot, Gabby Preston had been a constant presence, phoning several times a day with some new piece of gossip, turning up at the door at odd hours bearing various small "housewarming" gifts: a bouquet of orange blossom cut from the trees outside, a lemon cake baked by Viola, even a worn record player and a stack of old 78s. Margo was grateful. The little gifts and incessant chatter made the stark bungalow, with its smudged walls and furnishings that had seen generations of hopefuls come and go, seem almost like a home. Better yet, they helped to shut out the increasingly terrifying fact that she had walked out of her safe life with no idea what the future would hold. She was on her own now, but with Gabby there, she didn't feel so alone.

Still, Gabby's high-octane personality could be a little exhausting, and thanks to Dr. Lipkin and his miracle pills, her grasp on the concept of waking hours, as opposed to sleeping hours, was creative at best. It had been barely light that morning when Gabby had turned up at Margo's door, practically climbing out of her skin with excitement. "Did you hear? We're going out together on an engagement tonight! Aren't you excited?"

"I might be," Margo had said, rubbing the sleep out of her eyes, "if it weren't five o'clock in the morning."

"But a real engagement! I could just die!"

"Wait." Margo scowled sleepily in confusion. "An engagement? You're getting married?"

"Honestly, Margo, sometimes I think you don't know anything. An engagement is a night out on the town. The studio arranges it all. They choose your escort, dress you up in the most gorgeous gown, and send you out to one of the glamorous, exclusive places where all the stars go, and the next day your picture is in all the papers and everyone is talking about you. I've been on one or two before, of course, but only early in the evening, and always with Viola, which makes it all about as magical as a sack of lard. But not tonight! Tonight she's got to stay at home and knit, and guess who my escort is going to be!"

Margo blinked.

Gabby couldn't wait. "No, you'll never guess, I'll tell you. It's Jimmy! Jimmy Molloy!"

"Well, that's just swell," Margo said. *Swell* was about as enthusiastic as she could get before breakfast.

"*Swell* isn't the word for it! It's positively stupendous! I told you they're putting us together! It'll be announced any day, I'm sure of it. I can see the headlines now." Eyes shining, Gabby swept her hand through the air, across an imaginary front page. "Olympus's Singing Sweethearts Blow Up Box Office. No," she interrupted herself. "Singing *Steadies*. That's better than *sweethearts*, don't you think? More grown-up."

"Do I have an escort?"

"Don't you *ever* open your mailbox? Of course you do. You're being escorted by Larry Julius, and don't you dare look disappointed," she said, wagging a finger at Margo's obvious dismay. "You don't think he bothers with just anyone, do you? The studio couldn't give you a bigger stamp of approval if you walked in on the arm of Mr. Karp himself. By this time tomorrow, we're going to be the two most envied girls in Hollywood." Beaming, she hugged herself. "I could die of happiness!"

But now that they were at the Cocoanut Grove, Gabby looked anything but happy. Her small face was a thundercloud under a hairdo of beribboned sausages as she reached over to seize a handful of the silken skirt of Margo's dress, nearly knocking over the waiter who was opening the champagne for their table.

"That's pretty," Gabby grumbled.

In truth, Margo's dress was a lot more than pretty. After the banana dress incident, Margo had been a little apprehensive at seeing Sadie on her doorstep with a garment bag, but all her doubts had vanished the moment she saw the bias-cut satin gown with a plunging back in a shade of silvery blue that matched her eyes. The studio had lent her a delicate sapphire bracelet with earrings to match, and to one of the shoulder straps, done in a contrasting black velvet, she had affixed her little pearl pin. It was startlingly chic, more like something out of a fashion magazine than what your typical flashy Hollywood starlet would wear.

"Yours is nice too," Margo said, with as much enthusiasm as she could muster. Gabby had been coaxed, clearly against her will, into a frilly concoction of apricot tulle with a stiff crinoline skirt, the kind of dress a child might wear to a fancy party. "You look really pretty."

"Don't patronize me. I look like one of those creepy legless dolls Viola hides the extra roll of toilet paper under in the bathroom." Gabby's face crumpled. "Why do they make me wear these stupid baby dresses? Why can't I have a dress like yours?"

"Image, darling," Jimmy Molloy answered, politely holding out to the girls his gold cigarette case, which Larry Julius promptly declined on their behalf. "You can't go full glamour like the duchess here. You're Everyone's Kid Sister. But don't you worry, honey pie. There's a lot of money in being America's Sweetheart. Isn't that right, Margo?" He winked at her.

Margo wasn't quite sure what she thought of Jimmy. He was certainly awfully friendly, kissing her hand when they'd met and making a big show of pretending his eyeballs were popping out of his head when he saw her, like a wolf in a Tex Avery cartoon. But there was something a little bit *strange* about the way he never seemed to turn off.

"And, Gabby, you just be a good girl and do what the nice men tell you," Jimmy said, chucking her on the chin. "Before you know it, you'll have enough dough in the oven to get yourself a Schiaparelli for every day of the week."

"I don't need a shopperelly." Gabby pouted. "I just want a pretty dress."

"A Schiaparelli *is* a dress, silly." Grinning, Jimmy curled his finger below his nose like a Gallic mustache. "She is all zee rage with the *haute monde* in gay Paree."

"Oat mound? What on earth is an oat mound?"

"*Haute monde*. It means 'high society' in French," Margo said, instantly regretting it when she saw the humiliated look on her friend's face. The last thing she wanted to do was show Gabby up in front of Jimmy. "They probably only put you in that dress because they couldn't find anything else to fit you," she added quickly. "You've lost *so* much weight."

Gabby's face lit up. "Do you really think so?"

"I *know* so. If I didn't know better, I'd be worried."

Gabby beamed, smoothing the cloth of her dress over her svelte waist. Her hands, Margo noticed, shook slightly. "Yeah, well, now my chest is gone too. Just my luck. As if I didn't look young enough. Next time you see me, they'll probably have me in a baby bonnet."

"Look over there, Margo," Larry Julius interjected. With a subtle tilt of his cigarette, he indicated a raven-haired beauty draped in white silk and about fifteen ropes of huge black pearls gliding toward an adjacent table. "Hedy Lamarr. See the way she moves? Now, *that's the way you make an entrance.*"

"And look over *there*." Gabby smirked. Obviously, Viola had never told her it was rude to point. "*There's* that Amanda Farraday."

Her stomach clenching, Margo followed Gabby's accusatory finger to the gorgeous girl standing in the middle of the maze of tables. She was wearing black, as usual, but hers was a dress that Margo was pretty sure she'd never find on her own wardrobe rack: impossibly low-cut, and covered from top to bottom in jet paillettes, a diamond-shaped cutout just below the bust exposing a creamy swath of bare skin. One of her hands was tucked into a luxurious cloud of sleek fur. The other was clinging to the arm of a portly gray-haired gentleman nearly old enough to be her grandfather.

"She's not with Dane."

She whispered it under her breath, a private sigh of relief, but Larry Julius missed nothing. "Dane Forrest?" he asked, his sharp eyes coolly surveying Margo. "Did you expect her to be?"

"Oh, Margo and I saw them leave the commissary together the other day," Gabby said crankily. "They tried to slip out separately so nobody would notice them."

"But *you* noticed."

"Oh, sure," Gabby said. "Margo could hardly take her eyes off him, could you, Margo?"

"We had just shot my screen test together," Margo mumbled, staring down at her crystal saucer of champagne. "I was just wondering if I should try to say hello, that's all."

Larry Julius expelled a thoughtful cloud of cigarette smoke from what Margo was sure were terribly overwhelmed lungs. "Well. That's very interesting."

"Oh, that's not even the half of it," Gabby said cheerfully. "With that Amanda girl, I mean. Margo saw her earlier that same day, necking with some writer in his office." *God*, Margo thought, *doesn't Gabby forget anything?* For a girl who was so prone to proclaiming her academic ignorance, she had a mind like a steel trap. She could have made a heck of a trial lawyer, if anyone had ever bothered to teach her to read.

"Harry Gordon, I should think," Larry said.

"Harry Gordon?" Gabby's eyes were wide. "Not that Commie from New York who's supposed to be writing *my* next picture? The vaudeville musical?" Gabby had been crowing nonstop for days about her new picture. A standard rags-to-riches musical, it was nevertheless the first vehicle the studio had commissioned for Gabby to star in alone, and she was convinced it was going to make millions of dollars and win her every prize going, including an Academy Award. "Not some kind of juvenile Oscar either, like they gave Shirley Temple," Gabby sneered. "A *real* Oscar, for Best Actress. I mean, how could I lose? It's being written *just for me*! It's exactly the story of my life!"

"The very same," Larry said.

Gabby snorted. "Covering all the bases, just like I said to Margo. Good thing she can't sing."

"Let's have some champagne," Jimmy said quickly, raising his glass. "To old friends and new, to fame and fortune and dazzling success. To Hollywood!"

"To Hollywood." They all drank. Margo had never tasted champagne before. The golden bubbles, sweet and faintly sour, tickled her throat. An effervescent warmth spread down her neck and into her chest. *Like drinking a glass full of starlight*, she thought, her whole body tingling with pleasure.

"Who's that she's with, anyway?" The champagne had clearly not had the same tempering effect on Gabby, although she had drunk off her glass in a single gulp and was helping herself to another one. "He looks like he's ready for the grave."

Larry put down his glass, from which he had taken only the tiniest of sips. "His name is Oscar Zellman," Larry said quietly. "I'm surprised you don't know who he is. He ran a major production unit at Olympus until he left three years ago to set up as an independent. He's doing quite well for himself, much to Karp's dismay. Produced three of the ten Best Picture nominees last year, and without a studio behind him."

Jimmy hooted. "Atta girl, Amanda! There's a girl who knows where she's going."

"Well, I guess she wised up." Gabby tossed back her second glass. "I mean, Dane Forrest might be one of the biggest stars on the planet, but he's hardly the jackpot for any girl, is he?"

Margo could practically feel Larry Julius's eyes boring into her. "What do you mean by that?"

"Yeah, what gives?" Jimmy asked.

"Darlings, don't play dumb." The alcohol was loosening

Gabby's already loose tongue. "It's all out in the open now anyway, isn't it? In the papers he and Diana Chesterfield might have been on the rocks just prior to her, shall we say . . . *sudden departure*, but everybody knows what really happened."

Larry leaned toward Gabby. "Really." His voice had dropped to a dangerous purr, and his black eyes glittered like burning coals. Since she had arrived at Olympus, Margo had heard whispers about some of the more unsavory aspects of Larry's job, about the lengths to which he would go to keep the wrong story out of the papers or the right person quiet. For the first time she thought they might be true. "And just what does everybody know?"

"Well, far be it from me to spread nasty gossip," Gabby continued blithely. She was well into her third glass of champagne. "But I just heard she went off to have a baby. Among other things."

"What other things?" Larry prodded, in that same terrible voice. Out of the corner of her eye, Margo saw a uniformed cigarette girl begin to approach the table, only to scurry away at the last moment, like a tiny fish suddenly aware that the cave she is about to swim into is actually the open mouth of a shark.

Gabby flashed her dimples. "Things that a child of my tender years really ought not to know about. You couldn't possibly expect me to repeat them."

"Gabby Preston, you are one ripe tomato." Jimmy Molloy burst out laughing. "You play your cards right, honey, and you could give *Picture Palace* a run for its money. Now." Briskly, he snapped his fingers for the waiter. "Let's get some more champagne, since you drank this bottle all up yourself, you naughty little wastrel. And then I'd like everyone to put their attention back where it belongs: on me. I heard the darnedest thing happened at Warner Brothers the other day. . . ."

Jimmy launched into his story, a rambling yarn about some dim-bulb extra who became hysterical when she thought they were throwing a real baby out a fifth-story window during a firefighting sequence, as Gabby hung on his every word.

But all Margo could think about was Dane. Could Diana Chesterfield's mysterious disappearance have something to do with him? Had she really gone off to have his baby . . . or worse? Or maybe it was all just idle gossip. Margo didn't hold much truck with gossip, having been the subject of enough of it herself over the years. All those rumors Evelyn Gamble used to spread about her . . . If even half of that garbage were true, Margo would have had a past to rival . . . well, Amanda Farraday's.

But suppose, just suppose, this rumor *was* true? Suppose Dane had made a . . . mistake with Diana? So what? That didn't necessarily make him a cad, any more than it made Diana a "ruined woman." That way of thinking was like something out of the Victorian Age. The flappers of the twenties, the brash young women who bobbed their hair and drank gin and did as they liked with men, had done away with all that for good, and the Great Depression was supposed to have swept away what was left. Even in the rarified world of Pasadena high society, Margo had heard about the kind of distasteful things less fortunate women and girls, even the good, respectable, churchgoing types, had done just to survive in the hardscrabble early years of the Depression. Were those women ruined? Was Diana? Remembering the electric warmth of Dane's kiss the day of her screen test, Margo felt a stabbing pang of jealousy toward the

163

missing star. Maybe Diana was facing an uncertain future—or worse—but if you were going to be ruined, Dane Forrest was probably the most exciting way to do it.

Suddenly, the band struck up a lively Charleston. Scrambling couples flooded the dance floor. "Come on, Jimmy," Gabby squealed. "Let's dance!"

"Sit down, Gabby," Larry said. "You're drunk."

"I'm not! I'm just happy for once. And I want to dance. All of you are always making me dance, and now I want to for a change! I want to dance!"

The waiter was arriving at their table with their steaks. "Maybe you better eat something first, honey," Jimmy said. "Get something in your stomach before you go too crazy."

"Aw, don't be such a wet blanket!" Gabby shouted. "They're playing the shimmy shake, and I want to dance. I want to shimmy with you, Jimmy. Listen to that, I rhymed! I wanna shimmy with Jimmy," she chanted in a high-pitched singsong, lunging for Jimmy's arm. "*I wanna shimmy shimmy shimmy with my Jimmy Jimmy Jimmy* . . . everybody sing!" Suddenly, Gabby's chair gave way. She toppled over onto the waiter with a terrible crash. His tray went flying into the air, depositing steak, champagne, lobster Newburg, and an entire boat of gravy down the front of Gabby's dress.

"Gabby!" Margo cried, jumping to her feet. "Are you all right?"

Larry grabbed Margo's wrist. "Get her out of here."

"I don't feel so good," Gabby moaned.

"Margo," Larry hissed. The pack of photographers, having smelled fresh blood, was beginning to swarm. "*Now.*"

Margo dragged the protesting Gabby to her feet and beat a

hasty retreat through the palm trees, which formed a kind of protective canopy, making it impossible for cameras to get a clear shot until they reached the entrance of the ladies' powder room. *Smart*, Margo thought as she heaved Gabby through the door. *They must have planned it that way.*

Inside the powder room, everything was gold. Gold carpeting, gold wallpaper, gold dressing tables with mirrors in carved gold frames: the whole room glowed as though a pirate had just opened a chest of buried treasure. A gold velvet chaise dominated the center of the room. Languidly draped across it, her shimmering black gown providing the only contrast in the room, was Amanda Farraday.

"Oh!" Her smoky hazel eyes widened in surprise. She held a long ebony cigarette holder straight up in the air, like an exclamation point. "What do we have here?"

Margo racked her brain for a plausible lie. A sudden illness? A belligerent waiter? Hedy Lamarr? *That's it*, Margo thought wildly. *I'll blame it on Hedy Lamarr!* Hedy Lamarr, in a drunken rage, had flung a tray of lobster Newburg at an unsuspecting Gabby. Margo could see the headlines now: *Quelle Surprise! Hedy Lamarr Goes Cocoanuts at the Grove: Exotic European Hurls Homard at Starlet Songbird!*

"Oh my God!" The uniformed bathroom attendant leapt out of a marble toilet stall, fluttering her hands in front of her apron. "What happened to—"

Amanda interrupted her smoothly. "Carmen, leave us alone, please."

The woman's mouth tightened. "But the little miss," she cajoled, "her beautiful dress . . . surely I ought to tell somebody. . . ."

Amanda plucked a crisp twenty-dollar bill from her black

165

silk glove and brandished it under the astonished woman's nose. "You see this?" she hissed.

The attendant nodded dazedly. It was probably enough money to pay her rent for a month. "Yes, Miss Farraday."

"Good." Amanda ripped the precious bill in half and stuffed one piece into the woman's shaking hand. "Get lost for the next twenty minutes and the other half of President Jackson here is yours. Under one condition: You keep your mouth shut. If I hear that Perdita Pendleton or any of the rest of those *Picture Palace* hags got as much as one word out of you, I'll make sure this is the last piece of lettuce you see in this town that you don't find in a salad. You understand me?" The woman gave a quick nod as she made her way for the door.

"Now, first things first." Seizing Gabby's shoulders, Amanda steered her into a toilet stall. "She's got to get in there and bring up whatever she's got in the bread box."

"You don't mean . . ."

"Puke, vomit. *Regurgitate*. I don't care what you call it. She's got to do it."

"But I want to dance," Gabby murmured groggily. "I'm a swell dancer. I've been having lessons and everything."

"Sugar, for all I know you're Eleanor Powell and Ginger Rogers combined, but right now all you've got to do is make it come up." Amanda closed the stall door. A moment later, they heard retching. "Good girl," Amanda called encouragingly. "That's the way."

"Is that really necessary?" Margo asked tremulously.

"Are you kidding?" Amanda giggled. She looked younger up close, Margo noted, still beautiful, but with slightly crooked teeth and a spray of farm-girl freckles peppering her nose. She couldn't have been more than a year or two older than Margo herself. "She can barely stand. She's got to sober up, if you want to get her out of here with any kind of dignity intact, and believe me, this is the quickest way."

"Not that. I meant the whole business with the bathroom attendant."

Amanda's smile faded. "You want to see this whole episode in the gossip rags tomorrow? Where do you think they get their information? Bellhops, limo drivers, waiters, doormen, powder room attendants. The big shots don't even realize they exist, but believe me, they know everything about *everyone*. The columnists offer them five bucks a tip. Ten, if it's really juicy."

"But ratting out the people who keep you employed?" Margo said. "That's horrible."

"Is it? If you're trying to pay rent and carfare and feed and clothe a whole family on a buck fifty a day, do you really care what some reporter writes about a bunch of millionaires? If you want to keep them quiet, you have to make it worth their while. Just ask your friend Larry Julius." She shook her head. "Twenty clams, though, boy oh boy. That was every penny Zellman gave me for the powder room. Could have kept me in lipstick and stockings for two months."

"Why did you do it, then?"

"Oh, some kind of Olympus solidarity, I guess. Besides, Larry Julius owes me a favor now, doesn't he? Around these parts, a girl can't have too many powerful men in her debt."

"At any rate, it's terribly kind of you to help." Margo retreated into impersonal politeness. She felt uncomfortable with this world Amanda described, with its unethical journalists and paid informants and old men giving young girls exorbitant sums of money to go to the powder room. *Maybe it's true,* she thought. *Maybe everything my parents said about Hollywood was right.* "It all seemed to happen so quickly. We only just got here, after all. I don't know how she got so drunk so fast."

Amanda picked up Gabby's evening bag from the chaise. Undoing the clasp, she pulled out a small vial of pink pills. "Well, wonder no more."

"Those? That's nothing," Margo said defensively. "Just something the doctor gives her to help her with her diet, that's all."

"Sure. Her diet. And then she's so speeded up she can't sleep. So they give her these." Amanda pulled out another vial, yellow pills this time. "Nembies."

"Excuse me?"

"Downers. You mix these with a drink and it's good night, nurse. That is, unless they do you in altogether."

Margo swallowed hard. "You mean . . ."

"I mean, she better be careful. She wouldn't be the first nice thin girl to quietly drift off one night and never wake up, while the studio tries to figure out a way to cover up the fact that they drugged her to death. They'd get away with it too. They always do." *Diana,* Margo thought suddenly. Gabby had talked about Diana's taking pills for her weight too. *Could she be one of those girls?*

"The biggest mistake people make is thinking the studio is looking out for them," Amanda was saying. "It's all that happy-family crap Leo Karp talks. What a load of bull. The studio looks out for the studio. We're just products, and products have to make money or they're discontinued." Amanda pulled a gold compact encrusted with tiny green gems from her black velvet evening bag and began to repair her lipstick with a tiny brush.

"They can drape us in all the diamonds and furs they want. We're still the working class. All the real power stays at the top, same as it always was."

Margo laughed nervously. "You sound like a Communist."

"Do I?" Amanda studied her reflection critically in her mirror, making minute adjustments to her left eyebrow with the tip of her fingernail. "Maybe. The Communists are right about a lot of things. At least, that's what Harry says."

"Harry Gordon?" Margo said. "The screenwriter?"

Amanda's face softened into a dreamy glow. "Oh, you know who he is? He's awfully good, isn't he? And so passionate about his work and the world. He's from New York, from the theater, and he sees right through all that mercenary Hollywood bull."

"Why is he out here if he hates it so much?"

"He's got a widowed mother and three unmarried sisters back in Brooklyn to support," Amanda said simply. "And besides, he had a vision for the pictures. He wants to see if he can make something great."

"You seem to know an awful lot about him," Margo said.

"I'm just a fan, that's all." Amanda snapped the compact shut. "That's pretty," she said suddenly, pointing to Margo's pin.

Margo's hand flew up reflexively to cover it. "Thank you."

"It's unusual, isn't it? Obviously not the studio's. Where did you get it?"

"It's, uh . . ." Nervously, Margo twisted the pin in her fingers. It was one of the only things she'd been able to bear taking with her from Pasadena. It was a link to her old self, to things she wasn't ready to talk about yet with anyone, let alone a virtual stranger. "It was a gift," she said finally.

Amanda grinned. "Not-so-secret admirer?"

"Oh, no," Margo said, startled. "Nothing like that." She swallowed hard. Her parents were about the last thing she wanted to discuss with Amanda Farraday. "It's sort of an heirloom, I guess."

"That's right." Amanda's eyes narrowed. "You're supposed to be some kind of heiress or something, aren't you?"

"I . . . what?"

"You're Margo Sterling, right? I read all about you in *Picture Palace*. They made you sound terribly top-drawer. Where are you from?"

"I . . . um . . . I grew up in Pasadena."

"Well, la-di-da. And how did dear old mum and dad feel about daughter dearest going into the pictures?"

"Well . . ."

There was a deafening flush as Gabby, looking exhausted, emerged from the stall, wiping her mouth with a sheet of toilet tissue. Margo was grateful for the interruption. Surely Amanda hadn't meant any harm, but getting this unexpected third degree had unsettled her.

"Feeling better?" Margo asked Gabby.

Gabby nodded, pointing a damp finger. "What's *she* doing here?"

"Helping you, you ungrateful little bitch," Amanda said cheerfully. "Come on, let's get her out of here."

With the stains on Gabby's dress hidden by Amanda's strategically draped fox-fur stole—"It belongs to the studio anyway," Amanda said, when Margo protested—they managed to get Gabby back to the table.

"Gabs, there you are!" Jimmy exclaimed, rising to his feet and taking her by the waist in a well-rehearsed move. "I'm

170

feeling a little worse for the wear myself. What say you take me home? All right with you, chief?" He grinned at Larry.

"Sounds good to me."

Jimmy led Gabby away. Margo turned to Amanda to thank her for her help, but she was already snaking a path through the palm trees to Oscar Zellman's table. Her glittery black train trailed behind her like the fin of a mermaid's tail.

"Well, kiddo, I guess it's just the two of us," Larry said. "Have a drink."

"I'm not much of a drinker," Margo said. "You don't want two sick girls on your hands in one night."

"Just a little one. People are watching, you know, and it'll get that look off your face."

"What look?"

"Terror." Larry chuckled. "Abject terror."

Margo took a small sip of champagne. It had gone warm and flat while she was in the bathroom. Larry reached over to freshen her glass. "So," he said pleasantly. "I see you made a new friend."

"She helped me get Gabby cleaned up." Margo glanced over at Zellman's table, where Amanda was chatting animatedly, a generous expanse of cleavage spilling from the top of her black dress. Oscar Zellman couldn't take his eyes off her. *Will I ever hold a man's attention like that?* "She paid off the bathroom attendant and everything. To keep her from talking to the press, she said."

"Really?" Larry looked impressed. "Smart girl. How much?"

"Twenty dollars."

Larry whistled. "Big spender. I guess I'll have to put that on my tab." He stubbed out his cigarette. "Let's dance."

171

Margo suddenly felt very tired. "Maybe later."

"It's not a request," Larry said. "You've got to be seen."

The band struck up a lively version of "It Had to Be You" as Larry led her onto the floor, guiding her expertly to a clearing in the palm trees where the cameras could get a good shot. *It's like I'm a new car he wants to show off.*

"Smile, duchess," Larry muttered. "Come on. People are watching." *People are watching.* It sounded like something her mother would say. *Maybe nothing bad happened to Diana Chesterfield at all,* Margo thought suddenly. *Maybe she just needed to escape.*

The song ended, and the orchestra began to play a slow, romantic number. *"How Deep Is the Ocean,"* Margo thought. The Irving Berlin ballad had always been one of her favorite songs. The last time she danced to it was with Phipps McKendrick at the infamous Christmas dance. She'd worn a blue dress then too, she remembered, with the corsage of tiny pink roses she'd saved afterward. She wondered if it was still drying to dust in Pasadena in her top dresser drawer. Phipps had looked awfully handsome that night, with that soft lock of hair that had fallen over his forehead when he'd bent to pin the roses on her dress. It seemed like a lifetime ago. . . .

"Larry Julius," said a familiar male voice. "Aren't you the luckiest man in the room."

Startled, Margo spun around and found herself directly in front of Dane Forrest, looking devastatingly handsome in his dinner jacket and tie. She felt her stomach make a peculiar leap, as though it had suddenly decided to throw itself off the edge of a cliff.

"Dane." Larry scowled. "I didn't expect to see you here tonight."

"I didn't expect to be here. In fact, I was about to settle in with a good book and a glass of warm milk when I had the sudden and irresistible urge to dance with a beautiful girl. So I put on this monkey suit and came down here, and lo and behold, I see you've got the most beautiful one of the bunch all warmed up for me."

"Kiddo, I believe you've met Mr. Forrest," Larry said grudgingly.

"Oh, I've met the ravishing Miss Sterling. Although she was calling herself something different then. Lady Olivia, I think it was?" Gazing into Margo's eyes, he gave her a long, slow smile. Margo's head was spinning. *Oh God,* she thought. *What if I really am going to be sick?* "So what do you say?" Dane continued. "Mind if I cut in?"

Larry looked concerned. "I don't know if that's such a good idea."

"Oh, come on, Julius. You can't possibly keep her to yourself all night. They'll be scraping the remains of the brokenhearted men off the Hollywood sign come morning."

Larry's eyes darted toward the cadre of reporters hovering at the edge of the dance floor, notebooks and cameras poised to commit to press even the slightest hint of tension between publicist and star. "All right. One dance. *One.*"

"In that case, Margo, we better hurry." Dane smirked. "Or it'll be over before it's even begun."

Trembling, Margo moved wordlessly into Dane's arms. It was overwhelming to be so close to him again. She took a few deep breaths, feeling the weight of his warm hand on her back, inhaling the clean, musky scent of him from the collar of his jacket.

"Sterling," Dane said. "Not bad."

"I . . . Excuse me?"

"The last name. Certainly better than Funkhauser or Furgenbluger or whatever you started out with. And Margo. Very French, very marquee-ready. I wonder what genius came up with that."

Margo laughed. "As a matter of fact, my housekeeper used to call me that when I was a little girl."

"Housekeeper." Dane snorted. "That's right. *Picture Palace* made you sound pretty top-of-the-heap."

If he read that story in Picture Palace, *then he must have seen the one about Diana being declared officially missing,* Margo thought suddenly. But somehow, this didn't seem like the time or place to bring that up. "That story may have been a bit exaggerated."

"They usually are." Dane chuckled. "My studio biography says I'm descended from a line of pirate kings and I tamed my first wild Arabian stallion at the age of seven. But of course, that's all true, so maybe I'm not the best example. Anyway, it was a nice feature," he continued. "Nice picture too. Pity it had to be overshadowed by Diana. But then, she's always been good at that. Overshadowing people."

Margo drew her breath in sharply. It was a shock, hearing Dane speak Diana's name. *Of course,* she thought, *this must be horrible for him, unless . . .* Dane's face was perfectly neutral, but there was something dark and unreadable in his eyes.

"Now, never mind that," Dane said. "I want to hear all about you. How are you getting along?"

"Oh, fine, I guess . . ."

Dane smiled. "But?"

"Well, it's all terribly exciting, naturally," Margo said. "I mean, sometimes I wake up in the morning and just have to pinch myself to make sure I'm not dreaming."

"You don't have to give the studio-approved speech to me," Dane said. "I don't have a notepad at the ready."

Margo blushed. "Do you really want to know?"

"Sure. After your screen test, well . . . I've been thinking about you." Dane looked almost shy. "I guess I feel a little responsible, that's all. For getting you into this mess."

"Well, in that case . . ." *He's been thinking about me!* The very idea made Margo want to sing. "I guess it's not exactly what I expected. So far, it just seems like a lot of self-improvement."

"'A penny saved is a penny earned' and all that jazz? Or have they started bringing out the analysts?" He spoke in a fake German accent. "Vell, Miss Sterling, tell me about your saddest memories and zen I vill tell you how it vill help you cry on cue."

"Oh, no." Margo shook her head. "We haven't even discussed any acting yet. Mostly, we talk about my hair. Center part or side part? Should the curl go on the right side or the left? And then, when the subject of hair has been exhausted, we talk about eyebrows. How thin, how high, how arched? And don't even get me started on lips. The lips are an ongoing debate. Red or pink? Full or thin? Cupid's-bow or straight across?"

"Lips are terribly important," Dane said.

"Oh, I don't doubt it. But over the past four days I've gone from Clara Bow to Joan Crawford to looking like someone socked me in the mouth, and I still don't think the question has been resolved to anyone's satisfaction."

"Well, they look all right to me." His face was suddenly very close to hers. *Dear God,* Margo thought, her stomach churning with a mixture of joy and terror, *is he going to kiss me?* "And are you making friends?"

It was the last thing she expected him to ask her. "Making friends?"

Dane smiled sadly. "It can be pretty lonely on the lot if you don't have someone you can trust."

He's trying to tell me something, Margo realized. *What?* "Well, Gabby Preston has been very nice. Larry Julius's office sent over a big bunch of flowers when I first arrived. And there are so many people in and out all the time, and there's so much to do, the photo shoots and the wardrobe fittings and the movement lessons and etiquette lessons . . ." Margo wrinkled her nose, remembering the funny little man who had tried very hard to convince her that she was holding her soup spoon incorrectly, having had no idea of what a rigorous bastion of proper cutlery handling the Frobisher dining table had been. "I'm hardly ever alone."

"I asked if you were lonely." Dane's arms tightened around her, pulling her close. "That's different from being alone." Her cheek fell against his chest. To her startled delight, she realized his heart was beating almost as quickly as hers. For the first time in a long time, Margo felt safe. So safe and wonderful and warm that she didn't notice anything else.

Not Amanda Farraday's piercing stare. Not Larry Julius's furious expression as he came storming across the floor.

And certainly not the blinding glare of flashbulbs that popped everywhere around them.

FIFTEEN

Dancing Duo Says: Diana Who?

That was the headline all of Hollywood woke up to the next morning, trumpeted across the front page of *Variety*, from where it would trickle down to every two-bit gossip rag in town. In the movie business, bad news traveled at the speed of high-grade celluloid. By that evening, the consensus would be set: Diana Chesterfield was a vanished angel, a martyred saint. And Margo Sterling, a seventeen-year-old girl who barely two months ago was walking across a classroom in a girls' school in Pasadena with a stack of books balanced on her head, was a cold-blooded home wrecker who had probably gotten rid of poor St. Diana herself.

Naturally, Margo's newly installed telephone had been ringing off the hook.

Gabby, who seemed never to sleep, called at the crack of dawn promising to come by for "moral support and crisis management" just as soon as she could sneak away from the Tully Toynbee set. Next on the line was Amanda Farraday, which was more surprising, since one, she hadn't struck Margo as a particularly early riser, and two, she couldn't for the life of her think how Amanda had gotten her number.

"I think it's just terrible," Amanda had said, "the way these people twist the most innocent situations into something tawdry just to sell their lousy papers. It was bad enough when bottom-feeding scandal sheets like *Broadway Brevities* used to pull stunts like this, but *Variety*? They ought to be ashamed of themselves. I just want you to know I'm here for you, Margo. Anything you need to talk about, I'll listen."

She sounded so sincere that Margo was tempted to take her up on it. Dane's words from the night before rang in her ear: *You need to have someone you can trust.* There was really only one person she wanted to talk to. She politely hung up with Amanda and placed a new call.

"Winthrop residence," the familiar voice answered.

"Doris!" Margo could have cried. "It's you!"

"Yes, and who is this?"

"It's me," Margo said, confused. "It's Margaret."

"Oh! Margaret!" Doris sounded surprised. "How are you? Have you met Diana Chesterfield yet?"

What? "No," Margo began, "I—"

"What about Dane Forrest? Did you meet him?"

Margo was flabbergasted. The first time she'd managed to

178

get her friend on the phone since she'd come to Hollywood, and that was all she could ask? "H-haven't you seen *Variety* this morning?" she stammered.

"A variety of what?"

"*Variety*. They have it on the newsstand by school. It's a trade paper."

"What do you trade it with?"

"No, *trade*. As in *the movie trade*." Margo sighed. She had counted on Doris's already knowing everything that she didn't have the strength to explain herself. "It's like a movie magazine, except more, I don't know, businesslike."

"I guess I don't really keep up as much with that sort of stuff without you here," Doris said. "That was always more your thing, really. Oh! That reminds me! The invitations for my coming-out party arrived last week! I just sent yours care of the studio. I didn't know where else to send it."

"*Doris*," Margo scolded. "It'll get mixed in with the general fan mail that way. I told you to write me at that P.O. Box address I sent you."

"Oh." Doris sounded perplexed. "I guess I forgot. I'll put another one in the mail. But anyway, it's July seventeenth, at the club, of course. Please, please come, I don't care what my mother says, I want you to be there."

"Why?" Margo felt something in her neck tighten. "What does your mother say?"

"Oh, I don't know. . . . Listen, Margie, I have to go. Evelyn is honking the horn."

"Evelyn *Gamble*?"

"Uh-huh. Lucky duck. Her parents bought her a brand-new

179

Packard convertible for her eighteenth birthday—can you believe it? So we're driving down to the beach."

"You're going to the beach with *Evelyn Gamble?*"

"Oh, Margie, don't be like that. I know you two always rubbed each other the wrong way, but she's really not so bad when you get to know her. . . ." Doris put her hand over the receiver. "*Yes, Evvie, I'm coming!* Listen, I've really got to go. Talk to you later, movie star!"

Margo hung up the phone, feeling even worse than before. *"More your thing"?* *"What my mother says"?* *"EVVIE"?* Hardly two months had passed since Margaret had left Pasadena. Could things have really changed so much?

The doorbell rang. Hastily, Margo threw her dressing gown over her pajamas and went to the door. A studio gofer was staggering under the weight of an enormous bouquet of white and yellow daisies. "Delivery for Miss Sterling," he said through a mouthful of petals.

"Just put it down there," Margo said, pointing to the small coffee table. Her heart leapt. *Dane!* The flowers had to be from him; who else would have sent them? Surely this was his way of telling her they were in this together, that he felt the same way she did and meant to see it through. A small yellow envelope was tucked behind a fern. She tore it open greedily the moment the delivery boy was gone.

Wow wow wow! First night on the town and already a cover story! Here's hoping it rubs off on me. Best wishes, Jimmy Molloy

Gloomily, Margo shoved the card under the vase, where she wouldn't have to look at it. Really, it was preposterous; what would Margaret Frobisher have said if she could see her doppelgänger now, moping around in her dressing gown because the wrong movie star had sent her a huge bunch of flowers? And why should she have expected to hear from Dane anyway? He must have been mortified. For all she knew, he was still in love with Diana and devastated by her absence, just like the studio's last press release claimed. He was just being polite asking Margo to dance; she was the one who'd gone and fallen all over him like a rag doll. He probably blamed her for the whole thing.

Margo studied the front page of *Variety* for what felt like the millionth time that day. The picture was pretty nice, actually. Margo and Dane, surrounded by twinkling lights on the shimmering dance floor of the Cocoanut Grove, her head resting cozily on his shoulder, gazing up at him as though they were the only two people in the world. An awfully romantic scene, if you could ignore the poisonous words beside it:

Well, that was fast! Just days after his longtime paramour Diana Chesterfield's mysterious disappearance was confirmed, faithless film fiend Dane Forrest found solace in the shapely arms of stunning starlet Margo Sterling. The shameless Sterling, who bears an uncanny resemblance to Miss Chesterfield, made a beeline for the "grieving" Mr. Forrest's side, where the two shared an intimate dance that sent a ghoulish shiver down the spine of more than one concerned observer. Time will tell if the dilettante debutante can keep her cold little claws in the notoriously fickle star for more than, say . . . Nine Days'? Diana Chesterfield, if you're reading this, come home soon!

"Don't tell me you're reading that again?" Gabby, clad in her rehearsal leotard, stood at the open entrance of the bungalow. "Just throw it away."

"It won't help," Margo said miserably. "I've practically committed it to memory."

"Forget it."

"'The shameless Sterling'? 'Her cold little claws'?" Margo swept the paper off the table. It landed on the floor with an unsatisfying rustle. "How could they be so mean?"

Gabby shrugged. "It's their job."

"Well, it's a horrid job. Who wants to read that kind of sordid rubbish anyway?"

"Oh, Margo. Everyone." Gabby came inside and lay across the sofa, arching her back like a languid cat. Her legs looked like matchsticks in their dark rehearsal tights. "Haven't you heard the saying there's no such thing as bad publicity?"

"This is," Margo insisted fiercely. "For God's sake, Gabby, they make me sound like some kind of predator." She quoted again from the hateful text. "'Made a beeline for the grieving Mr. Forrest'? Dane was the one who asked me to dance! I didn't even see him until he started talking to Larry."

"If you say so. I wasn't there." *No,* Margo thought, *you were practically unconscious and had to be carried home with vomit stains all over your dress.* "What does Dane think about this?"

"Horrified, probably. I can't even think about it."

"Well, who are the flowers from, then?" Gabby jerked her pointy little chin toward the daisies.

"Jimmy."

"Jimmy Molloy?" Gabby's forehead wrinkled. "Why is he sending *you* flowers?"

Margo shrugged. "He seems to think this is a good thing."

"Well, everyone knows who you are now." Gabby narrowed her eyes. "Different flowers are supposed to mean different things, aren't they? What are daisies?"

"I don't know." Margo thought back to the interminable flower-arranging sessions in Miss Schoonmaker's Poise and Presence class back in Pasadena. "Friendship, I think."

"Oh." Gabby seemed mollified. "That's all right, then. But you really haven't heard from Dane?"

"Not a whimper."

"Well, it's still so early. Maybe he hasn't seen the papers yet. Maybe he sleeps late. Or maybe he's been up for hours, planning to send you some kind of elaborate and lavish gift that you couldn't possibly have received yet. Like a diamond. Or a car. Or a horse. Or . . ." Before Gabby got any farther down the wish list, the doorbell rang again.

"Urgent delivery for Miss Sterling," said the delivery boy in the doorway. Margo pounced on him, ripping the thin tissue-paper envelope open like a wild animal.

"What is it?" Gabby cried breathlessly. "Is it from him?"

"No." Margo was pale. "It's from Mr. Karp's office. He wants me to come in for a meeting this afternoon."

Neither girl had to say out loud how serious this was. In the best-case scenario, a summons to the office of the all-powerful studio chief might mean something wonderful, like you'd been nominated for an Oscar. On a day when the biggest movie magazine in the country had chosen to run a scandalous story about you, it was very bad news indeed.

Gabby finally spoke. "Remember. Talk about America. America, and Pasadena, and how much you love it there, and your wonderful mother . . ."

"Gabby." Margo silenced her with a grim laugh. "If I could do that, I'd be the greatest actress in the world."

SIXTEEN

"Have a seat, dear." The secretary gestured toward a low stool against the wall, wedged between two miniature palm trees. "He'll be with you in a moment."

Feeling meek and small, Margo did as she was told. It was exactly as though she were sitting outside the headmistress's office at Orange Grove. Anxiously, she wiped her sweaty palms against the scratchy fabric of the pleated plaid skirt she had chosen to wear, a holdover from her old life. *If I'm going to be punished like a naughty schoolgirl,* she thought, *I might as well look the part.*

A tall, distinguished-looking gentleman strode briskly through the office door and into the reception area. The secretary sprang abruptly to her feet. "Mr. Payne! You're finished so soon!" She was practically standing at attention. "Shall I call a car to take you to the airport?"

The man ignored her. Instead, he cast his hooded gaze toward Margo, raking his eyes lazily from the top of her head to the tips of her toes—with a lot of meaningful lingering on certain parts in between. "No need. I've got my driver waiting outside."

"Of course. Of course, Mr. Payne. Have a safe journey, and we're so looking forward to seeing you again."

"Hmmm." The man looked thoughtful. "How I wish I could say the same."

So that's Hunter Payne. Now that Margo saw him in person, it all made perfect sense. Hollywood, for all its bluster, was a glittering colony of strivers, scrappy immigrants, and small-town dreamers, but everything about Hunter Payne, from the knife-edged crease in his trousers to the easy grace of his walk, reeked of privileged entitlement, of a man who had never known a moment's humiliation, heartbreak, or doubt. *A man like my father,* Margo thought, the kind of man she'd known all her life. No wonder everyone was afraid of him.

The secretary took a moment to recover after he had gone before she turned to Margo. "You can go in now, Miss Sterling."

Fingering her little gold-and-pearl pin, affixed to the Peter Pan collar of her blouse, Margo took a deep breath and opened the door.

The inner office of Leo F. Karp was furnished to look like an ocean liner. Not a ship's cabin or even an officer's quarters, but the ocean liner itself. Since her arrival at Olympus, Margo had overheard a few competing theories as to the reason for the nautical theme. Some said it was meant to evoke the great ship on which Karp had sailed to America as a small boy; other, more cynical types whispered that the studio boss, famously

186

extravagant (at least when it came to himself), had simply re-solved to choose the most lavish and ruinously expensive de-sign scheme his designer could imagine, and this turned out to be the winner. But whatever the motivation, there was no denying the grandeur of the place. Long, curving walls were covered in creamy white leather, punctuated by baseboards of inky mahogany. A luxurious white silk carpet, laid in narrow panels, emulated a newly whitewashed deck. The windows were round, like portholes looking out onto the sea. And all the way at the back, behind an enormous white prow of a desk and dressed in a crisp suit of nautical navy, was Leo Karp himself, the fearless captain at the mighty helm. It looked like a fantasy out of a movie, which of course was exactly what it was.

Tentatively, Margo inched forward, wondering what the protocol was. Should she curtsey? Should she wait for him to speak, as one did with the king of England?

To her surprise, the all-powerful head of the biggest studio in Hollywood came barreling excitedly toward her with his arms outstretched.

"My darling Miss Sterling! How marvelous to see you at last!" He seized her hands, planting noisy kisses on each of her cheeks. "I can't tell you how grateful I am to you for stopping by on such short notice."

As though I had a choice, Margo thought. "Of course. I'm thrilled to be here."

"Let me look at you." With her hands still clasped in his, he held her out at arm's length, as though to get a better view. She took the opportunity to conduct an examination of her own. Mr. Karp was short. Very short. Even for Hollywood, where, in Margo's still inexpert opinion, people were by and large shorter than any grown people had a right to be. Though she was wearing her flat oxfords, he barely reached her nose, and his feet, clad in highly polished spectator wingtips, looked no bigger than a doll's. But he was solidly built, broad shouldered and barrel chested in a way that almost made you forget his diminutive stature and twinkling eyes. Sure, he looked a little like a teddy bear, but a teddy bear who could beat the hell out of you if he wanted to.

"My latest acquisition." Mr. Karp sighed with pleasure. "Ah, but you're a vision. The photographs don't do you justice."

Margo flushed. "Thank you."

"Don't thank me, darling. It's me who should be thanking you. I get to sit here looking at a glorious girl, while you're stuck staring at my ugly mug." He gestured to a white quilted leather armchair. "Won't you sit down?"

She sat, waiting for Mr. Karp to do the same. Instead, he began to pace in circles around her chair, as though she were a suspect brought in for questioning. Was this some sort of intimidation tactic? Was he stalling for time? Figuring out the best way to give her the bad news?

She couldn't take it anymore. "Mr. Karp . . ."

He held up a hand to cut her off. "Miss Sterling, please. I know what you're going to say. A beautiful new player comes to my own studio, joins my orbit, if you will, and I don't come to meet her? Of course, I'm a busy man; of course, I have meetings to attend, pictures to produce, papers to sign, money to make. But still, Miss Sterling, I ask you, what way is this for a gentleman to treat a lady such as yourself? You must be furious with me. Particularly under the circumstances."

She flushed. *What is he playing at? What circumstances?* "Mr. Karp, really—I . . ."

"Miss Sterling—may I call you Margo?" At last, he sat, leaning toward her with a comically grave expression on his face. "Margo, darling, I'm going to speak frankly. Larry Julius told me about how it was that you came to us. The troubles with your mama and papa."

"I—I don't—"

"Please, my darling, there's no need to explain." He shook his head sadly. "It's a terrible thing, to have troubles in one's family. As happy as we are to have you here with us at Olympus, I can't help feeling in some way responsible. So I hope that what I'm going to tell you will come as a small comfort to you."

He's firing me, Margo thought wildly. *He's going to tell me to go back to Pasadena and make peace with my parents.*

"I want you to know, lovely Margo," Mr. Karp continued, "that I look at everyone, every single man, woman, and child here at Olympus, as if he or she were a member of my own family. I hope, in time, that you'll be able to think of me like a father. Or maybe more of a grandfather; after all, you're so young." He smiled. "But if something or *someone* is troubling you, I'll do anything, *anything,* within my power to help, just as if you were my own daughter. Do you understand?"

"Yes," Margo whispered.

"And does that make you happy?"

"Yes." It was the truth. Even if what Mr. Karp was saying was partially for effect, it *did* make Margo feel better to hear it. Maybe she wasn't about to be fired after all.

Mr. Karp walked grandly back over to his enormous desk

and sat down, his arms crossed over his chest like a benevolent pasha. "I'm very glad to hear that. Because I'm about to ask you for a rather large favor." He drew a well-worn script from the drawer and slid it across the desk toward her. Margo read the title page.

THE NINE DAYS' QUEEN

BY

HARRY GORDON

Mr. Karp peered at her keenly over his glasses, studying her reaction. "You recognize it?"

Margo struggled to locate her voice. "I . . . it's . . . isn't this the picture Diana Chesterfield was making before she . . ."

"Before she went on extended vacation, yes," Mr. Karp said firmly. "And you can imagine how that left us in the lurch. The studio has invested, shall we say, *significant* resources in *The Nine Days' Queen*. Weepy history pictures with female leads are big business right now. This was supposed to be our answer to *Marie Antoinette*, to *Jezebel*, to that *farkakte* Civil War movie David Selznick claims to be making, if he can ever find the right girl, what's it called, *Gone with the Wind*. When I first heard that title, I said, what's the picture about, his bank account? I mean, what kind of *schlemiel* green-lights a picture and blows through a million bucks in preproduction alone, without a star attached? Some people say, who cares, what's it anyone's business if some crazy producer wants to ruin himself? Not Leo Karp. Leo Karp says that when one man does bad business, it's bad for everyone in the business. If it was up to me, I'd have him run out of town." He shook his head. "Now, God help me, I feel bad for the poor *schmuck*. Because you do everything right, get the best directors and designers in the business, real *machers* who know how to stick to a budget and do it right, you go into production, everything is perfect, solid, you're on top of the world, and then poof!" Margo jumped as he brought his surprisingly large fists down on the desk, scattering a pile of papers onto the plush white carpeting. "My biggest star is gone. Three-quarters of a mil already gone in preproduction, budgeted, plus ten grand a *day* it's costing me to keep it on hold. I say fine, we'll shut production down, the studio will take a million dollar loss and Hunter Payne and the banker boys in New York—if you'll pardon the expression, dear—will have my balls for breakfast, but fine, I'm a big boy, I've got deep pockets, I'll take the hit. And then what do you think happens?"

Margo shook her head in disbelief. Never in her life had she heard someone speak this frankly about money. While money cast its gritty pall over everything and everyone in Pasadena, on the rare occasions when it was actually discussed, it was spoken of in euphemisms, in the same way as death, or illness, or, God forbid, *sex*. As though it were an unseen force of mystical power, a sleeping dragon better left to lie. Leo Karp, on the other hand, had no such inhibitions, throwing out figures with the fiduciary frankness of a riverboat gambler. She was utterly enraptured.

"I'll tell you what happens," Mr. Karp continued furiously. "The screenwriter of this white elephant, Harry Gordon, this little Commie *pischer* from New York threatens to sue. Breach of contract, he says. He can't win, but he can make things pretty difficult if he wants to, make me tie up our lawyers, throw even more money down the toilet for a movie I'm not going to make. I'll probably wind up tripling his salary just to shut him up. And I thought Communists didn't care about money." Mr. Karp took a fat cigar from the polished humidor on his desk and twiddled it absently in his hand. "It turns out they just don't care about anyone else's. So you see, darling Margo, it turns out we've got to make the picture anyhow, and I'm an actress down. We've got nobody here who can fill Diana's shoes, and no one who wants to try, so I go to MGM, I say 'Let me have Katie Hepburn.' They get all hoity-toity—'Oh, Leo, at MGM we never loan out our stars to another studio'—and in the very same breath, they offer me Joan Crawford. I say, you've got to be kidding. This character in the picture is a seventeen-year-old girl; Crawford is thirty-five if she's a day, which means she's forty. He says, it's Crawford or nobody, so fine, it's nobody. Paramount, forget about it, the only girl they've got who's not ready for the nursing home is Lombard, and Lombard doesn't do costume drama. Columbia, please, who am I supposed to put in a ball gown, the Three Stooges? So I ask Jack Warner to help me out, but de Havilland is unavailable, Stanwyck's all wrong, and Bette Davis is not interested. Not interested!" His jaw dropped in feigned shock. "What is she, crazy? Not interested in the greatest part out there for an actress since *Anna Karenina*? But no, apparently she thinks she's got the Oscar all sewn up with *Jezebel* this year and she's not interested in any competing projects." He snorted. "Well, we'll show her a thing or two, won't we, Margo?" Margo hesitated as Mr. Karp paused to light his cigar, unsure whether she was supposed to answer. "Well?" he asked, exhaling a large cloud of noxious smoke. "Won't we?"

"I . . . I don't think I know what you mean, sir."

"What I mean is, we've been reduced to testing unknowns. Just like Selznick, the poor *schmuck*. Young hopefuls, contract players, extras down at Central Casting. Even a few some scouts picked up off the street." *Or at the lunch counter at Schwab's,* Margo thought drily. "Maybe twenty, thirty girls in all. Kurtzman—Raoul Kurtzman, that is, the director of the picture—isn't impressed. Says they reflect poorly on the state of the American actress." His face darkened. "The guy would be in Dachau right now if it wasn't for the largesse of this great country and its people, but that's gratitude for you. Turned up his nose at every girl we tested, except for two." Mr. Karp put down his cigar. "One of them, Margo, was you."

Margo felt the blood slowly drain from her face. She gripped the arms of the chair. "Me?"

"We already have you under contract. Raoul Kurtzman has named you his first choice to play Lady Jane Grey," Mr. Karp said. "And we know you have some chemistry with your costar. And therein lies the problem." With excruciating slowness, Mr. Karp reached into his desk drawer again and pulled out the offending issue of *Variety*. Very carefully, as though he were holding some kind of forensic evidence, he laid it next to the script. On the bare surface of the white lacquer desk, the headline seemed written in letters about three feet high.

"Mr. Karp," Margo began. "I can explain—"

He cut her off sternly. "Darling, there's no need to make excuses. The only thing that matters is what happens next." Taking off his glasses, he began to slowly polish the lenses with a soft checked cloth, his eyes boring into hers. "Margo. You will be given the part in *The Nine Days' Queen* under one condition: whatever is going on between you and Dane Forrest must come to an immediate end."

Margo felt the tears well up in her eyes unbidden, threatening to spill. *Don't,* she commanded herself sharply. *Not in front of Leo Karp.* "But there's nothing going on between us," she whispered. "Not the way they made it sound."

"And there never will be," Mr. Karp said. "Not in the way you hope."

It was the word *hope* that did it. The tears started to fall, hot and slick, down her nose.

In a fluid, practiced motion, Mr. Karp plucked the white silk handkerchief from his breast pocket and handed it to her. *How many girls has he had crying in front of his desk?* Margo wondered as she carefully wiped her eyes.

"I don't blame you, my dear," Mr. Karp said. "I know exactly how irresistible a man like Dane Forrest is to a young girl; after all, we designed him this way. As for his attraction to you—how shall I put this delicately?—you're certainly his type. But the public would never accept it. Not after this"—he seemed to search for the word—"*situation* with Diana. There would be a terrible scandal. It would sink the movie. It could sink your potential as an actress for good. And on a personal note," he added gently, "just so you know it's not all dollars and cents. Dane Forrest is not the boy for you. There are things about Dane, things in his past . . . well." With a sigh, Mr. Karp replaced his glasses. "It's not appropriate to go into specifics in front of a young lady such as yourself. But for your own good, you're to have nothing to do with him. You'll star in the picture together. That's all right, Dane's a decent actor; there's a lot you

194

can learn by watching him. But that's as far as your relationship will go."

An image of Dane swam into Margo's head. She remembered the soaring feeling of being in his arms, the unspoken promises in his warm green eyes. "What will he say?"

"Dane's already agreed," Mr. Karp said flatly. "He's in enough hot water as it is with this Diana business. Dane was in Hollywood a long time before he made it, and now that he has, you better believe he's enjoying the perks. Trust me, darling, he's not going to give it all up for one little teenage virgin, sweet as she might be."

His words hit Margo like a sledgehammer. *A teenage virgin.* She winced in shame. Was that what they thought of her? No wonder Dane had given her up so easily. What use was a girl like that to a man of the world like Dane Forrest? What a fool she'd been, what a stupid, naïve, arrogant little fool, to think he could ever have cared for her at all.

"But there's exciting news too," Mr. Karp was saying. "You see, just to be certain that you won't be tempted, that there can't possibly be any hint of anything between the two of you, you are going to begin a very conspicuous, very well-publicized romance with someone else." He grinned. "Jimmy Molloy."

"Jimmy?" Margo gasped. "But what about Gabby?"

"Gabby?" Mr. Karp looked confused.

"Gabby Preston. She's crazy about Jimmy," Margo protested. "They're starring together in the new Tully Toynbee movie, and especially after last night, when he escorted her home after . . ." She stopped herself before she gave away any more details of Gabby's precipitous departure. *No point getting Gabby in trouble too.*

"Gabby Preston is a little girl," Mr. Karp said. "Don't worry about her. We'll find someone nice for her when the time comes. In the meantime, Jimmy Molloy is the boy for you."

"But it's absurd," Margo pleaded. "I hardly know Jimmy."

"You hardly know Dane Forrest."

Margo shook her head. "That's different."

"Darling, listen to me." Mr. Karp came around from behind the desk. "When I was a small boy, long before I came to this wonderful country, I lived in a small village in Russia called Plodov. And in Plodov, as in every village of its kind, there lived a matchmaker, and when it came time for the sons or the daughters of each family to marry, the matchmaker would make for each of them a proper match. My own beloved mother, may her soul rest in peace"—he paused to roll his eyes heavenward—"never even met my dear departed father before their wedding day. Fifteen years old she was, and the night before she was to be married she cried her eyes out. 'Papa,' she begged of my grandfather, 'how can I marry a perfect stranger?' But she married him, and they had six children and were happy all their days, and all her life she was glad she listened to her papa. Because to do otherwise would have been unthinkable." Kneeling beside her chair, he took her hands in his. The metal of his thick wedding band felt cold against her skin. "Do you understand what I'm saying to you, Margo?"

Yes, Margo thought. *You're telling me I don't have a choice.* She closed her eyes, struggling to compose herself. In her mind's eyes, all she could see was Dane. *Dane has already agreed.* "And if I refuse?" she whispered.

Mr. Karp got up off his knees. "Then we'll have no choice but to terminate your contract with us. I suppose you could try

196

to go to another studio, but I doubt anyone would be interested in an actress who was willing to throw away an opportunity a million actresses would cut off their right arms for. And please, darling," he cautioned, "I know how romantic young girls can be, but don't get any ideas about giving it all up for the love of Dane Forrest. He'll have forgotten all about you before your car even pulls off the studio lot."

Margo pressed her lips together, willing herself not to cry again. "And *The Nine Days' Queen?*"

Mr. Karp smiled. "Then the part of Lady Jane Grey will go to the other girl. Gene Tierney is her name. She's just your age. From a good family in the East. A debutante, just like you. And I understand her parents are very supportive of her career."

Her parents. It was the trump card. The final reminder of what Margo had signed away. Olympus Studios was mother and father to her now. If she defied this new set of parents, she would have nowhere to go. Leo Karp had given her a choice that was no choice at all.

Slowly, very slowly, she reached for the script.

"Good." Mr. Karp expelled a little gasp of air as he bowed his head. She wondered if, even for a moment, he had doubted she'd say yes. "Very good. I knew you'd make the right decision. Now go back to your bungalow and start studying your lines like a good little schoolgirl. But first, come here and let me kiss you, like a proud papa."

Mechanically, she rose from the chair. Clutching the thick bundle of the script against her chest, as though it were a plate of armor, she allowed him to briefly press his lips, damp and tobacco-dusted from the cigar, against her forehead. "Mr. Karp," she said, "may I ask you something?"

His eyes glinted as he nodded his assent. Margo took a deep breath. *It's now or never,* she thought. She might never get another chance. "Where is Diana Chesterfield?"

"Diana Chesterfield," Mr. Karp repeated. Margo had expected him to look angry, or shocked that she'd been so bold to ask the question directly, or incredulous that she'd assume he would know. Instead, he just smiled. A calm, thin smile that somehow chilled her to the bone. "Margo dear, if I were you, I wouldn't be quite so eager for Diana Chesterfield to be found."

"But why?"

"Because, darling." He spoke in the same calm voice one might use to placate a child who kept asking why the sky was blue. "If Diana Chesterfield was here, why on earth would we need you?"

SEVENTEEN

*N*ever let your guard down.

Some people embroidered their favorite adages on cushions; for years, Amanda Farraday had imagined her own practically pulsating through her body. As though she'd swallowed the letters, one by one, until they were visible, raised and blue as veins, beneath her pale skin. But lately, something had changed. The icy motto was fading. A trumpet had been sounded, and that old wall of Jericho was slowly crumbling, if not quite tumbling, down. For why else would she be here, waiting patiently outside the cloakroom of the Trocadero supper club, listening to Harry argue good-naturedly with the maître d', who had had the misguided temerity to suggest that "Monsieur might be more comfortable" if he borrowed a jacket and tie from the restaurant to wear.

"If Monsieur thought he would be more comfortable in a

jacket and tie," Harry replied, "Monsieur would have arrived in a jacket and tie. If it's a question of *your* comfort, then have the decency to say so directly."

"Monsieur, it seems it is simply a question of semantics."

"But semantics are everything!" Harry cried. "Semantics are the difference between transparency and exploitative obfuscation. Semantics are how dictatorial governments turn workers and other benighted classes against their own best interests. Semantics are the scaffolding upon which fascism is built!"

Amanda sighed fondly. Harry couldn't have been more unintelligible to her if he were speaking French. Normally, she found some excuse to decline Harry's suggestions for a night out on the town. Not because of outbursts like these—on the contrary, there was something perversely appealing about Harry's almost missionary zeal for discussing the tenets of radical politics with every waitress, janitor, or gas station attendant who wandered across his path. Amanda was simply afraid of being recognized by the wrong sort. Harry was so astute, so quick to pick up on the smallest things, that it wouldn't take much: the wrong kind of look, a misplaced word or two, and she'd have an awful lot of quick explaining—not to mention lying—to do to recover lost ground. Lucky for her, Harry's invitations were few and far between; the naturally hermetic life of a writer more easily lent itself to long private drives through the mountains in her pearl-gray Packard convertible, or sandwiches hastily munched between kisses on the couch in his office. But when Harry had called that day, insisting that they go out to dinner at the Trocadero, she'd surprised herself by saying yes. Maybe she was feeling more confident; surely the more time that passed, the less likely she was to be found out.

Or maybe it had to do with Olive Moore.

Amanda had been apprehensive when Olive Moore had summoned her, anxious to hear what her protégée had dug up on Margo Sterling. Try as she might, Amanda had been unable to find out Margo's real name. The girl had rebuffed all overtures of friendship. The only information Amanda had to offer Olive was that she thought Margo had been raised in Pasadena, and that she seemed fond of a little gold-and-pearl pin that looked a lot like the one Olive wore.

"Are you sure?" Olive had asked. "The same pin?" Amanda said that she wasn't, she'd only seen it for an instant, but it looked awfully similar.

"Thank you, dear," Olive had said, her blue eyes imbued with a faraway glow. It was only then that Amanda noticed the assortment of movie magazines spread across Olive's desk, each open to a story about the dashing Miss Sterling's new romance with teenage sensation Jimmy Molloy. *America's Sweethearts,* blared one. *Girls Across America Lament: Has Love Finally Found Jimmy Molloy?* As usual, *Picture Palace* carried the biggest scandal: *Jimmy and Margo . . . and Baby Makes Three?* Amanda shook her head. She couldn't begin to imagine the source of Olive's fixation on the pretty blonde. If Margo were a former employee, Amanda would surely know, and as for one of Olive's . . . *extracurricular* interests, well, Margo Sterling didn't seem the type. Perhaps it was the resemblance to Diana. The only thing Amanda cared about was that her part in it seemed to have ended, at least for now.

It was terrible, living under this constant threat of blackmail. If she could only break through, get a good enough part, become a big enough star that the studio would have to protect her.

Sometimes she almost felt like throwing in the towel, taking the big mason jar full of cash she'd managed to squirrel away from her salary and the sale of some jewelry and the money her dinner dates gave her and go north. San Francisco, maybe, or Seattle, or even New York; somewhere no one would recognize her, where she could start over with nothing to fear. But then she'd think of Harry, with his loud voice and soft lips. Harry, who even now, as the maître d' at last settled them into their banquette and a trio of scantily clad cigarette girls who looked as though they had all been small-town beauty pageant winners in a former life descended on their table, making sure they were adequately lit and tobaccoed for the night, was still looking at her as though she were the only woman in the world.

"So," Harry said, once they were finally alone. "I guess we're still in mourning?"

"What do you mean?" Amanda asked.

"*'Tis not alone my inky cloak, good mother,*" Harry intoned solemnly, "*nor customary suits of solemn black . . . that can denote me truly.*" He was quoting Shakespeare, probably. Harry always got that tone when he was quoting Shakespeare.

"I don't know what you're talking about," Amanda said. "If you have something to say to me," she added with a mischievous grin, "have the decency to say it *directly*."

"Touché," Harry said with a laugh. "I meant your dress."

"Don't you like it?"

Harry frowned slightly. "It's black."

"It's Mainbocher," Amanda retorted hotly, smoothing the thick crepe fabric lovingly with her fingers. Bought on credit, otherwise it would have emptied her money jar at least three times over. "Anyway, what do you know about clothes, Mr. Borrowed Sports Coat?"

Grinning, Harry fingered the too-long sleeves of the frayed blazer into which the maître d' had finally managed to wrestle him. "It's *Monsieur* Borrowed Sports Coat to you, missy. Besides, it could be worse. Back home in New York there's places that when they make you borrow a jacket you know it came off the body of the last wiseguy who got whacked there."

"No!"

"Would I lie to you? There's a place on Mulberry Street I used to go to with my producer. Best linguini with clam sauce in the city. One day I show up in short sleeves, straight from rehearsal, and the waiter gives me a jacket with a bullet hole, bam, clean through the lapel." Arranging his hand in the shape of a gun, Harry mimed being shot in the chest.

"That's terrible!" Amanda exclaimed. "Wasn't it too creepy?"

"Nah." Harry grinned. "Not for a tough guy like me. Hey," he continued, leaning forward over his menu, "that's not your story, is it? You're not some kind of Sicilian widow? Because if so, you better tell me now before a bunch of goons burst through the door and ruin yet another perfectly good sports coat."

"What if I told you I just happen to *like* wearing black?"

"I wouldn't believe you. I'm a writer, Amanda. It's my beat to look for the story. A beautiful young girl who dresses only in black? That's what we in the business would call a character choice. There's got to be a reason for it or it's just bad writing. So maybe she's not a widow." Harry scratched his upper lip thoughtfully. "Maybe she's in mourning for something else. A parent? A child?"

"Maybe she's a cat burglar," Amanda suggested. "Or one of those Japanese assassins, like in the Charlie Chan pictures."

"A ninja. Very imaginative." Harry nodded. "Let's think closer to home. More believable. In these troubled times, maybe it's political. Maybe she's an anarchist. Or even a Fascist."

"Never a Fascist!"

"Never? The lady doth protest too much, methinks."

"No!" Amanda laughed helplessly. "No more Shakespeare, please!"

"Then tell me what the deal is with the black."

Amanda hesitated. "Do you really want to know?"

"*'Tis now the very witching time of night, when churchyards yawn and hell itself breathes out . . .*"

"Fine!" she cried, jokingly clamping her hands over her ears. Harry made her feel like such a little kid sometimes. "I'll tell you. But you have to promise not to make fun of me."

"Never." Harry leaned toward her again, staring at her with that burning gaze of his. "I would never make fun of you."

"Okay, well . . ." Amanda dropped her eyes to the tablecloth. *And another brick slides out of the wall of Jericho.* "Well, when I first came out here, to Hollywood—"

"From where?" Harry interrupted.

"Oklahoma," Amanda said, too startled to lie.

"The Dust Bowl," Harry said, raising his eyebrows. "You never told me that before."

"Didn't I?" She meant it to sound lighthearted, but it came out a quavering whisper. "A tiny little town called Arrowhead Falls. You'd never have heard of it in New York, it's not on any map—"

Harry shrugged. "Honey, in New York we'd barely heard of Oklahoma."

204

"Right. Anyway, I was very young then. A kid, really—"

"You're still a kid."

"Stop interrupting me or I'm not going to tell you," Amanda said.

Bowing his head in apology, Harry made a zipping motion across his lips, as though to fasten his mouth shut.

"Thank you," Amanda said. "I didn't know anyone here. I didn't have a job or a school to go to or anything. My parents had . . . had passed away." Harry opened his mouth as though he was about to say something but thought better of it. "So to pass the time, I used to walk for hours up and down Wilshire, looking at all the fine shops where the rich ladies would go. The things in the windows were so beautiful. Silk dresses, ropes of pearls, perfume in bottles that looked like they were carved out of diamonds. I'd never seen those kinds of things before; in Arrowhead Falls not even the pictures in magazines looked like that." She traced a pattern on the tablecloth with her finger, remembering. "I always wanted to go inside, but I didn't dare; how could I, in my broken shoes and calico dress, talking in that hick accent—honestly, Harry, when I opened my mouth, people thought I was an immigrant, a foreigner, that's how bad it was. But I told myself, 'Amanda, one day, you're going to be a fine lady with money in your pocket. And you'll go into these shops and the salesgirls will bring you all these beautiful things to look at, each one more beautiful than the next, and you'll turn up your nose at all of it, just like the fine ladies do.'"

Harry laughed. "And did you?"

Amanda took a deep breath. "Well, I eventually got a job." *You could call it that,* she thought. "And the first time I got paid, I bought a new dress from Woolworth's, a plaid taffeta, purple and green. Shoes too, to match, and then I splurged on a lipstick at Bullocks. It cost fifty cents and came in a beautiful gold case. And I got all dressed up and walked over to Wilshire and walked into the first store I saw. A jewelry shop."

She squeezed her eyes shut for a moment, summoning the memory. "I stood there at the counter, proud as a peacock in my new Woolworth's dress, waiting for the salesgirl to bring me whatever I wanted to see. Like a lady." With a hard swallow, Amanda shook her head. She hated this part of the story. "Well, that salesgirl looked at me like I was something she scraped off the bottom of her shoe. It was like she saw right through me. She knew I was just a cheap little piece of Oklahoma trash who'd gotten above herself. Didn't say hello, didn't ask if she could help. Just stared at me until I was too embarrassed to stand there any longer."

"That must have been terrible," Harry said softly.

"It was one of the worst afternoons of my life," Amanda whispered. Even now she could still feel her cheeks burning with the shame of it. "But at least I got a good long look at what was in those glass cases. Diamonds and rubies and pearls, on beds of black velvet. I know it sounds crazy, but standing there in that stupid loud taffeta dress, which I'd spent all my money on and was now too ashamed to wear, I looked at that velvet and I thought, 'Black. I'm going to wear black.'" She looked up at Harry, tears glistening in her eyes. "No one can feel ashamed in a black dress. It doesn't matter if it cost one dollar or a thousand. You might look dull, you might look serious, you might look sad. But one thing you won't look like is an ignorant little hick from Arrowhead Falls, Oklahoma, who a salesgirl can treat like a dirty old shoe."

Harry's eyes were very bright as he took Amanda's hand and squeezed it, hard. "Thank you for telling me that."

"You're welcome," she said quickly. The waiter, arriving with their drinks, saved her from having to say any more. Seizing her martini by the stem, Amanda took a long, restorative sip. "Okay, buddy," she said, feeling steadier. "Now it's your turn."

"My turn?" Harry looked puzzled.

"Didn't you have something to tell me?" she asked pleasantly. "That's how you made it sound on the telephone."

"Aha." Waggling his eyebrows up and down like Groucho Marx, Harry took a small sip of his drink. "If you mean to suggest, my dear Watson, that I would need a special reason to escort you to an establishment at which the price of a simple chicken dinner for one could feed a hungry family of five for a week, then congratulations, because you are absolutely correct."

Amanda smiled. Despite its faux French menu and the swanky cream-and-gold interior—not to mention the high-stakes gambling tucked discreetly away in the back room— the Trocadero was actually one of the more reasonably priced places on the Sunset Strip. God help Harry if she ever managed to drag him to the Cocoanut Grove or the Vendome. He'd probably drown himself in the lobster bisque. "Well, what is it?"

Harry's face was lit up like a candle. "It's good news. Very, very exciting news." He paused dramatically, taking another sip of Scotch. "As of this week, I will no longer be Harry Gordon, nominal screenwriter, glorified errand boy, and knock-around slob. No, no." He puffed out his chest proudly. "I am going to be Harry Gordon, *actual* screenwriter, with an actual, genuine, honest-to-God movie to my name."

"Harry!" Amanda squealed. "You don't mean—"

"That's right. As of tomorrow, *The Nine Days' Queen* officially goes back into production."

Amanda felt her jaw practically drop to the floor. "They found *Diana*?" she gasped. "Diana's back?"

"Even better." Harry beamed, pointing in her direction. A burst of desperate, unreasonable hope suddenly surged through Amanda. *Me?* she thought, with joyful disbelief. *They're giving the part to me?* "Look over there."

Deflated, Amanda followed Harry's extended finger to the doorway, where a phalanx of photographers, like musicians directed by some invisible conductor, had suddenly converged. Through the blinding flash of popping lights, Amanda caught a glimpse of Jimmy Molloy's grinning face. Beside him stood the dark outline of a slim blonde in a silver dress, her face shrouded in a gauzy evening veil. Standing regally at attention, her pale hair gleaming white, she lifted the veil and turned her face toward the light. Amanda couldn't hold back her astounded gasp. She looked so much like Diana it was like seeing a ghost.

"Margo Sterling," Harry said proudly. "Pretty amazing, don't you think?"

"Smile, Margo," Jimmy muttered through his clenched teeth. "Smile for the nice men."

Obediently, Margo turned up the corners of her painstakingly painted mouth, careful to keep her chin tilted down and her cheeks held in, the way her smiling instructor had shown her. *A smiling instructor.* He had been waiting outside her bungalow the moment she'd returned from her fateful audience

208

with Leo Karp, ready and eager to tell her that her right incisor was deformed and her eyes crinkled unflatteringly, so she must always be careful not to smile too wide. After mercilessly coaxing her lips and cheek muscles through a variety of iterations, all of which seemed to have their own unsettling name—the Princess Pout, the Girl-Next-Door Grin, the Southern Belle Simper—they had finally settled on a bemused Mona Lisa Smirk, which radiated oodles of glamour and absolutely no joy.

"That's a good girl," Jimmy muttered as flashbulbs popped all around them inside the Trocadero. "Now turn. Let them get a good shot of the dress."

Even with the double-layered rubber girdle she was wearing, she felt as though her dress were bursting at the seams. "I can't breathe," she murmured back to Jimmy. "I feel like a trussed chicken."

"Darling, don't be silly." Jimmy replied smoothly, expertly pivoting her to the front again. "It's only how you look that matters."

Isn't that the truth, Margo thought. Nothing had prepared her for the scrutiny she found herself under as Jimmy Molloy's latest sweetheart and Olympus Studio's newest star. The smiling instructor had just been the tip of the iceberg. Experts descended on her normally quiet bungalow, day and night, each one eager to perform a dizzying and (she was assured) highly necessary array of beauty treatments and therapies. The "improvements," as they were called, had one major element in common: each one was more painful and invasive than the last. A team of hairdressers peroxided and straightened her hair. Makeup artists plucked and waxed her eyebrows until beads of blood stood out on her brow. A team of dressers had wheeled in rack after rack of heart-stoppingly stylish clothes personally selected by Rex Mandalay, the young Australian genius newly in charge of Olympus's wardrobe department.

"There must be some mistake." Margo had gasped for breath as Rex gave the zipper of a tiny lavender column of bias-cut satin a last futile tug.

Rex snorted. "I'll say. You're going to have to reduce." He was wearing pants as tight as a ballet dancer's.

"Reduce?" Margo looked down at her body, packed like a sausage into the minuscule gown. "But most of these clothes wouldn't fit a child!"

"The camera adds ten pounds," Rex said, "which means you need to lose twenty. I'll tell the commissary to start you on the official studio diet. Grapefruit for breakfast, a very small steak for lunch, nothing for dinner. No bread, no sweets, and absolutely no eating between meals. The weight will come off in no time."

I'll starve, Margo thought helplessly. *They're trying to starve me to death.* "And if it doesn't?"

"Then you'll go to the studio doctor and he'll give you some pills."

Margo thought of Gabby and the vials in her handbag. "No," she said firmly, "no pills."

Rex shrugged. "I suppose you could always have your bottom ribs removed."

Margo yelped. "Why on earth would I do that?"

"Everyone's doing it now, now that the waist is back. There's a marvelous man in the Bahamas who did the Duchess of Windsor's." Thoughtfully, Rex placed a hand on each side of his own slim midsection, squeezing the sides into a tapering V.

210

"Something to think about. Mark my words, this time next year, the wasp waist will be back with a vengeance." Stepping closer, he peered into her face with an appraising look. "We might do something about your nose as well."

"My nose?" Margo repeated. "What's wrong with my nose?"

"The tip is a little on the bulbous side. And there's a bump, right here." His finger felt like ice as he tapped it. "You might not notice now, but on the screen you see every little imperfection. There's a man in Berlin who could do the job, if we can get you over there before they start another war. It would really look much better on camera."

On camera. Everything was for the camera. She wasn't Margaret Frobisher anymore; she wasn't even really Margo Sterling. She was a thing on display, powdered, primped, and starving, in a dress that didn't fit, on the arm of a man she didn't love. The camera ruled them all.

"Aw, shucks, I knew Margie was the girl for me the first time I saw her," Jimmy was saying now as a man from the *Hollywood Reporter* scribbled notes in his pad. "And then I just did what any fella would do. I wooed her. Sent her present after present, each one nicer than the last, until she finally said she'd be my girl. And the best part is, you and the folks at home can read all about it, just as soon as the newest issue of *Picture Palace* hits newsstands next week." He chuckled heartily, jiggling his arm around her waist. "Isn't that right, honey?"

"Sure," Margo said, gritting her teeth at the memory of that asinine photo shoot they'd suffered through the day before. Jimmy, mugging wildly in a Santa hat, while she pretended to unwrap box after box, oohing and aahing over the contents— an enormous stuffed panda, a string of pearls, a white mink cape, all of which would be promptly returned to the studio's props department as soon as the photographer left. Jimmy, who was drinking heavily and prone to disappearing for long periods of time between shots, had barely spoken to her, except to tell her and anyone else who would listen what an idiot he felt like. That was what *Picture Palace* would hold up to its readers as the epitome of young love. To think she actually used to take that stuff seriously! She'd had more romantic afternoons at the dentist's office.

"Culminating with a pony, is that right?" the reporter asked.

Jimmy nodded proudly. "A genuine Thoroughbred California palomino. To match her beautiful hair. We'll be posing for photographs with it up at the stables in a few days, so stay in touch with the press office before all the good shots are taken."

"And what about you, Miss Sterling?" asked a woman in a purple dress. "When did you realize how you felt about Jimmy?"

When Leo Karp sat me down in his office and told me it was either Jimmy or my job. Helplessly, Margo cast an eye around the supper club, trying to stall for time. Like an iron filing to a magnet, her gaze was drawn directly to Dane Forrest.

Of course he'd be here, she thought bitterly. He was standing next to a table, his arm around a peroxided blonde in a blue fox stole. Margo had never seen her before, but even from across the room it was clear she was not the sort of girl who would ever darken the doorway of the Orange Grove Academy. The blonde was laughing uproariously at something Dane had said, throwing her head far enough back to make sure he got a good look down her red sequined gown. He glanced up as he pulled out a chair for his companion, and for a single, breathless moment, Margo thought he caught her gaze. Even from all the

212

way across the room, she could make out the deep green of his eyes.

"Miss Sterling," pressed the woman. "How did you know Jimmy was the guy for you?"

The words fell out in a tumble. "I'd loved him ever so long, from the pictures. And then we met by chance my first day on the lot. I was awfully scared, and he was so kind. I felt as though he understood me. As though we could understand each other. As though I could tell him anything and he'd understand."

"Not bad," Jimmy murmured, so only she could hear. "Not bad at all."

"How about a kiss?" asked a reporter.

"Sure!" Jimmy said. "Whaddya say, honey? Aw, look at the kid, she's shy."

Dane had his arm around the blonde again. He was staring into her eyes with that special attentive gaze that made you feel like you were the only girl in the world. He had looked at Margo that way. And Diana. *And who knows how many other hundreds of girls.*

Suddenly, Dane was gone. Jimmy's face loomed before her, blocking her view. "Come *on*, Margo," he hissed. "Just one. For the *camera*."

Oh God, *no*. They were kissing. They were actually *kissing* right there for everyone to see. And of course, the flashbulbs were popping away.

Under the table, Gabby dug her fingernails so hard into her palms she thought she would draw blood. She almost hoped she did. She imagined the blood running warm and sticky and red down her wrists, smeared thickly all over the front of her white taffeta dress. It would be like something out of a horror movie, like the Bride of Frankenstein. Then maybe her outsides would match the way she felt inside.

America's Sweethearts. America's Cinderella Lands Prince Charming. The day those headlines started running was one of the worst of Gabby Preston's young life. Maybe *the* worst, if you didn't count the day her sister Frankie ran off. While all those little nobodies out there were swooning over the photo spread of Jimmy in white tie and tails, laughingly pretending to fit a glass slipper on a ball-gowned Margo's dainty foot, all Gabby could see was the boy she'd danced with, daydreamed of, even thought she *loved* for more than a year, proclaiming his undying affection for her best friend. *Best friend.* That was a laugh. Some friend Margo had turned out to be. It was like Viola always said. In show business, the only real friend you had was yourself.

For at least a week, all Gabby had wanted to do was go to sleep and, if she was lucky, never wake up. It was Viola who had dragged her out of bed and forced the new green wake-up pills down her throat. The pink ones had stopped working weeks ago.

"So the good Lord Jesus decided it was the Sterling girl's turn right now." Viola always went very Catholic in times of strife. "It'll be your turn next, baby, you'll see. So go out there and sparkle, because the Lord helps those who help themselves." And with that, she bundled Gabby off to the rehearsal studio without so much as a second glance.

If it weren't for Dr. Lipkin and his pills, Gabby didn't know how she'd survive.

Especially not tonight. She'd been hoping to spend the evening alone in her bedroom in the house on Fountain Street, listening to records on her new phonograph and crying periodically, but Viola had burst into her trailer on the Tully Toynbee set, brandishing a new white taffeta evening gown as though it were a flag of war. "I've just come from a meeting about the vaudeville picture. You've got above-the-title billing and it's confirmed, Harry Gordon is writing it just for you. A Gabby Preston vehicle, pure and simple. You're doing all right, kiddo. You've got heat. And if you want to keep it, you better stop moping and stay in the public eye. Remember, the whole world is watching."

So like the good little girl everyone expected her to be, Gabby got dressed up and went to the Trocadero. Jimmy was there with Margo, who was looking like Diana Chesterfield to a creepy—and frankly tacky—extent; Amanda Farraday, acting all fake and gooey-eyed over Harry Gordon, was sitting at a table right in the center of the room with Dane Forrest, of all people, and a very glamorous-looking blonde in a sparkly red dress.

And who was Gabby Preston sitting with? Her mother and that goofball from the publicity department, Stan or whatever his name was. If there was a more humiliating scenario, Gabby didn't want to hear about it.

Her heart was pounding—no, not pounding—it was trying to *get out*. Throwing itself violently against her rib cage, like a lemming diving into the sea. *Am I going to be sick?* Gabby wondered. *Oh, please, don't let me get sick. Not tonight.*

"Gabby." Viola pinched the delicate skin of Gabby's forearm hard enough to bruise.

"Ow! That hurts!"

"Then pull it together. People are watching." Viola leaned in closer. The whiskey on her breath mingled with the powdery scent of the Shalimar perfume Gabby had bought her for her birthday. "How many green pills today?"

"It doesn't matter."

"You're sweating bullets." Viola took a pillbox from her handbag and forced a blue capsule into Gabby's hand. "Take it."

Gabby glanced nervously at Stan, but he was too busy gazing at Margo with a rapturous expression on his big-billed face. "Those are for bedtime."

"It's just one, and believe me, you need it." Viola pressed her half-full glass of Scotch into Gabby's hand. "Wash it down with this. Then go to the ladies' room and fix your face."

The ladies' room at the Trocadero had no grand sitting rooms or uniformed attendants. *Good*, Gabby thought. She was glad to be alone. Leaning over the sink, she examined her face carefully in the mirror. The heavy pancake makeup she wore to even out her complexion was smeared with sweat. Black streaks of mascara had pooled in the hollow purple shadows beneath her dilated eyes. The clump of dark curls sticking to her damp neck was deflated, like a fallen, burnt soufflé. *Viola was right*, Gabby thought with a shock. *I really do look like hell.*

It was funny about the pills, she mused as she reached for her powder puff. They made you feel so marvelous at first, strong and brave and beautiful, as if you could do anything in the world. But that feeling went away so quickly, and pretty soon you just felt like yourself again, only a little smaller, a little more scared, and then you just felt tired. So you had to take a few more pills, and before you knew it, you had crossed the threshold from tired to wired to another feeling entirely. *Dread* was the best word Gabby could think of for it. A creeping, heart-pounding feeling of dread, as though something horrible was about to happen. She'd felt that way tonight, at least until Viola had given her the blue pill. *Sweet, good Viola*, Gabby thought, lazily dragging the velvet powder puff over her skin. *She always looks out for me.*

The door began to open. Someone was coming in. *Damn it,* Gabby thought. She couldn't let anyone see her like this. She darted into an empty stall just in the nick of time, locking the door behind her. The door went all the way to the ground, hiding her completely, but through the small crack at the side she could make out a flash of black dress and red hair that she knew belonged to Amanda Farraday. The other girl was the blonde in the sparkly red dress. *Dane Forrest's girl.*

"Lucy," Amanda hissed in a low voice. "What the hell are you doing here?"

"Same thing as you, honey," the girl replied. She had a high, squeaky voice, the kind the chorus girls always had in gangster pictures. "Enjoying a night out on the town on the arm of a handsome gentleman."

"Get real."

"Aw, come on, Ginger, cool it, will ya?" *Ginger?* Was that Amanda's real name? "Dane came storming into Olive's place drunk as a skunk and looking for some action. Olive didn't want any trouble, so she gave him a cup of coffee and said someone would take him out."

"And he picked you." Amanda's voice sounded flat.

"Truth is, Olive asked me to take care of him. On account of I've been around long enough I ain't likely to cash out to the tabloids with a story about how Dane Forrest showed up three sheets to the wind and looking for girls at Olive Moore's house."

Olive Moore! Gabby had to clap her hands over her mouth to keep them from hearing her gasp. She knew who Olive Moore was; everyone in Hollywood did, unless they were prissy little Margo Sterling.

"But Olive's girls have always been discreet," Amanda said.

"Used to be. Things have changed since your day, Gin. The new ones she brought in, well, let's just say they aren't all exactly fresh from finishing school, if you catch my drift."

Amanda's dress made a silken rustle. "You should have brought him someplace else. Someplace less conspicuous. Olive won't like it."

"This was where he wanted to go. What am I going to do, say no? Besides, how was I supposed to know you were here? Hey"—Lucy's voice dropped about an octave—"you're not still hung up on him, are you?"

"Don't be ridiculous." Amanda snapped her purse shut. "That's all been over for ages. Over before it even began."

"That's what I thought," Lucy said. "And I guess that's the new fella?"

"He's a fella, yes."

"And I suppose he doesn't know about all this."

"He certainly does not," Amanda said. "And he's not going to."

"Relax, Gin. He's not going to get anything out of me. I'm not out to ruin things for you. Although . . ." Lucy paused. "It would be nice to feel like a big star like you remembered her old friends every now and again."

A sharp edge, like the blade of a knife, crept into Amanda's voice. "What do you want, Lucy?"

"Nothing! Just a letter now and then, that's all. Golly, you've gotten hard in Hollywood."

"I'm sorry, Lucy. I didn't mean it to come out that way."

"That's all right, Ginger." Lucy's voice was gentle. "But you have to know we're rooting for you. Maybe not Olive, but I am. And I know it can't be easy."

"It would be a lot easier if you'd stop calling me Ginger."

Lucy let out a peal of laughter. "Excuse me, *Amanda*. But I do think I played it off pretty well though, don't you think? 'Well, I do declare, Mr. Gordon, Ginger is just what we call all the redheads back home! Just a term of endearment down in little ol' Kentucky!' He never doubted it for a second!" Their laughter echoed through the door as it swung shut behind them.

Alone again, Gabby finally dared to breathe. Her heart was pounding harder than ever, but her mind was perfectly clear. *Amanda Farraday worked for Olive Moore.* And she and Dane had had some kind of relationship, had been lovers, even. *Oh boy.* This was a doozy.

Knowledge is power. Gabby didn't know who had said it first, but she knew it was true. She knew so many things now. About Amanda, about Dane, about Jimmy, about Margo.

Smiling, Gabby sat back on the toilet seat, the blue pill beginning to send its calm blue warmth through her veins. If knowledge was power, then Gabby Preston was about to become the most powerful person in Hollywood.

EIGHTEEN

"Here, Sophie." Standing at the paddock fence, Margo took an apple from the folds of her heavy gown and held it against the mare's velvety snout. The horse turned her large dark eyes on Margo as though she'd never seen her before. "It's a cooking apple, just like you like," Margo urged. "Go on, eat!"

She heard a quiet chuckle. Owen, the head groom of the Olympus stables, stood behind her, twisting his checked cap in his hands. "Begging your pardon, Miss Sterling," he said in his soft Irish brogue, "but they're nearly ready for you on the set. They've sent me to come and fetch you."

"Oh, Owen," Margo said mournfully. "I don't think Sophie recognizes me."

Owen laughed again. "Telling the truth, miss, in that getup I'm not sure I'd have recognized you myself."

Margo looked sheepishly down at her costume, a vast

220

Tudor-style riding habit of heavy brick-colored velvet—which Rex Mandalay insisted would photograph as black—with enormous padded panniers over the hips and a tightly laced stomacher that made the front of her torso look like a flat inverted V. Along with the huge feathered riding hat and the thick hank of false hair gathered into a spangled net at the back of her head, she was about three times the size she usually was when she came to the paddock, in jodhpurs and a button-down shirt. "I see what you mean."

"Don't you worry, Miss Sterling. She'll know it's you as soon as you're on her back. Horses always do." Owen gave Margo an awkward pat on her wrist, the only part of her he could easily access. "Now, we can walk down to the set if you'd like, but if you don't mind, I'd rather you ride. Sophie's all saddled up, and I'd like to get a sense of how the weight of that skirt feels in the sidesaddle before you start filming. Then I'll lead you down."

"That sounds very sensible, thank you."

Putting on his cap, he knelt next to the horse and put out a sturdy palm to boost Margo into the saddle. His brow knit in concentration as he carefully arranged the capacious folds of her dress over the mare's chestnut haunches. "I'm sure the dressing girls will have another go at it," he said, giving the fabric a final tug, "but in the meantime, how does that feel?"

"Fine," Margo said, settling into the saddle. "More importantly, how does it look?"

Owen pushed back his cap, wiping the sweat from his brow. "Before I came to America to seek my fortune, I was a groom in the stables of the Earl of Kimbrough, back in Tipperary. I thought never to see a finer horsewoman than his countess."

He grinned. "And I still never have. But for an American girl, I guess you'll do."

"Owen!" She tossed a glove at him playfully. "As though I'm not nervous enough!"

"Begging your pardon, Miss Sterling, I was only joking. You've the best seat I've seen around these parts. Excepting . . ." Owen suddenly stopped himself.

"Except who?" Margo asked.

Owen looked straight ahead, not daring to meet her eye. "Excepting Miss Chesterfield, miss."

I should have known, Margo thought. "Diana was good in the saddle, was she?"

"Better than good," Owen said reverently. "Had a real sixth sense for the animal, she did, as though she could tell what it was feeling. It's rare, that is, although not so much for those that grew up on a farm."

"Diana Chesterfield grew up on a farm?" Margo asked in disbelief. "I thought she was supposed to be a socialite in England or something."

"Ah, come to think of it, I could be mistaken, Miss Sterling," Owen said, obviously embarrassed to have revealed something he realized he shouldn't have. "Perhaps that's a tale of my own invention. On account of how natural she was with the horses."

"What about Dane Forrest?" Margo pressed, unable to stop herself. "How is he in the saddle?"

"Oh, fine, fine," Owen said quickly. "A bit rough for the mares, perhaps, but I can't fault him on a stallion. But you'll see soon enough, won't you?"

"Yes," Margo said. "I suppose I will." Today would be her first day filming with Dane and their first interaction since that fateful night at the Cocoanut Grove, if you didn't count that horrible night at the Trocadero, when he could barely bring himself even to glance at her. Perhaps the anticipation of seeing him, more than the thought of toppling off her horse from the weight of her dress, accounted for the butterflies in her stomach—or rather, under her stomacher.

Margo gave Sophie's flank a gentle kick. The horse trotted obediently out the paddock gate as Owen walked ahead, holding the reins.

It was a beautiful morning. The last orange streaks of sunrise had retreated, and the sky over the canyon was dazzlingly blue. As they made their way down the rocky path from the paddock, Margo caught her first glimpse of the hollow. It was utterly transformed. The ground was laid with what looked like nearly an acre of sod, transforming what had been a scrubby Southern California canyon into one of England's verdant hills. In the middle of the lawn stood two turrets, festooned with the royal standard and the Cross of St. George. Between them milled about thirty extras in plates of armor and Tudor livery, doubtless indulging in the traditional film extra activities of chain-smoking and complaining about the weather and/or the breakfast they had just been fed. At the end of the grass was the enormous modern camera, surrounded by a forest of clanking generators and cylindrical lights. It was utterly incongruous, utterly magical, utterly mad. Utterly Hollywood.

At the center of it all was the small figure of Raoul Kurtzman, bundled tightly in overcoat and scarf despite the incipient heat. Beside him was Dane, astride a giant black charger. In a dark velvet doublet and loose white shirt left open at the throat, his perfect profile finely etched in shadow by the rapidly rising sun, he looked more handsome than Margo had ever seen him. *Damn,* she thought furiously. *Damn, damn, damn.*

"Good luck, Miss Sterling," Owen said. "I'll be standing by if you need me." He let go of the reins.

Taking as deep a breath as her costume would allow, Margo trotted Sophie gingerly over to her director and costar.

"Margo," Dane said curtly, glancing up at her. The makeup department had affixed some kind of jaunty little mustache to his upper lip, but he could make even that look good. "Nice of you to join us." Clearly, he was itching for a fight.

"Hello, Dane."

"Miss Sterling, there you are." Mr. Kurtzman clapped his hands together. Most people went sort of craggy and pale over the course of a movie shoot, as though the strain of the filming and lack of sleep were slowly turning them to weathered stone. Not Raoul Kurtzman. Over the past few weeks, he had completely transformed from the tired little man she had first met on soundstage fourteen into a smiling, effusive, rosy-cheeked bundle of energy. *He needs to be making a picture,* Margo thought. *It's like oxygen to him.* "Let me look at you." Margo obliged, pulling Sophie back a few steps. Mr. Kurtzman surveyed them with an appraising eye. "Very good," he said. "Very good indeed. Just a small adjustment we need in the arrangement of the skirt. . . . Wardrobe!" He snapped his fingers and two women in smocks came hustling forth to fussily rearrange the folds of cloth over Sophie's hindquarters, seemingly heedless of any possible unpleasant surprises from that end.

"Now." Kurtzman clapped again. "Today, we begin with a very simple shot. Simple for you, that is, not simple for me. It is the moment when Lady Jane Grey"—he gestured toward

224

Margo—"and Lord Guildford Dudley, her betrothed"—he bowed toward Dane—"meet. When I call action, Lady Jane, accompanied by her father, the Duke of Suffolk"—he nodded toward the cluster of director's chairs in the shadow, where Sir Benjamin Cattermore, the august and elderly British actor playing the role, was poring intently over a racing form—"and her liveried men, will ride out from the castle. From the other end rides Lord Dudley with his armored men. And you meet in the middle. Understand?"

"Mr. Kurtzman!" a man called from behind the camera. "We need you to look at these lights."

The director turned back to Margo and Dane. "You just stay here and—how do you say it in English—sit tight? Sit tight until I call places, yes?" He darted away.

Margo twisted Sophie's mane idly between her fingers, not daring to meet Dane's eye. She could sense that beside her, he was doing the same thing. *Well, this is comfortable,* she thought. The initial thrill of moviemaking wore off quickly, Margo had found. The acting part was exciting, but mostly you spent a lot of time sitting around doing nothing as they calibrated the lights, then recalibrated them, then moved the camera three inches to the left, then back again. It was trying enough in the best of circumstances. If she and Dane couldn't bring themselves to talk to each other, the day was going to be excruciating.

Dane finally cracked. "So," he said. "How's it going for you?"

"How's *what* going for me?" Margo replied. Grateful as she was to him for initiating the conversation, she had no intention of making this any easier for him than it had to be. After all, he was the one who'd agreed to shut her out first.

225

"The picture." He offered a wan smile. "At least, let's start with that."

"Fine," she said. "Although you'd know that already if you'd stopped by the set."

"It's not a school play, Margo," Dane said testily. "I come when I'm called. Otherwise my time is my own. And besides," he added, giving his charger's reins a little tug, "I may be listed as a costar, but this is your show. My role is actually pretty small. Most of my scenes were shot before you even started."

"Oh?" Margo raised her eyebrows loftily. "I didn't realize that."

"Margo, please. Don't pull that high-and-mighty duchess bit on me. You know very well what a rush job this was. They're massively over budget as it is. Karp has to please New York, and New York likes things cheap."

"Like me, I suppose," Margo said. She twisted Sophie's reins tightly around her hand. "Nice and cheap."

"Margo—"

"Just a nice, *cheap* replacement for Diana."

"I didn't say it," Dane replied coldly. "But if that's your aim, I have to say you're doing a pretty good job."

"What's *that* supposed to mean?"

Dane's charger let out a whinny, rearing back on his hind legs as a desert lizard scuttled across the path. Pulling back on the reins, Dane patted his neck soothingly. "Nothing," he said when the horse was calm. "Forget it."

"No," Margo insisted. "Say what you mean, Dane."

Dane kept patting his horse. "How *is* Jimmy, Margo?"

There. There it was at last. The all-singing, all-dancing, ten-ton elephant in the room—or rather, on the hillside. Margo

226

glanced over at the liveried extras standing in a cluster as they received direction from an assistant director. The smoke from their cigarettes formed a small cloud above their heads. "Marvelous, thank you."

"From what I read, the two of you have certainly been painting the town red."

"Since when do you read the gossip columns?"

"Oh, I pick up the odd rag here and there. Doctor's office, barbershop, that sort of thing. I saw quite a precious little photo spread of the two of you the other day. Jimmy prancing around dressed as an elf, I think it was?" He paused. "Or perhaps was it a fairy?"

There was a cruelty to his tone that Margo didn't care for. She and Jimmy knew how foolish they both looked, but that didn't give Dane any right to mock them. "It was Santa Claus, as it happens," she said coolly.

"Santa!" Dane snapped his fingers. "How could I forget? Curious, though, that they should run it in the summer instead of waiting for the holidays—unless they don't expect the two of you to make it that long. But I suppose they'll let you know when you've served your time. And I suppose we'll see if I've got any appetite for Jimmy Molloy's sloppy seconds."

"Flattering a thought as that may be, Mr. Forrest, I hardly think we'll get to find out." Her tone was icy, hard, bemused. *Vintage Mildred Frobisher,* she thought with a surprising burst of gratitude. *At least Mother taught me something.* "Things are going very well between Jimmy and me. So well, in fact, that he's escorting me to Pasadena tonight. We'll be attending the coming-out party of a *very* dear friend at the club there."

"Bringing him home to the folks, huh?" Dane gave a hard

laugh. "Well, that's just swell, Margo. Really swell. It does my cynic's heart good to hear it. I suppose we'll be reading all about the engagement ring in *Picture Palace* any day now. *America's Princess, A Fairy-Tale Bride*. I can see the pictures now. Of course, they'll recast your father if he's too bald and your mother if she can't cry on cue, but what does that matter? It's a small price to pay for being the envy of every girl in the world." He looked her straight in the eye. "Just as long as you know that deep down, they all hate you."

"Dane!"

"It's true, you know. They hate us. They say they love us, but deep down, they hate us. Because we remind them that life is unfair."

Margo was silent for a minute. "Well, they're right. Life is unfair. About Karp . . . I—I had no choice," she said, her voice breaking. "You would have done the same thing."

Dane shook his head. "I don't know about that, Margo. Because you went into Karp's office with more power than anyone in the business, and you came out with nothing."

"What?" Margo blinked back astonished tears. "What do you mean?"

"You had the most powerful thing of all," Dane said sadly. "The power of having nothing to lose. You aren't like the rest of us—the gypsies and strivers and walking wounded. You could have walked away. Gone back to your beautiful house in Pasadena, and your canopy bed and your swimming pool and the long line of nice, solid, honest young men who would give their eyeteeth for a chance to make you happy. You could have kept your soul."

"What do you know about my soul?" she hissed. Suddenly,

she wanted to hurt him. She wanted to slap that fake mustache right off his smug face. "What do you know about my *life*? You barely know me!" She had never spoken like this to anyone before, let alone a grown man, but she was too furious to stop. "You're the one who got me into this mess in the first place. You *knew* the tabloids had it in for you. You knew they'd jump all over any girl you so much as smiled at, like a pack of hounds who smelled blood. God, it's so sick, it's like a game to you! And it's not just me, is it, Dane? There's that blonde you were out with at the Troc the other night, and Amanda Farraday . . ."

"Margo—"

"And Diana! Because it all comes back to her, doesn't it? It all comes back to Diana. And you know where she is, don't you? You know exactly what happened to Diana. Why won't you tell the truth, Dane? *Why won't you tell the truth about Diana?*"

Dane grabbed hold of Sophie's reins, pulling Margo close, horse and all. His eyes blazed, searching hers. *He's going to kiss me,* Margo thought wildly. *Or hit me.* Or maybe both.

"Places, boys and girls!" Raoul Kurtzman's shout, amplified through the megaphone, echoed through the canyon like the voice of God. "Places, please! Let's try it from the top!"

Dane kept his hand on Sophie's reins. His face was so close to Margo's she could feel the heat radiating off his skin. She could smell the sweat. "Because I'm afraid, Margo," he whispered hoarsely. His hot breath tickled her neck. "Because I'm a coward."

And then he galloped away to begin the scene.

NINETEEN

*T*wo greens, one blue.

After all this time, Gabby Preston had finally figured out the pills. It was just like when she was little and Viola used to buy her a sack of raisins and almonds as a treat. She spent what seemed like ages trying them out in different combinations until she hit on the perfect ratio: two raisins, one almond. The perfect balance of sweet and salty, soft and crunchy.

The pills were like that. *Two greens, one blue.* Not too wired, not too sleepy. She was bursting with energy, but her thoughts weren't all jumbled up the way they used to be. She was thinking clearly, so clearly that her thoughts were practically like the paving stones of a shining road, and all she had to do was follow it. It was like Viola used to say back in the old days, when things got a little hairy: "Don't worry, baby, I've got a plan."

Well, now Gabby had a plan. Even if she was the only person who could see it clearly.

Okay, Gabby thought as she approached Margo Sterling's bougainvillea-draped door—leave it to Margo to somehow wind up with the prettiest bungalow on the lot. *Step one.* She took a deep breath, smoothing down the skirt of her plaid dress. To some people it might seem the teeniest, tiniest, eensiest bit, well, *mean,* what she was about to do. But getting Jimmy back was the first part of the plan. However you sliced it, Gabby and Jimmy belonged together. They were like Mickey and Judy, Fred and Ginger, bacon and eggs. On their own, they were great, but together, well, they just made *sense.* Gabby knew it. Jimmy knew it. Even the studio knew it, or they wouldn't keep putting them together in picture after picture. All she had to do was make Margo see, and everyone would be better off. The order of the universe would be restored. And she and Margo could go back to being friends again. Proper friends. *Best* friends.

She raised her hand to knock, but the door pushed open at her touch, revealing the darkened room.

"Gabby?" Margo was stretched out on the divan in a silk slip, her bare white arm tossed carelessly above her head.

"The door was open," Gabby apologized. "I hope I'm not disturbing you."

"Not at all! It was just a long day. Please, come in."

Gabby took a tentative step inside. It had been weeks since she'd been in Margo's bungalow. Normally, the place was neat as a pin and sparsely furnished, but now, crammed with dressmaker's dummies wearing bits of half-constructed costumes, it looked as though a tornado had hit it. Bolts of dark velvets and somber brocades were heaped on every available surface. The wastepaper basket overflowed with off-cuts and discarded pattern pieces, and the floor was littered with scraps of tissue paper and muslin and tangled skeins of loose thread. "Is this all for you?" Gabby asked. "For *The Nine Days' Queen?*"

Margo rolled her eyes. "Twenty-eight costume changes. Can you believe it? I don't think the script even has twenty-eight separate scenes." Stretching delicately, she shrugged on a gorgeous Japanese silk kimono and plunked herself down at the dressing table to rake an ivory comb through her already perfect hair. "I really should hire a maid, but who has the time to interview candidates? I shoot for *hours* every day, then I have to get out of those costumes, which weigh at least twenty pounds each, and get into hair and makeup and evening clothes for engagements with Jimmy. Honestly, it's torture." Putting down the comb, Margo took a pair of eyebrow tweezers out of a small dressing case. The case was beautiful, made of blue leather and lined in cream-colored velvet with her initials embossed on it in gold. "You're so lucky, Gabby, not to have to go out."

Well, well, well, Gabby thought, hypnotized by the fluid motion of tweezers in Margo's hand. How things had changed. No more meek little wide-eyed Margo, so sweetly, pathetically grateful for any little crumb she was thrown. This sleek, gorgeous girl, with her newly acquired platinum hair, fashionably boyish figure, and untroubled air of haughty self-possession was a different creature entirely from the one she'd seen wandering shy and starry-eyed around the Olympus commissary all those months ago. Gabby couldn't help feeling a kind of resentful admiration toward her. She was reminded of the way Viola used to scold her when Gabby would leave the house with her hair uncombed or her blouse untucked: "If you want people to think you're a star, you better start acting like one." Margo looked like a star.

"You're going out with Jimmy tonight?" Gabby asked, although she already knew the answer.

"Yes." Catching Gabby's eye in the mirror, Margo turned around to face her. "Look, Gabby, I've been meaning to talk to you. I know how upset you must have been when it all . . . I—I meant to call you. . . ."

"Why didn't you?"

"I don't know. I suppose I couldn't find the right words. And then when you stopped coming around, and I didn't see you, well . . ." Margo looked down at the tweezers. Gabby noticed that they were plated in gold. "I guess I thought you didn't really want to talk to me."

"Oh no!" Gabby strove to keep her voice light. "Not at all! I've just been so busy, with filming and rehearsals and recording sessions and dancing lessons and goodness knows what else."

"So you aren't mad? About me and Jimmy?"

"Well . . ." Gabby paused, choosing her words carefully. If she denied it totally, Margo would never believe her, but she couldn't just come right out and tell her. The whole plan would be ruined if Margo didn't trust her, and anyway, Gabby had *some* pride. "Maybe just a little at first. But Jimmy explained everything." That was a lie, but it sounded good. Lying was part of the plan. "And I'm not ready to be part of a couple just yet. I'm so busy, and things are going so well. The Harry Gordon picture, for example."

"Have you seen the script yet?" Margo asked.

"No, but it's going to be a doozy, I can tell. I mean, it's written just for me. Viola got me top billing too, above the title and everything."

"Gabby!" Margo's smile was disconcertingly genuine. "That's great!"

"And that's not all," Gabby continued. She knew she shouldn't talk so much about everything before it was settled, but she was so excited she couldn't help herself. "Larry Julius promised Viola that if everything goes as planned, the studio will make a big push for me come Oscar time. All I have to do is stay thin and keep my wits about me and I'm practically guaranteed a nomination next year, if not the little guy himself. There will be plenty of time for romance after that." She gave Margo her most sparkling smile. "I'm sure Mr. Karp will suggest someone wonderful."

"Sure he will," Margo said. "And I have to say, I'm so relieved to hear you aren't sore about Jimmy. All this time, I kept thinking—"

"Not at all," Gabby said firmly. "In fact, Jimmy's the reason I'm here. He asked me to give you a message."

Margo's eyebrows shot up. "Oh? What's that?"

Gabby didn't hesitate to hand over the envelope. One of Jimmy's special yellow ones, the kind that had been tucked in that big bouquet of daisies he'd sent Margo after that first night at the Grove. How clever Gabby had been to sneak it out of the desk in his office that day! A green-pill brainstorm, if there ever was one.

"Oh no," Margo moaned, scanning the contents. "Rats, rats, rats."

"Why?" Gabby asked, although she knew full well what the

note said. She'd copied it out about six times, to make sure she got the spelling right. "What does it say?"

"Only that shooting ran late on the Toynbee picture and he can't come to pick me up." Margo sighed. "Did you know anything about this?"

"I was off today." Gabby shook her ringlets innocently. "So I guess he can't take you out tonight?"

Margo shook her head. "No, he says to get the car and pick him up at the Chateau Marmont instead. I don't even know what bungalow he's in!"

"Number seven," Gabby said automatically. "By the pool. Until the house in Malibu is finished."

"Oh," Margo said. "But still, I have to start getting dressed now or I'll never make it in time."

"Where are you going?" Gabby asked. "The Grove? They'll hold the reservation."

"Not the Grove." Margo was already on her feet. "Pasadena."

"Pasadena?"

"Yes. It's my old friend's debutante party, and Jimmy promised to escort me. Doris always had the most terrible crush on him, and I thought . . . well . . ." Margo had a faraway look in her eye, as though she was imagining something she'd rather not. "I don't know what I thought."

"Are you nervous?"

"It's been a long time since I saw any of those people," Margo said softly. "If it were anybody but Doris . . ." She shook her head. "God only knows what they've all been saying about me. The thought of all those beady little eyes on me, judging me . . . It's daunting, to say the very least. And what on earth am I going to wear?"

"Haven't you picked something out?"

"A million things. But I keep changing my mind. And then changing it back again. It's hopeless."

She sounded and looked so much like her old self in that moment, so much like the sweet, funny, humble girl Gabby had been so proud to have as her very first friend. For a moment, Gabby forgot all about movies and publicity and Jimmy. "I'll help you."

Nimbly sidestepping the piles of pattern paper and pins, Gabby threw open the doors of the wardrobe, pushing past the neat rows of everyday blouses and skirts to where the evening gowns hung at the back on satin hangers, stuffed with tissue paper and separated by hangings of silk. She shook her head at the flounced pink taffeta, flicked past the pale blue silk, rejected a yellow dotted Swiss with ruffled sleeves that was frankly too cute for its own damn good.

Then she saw it, hanging at the end of the rail. A sinuous gown of softest silk velvet, in a crimson as rich and deep as a stream of fresh blood. With a plunging neck and a daringly low back, it was a dress to die for. So sophisticated and sexy and fabulously unapologetic, it was practically sinful.

"This one," Gabby breathed. "This is it."

"That?" Margo looked doubtful. "Some atelier sent it over from Paris; a present, I guess, but I don't know if I can carry it off. I mean, it's awfully—"

"Perfect," Gabby interrupted. "Think about it. You're going to stand out anyway, so you might as well make the most of it. There won't be a man in that room who'll be able to take his eyes off you. You'll be the talk of the entire season. And you know what Viola says, the only thing worse than being talked about is not being talked about."

"I think Oscar Wilde said that."

"Oscar Wilde?" Gabby thought she'd heard that name before. "Is he at Warner Brothers?"

"Oh, Gabby." Margo laughed. "I've missed you."

"Me too," Gabby said. The plan was working. Her hand was already in her pocket, fingering the next round of pills. *Two green, one blue.* "I've missed you too."

TWENTY

The most famous hotel in Hollywood was practically invisible.

Perched as it was on the first ridge of the soaring Hollywood Hills, you couldn't even see it until you came around the curve on Sunset Boulevard, and suddenly there it was, a looming edifice of white stones and gables and lofty turrets, hidden again the moment you rounded the next curve. Like Brigadoon or Shangri-La, it seemed to disappear into the ether from which it had come.

Perhaps it was just this quality that made it the destination of choice for famous people looking to do things they didn't want anyone to know about. As long as the right palms were greased and the wrong sorts kept out, no one ever would. Not for nothing had no less a Hollywood personage than Harry Cohn, the famously naughty head of Columbia Pictures, liked to say to his stars: "If you must get into trouble, do it at the Chateau Marmont." It was like no other place in the world.

And as far as anyone knows, Amanda thought, pulling her little gray Packard coupe up its graveled driveway, *I've never been here before.*

The uniformed valet jumped forward to help her out of the car. "Ah! Miss . . ."

"Farraday," Amanda said quickly. "Amanda Farraday."

"Miss Farraday, of course. How nice to see you again."

"You must be mistaken," Amanda cooed, pressing into the man's hand one of the folded ten-dollar bills she'd tucked into the wrist of her black kid glove for just this purpose. "This is my first visit to the Chateau."

"My mistake, Miss Farraday, of course." The valet discreetly pocketed the bill. "I must have recognized you from one of your pictures."

As he drove off with the car, Amanda put on her dark glasses and adjusted her black silk driving scarf so it completely covered her distinctive red hair and most of her face. *Maybe I should sell the Packard,* she thought. There were too many people who recognized it from her previous life, and God knew she could use the cash. But she couldn't stand the idea of being trapped on the Olympus lot, having to order a studio car every time she wanted to go anywhere, with a chauffeur who was compensated handsomely to report the movements of his passengers directly to Larry Julius. Maybe she could just have it repainted a less conspicuous color, like black, or maybe that funny ecru everybody was so mad for that looked to Amanda like curdled milk. But she loved the dreamy pearl-gray. Amanda dressed in black, but gray was her favorite color. It was chic without being

239

affected, melancholy without being hopeless. Gray had . . . possibilities. It reminded her of the movies.

The clerk at the front desk didn't blink an eye at Amanda's veiled face. If there was one thing the staff at the Chateau Marmont was accustomed to seeing, it was beautiful people conspicuously trying not to be noticed. "May I help you?"

"Mr. Gordon's room, please."

"I'm afraid Mr. Gordon has asked not to be disturbed."

Amanda regretfully slid another ten-dollar bill from her glove. "I'm Jane Austen? He's expecting me."

"Of course." The money had already vanished. "He's on the fifth floor. Room F. At the end of the hall."

Amanda was relieved, frankly, that Harry had chosen a regular room. The Chateau's poolside bungalows might be more luxurious, but they were outside, leaving them that much more vulnerable to photographers, some of whom were resorting to increasingly absurd measures to get their shots. She'd heard a truly crazy story about a guy who'd been so desperate to get a shot of Clark Gable and Carole Lombard that he'd scaled the fence under cover of darkness and actually hidden *in* the pool for hours, breathing through a straw. The poor guy's skin had practically fallen off when Clark Gable himself had hauled him out in the morning, thinking he was a hotel guest who'd drowned. When this turned out not to be the case, so the story went, Gable was none too pleased, although the famously gracious King of Hollywood did offer the man a blanket and a restorative glass of brandy before he smashed his camera and called the police.

Amanda knew she'd been lucky so far. She wasn't naïve enough to think that *nobody* in Hollywood had managed to make the connection between elusive starlet Amanda Farraday and Ginger, party girl for hire, but for whatever reason—honor, shame, or simple disinterest—they hadn't come forward. If only she could get a good part in a picture. Something juicy and important, beyond the gun moll and dizzy showgirl roles the studio kept assigning her. Something that could make her a real star. Then she'd be an asset to the studio, one they'd protect at any cost. She'd be untouchable.

Except when it came to Harry. Now, there was irony for you. The one person she wanted to share everything with was also the only one who could never know the truth.

"Amanda!" Harry answered the door. "You're here!"

"Sure, I'm here. I told you I was on my way."

"I know." Harry smiled sheepishly. "But I was worried you were sore at me. You are sore at me, aren't you?"

"I was a little . . . perplexed, that's all," Amanda said carefully. That was the understatement of the year. She'd been racked with terror when Harry had failed to be in touch for a few days, certain he'd found her out somehow and didn't know how to face her. When at last she'd heard from him that afternoon, she'd nearly wept with relief, until the thought occurred to her that maybe he had only summoned her to break up with her, and she was terrified all over again. "But I know a man needs his space sometimes," she said, her stomach tying itself in knots. "I . . . I just wish you'd told me what you were doing."

"Well, Miss Farraday, step inside and all your questions will soon be answered."

He ushered her into the room. A luxurious suite with a long terrace and a dazzling view of the Sunset Strip, it was a far cry from his cramped, paper-strewn office in the writers' building at

Olympus. An enormous bouquet of roses and peonies perfumed the air; a small table against the wall held a series of room service trays covered with silver domes. Beside the table, a bottle of champagne cooled in a silver bucket.

"What's all this?"

"Dom Perignon." Harry walked to the table and lifted one of the silver domes. "And caviar. And lobster. And profiteroles. Basically, everything I could find on the room service menu that was obscenely expensive and wasteful. You know, all the things you like most."

"Are you feeling okay?" Amanda said. "Do we need to call the doctor?"

"Absolutely not." Harry grinned. "This is a private celebration."

"Oh." Amanda took a step closer to Harry. "And may I ask what we're celebrating?"

"My movie, of course."

"*The Nine Days' Queen?*" Amanda frowned. "I thought that didn't finish shooting until next week."

"Not *The Nine Days' Queen.*" Harry lifted the last, largest dome. On the tray beneath it was a script. Neat and freshly bound, it was so new Amanda could smell the ink on the page.

AN AMERICAN GIRL

By Harry Gordon

"The Gabby Preston picture!" Amanda looked up at Harry with a smile. "You finished it! Oh, darling, that's wonderful!"

"I finished it, all right." Harry stroked the title page lovingly with an ink-stained finger. "But it's not a Gabby Preston picture. Not anymore."

"Oh, Harry." Amanda slipped her arms around his waist. "Don't worry. I'm sure she'll change her mind. And if not, you can take it over to Metro. I know a producer there who says they're desperate for something for Judy Garland."

Harry placed a finger over her lips. "I don't need her to change her mind. And I'm not taking it to Metro." He paused to take a deep breath. "*An American Girl* is not going to be a Gabby Preston picture because . . . it's going to be an Amanda Farraday picture."

"*What?*" Amanda gasped. She thought her heart would stop. "You heard me."

"But, Harry, you can't be serious. How can I headline a musical? I can't sing, I don't dance really, I—"

Smiling, Harry shook his head. "It's not a musical anymore. I rewrote the whole thing. That's what I've been *doing*, holed up here all this time." His eyes were alight with excitement. "Ever since that night at the Trocadero, I haven't been able to get that story you told me out of my head. All those details— the plaid dress, the haughty salesgirl—it's a perfect allegory for what's *happening* in this country. The haves and have-nots, all the people out there with nothing but their dreams. And I thought, who needs another cheerful little vaudeville picture that's just a few lines stringing some dance sequences together? Here's a chance to do something *real*. The kind of thing Odets is doing for the theater, but in the pictures, where so many millions more people will see it and be affected by it. The story of a poor girl clawing her way to the top by any means necessary. What does she leave behind, what does she have to compromise? It's the American dream personified. It's *your* story, Amanda. I wrote it for *you*."

Amanda grabbed the side of a chair for balance. "But . . . has Mr. Kurtzman seen it? Mr. Karp?"

"This isn't for Kurtzman. This needs a young director, someone who really understands America, the kind of things that are happening now. There's a young guy called Elia Kazan doing interesting work in the theater; he might be willing to come out, with the right script. Karp's reading it as we speak, but he'll be on board. He has to be. I'm the golden boy right now. And then once we start shooting, and once *The Nine Days' Queen* is a hit, I can renegotiate my contract, and we'll have enough money to get married."

"Harry!"

"Amanda, listen. I know it seems sudden, but I've been thinking a lot about this." He held her out at arm's length, drinking her in with his eyes. "These last months have been the happiest I've ever had, and it's all because of you. Everything good in my life came because you're in it. This picture"—he pressed his hand against the script as if he were pressing his heart—"is the best thing I've ever written. You're my lucky charm, my muse. Now that I've found you, I don't ever want to let you go."

"Oh, Harry . . . ," Amanda sighed. "I love you."

She'd never said that before, not to anyone, at least not since she was a very little girl. Suddenly afraid, she looked down at the carpet, wondering if there were some way to take it back. Harry took her chin in his hands, tilting her face to meet his. "I wish you'd let me say it first," he said. "But I love you too."

They melted into each other's arms. She felt her heart pound-ing . . . or was it Harry's? She couldn't tell where she ended and he began anymore.

"There's one more thing," Harry murmured, when they fi-nally broke apart. "Something I want to give you."

He reached under the table and pulled out a large white box tied with a black silk ribbon. Harry had never given her a pres-ent before, let alone something that looked as expensive as this.

"Harry . . ."

"Go on," Harry urged. "Open it."

Amanda untied the black ribbon and lifted the lid. Beneath folds of tissue paper she saw a flash of pink silk. She carefully lifted the pink silk thing out of the box and held it up. It was an evening gown. The most gorgeous one she'd ever seen, the palest of pinks, overlaid with a shimmering spiderweb of silver lace so delicate it looked as if it had been woven by a fairy.

"The woman in the shop said it was a Mainbocher," Harry said shyly. "I guess that's good. I know it's not the sort of thing you usually wear, but I thought, if you ever wanted to give the black a rest . . . Do you like it?"

"Harry." He looked so anxious and frightened and proud that Amanda thought she would die of tenderness. "I think it's the most beautiful thing I've ever seen."

"I . . . I don't suppose you'll try it on for me, will you?" Harry whispered, taking her in his arms.

The smile on Amanda's face was like a rainbow breaking through a cloud. "Only if you'll help me out of this one first."

TWENTY-ONE

"*Damn it!*"

The train of Margo's dress caught in the hinge of the small gate at the end of the pebbled path that led to the Chateau Marmont pool. Irritated, she crouched to the ground, gingerly attempting to disentangle it without damaging the delicate cloth. In the dim light, her hand slipped and the sharp edge of the hinge sliced the soft flesh of her hand, leaving behind a thin stripe of bright blood. "Damn, damn, damn!"

This whole ordeal was really Jimmy's fault, Margo thought as she applied pressure to her palm with her thumb. It was terribly ungentlemanly of him. The least he could have done after she'd gone to all the trouble of arranging the car herself was wait for her outside, or at least in the lobby. She had asked Arthur to fetch him, but the chauffeur had shaken his head.

"They won't let me in the Chateau, miss," he had said. "Not up in any guest rooms, that is."

"But that's ridiculous!"

Arthur had let out a bitter laugh. "Maybe so. But it ain't gonna change this evening, and nothing you can say is going to make a fool's worth of difference." So instead, here she was, bleeding and having to chase down Jimmy as if she were his mother. *He's going to get an earful from me in the car,* she thought angrily. *That's for sure.*

Bungalow seven was on the far end of the kidney-shaped pool, nestled behind a small private grove of fragrant flowering bushes. Margo knocked gently on the door. There was no answer. Impatiently, she jiggled the knob, and to her surprise, the door swung open.

Margo knew it was horribly rude to just barge into someone's house like this. But Jimmy was expecting her, and Pasadena was at least forty-five minutes away. If they didn't hit the road soon, they were going to be unforgivably late.

The front sitting room was empty but showed clear signs of habitation: an overflowing ashtray, a couple of half-consumed glasses of watery Scotch on the coffee table. A record, having finished, spun silently on the phonograph.

"Jimmy?" she called. "It's me, Margo." There was no answer, but she heard an unmistakable scuttling sound coming from the back of the bungalow, as if someone was trying to move around without being heard. "Jimmy, come on, I know you're in there."

There was no answer, only a hissing noise, like someone trying to talk without being heard, coming from a closed door that she assumed led to the bedroom.

She was just about to try the knob when the door opened a crack and Jimmy's head popped out. "Margo!" Holding the door firmly in front of him, he flashed her a queasy attempt at his famous smile. "What are you . . . what are you doing here?"

His face was damp and his hair disheveled, as if he'd just been for a run. *God*, Margo thought, *he isn't even dressed yet*. By the time he'd taken a shower and put on a dinner jacket, they'd have practically missed Doris's entire party. "We have a date." Margo glowered. "You're supposed to take me to Pasadena tonight, remember?"

"Of course I do!" Jimmy said, a bit too quickly to be convincing. *He isn't really that good an actor*, Margo thought. "Good old Pasadena, I can't wait! It's just . . . um . . . I'm in the middle of something . . . in here, so be an angel and wait in the sitting room, won't you, darling? Or out by the pool, that's much nicer. I'll be out in two shakes of a lamb's tail."

Margo held her injured hand in front of Jimmy's face. "I'm bleeding," she snapped. "I've got to go to the bathroom and clean up."

"But I'm not dressed," Jimmy protested desperately.

"I don't care!" Margo could have strangled him. "I cut myself on a rusty hinge. It needs to be cleaned right away or it will get infected."

"Go back to the main building, then. The bathroom attendant will help you, and I'll meet you in the lobby for a drink before we go."

Margo's hand was starting to throb. "This is ridiculous. I'm going to bleed all over my dress. Just let me in!"

"No!" Jimmy shouted.

Suddenly, it hit Margo like a flash. The two half-drunk

glasses of Scotch, the spinning record. Jimmy hadn't been expecting her at all. *He's got someone in there,* she thought furiously. Probably some chorus girl. *And Gabby knew.* That was why she'd told Margo to come to the Chateau. So she could catch them red-handed. "Let me in, Jimmy!"

"Margo, no, please!"

She seized the side of the door. Jimmy wedged his body against the jamb, trying in vain to hold her back.

The door swung open, and so did Margo's jaw.

Jimmy had someone in there, all right. Lying bare-chested in the king-sized bed, entangled sexily in the musky sheets. Only it wasn't a girl.

It was a *boy.*

"It's . . . You . . ." Margo tried to speak, but her tongue was in knots. *Tongue-tied,* she thought. Now she knew what it really meant.

The boy stared at her from the bed, calmly smoking a cigarette with long, languorous drags. The edge of the sheet was tucked below his smooth, olive-skinned chest. *He's a handsome boy,* Margo thought, in spite of her shock. *A very handsome boy.*

"Margo," Jimmy said. "Go into the sitting room. Please."

Numbly, she did as he said and sat down on the sofa as Jimmy closed the door behind her. From the bedroom, she heard a buzz of slurry whispers, but she couldn't make out the words. *Jimmy will come out in a minute,* she thought dazedly. *What on earth am I supposed to do then?* Orange Grove Academy for Young Ladies had prided itself on preparing its students for any possible social situation, but the proper mode of decorum for when one had just discovered an unclothed boy in one's pretend boyfriend's bed had been conspicuously absent from the curriculum. With her uninjured hand, she carefully arranged the folds of her gown so it draped more gracefully over the sofa. Whatever was about to happen, she thought, she'd feel better facing it in an unwrinkled dress.

Jimmy emerged from the bedroom in his bare feet, dressed in slacks and a button-down shirt open at the neck. His damp hair was combed back slickly from his face. Wordlessly, he went to the bar and poured out two stiff drinks.

"Here," he said flatly, handing Margo the glass of Scotch.

"Jimmy . . ."

"Drink it." Even his voice had changed. Gone was the cheerful, mugging Jimmy she had heard "aw shucks" his way through so many interviews and public dates over the past several weeks. This Jimmy sounded terse, matter-of-fact, almost dangerous. Awfully ironic, Margo thought, that this of all possible situations seemed to have transformed silly, tap-dancing Jimmy into Humphrey Bogart. *Funny*, she mused, *I actually like him better this way.*

"Drink," Jimmy repeated. "Don't make me ask you again."

She tossed the liquor down her throat in a single swallow, wincing at the burn.

"Good girl," Jimmy said. He refilled both drinks. "Again." He waited to speak until they'd drained their drinks for the second time. "Now tell me what you're doing here."

"It was Gabby." Margo felt dizzy, as if a warm, spreading light were shining directly into her eyes. "Gabby said—"

"What? What did she say?"

"She told me you said to come here. To pick you up," Margo

said helplessly. "She must have . . . she must have known you'd be . . ." She didn't quite have the words to go on.

"It certainly looks that way," Jimmy said grimly. He poured himself another drink and held out the bottle to Margo. She shook her head. "She must have overheard me making arrangements with Roderigo on the phone today."

Roderigo. It was shocking, somehow, knowing the handsome boy's name. Margo wondered if he was listening to them through the door. "You mean . . . Gabby . . . knows about . . ."

"I don't know what she knows and what she doesn't. She probably thought it was a dame I was meeting. Maybe not. Gabby may act like a little kid, but she's been around show people her whole life. She's not exactly an innocent flower when it comes to this sort of thing."

"But why? Why would she do such a thing?"

"Oh, I'm sure she had her reasons. Maybe she was bored and wanted a laugh. Maybe she was jealous, or maybe she figured it'd scare you off and she'd inherit me. Who knows what's going through that pill-crazed little mind of hers right now?"

"Gabby's in love with you," Margo said suddenly, although she wasn't sure why she felt the need to defend her faithless friend.

"No." The ghost of a smile played across the shadow of Jimmy's face. "Gabby Preston is in love with the idea of me, or more accurately, the idea of herself with me. She wants to be America's Sweetheart, part of an iconic couple. As far as she's concerned, this"—he gestured toward the closed bedroom door—"is no barrier to entry." He swallowed his drink. "Don't be sore at Gabby, Margo. However selfish her reasons, in a way

251

it's rather a relief you found out. Not the ideal situation, perhaps, but at least you didn't have to hear it from someone else."

"Someone else? What do you mean, someone else?"

Jimmy let out a short bark of a laugh. "Oh, come on, Margo. You don't think it's just by chance the powers that be oh-so-patiently nurtured our young romance into being, do you? And just after your little tête-a-tête with Dane Forrest too? One star, one ascendant: nasty gossip dogging both. Put them together and it cancels out the scandal. Publicity 101."

"If you don't like what they're saying, change the conversation," Margo said quietly.

"The oldest trick in the book. And as an added bonus, with a guy like me they wouldn't have to worry about you getting into trouble. In the family way, I mean." Jimmy smiled at her, with what looked like real kindness this time. "Poor little Margo. I bet you didn't know this kind of thing even existed."

"Don't be ridiculous," Margo said defensively, although she couldn't help thinking what her father might make of this. Nervously, she fingered the gold-and-pearl pin she'd fastened at the last moment to the strap of her evening dress. It had made her feel better when she was dressing, to think she was going back to Pasadena with a little piece of it still with her; now she was just glad she had something to do with her hands. For the first time, she understood why so many people took up smoking. "I just . . . well, I just didn't think I'd ever . . . you know, meet one in person."

Jimmy chuckled. "I'll bet my bottom dollar that you've already met about a hundred of them. Show business is crawling with us 'artistic types,' I'm afraid."

"But isn't it awfully . . ." Margo searched for the right word. "*Unhealthy*, I guess?"

Jimmy's smile faded. "I suppose the next thing you're going to tell me is that I'm going to hell."

"No! I don't think that's for anyone to say!" Margo didn't know what to say. She supposed she ought to disapprove, or be angry at having been deceived, but Jimmy had never made a secret of the fact that their relationship was more business than pleasure. And what really was so wrong about a man wanting to be with a man, or a woman to be with a woman? She remembered the vague, sinking feeling of entrapment she'd always felt whenever her mother began talking excitedly about her future marriage prospects. The way she felt her heart cracking in two when Mr. Karp had told her she could no longer hope for Dane. How much worse must that be for someone like Jimmy? To feel that not just one person but all of society would never allow you to be with the one you loved? The whole thing seemed about as senseless as keeping Arthur out of the stupid lobby of the hotel. "I just . . . well, maybe you just haven't met the right girl," she finished lamely.

"Margo, I'm a movie star," Jimmy said. "I could have any girl on the planet if I wanted. The problem is, I don't." Finishing his Scotch, he calmly poured himself another. "But look, I have to say, you're taking this all very well. Like I said, it's a relief."

"For me too."

"I'm glad to hear it," Jimmy said. "And anyway, there's no reason why we can't carry on as before."

"What?" Margo shook her head. "How can we do that?"

Jimmy came to sit beside her on the couch. "Darling, look.

Ninety percent of Hollywood romances are just business anyway, whether the parties go to bed together or not. And we're doing good business. We've got a public profile. We've got fans. There's no need to derail all that. We might as well keep it up. If you want, we can even get married."

Married? "Why would I want to do that?"

"The studio would like it, for one. Karp's made that abundantly clear. It would keep the gossip columnists from breathing down my neck for a while. As for you, well, you could move off the lot, have some space, some privacy. I'm building a big house in Malibu, and I've got another one in Beverly Hills. Both of them could use a woman's touch. And I'd make it worth your while, financially, that is. My lawyers can renegotiate your contract after *The Nine Days' Queen* comes out, see that on your next picture Karp gives you what you're worth. And Hollywood's been good to me over the years. I'll gladly supplement your salary with a generous allowance. And if there should ever come a time when we agree to . . . well, *dissolve* our arrangement, I'll see that you're well taken care of. In return for your discretion, of course."

"Of course," Margo said mechanically. She could hardly believe this was happening. *Our arrangement. Your discretion.* A desert breeze was drifting through the open window. Suddenly, she felt very cold.

As if he could read her mind, Jimmy reached over and gave her hand a squeeze. "Look, I know it's not exactly the proposal that every girl dreams of. And none of this has to be decided now. But believe it or not, I'm fond of you, duchess. I know I haven't always shown it. . . ." His eyes wandered toward the closed bedroom door. "But we could be good friends for each other, if you'd like to try. And in the meantime, I'd be more than happy to let you pursue whatever interests you had on the side. Believe me, I'll be a hell of a lot easier to get around than Larry Julius, that's for sure."

"What do you mean?"

"Dane Forrest?" Jimmy raised his eyebrows mischievously, and for a moment he looked like his old self. "God knows he'd be a lousy husband. But as a part-time lover? It's the role he was born to play."

Margo forced herself to put that thought to the side. Future clandestine meetings with Dane Forrest were the last thing she could think about right now, especially after that scene on the set today. If she started thinking about the mystery of Dane Forrest, not to mention Diana, she might never stop. "I still don't see what's in it for you," she said stubbornly.

"For me? I thought I told you." Jimmy looked surprised. "I get to keep the thing I love."

"Roderigo?"

Jimmy chuckled. "Touché."

"No, I mean, wouldn't you rather let people know who you really are?"

"But they already do."

"Jimmy, I'm being serious."

"So am I," Jimmy said intently. "Because before I am anything else in the world, before I'm a son or a friend, or a brother or a lover, I am a *performer*. It is the first, last, and only thing I am."

"But it can't—"

"Listen to me, Margo." He leaned in very close to her. His boyish face was as grave as a judge's. "Some people are in the business for the cash. I'm not going to name names, but they get addicted to the lifestyle, the luxury, the fame. I don't care about all that."

"Neither do I, Ji—"

"It's different for you," Jimmy interrupted. "You grew up with money. You don't care about it because you can't imagine a world where it doesn't exist. But my father was a hobo. We used to ride the rails, he and I, and I started singing and dancing so people would throw pennies at us, or pieces of bread. And it turned out I was good at it. Really good. Better than anyone else in the world."

Jimmy's face had taken on an almost beatific glow. He looked like one of the angels singing in the painting above the altar in the chapel at Orange Grove. "I dance dances that are created by geniuses, like Tully Toynbee," he said. "I sing songs written by Cole Porter, Irving Berlin, the Gershwins, Dorothy Fields: the greatest poets of the modern age. I bring joy to millions of people who have nothing else to be happy about. Men who've been out of work so long they don't feel like men anymore. Women who don't know how they're going to put dinner on the table every night. People everywhere, living under the thumb of poverty and oppression. They need me, Margo. There's nothing in the world I wouldn't sacrifice to keep giving that to them. Nothing I wouldn't hide." He put down his glass. "If you want to be a star, a real star, you have to be willing to give up everything else. *Everything.* And anyone who says otherwise doesn't belong in Hollywood."

Reaching out to Jimmy, Margo stroked his damp cheek. Smoothing her dress, she stood from the couch and walked to the door. "Then I guess I'd better go back where I belong."

TWENTY-TWO

The row of orange trees standing guard along the gravel drive of the Pasadena Country Club was ablaze with tiny balls of lights. Not cheap Christmas-tree strings that came coiled in a box at the five-and-dime, but individual Chinese lanterns no bigger than an infant's fist, each painted with the initials *DW* entwined in the petals of a miniature orange blossom. Dangling from every glossy green branch like beacons lighting the way for a battalion of fairies, they cast a magical glow on grounds that for Margo were already imbued with a hazy mist of memory.

Here was the lawn where she had spun in circles in her first new party dress, until she'd gotten so dizzy she'd had to lie down behind the bushes. There was where she and Doris had gone sledding on tea trays that one December when Los Angeles had had snow; below it was the pool where they'd eaten countless club sandwiches and horrified the more old-fashioned members with their newly stylish suntans. Above her head was the flower-bedecked terrace where Phipps McKendrick had pulled her hair during their first cotillion tea, with the long walkway down which she used to dream of gliding on the arm of her beaming father at her own coming-out ball, and at her wedding soon after. The word swam into her mind unbidden, stinging her eyes with tears. *Home.*

In the main ballroom, branches of fragrant mimosa soared from crystal vases encircled in white hyacinths and roses the color of milk. Debutantes in white glided by, their full gowns as silken and bell-shaped as Easter lilies, their slender gloved arms threaded through the white-jacketed elbows of their escorts. Margo had forgotten how clean everything would be, how beautiful, how *pale*. In her crimson velvet, she looked like an unwelcome streak of blood on a white handkerchief.

"Margaret!" Doris came rushing over, an astonished expression on her face. With her white ruffled skirt bobbing along behind her, she looked as though she were poking her small head out of an enormous cake. In her hand she held a wreath of gardenias, waiting to be pinned in place in her hair. "What are you doing here?"

"I wrote to tell you I was coming," Margo said. Her arms were suspended in midair, as though she were anticipating an embrace. Feeling foolish, she lowered them. This was hardly the warm welcome she'd been expecting. "Didn't you get my note?"

"Oh, perhaps Mother opened it. Isn't it awful? I've been far too busy preparing for the Season to keep up at all with my correspondence." Doris stretched her mouth in a wide, forced smile. "Anyway, you're here now! My, how you've changed!"

I'm not the only one, Margo thought. Doris was as small and spritely as ever, but the unruly girl had been smoothed down, the girlish freckles expertly powdered away. Even her voice sounded different, its bubbly, musical excitement having given way to a clenched, metallic quality, her words forced through her teeth as though moving her jaw were an effort she really couldn't be bothered to make. "Well, you look just beautiful." It seemed like the only thing to say. "What a lovely dress."

"Do you think so? I hoped for something a bit sleeker, but Mother insisted on a crinoline. It seems everyone is doing ball gowns this year. Much easier to make over into a wedding dress, if there's actually going to be some ghastly war and it's impossible to order a proper one from Europe." Doris shook her head. "Isn't it awful? Those poor people."

"Oh, I know," Margo said fervently. "There are so many people at the studio now who had to leave Germany. My own director—"

"Oh, I'm not talking about *those* sorts of people, silly. I mean the poor Germans. Just because they finally have a leader willing to stand up for what he believes in, they have all these people jumping down their throats. My father went to Berlin last month on business and he said the city hadn't been so pleasant since the kaiser was in power. All the more unsavory elements are gone. He said it's finally a place where you can feel your wife and children would be safe."

With great effort, Margo managed to suppress a snort. *If only Raoul Kurtzman or Harry Gordon were here,* she thought. She'd love to hear what they had to say to that. Then she remembered where she was. The Pasadena Country Club was restricted. Raoul Kurtzman and Harry Gordon—or even Leo

Karp, or L. B. Mayer or Adolf Zukor or Sam Goldwyn or any of the men who had the power of emperors in her new world—would never be allowed through the front door. "Thank goodness for Neville Chamberlain," Doris continued, in that same metallic voice. "If anyone can sort this whole mess out, he can."

"I never realized you were so interested in politics," Margo said. When they used to go to the pictures together, Doris would always be overcome with a craving for popcorn or Milk Duds so strong she had to duck out to the concession stand the moment the newsreel came on. That she could suddenly identify the British prime minister and his stated policy of appeasement was nothing short of astonishing.

"Oh, it's very good for dates," Doris said, without a detectable trace of irony. "I mean, we're not living in the olden days anymore. Eligible young men expect a girl to be up to date on current affairs."

Who are you, Margo wanted to scream, *and what have you done with my friend? It was as if Doris had been brainwashed. But by whom?*

"Doris! There you are!" Even in her pristine white gown, Evelyn Gamble looked like a giant bird of prey, swooping down on Doris as though she were a helpless mouse. *So that's the answer to that question,* Margo thought. "I've been looking all over for you. Where have you been? And what on earth happened to your hair?"

Doris looked sheepishly at the flowers in her hand. "They won't stay put."

"Well, go to the powder room and have Prissy use extra pins. They cover your ears, you know."

"Hello, Evelyn," Margo said loudly. "How are you?"

"Margaret." The color drained from Evelyn's face, but her voice was as steady and sharp as always. "What a surprise to see you here."

"Yes," Margo said coolly, shooting Doris a dark look. "It seems to have come as a surprise to everyone."

"Well, I suppose we all thought you'd be far too busy for us, now that Hollywood has claimed you." Evelyn gave Margo her sickliest sweet smile. "I trust everything is going well?"

"Very well," Margo replied. She turned back to Doris. "I've got so much to tell you. Things you wouldn't believe, all about the studio, and how a picture is made, and what the stars are really like—"

Doris's face brightened, her eyes opening wide. *Like her old self,* Margo thought happily. "Did Jimmy Molloy come with you?" she asked.

"Ah . . . n-no," Margo stammered. "I'm afraid Jimmy had a previous engagement."

"Oh." Doris's face fell. "That's too bad. Maybe he could have sung a song or something."

"Never mind about that, Doris." Evelyn slipped her long-gloved arm through Doris's. "Your father was looking for you earlier; that's why I was sent to fetch you. He wants to practice your father-daughter waltz. He's terribly afraid he'll trip on your dress and spoil everything."

"Oh!" Doris brought a tiny hand up to her mouth. "We'd better go. I'll see you later, Margie?"

"Sure," Margo said.

"Lovely to see you, Margaret." Evelyn flashed her a Cheshire cat grin as she pulled Doris away. "And by the way, that really is *quite* a dress. Very . . . *red.*"

261

My God, Margo thought as she watched them go. Was it always like this? Had Doris always been so changeable, so easy to manipulate? She remembered what Doris had said about the pictures on the phone: *You were always more into that stuff than me.* As if she were a sponge, indiscriminately absorbing whatever was around her. Maybe Doris hadn't really changed at all. *I'm the one who's changed*, Margo thought bitterly. All these months spent in Hollywood, the World Capital of Phonies, had left her with the horrible ability to see people for what they really were. She didn't know if it was a blessing or a curse.

"Looks pretty good to me," piped up a male voice behind her.

Margo spun around and saw Phipps McKendrick, resplendent in dinner jacket and bow tie, slouching against an ornately carved pillar. "The dress, I mean." Reaching up to push his studiedly disheveled blond forelock off his forehead, he gave her what she knew he considered his most devastating grin.

"Thanks," Margo said coolly. If memory served, it was important not to seem too impressed by Phipps. God knew he was impressed enough for the both of you.

"No, I mean it," Phipps said, taking a step toward her. "It's refreshing to see a girl who lets it all hang out like that."

"I'm not sure I like your implication," Margo said hotly.

"Aw, come on, Margie." Phipps held up his hands. "I didn't mean it like that. It's just that it's nice to see a girl dressed like a *woman*, for a change. I mean, look at them." Phipps tilted his head in the direction of Mary Ann Nesbit, who was wearing a very frilly white dress and speaking with uncharacteristic animation to an equally frilly girl Margo didn't recognize. "They look like a couple of babies in a christening gown. Who wants to dance with that?"

In spite of herself, Margo smiled. Phipps had always been charming when he wanted to be. He wasn't handsome and brooding like Dane, but he was awfully good-looking in his cocky, prep school way. And they did have a history together. That had to count for something. "Well, I'm glad you approve," Margo said. "To tell you the truth, even before Evelyn said anything I was feeling very Julie Marsden."

Phipps frowned. "Who's that? Not that really tall girl at Briarcliff? The one from the field hockey?"

"No." Margo laughed. It was funny, how much Pasadena and Hollywood had in common, actually. Each sequestered in its own way, with a complicated lexicon of symbols and references that no outsider could ever hope to understand. She wondered how many other people had ever seen so far inside both. "Julie Marsden is the character Bette Davis plays in *Jezebel*. She's a headstrong Southern belle. You know the type. She insists on wearing a red dress to a ball, and it causes such a scandal that she's shunned from society forever. You must have seen it, it came out months ago." Margo paused for a moment. She remembered seeing *Jezebel* with Doris, just before that fateful afternoon at Schwab's when everything changed. They had cried over Bette Davis's plight in the theater, of course, just like you were supposed to do, but Margo had no idea just how hard the story would eventually hit home. "Bette was just marvelous," she added quickly, recovering. "Everyone in town is sure she's going to win the Academy Award."

Phipps shrugged. "If you say so. I never remember pictures myself. Mostly I just go to the theater to neck."

He's trying to shock me, Margo thought. *It was almost endearing.* "Spoken like a true gentleman," she said.

"Hey, at least I'm honest." Phipps laughed. "Speaking of pictures, aren't you making one? What's it called again?"

"*The Nine Days' Queen.*"

"Well, that one I'll watch all the way through. Scout's honor." He took a step closer. "Really, Margie, you really do look good. All shiny or something. Kind of like that actress you used to be so crazy about, remember? What was her name?"

"Diana Chesterfield."

"That's her." Phipps looked at Margo intently. "I guess I never noticed it before, but you really do look like her. Does she look the same in person?"

"I don't know." Margo felt a sudden chill go through her. "I haven't met her."

"Oh, that's right." Phipps frowned. "She ran away, didn't she?"

"Something like that," Margo said quietly.

"I remember hearing about it on the radio," Phipps said. "Lucky for you, isn't it?"

"What do you mean by that?"

"Well, I mean, if she comes back . . . what would they do with two of you?"

Margo was furious. She worried about that enough as it was, when she heard it from people who knew what they were talking about. The last thing she needed was to hear it from some arrogant Pasadena twit like Phipps McKendrick.

"Margie, wait." Phipps caught her by the hand before she could storm away. "What? What'd I say?"

"You know perfectly well," Margo said. "That was rotten and you know it."

"I'm sorry," Phipps said.

"That's nice for you."

264

"Margie, come on. I was just teasing, I didn't mean anything by it, really. I'm just . . ."

Margo tapped her foot impatiently. "You're just what?"

Phipps looked down at the floor. "I don't know. I mean, I haven't seen you in so long, and you look so gorgeous and you've been off . . . well, *hobnobbing* with all these stars . . . I guess I'm just a little nervous, that's all."

Margo felt her irritation subside. With his hair flopping over his forehead and his downcast eyes, he looked like a little boy who had just been scolded by his mother. In spite of herself, she smiled. "Nervous?" she said. "Why would you be nervous? I thought you were going to be the governor of California someday."

Phipps's face settled back into its familiarly rakish grin. "That's the plan." Still holding her wrist, he gently caressed the back of her hand. "A future governor and a future movie star. You have to admit, we make quite a pair."

In the ballroom, the band had reconvened. The music wafted in through the open doors.

"How Deep Is the Ocean."

The song she'd danced to with Dane Forrest at the Cocoanut Grove, the night she'd felt as though all her dreams were suddenly coming true.

But she'd danced to it with Phipps first.

Dane didn't want her, not enough. And Jimmy didn't want her—at least, not for the right reasons.

But Phipps McKendrick wanted her. Wanted her without complication, reservation, or hesitation. Without any backroom deals or calculations or worries about what the papers would say. She was the most beautiful girl in the room, and he was the most desirable boy, and he wanted her. It was as simple as that. She looked at him. "How about we get a breath of fresh air?"

It was cold outside, the kind of brisk chill in the night air that reminded you, somehow ominously, that you were living in a desert. Phipps took off his jacket and placed it over her bare shoulders. *He's a gentleman,* Margo thought.

He leaned over to kiss her. She kissed him back.

She remembered the first day of school every year at Orange Grove, how as soon as the bell rang it seemed as though summer vacation had never happened, as though it had all been just a dream. That was how she felt now, sitting on the lawn of the club with Phipps. As if she were just picking up where she'd left off. As if she'd never been to Hollywood at all.

His mouth was still on hers, but she felt him fumbling around in his lap. There was a faint, sandpapery rasp of a zipper. Before she knew quite what was happening, he had seized her hand and was forcing it into his pants.

"Phipps, what are you doing?"

"Oh," he murmured, "I think you know."

"Well, stop it." She pulled her hand away.

"Come on, Margie," he groaned, palpating his lips messily against her neck. "Don't you want to make me feel good?"

"Not like that!"

"Oh please." Phipps's mouth, smeared with her lipstick, contorted into a sneer. "I'm not an idiot, Margaret. I know all about the kind of things girls like you do in Hollywood."

"I'm sure I don't know what you're talking about," Margo said coldly. *How did I ever think he was nice?* "I'm going back inside."

"Not so fast." Phipps grabbed her wrist, tighter this time.

"You don't think you can just ask me out here and not deliver, do you?" His blue eyes glinted cruelly in the darkness. Margo felt a sudden shudder of fear. "Actresses are *whores*," he hissed, so close she could feel his spittle sting her face like a hail of tiny bullets. "And whores don't just get to walk away."

"Phipps, stop it! Let go of me! *Let go!*"

She tried to get to her feet, but the ground seemed to rise up to meet her as her injured hand shot out to cushion the fall. Wincing in pain, she gasped. Phipps was on top of her, pinning her arms to the ground. His face was angry as it came closer to her, blocking out the sliver of moon visible through the trees. Blocking out everything.

"No!" Margo cried. "Please, no."

Suddenly, a voice cut across the lawn. "Miss Sterling. Is that you?"

"Arthur!" Margo cried desperately, air flooding back into her lungs. Startled, Phipps loosened his grasp, allowing her to wrench free. "Over here!"

Arthur ambled into view, a look of concern etched across his dark face. "I thought I heard you holler," he said. "Are you all right?"

"She's fine," Phipps spat. "Just tripped, that's all. Go back to your car and leave us alone."

Arthur glanced at Margo. "No, sir, I don't think I will. Not unless it's what Miss Sterling wants."

"Damn you, I said *leave!*"

"What the hell is going on out here?" Doris's father came barreling across the lawn, a small group of partygoers trailing behind. Through the trees, Margo caught a glimpse of Doris's face, small and bewildered beneath its halo of gardenias.

267

"We heard somebody shouting," Doris offered weakly.

"Please, Doris, I'll handle this," Mr. Winthrop snapped. "Now, just what is the meaning of this? Who is this man?" He jabbed an accusatory finger in Arthur's direction. "Roberts, Norris, hold him. See that he doesn't get away."

Margo watched in horror as two uniformed attendants seized Arthur by the arms. The chauffeur remained stoic, but she could see his face twitch with fear. "Mr. Winthrop—"

"*Quiet!*" bellowed Mr. Winthrop. He turned toward Phipps. "Phipps, my boy, perhaps you can explain what all this is about."

Cigarette in hand, his hair already smoothed back from his face, Phipps looked as cool as a cucumber. "Well, Horace," he began pleasantly, "I really don't know. You see, Margaret invited me to come outside for a—how shall I put this?—a breath of fresh air"—he shot Mr. Winthrop a slightly abashed "just-between-men" kind of smile that engendered in Margo a terrible wish to make sure Phipps McKendrick would never be able to think of himself as anything resembling a man ever again—"Margo tripped, and I was trying to help her to her feet, when this fellow suddenly accosted us out of nowhere. Frankly, I can't think how he got on the property. It was almost as if he was lurking in the bushes."

"I see." Mr. Winthrop gave a short nod toward another uniformed attendant. "Franklin, call the police."

"No!" Margo shouted, heedless of anything resembling decorum. "That's not true!"

Mr. Winthrop gave her a look as though she'd just gone to the bathroom on the lawn. "I *beg* your pardon?"

"Please, Mr. Winthrop," Margo said desperately. She couldn't let anything happen to Arthur, not on her watch. "Arthur

268

drove me here. He only came running over because he thought I was in danger."

"Danger?" Mr. Winthrop's red face was incredulous. "Surely not from Phipps?"

"As a matter of fact, yes," she insisted.

"But why on earth could that be?"

"Yes, Margaret," Phipps chimed in. His voice was calm, but she saw the shadow of the threat in his eyes. "Why is that?"

"He was . . . trying to . . ." She looked around at the sea of faces, many belonging to people she'd known her whole life, staring at her with hard, judgmental eyes. *The way they look at an outsider.* She felt her face grow hot. "Let's just say he wasn't acting like a gentleman," she finished, looking down at the grass.

"I was trying to help you," Phipps pressed, his voice hard. "What could be more gentlemanly than that?"

"Let's get one thing straight." Mr. Winthrop held up his hands, signaling the end of debate. "Phipps came out here with you at your invitation, is that correct?"

"In a way, but—"

"Did you ask Phipps McKendrick to accompany you outside, away from any chaperone, or did you not?"

"Yes," Margo said quietly.

"It's not the first time she's done it either." Evelyn Gamble, her lips contorted into a disapproving grimace, materialized behind Mr. Winthrop. The unwelcome sound of her unmistakable bray was like a knife through the ear. "She did the same thing with him at the Christmas dance last year. Everybody saw them."

Mr. Winthrop looked as if he were about to explode. "Doris? Is this true?"

Trembling from head to toe, Doris was wringing her hands against the ghostly skirt of her dress. "Well . . . ," she whimpered.

"Good grief, Doris, answer me! Is what the Gamble girl says true or isn't it?"

"It's . . . ," Doris squeaked. Her eyes met Margo's for only the briefest second before she dropped them back to the grassy patch before her father's feet. "That's what I heard," she whispered.

"Right." Mr. Winthrop gave a sharp nod. He turned to Margo with eyes cold as ice. "Miss Frobisher, I think you'd better leave."

"He's lying!" Margo cried. The humiliation of his dismissal was almost too much to bear. "If you'll just listen to what happened—"

"I've listened enough!" Mr. Winthrop raged. "Margaret Frobisher, or whatever you've taken to calling yourself, you have been a corrupting influence on my daughter long enough, not to mention the doubtlessly corrosive effect you've had on the morality of other young ladies of her cohort. It's time somebody put a stop to it once and for all." He paused, fixing her with a terrible glare. "My only regret is for your poor parents. I can't think what they did to deserve the shame you have singlehandedly brought upon them."

Margo reeled back as though he had slapped her. A faint murmur of shock went through the assembled crowd. Even by the merciless standards of Pasadena society, that was a low blow.

"Now, if this man is indeed your driver," Mr. Winthrop continued, "then I suggest he drive you someplace else, unless you'd prefer to wait for the police."

Call the police, Margo was about to shout, until she saw Arthur's body tense, panic flashing in his dark eyes. It was so unfair. The Pasadena police would never take the word of a "ruined" girl and a colored man over Horace Winthrop's and Phipps McKendrick's. She couldn't risk getting Arthur in trouble, after what he'd done for her. Margo bowed her head, hiding the furious tears stinging her eyes. "Fine," she said in a low voice. "We'll go."

"See that you do. Phipps." Mr. Winthrop clapped the boy on the shoulder. "So sorry about all this. No hard feelings, I hope."

"None at all."

"Come back to the party and we'll have a drink. That goes for everyone!" Mr. Winthrop commanded. "Back to the party. Nothing more to see here."

Slowly, the crowd began to obey, turning their backs on Margo one by one. "Doris," she called, stretching her arms out as her friend walked past her. "Wait."

Doris spun on her heel. In the darkness, her huge gray eyes were almost phosphorescent with anger and disbelief. "You ruined my party, Margaret."

"I'm so sorry. If you'll just let me explain . . . ," Margo pleaded.

"No!" Doris cried. "Evelyn told me not to invite you. Why didn't I listen?" Her face was nearly as red as her father's. "You always have to make everything about you. As if you don't get enough attention already."

"Doris, please—"

"How could you, Margaret?" She shook her head from side to side, the way she used to do in French class at a sentence she couldn't understand. "How could you?"

Speechless, Margo watched as she walked away, as they all

walked away, making their way slowly up the hill. A procession of mourners abandoning the site once the grave was full. She was dead to them now. She was the corpse, left alone to be forgotten in the ground, while the living trudged back to their everyday lives.

"Miss Sterling." She felt Arthur's comforting presence at her side.

"Oh, Arthur." It came out like a strangled sob.

"Oh no you don't, Miss Sterling." Arthur grabbed her arm. "Don't you cry. They aren't worth it. Not a single one."

"I don't know."

"I do. Not a single one of them is worth even a single tear of yours. You just remember what Miss Chesterfield used to say."

Margo turned toward the chauffeur, mouth agape. "Diana? What did she say?"

"She used to say, 'Arthur, I've cried so many tears in my life, I promised myself I'll never shed another one unless it's for the camera.'"

Margo shivered. "For the camera."

"That's right." Gently, Arthur laid his coat over her bare shoulders, to replace the one that Phipps had ripped away. "Come on, Miss Sterling. I'll take you to the car."

TWENTY-THREE

Arthur didn't like this, not one bit. "Won't you just let me take you back to the studio, Miss Sterling?" he pleaded, even as he pulled up to the curb outside Schwab's. "After the night you've had, you really ought to be getting some rest."

"Absolutely not," Margo said firmly. Her hand was already on the car door. "But you go on, Arthur. Go home and be with your family. I'll be all right."

"How are you going to get back?"

"I'll have them call me a cab. Or I'll hitch a ride with someone. Don't worry," she said, leaning over the seat. "I lived seventeen years before I had a driver, and somehow I always managed to get where I was going."

"Respectfully, Miss Margo," Arthur said, "my job wasn't dependent on it those seventeen years."

She had to take down three different phone numbers—

including his personal number—and solemnly swear to call any of them, at any hour, the moment she got in trouble, before he would leave. When he had at last pulled away, Margo stood on the sidewalk for a moment, staring up at the flashing neon sign that had once held for her such promise, such hope, like the first glimpse of land after months spent at sea.

Schwab's Pharmacy

She needed to be here. She needed to be where it had all begun.

It was late, still the store was unusually empty for a Friday night. All the Hollywood hangers-on who made Schwab's their headquarters, the has-beens and never-weres and still-to-bes who set the air abuzz with their jabber and complaints, their gossip and gloats, were nowhere to be seen. Margo made her way down the quiet main aisle and sat down at the horseshoe-shaped lunch counter in the back, which was empty apart from a man in a trench coat reading the late edition of the newspaper over coffee and apple pie. He had on one of those soft felt hats that were worn only by undercover detectives or men who played them in the movies, and for once in her life Margo wasn't interested in guessing which one he was.

The soda jerk, a kid about her own age clearly stuck on the dead late shift due to lack of seniority, came rushing over. "Miss Sterling!" he exclaimed, placing a paper placemat in front of her with a flourish. "How nice to see you. Are you alone?"

"Yes," she said. "All alone."

"Oh! Well, in that case, um, what can I get for you?"

"Just a cup of coffee, please."

"Sure thing." The kid hesitated. "Are you sure you don't want anything to eat?"

He looked so earnestly let down that Margo cracked. *I'm probably one of the only customers he's had all night,* she thought. And she couldn't deal with seeing that look of disappointment on anyone else's face. Not tonight. Not with the day she'd had. "I'll have a cheese dream, I guess. With bacon, if you have any left. And a chocolate soda . . . no, a black-and-white."

"Yes, Miss Sterling!" The kid looked as if she'd just offered him a million bucks. "Coming right up!"

Where is everybody? Margo thought as the kid dashed off to the icebox. There was something downright eerie about Schwab's devoid of its cast of usual suspects. *Maybe they're all off together someplace.* Some teeming party in one of their shabby, cramped apartments over on La Cienega, all of them drinking fruit punch spiked with cheap gin from mason jars as they jabbered grandly about the dreams that for most of them would never come true. In a way, Margo envied them. Her own rise, while certainly not without enormous cost, had been so unimpeded, such a case of dumb luck. If *The Nine Days' Queen* was a hit, she would be a star, but it could just as easily—and even more probably—bomb, and she'd be back where she'd started, without the years of hard work and high hopes and good friends that would not only make success all the sweeter, but also cushion failure's blow. Still, the one thing she could never say was that she hadn't gotten a fair chance.

She glanced over at the kid at the icebox scooping vanilla ice cream into her tall soda glass. Would he one day, years from now, tell some starry-eyed teenager how he used to make black-and-white sodas for Margo Sterling? It seemed like a lifetime ago that she'd sat here with that stack of movie magazines in front of her, in her sweater, wearing that ridiculous scarlet lipstick she'd thought was the height of sophistication, and, of course, her funny little gold-and-pearl pin. Instinctively, she reached up to feel the familiar comforting coolness of the pearl against her skin.

But her fingers met only cloth.

The pin was gone.

Frantically, Margo lifted the paper placemat, the roll of the silverware, the napkin holder, scanning the counter in desperation. She searched the folds of her gown; she squatted beside her stool, methodically examining every square inch of the floor. It was no use. The pin was gone. It must have come loose during the horrible tussle with Phipps on the lawn.

"Oh, God," Margo gasped, "oh God, oh God, oh God."

"Margo? Is that you?"

Dane Forrest stood in the middle of the aisle, holding a couple of newspapers and a packet of cigarettes still in the cellophane wrapper, a quizzical expression on his face. Margo sat up with a start, banging her head hard against the bottom of the counter. "Dane! What are you doing here?"

"I should ask you the same thing," Dane said. "You're a little dressed up for Schwab's, aren't you? Not to mention mucking around on the floor. Are you trying to be discovered again?"

"Dane, please don't be horrible to me," Margo pleaded. "I just can't take it right now."

"What's the matter?" Dane smirked. "Cozy dinner with the folks at home didn't go quite according to plan?"

"No," Margo whispered. She didn't know if Dane was trying to be unkind, but the edge in his voice was the last straw, the raindrop that started the flood. She started to sob. Horrible, racking, ugly sobs that made her body spasm and heave.

"Oh no, Margo, please." Dane rushed toward her, looking horrified. "Please, sweetheart, don't cry. I didn't mean anything by it."

"It's not you," Margo wept. "It's just . . . just . . ." Before she could go on, a fresh round of sobs overcame her, even worse than the first. Her stomach contracted, as though her body were trying to expel some kind of poison.

"There, there," Dane murmured. "Take my handkerchief. Not once, in any emotional crisis since I've known you, do you ever seem to have your own handkerchief." Margo accepted the folded cloth he held out, grateful for the small gesture of kindness.

"Good girl," Dane said gently, taking a seat and motioning Margo to do the same. "Now suppose you blow your nose and tell me what's wrong."

For a moment, Margo hesitated, but she was so tired of secrets, so tired of pointlessly hiding the worry and strain of the last few months. It all spilled out: how her parents had thrown her out of the house and out of their lives; how she'd given up her high school graduation, her prom, her debutante ball. She told him about Mr. Karp, and Jimmy, and Gabby's betrayal, and the horrible thing that had happened on the lawn with Phipps McKendrick.

She told him everything that was bothering her—everything, of course, except anything that had to do with Dane Forrest himself, or a certain other person whose first name also began with the letter D.

The moment she finished, Dane called out to the soda jerk. "Donny, give me a glass of whiskey, will ya? Not the house brand. There's a bottle of Glenfiddich Leon keeps for me under the cash register."

"Right away, Mr. Forrest."

Margo looked at Dane in disbelief. She'd just poured out her whole life story. "Did you not listen to anything I just said?"

Dane's face was grave. "I listened to every word, Margo. Which is why I need a drink, before I drive straight to Pasadena to murder this Phelps character with my bare hands. Along with anybody else unlucky enough to cross my path."

"Phipps," Margo corrected automatically. But on the inside, a tiny part of her was soaring. Dane wanted to avenge her! He saw her as somebody it was his right, his duty, to defend. He cared about her. In his mind, on some level, she was *his*. The thought threatened to make the tears come all over again. "I lost my pin," she said.

Dane was sipping his drink. "Your what?"

"My pin. That's what I was looking for when you came in. I think it must have come off when Phipps was . . ." She trailed off. "Anyway, it's gone."

Dane frowned. "Not that one you always wear? The funny little gold one, with the pearls?" Margo nodded. "That's too bad."

"I'm surprised you remember it," she said.

Dane grinned at her over the rim of his glass. "Margo, I hope you don't take offense at this, given the night's ordeal, but I, along with, I imagine, every other man in Hollywood, have spent more than my fair share of happy moments contemplating the precise placement of that pin on your chest."

In spite of herself, Margo laughed. "Not *every* man in Hollywood."

"No, I suppose not," Dane murmured, clearly getting her meaning. "Poor Margo. Did Jimmy give you a terrible shock?"

278

"At first, yes," Margo said thoughtfully. "I was shocked, but also terribly sad."

Dane tilted his head. "How do you mean?"

"Well, it seemed so unfair. I mean, it's terrible, isn't it? To have to hide so much of who you are, to never be able to properly be with someone you love. But then I was thinking about what Jimmy says about his career, about how important it is for him to bring joy to people. How he cares more about that than anything else."

"About his career?" Dane muttered darkly.

"No, about being a star. Stars make people happy." Margo raised her chin. "*I'm* going to make people happy. It's the most important thing in the world. And I'll show everyone back in Pasadena how wrong they were. Everyone who was ever mean to me: Evelyn Gamble and Phipps McKendrick and Doris, and my parents. Especially them." Emboldened, she reached over for Dane's glass of Scotch and took a sip. "I'll show them all."

"Oh, Margo," Dane said. He took her hand in his. His touch sent an electric jolt through her body, leaving her feeling as if she were being pricked all over by tiny needles. "What did I tell you? The only thing being famous does is let people recognize you in restaurants. It doesn't make anybody love you."

"Then what does?" she asked.

Dane's liquid green eyes were as sad as she'd ever seen them. "When you find out, be sure to let me know." Draining the last of his drink, he reached into his pocket for a money clip and threw down a twenty. "Come on," he said. "I'll take you home."

It was a gorgeous night. A soft, warm wind from the west rustled the leaves of the palm trees. Bathed in the silvery glow of a three-quarter moon, Olympus looked more like an enchanted city than ever.

Dane parked the car at the far gate, and together they walked through the deserted lot, their footsteps echoing off the false fronts of the make-believe streets. A cluster of pretty suburban houses, a New York tenement block, a creaking wooden sidewalk supporting a row of rickety shops straight out of the Wild West: paint and plywood with nothing behind them. Margo had always found the staged street a little creepy. The emptiness behind their brightly painted, perfectly rendered facades seemed to hint at something more than the smoke and mirrors of Hollywood, something about the illusory nature of life itself. But tonight, with Dane by her side, she thought it was her favorite street in the world.

"Do you want to come in?" she asked breathlessly, when they stood at her door.

Dane was toying with one of the bougainvillea flowers, rubbing the bright pink blossom between the tips of his fingers until the petals crumbled to dust. "I don't know if that's such a good idea . . . ," he said slowly.

"Just for a minute." She couldn't bear the thought of seeing him go. "I don't want to be alone. Not yet."

Wordlessly, he followed her inside. He looked so big in her little room, Margo thought, so conspicuously, beautifully out of place. "Do you have anything to drink?"

"There's some Scotch in the cabinet," she said. "Not Glenfiddich, but it'll have to do. Help yourself."

What was she supposed to do now? Dane had his back to

280

her, rooting around in the cupboard for some glasses. Should she sit down? Take off her shoes? Affect some flattering pose on the couch that would make him fly to her side? Her eye fell on Gabby's old phonograph on the end table. *Of course.*

"I'm just going to put on some music," Margo called. Quickly, she flicked through the small stack of records until she found the one she wanted.

"How Deep Is the Ocean."

The familiar clarinet line floated through the room, sweet and sharp and sad. Dane turned around slowly to face her. They stood looking at one another for a moment that seemed to last forever. Finally, Dane spoke.

"Margo."

The way he said it, it wasn't a question, or the beginning of a sentence, or an opening to say something else. It was just a simple declaration. All on its own. As though her name were the only thing present in his mind.

Shyly, she stepped toward him. "We danced to this, do you remember?"

"Yes."

"At the Cocoanut Grove that night. When you cut in on me dancing with Larry Julius. Remember that?"

"Yes, Margo, I remember." Dane's smile was gently mocking. "I remember everything about that night. I remember your blue dress and your pearl pin and how your hair smelled of lilacs. I remember the first time I saw you crying your eyes out on that bench by the soundstage, the way you balled my handkerchief up in your fist like it had done something to you; I remember the look on your face in the commissary later that day, when I spoke to Amanda and not you. And I remember you on the set this morning, riding toward me with the face of a queen and the eyes of a sad little girl."

"Dane—"

"I remember everything about every time I've ever seen you." Dane sighed. "Oh, Margo, what makes you think that you're the only one?"

She fell into his arms. His open lips descended on hers urgently, hungrily, as though her kiss were the only thing that could keep him alive. *This*, Margo thought, feverishly pressing her body against his, pure joy coursing through her veins, his lips moving with hers as though the two of them were speaking their own private language, *This. This is the only thing there is.*

"Margo," Dane whispered hoarsely. "Margaret."

"What?" She clung to him desperately, trying to pull his lips back to hers. "What is it?"

"This . . . we have to stop."

She looked up at him in shock. "What?"

Dane looked at her mournfully. "You've been through so much tonight. I never should have . . . I should go."

"No!" She gasped, feeling as though he had struck her. The thought of his absence, of him being gone from her arms, seemed to cause her almost physical pain. "You can't!"

"Please, darling." He unwrapped her arms from around his neck. "It's very late. You're tired, you're confused . . . I should never have taken advantage of that."

"I'm not a child!" Margo cried, suddenly furious. How dare he open her eyes and then insist she force them back shut? "I know my own mind."

"Darling, you don't know what you're saying. . . ."

"I do!" Margo insisted. "I'm not a china doll, Dane. I know

what it means. You're not forcing me into anything. It's not like that between us. I make my own decisions. And what I want is to be with you! I'm not afraid, and I'm not asking for any promises. I just want to be with you the same way Diana was, for us to do the same things you did with her. Please don't leave now, please. . . ."

"What?" Dane suddenly pushed away from her, holding her at arm's length. "What did you just say?"

"Don't leave."

"Not that!" His expression was angry. "What did you say about Diana?"

"Nothing, it doesn't matter!" Margo cried, suddenly frantic. "I didn't mean anything by it, only that—"

"I have to go."

"You can't!" In a panic, she threw herself on him, clutching at his shirt, trying to pull his jacket from his hands. She knew she must look like a maniac, but she couldn't let him go. Not now. Not after everything. "Don't go!"

"Margo, *please*." His voice was a horrible, broken rasp. The raw anguish of it froze her in her tracks, long enough for him to get to the door.

"Dane," she whispered.

The door slammed behind him.

Shaking, Margo fell to her knees. *He's gone,* she thought. *I threw myself at him and he's gone. I'm all alone.* She crossed her arms over her chest, swaying gently back and forth. *I'll always be all alone.*

Her swaying torso bumped against the coffee table, knocking over Dane's glass of Scotch. The sharp, sickly smell of the alcohol seeping into the carpet brought her to her senses.

Leaping off the floor, she pushed through the door, running. She ran past the bungalows, through the orange grove, out into the maze of fake streets, searching for him, willing him to somehow come back into view, wanting only to see the familiar shape of him looming toward her.

But it was no use. He was already gone.

She felt the heaving sobs well up in her again. She pushed them back. She wouldn't cry. From now on she would be like Diana. She would only cry for the camera.

She stood in the middle of the street that led nowhere, surrounded by beautiful houses that no one could live in. There was nobody to hear her.

Margo screamed.

TWENTY-FOUR

"Jesus!" The champagne cork popped out of the bottle with such a ferocious bang that Amanda Farraday actually ducked for cover. "That has to be the loudest cork I've ever heard."

"Oh yeah." Harry grinned as they watched a waiter upend the fizzy contents of the bottle over a towering pyramid of champagne saucers, letting the golden liquid run in rivulets down the sides to fill the goblets below. "They're bringing out the heavy artillery tonight."

"I guess *so*," Amanda said, accepting the glass Harry handed her from the top of the stack. Principal photography had ended on *The Nine Days' Queen* only two days before, but from the look of things, Leo Karp—or rather, the small army of housekeepers and butlers and cooks and maids to whom Leo Karp entrusted the care and feeding of his palatial estate— had been planning this party for months. The grounds of the

Spanish-style mansion had been transformed into a picture-perfect stretch of English countryside, complete with wild roses, climbing ivy, and a carpet of real bluebells, which had been carted in by the boatload all the way from Kent. On a shimmering lily pond that may or may not have been dug especially for the occasion floated a pair of pure white swans wearing tiny gold crowns, tiny cloaks of ermine, and admirably, Amanda thought, not the slightest expression of humiliation. Apart from the multitiered champagne fountains on every surface, there were endless silver trays of the most delectable tidbits—fresh California dates wrapped in bacon, paper-thin *blini* spread thickly with sour cream and caviar, tiny china eggcups filled with the famous Olympus chicken soup—all served to the assembled crowd of Hollywood's good and great by a small battalion of waiters costumed in livery distinguishable from that of the court of Henry VIII only by the Olympus insignia, a lightning bolt piercing a crown of laurels, which replaced the Tudor rose. "If this is the wrap party, I can't imagine what he's going to do for the premiere. Fly in the king himself?"

"Well, they can probably get the one who quit, at least," Harry said darkly. "That is, if they can tear him away from Berchtesgaden." Amanda shook her head with a rueful smile. In Harry's eyes, and in Amanda's, for that matter, the former Edward VIII was never going to live down that chummy little post-abdication visit to his buddy Adolf Hitler. "But you have to understand," Harry continued, "this isn't exactly your run-of-the-mill wrap party."

"Oh no?"

"No." Harry's eyes twinkled. "What this is here is nothing short of a resurrection."

286

Amanda laughed. "And you're Jesus Christ, I suppose."

"Depends on who you ask," Harry said. "I mean, every Jewish mother thinks her son is the Messiah." Amanda laughed. "But no. I'm no expert on the New Testament, but I was thinking more along the lines of Lazarus. One day, he's lying there dead as a doornail, then some guy in sandals shows up, says the magic words, and boom! He's up on his feet, back to work the next morning. Isn't that how the story goes?"

"Something like that." What would those old busybody church ladies back in Oklahoma say if they could see her now, getting a lecture on the Bible from a radical New York Jew in the house of the highest-paid man in America? "Does that mean Margo Sterling is Jesus?"

"Well, I never said it was a perfect metaphor." Harry followed her eyes across the room to where Margo Sterling stood, being shown off by an ebullient Mr. Karp to a bunch of older men in double-breasted tuxedos—investors, probably, or moneymen from New York. Margo looked as sleek and beautiful as ever in her fluttery lavender beaded gown—clearly a Rex Mandalay original—but even from some distance Amanda could see the listlessness of her manner, the tightness of her practiced smile. *She doesn't look happy,* Amanda thought. *She looks like she'd rather be anywhere but here.* "Hey," Harry said brightly. "Have I told you how gorgeous you look tonight?"

Amanda flushed. "Do you think so?" She was wearing the blush-colored gown Harry had given her at the Chateau Marmont. The dress fit like a glove, showing off her narrow waist and pale shoulders to their best advantage, but after all that black, she felt a little shy in something so frothy, so feminine, so *pink*.

"Absolutely." Harry gave a wolf whistle. "Pink is your color, sugar. I've got great taste, if I do say so myself."

Amanda giggled. "I feel like such a girl."

"You *are* a girl." Harry turned again toward Margo, now stiffly holding court with yet another group of well-wishers. "And next year, that's going to be you over there with the big shots fawning all over you. This time next year, you're going to be a star."

Amanda looked back at Margo's sad eyes, her fixed smile.

She looked back at Harry. Next year couldn't come too slowly.

It should have been a perfect night.

The Nine Days' Queen had finished shooting. The picture everyone had once thought was dead had somehow been made. The raw footage, according to the handful of executives, press agents, and general studio yes-men who had seen it, promised a feat of epic moviemaking equal to anything Olympus's rivals had yet produced. Most miraculously of all, it had somehow come in under budget, which meant that as far as the studio was concerned, Raoul Kurtzman was the greatest leader of men since Alexander the Great, Harry Gordon was the next Shakespeare, and Margo was the belle of the ball.

Claudette Colbert, Errol Flynn, Olivia de Havilland—stars who just six months before had been little more to Margo than faces in magazine clippings pasted to her bedroom wall—were practically waiting in line to congratulate her and, in the case of Errol Flynn, to lean forward and whisper a deliciously unspeakable suggestion in her ear. Gabby, in a puffy blue dress that made her look like a giant hydrangea, had squealed with joy, clinging to Margo's neck as though she'd just come home from a war, and Larry Julius, who could make a grown man cry just by looking at him, was near tears himself, telling her how proud he was of her, how he knew she had it in her all along. She even met Clark Gable, who had laughed his famous uproarious laugh and immediately scribbled "To My Best Girl, Emmeline, with Lots of Love from Clark Gable" on a cocktail napkin when Margo told him the housekeeper's single condition for her help all those months ago.

And then there was Leo Karp himself, parading her around on his arm like a trophy, telling her over and over again that she could have anything she wanted. Did she want something to eat? Why not, the filming was finished, she could eat an entire chocolate cake if she wanted, he'd feed it to her himself. Something to drink? He'd crush the grapes, distill the juniper berries, chip the ice. Did she want to go for a ride? She could go down to the garage, pick out whichever of the twenty-nine cars there she wanted, he'd give her the papers, it was hers.

But the one thing Margo wanted was the one thing she couldn't have.

Dane.

The last few days of shooting had been torture. In their final few scenes together he'd been loving, gallant, heartbreaking—everything Lord Guildford Dudley was supposed to be—until Kurtzman called "Cut!" and it was as if a brick wall had descended between them. He didn't speak to her between takes, he didn't praise her at the end of the day, he gave not the slightest indication that what had transpired between them in her bungalow that night would ever be repeated or discussed, or that it had even happened at all. It was as though he had simply willed himself not to see her, which made his tenderness toward her in their scenes together all the more maddening. *Who can go back and forth like this?* Margo thought wildly. Veering between these two extremes, on camera and off, not knowing what was real and what wasn't—it was positively schizophrenic. *No wonder actors go crazy.* If she didn't talk to him soon, she was going to lose her mind for good.

He was standing alone at one of the bars, blending in among the sea of tuxedos, downing what she was fairly sure was meant to be one of many tumblers of Glenfiddich. Margo waited to slip away until Mr. Karp was deeply immersed in an intensely boring conversation about box-office returns with a couple of managing officers. Nervously, she grabbed a saucer off the top of one of the champagne fountains and downed it in one gulp; she grabbed a second one for good measure and drank that too. Fortified, she sidled up to Dane at the bar and very gently laid a hand on his sleeve.

"Hello, Margo." Dane was funny when he drank, she'd noticed. He didn't get slurry or vague or cloudy-eyed the way other people did; in fact, he somehow seemed sharper. As though an invisible camera had trained its lens on him and thrown everyone around him into an indistinct blur. "You look nice," he said quietly.

The faintest hint of a smile on his face gave Margo the strength to continue. "I've been looking for you all night," she said urgently.

"Really." He drained the Scotch from his glass. "I don't remember hiding behind Clark Gable."

"Dane, please. We need to talk."

Dane frowned. "Do we?"

"Don't you think so?"

"I don't think this is really the time or place."

"Then *when is?*" She tried to keep her voice down, but she knew her desperation was written all over her face. "You won't talk to me here, you won't talk to me on set, you don't return my phone calls. Why are you doing this to me? What did I do to make you treat me this way?"

Dane's voice softened. "Margo—"

"Here they are! My two stars!" Leo Karp came barreling over to them, clapping a surprisingly strong hand on each of their shoulders. *Showing us who's boss,* Margo thought bitterly as he pushed both of them insistently toward his companion, like a couple of cheap souvenirs he was trying to get the man to buy. "Now, Dane Forrest, of course, you've met before," Karp was saying, "but this is Margo Sterling. Our newest star." Mr. Karp beamed with pride. "Margo, darling, this is my partner and dear, dear friend, Mr. Hunter Payne."

So this is the notorious Hunter Payne, Margo thought. Up close, he looked much younger than when she had seen him coming out of Mr. Karp's office. Naturally, the prematurely silver hair aged him a bit, but his face was unlined and his hazel eyes sparkled with youthful mischief. He was easily young enough to be Mr. Karp's son.

"Margo Sterling, I'm enchanted," Hunter Payne said, leaning forward to brush his lips lazily against her outstretched hand. Beside her, she felt Dane's entire body stiffen. *Good,* she thought. Let him see another man be interested in her for once. Let him be jealous and afraid and uncertain. *Give him a taste of his own medicine for a change.*

"Enchanted?" Leo Karp crowed. "Dane, I'm telling you, you should have heard him just now. All night, it's 'Leo, tell me, who is that girl? When will you introduce me to that girl?'"

Hunter Payne laughed. "I'm afraid I was an awful nuisance."

"Who can blame him?" Karp chortled. "Who isn't smitten with our little Margo?"

"Well, Mr. Payne," Margo said, in her sweetest finishing school voice, the kind of voice F. Scott Fitzgerald must have had in mind when he'd written that Daisy Buchanan sounded like money. "I'm sure I'm terribly flattered." Satisfyingly, she saw a muscle in Dane's jaw jump.

"Call me Hunter. All my friends do."

"And what about your enemies?" Dane's voice was cold as ice.

"Dane, there you are!" Larry Julius suddenly materialized at their side, as though he'd been conjured out of thin air. "So sorry to interrupt. That woman from *Picture Palace* has been asking for an interview all night. If we don't oblige her, God knows what kind of poison she'll write."

"Well—"

"I'll come with you," Mr. Karp said. "A star and a studio boss. Some scoop for the old bag, huh?"

It all happened so quickly, so smoothly, that Margo was sure it had all been worked out in advance. Larry must have been hovering on the sidelines the entire time, ready to whisk Dane away at the first sign of trouble. But how did Larry know there would be trouble between Dane and Hunter?

Hunter was smiling at her—the expectant smile of a man who was used to being entertained. *I have to say something.* "Mr. Payne—" she began.

"Please." He cut her off. "Hunter."

"Hunter," she said shyly, glancing up at him through her eyelashes. He wasn't as handsome as Dane, but he had a confidence, a kind of calm authority, that made him seem better-looking than he was. "I do hope you'll excuse Mr. Forrest—"

Hunter cheerfully interrupted her again. "Why are you apologizing for him?"

That's a good question, Margo thought. When had Dane ever stuck up for her? When had Dane ever done anything but jerk her around? Throw her a crumb when it suited him, just enough that she never knew if she was coming or going, and then make it somehow seem as though it were all mysteriously her fault? "I suppose I just don't want him to be in any trouble," she said.

"Well, that's very noble." Hunter chuckled. "But I wouldn't worry if I were you. I may be a staid New York moneyman, but I know how moody these creative types can be. Besides, we'd better give Mr. Forrest the benefit of the doubt. This must be a difficult night for him."

Margo drew her breath in sharply. "What do you mean by that?"

"Well, it's never easy for an old star when another one ascends, is it?" His hazel eyes danced. "Sure, the old one might flame out in a glorious supernova, but the new one gets to stay and reflect all the light."

"I don't know what you're talking about."

"I'm talking about *you,* Margo." With one smooth motion, he swept two full champagne flutes from the silver tray of a passing waiter without ever taking his eyes off her face. *How on earth did he do that?* "Here. Now drink that down like a good girl and forget all about the fantastic Mr. Forrest. At least for one dance."

Margo smiled. It was impossible not to. Robert Taylor and

William Powell and even Dane might all playact different versions of the urbane gentleman, but Hunter Payne was the real deal. "One dance would be lovely," she said. In reply, he presented her with another glass of champagne.

The orchestra was playing outside, on the rose-bedecked ivory-colored terrace. A hush fell over the crowd as Hunter led Margo onto the dance floor below. "I guess you better get used to the stares, Margo," he murmured under his breath, wrapping his arms around her tightly. "This is your life from now on."

Hunter was a marvelous dancer, with grace and surefootedness that were clearly the product of a lifetime of cotillions and parties and balls. But there was a whisper of danger in the proprietary way he clasped her waist, the way he looked at her with a kind of careless fondness, as though she were a prize he'd already claimed. Margo wasn't sure she liked that, exactly, but she liked him. She liked the idea of him. And she especially liked the idea that Dane was watching. And seething.

"*The Nine Days' Queen* will do good box office," Hunter was predicting. "There's enough interest around it, due to everything that's . . ." He paused for a moment. "Everything that's happened. And it's always exciting to see an unknown in a juicy role like that. Even if they stink, it's still fun."

Margo felt her stomach lurch. "You don't mean—"

"That you stink?" Hunter laughed. "Darling, even if I'd seen the finished picture, I honestly couldn't tell you. I'm strictly a numbers man. And right now the numbers are saying that in general, this kind of big historical picture is done. *The Nine Days' Queen* is one of the last of its kind, and if you want to stay on top of the game, you've got to get yourself out of the swords-and-corsets racket, if you know what I mean."

"And what do the numbers suggest I do instead?" Margo asked, genuinely intrigued. No one had ever spoken to her like this before, as though she had a say in controlling the trajectory of her career.

"Well, there's a real gap in the market right now for a modern, highbrow, sophisticated leading lady. Myrna Loy, but she's too old for the ingénue roles, or she seems like she is. Katharine Hepburn's got the breeding and the chops, but if there's a single red-blooded man in the whole forty-eight states who honestly wants to go to bed with Kate Hepburn, then I'm the king of the Belgians. Lombard's the closest." He nudged their clasped hands in the direction of the gorgeous blond star, who was wearing a hooded gown of the palest blue silk and gazing deeply into Clark Gable's eyes. "But she can't do drama; at least, the audiences don't think she can. So if you ask me, the numbers all add up to a hostile takeover by Miss Margo Sterling. Of course, you could benefit from being party to some real sophistication. Not all this trashy Hollywood flash. You should spend some time in New York. Maybe London, or Paris. Spend some time with people who have had money long enough to be bored by it."

"And I suppose you think you're the one to take me there?" It was a bold thing to say, but Margo was feeling bold. Hunter seemed to expect it. It was as if he'd already written the script. All Margo had to do was say the lines she was given.

"I might be." He gave her one of his careless smiles. "I'd certainly be open to discussing it further. I wonder if we might go someplace a little more private?"

Margo felt a sudden stab of fear as the image of Phipps McKendrick and his angry smirk swam into her mind. "Someplace . . . private?"

"Sure," Hunter said casually. "After all, I'm not one of you Hollywood exhibitionists. You may be used to going through life being stared at, but I'm feeling a little self-conscious having everyone looking at me as though I were a trained monkey." He grinned. "Besides, it's for Leo. Apparently he spent a fortune setting up a gazebo and a hedge maze and all manner of English-style nonsense out on the grounds, and he's positively livid that nobody seems to want to move very far from the booze and the food. So what do you say? Should we do the old man a favor?"

Margo felt a little dizzy. All those glasses of champagne in quick succession had gone straight to her head, just like people were always saying they would. She knew she ought to be cautious about this sort of thing after that horrible episode with Phipps, but that wasn't Hunter's fault. Hunter would never try anything like that. Hunter wasn't a hormone-crazed adolescent animal like Phipps. Hunter was a gentleman, one she was pretty sure didn't need to force a girl into anything. Nothing would happen, but just think of the look on Dane's face when he caught a glimpse of her coming back from the hedge maze with a man who had the power to buy and sell Leo F. Karp.

"Sure," she said finally. "Why not?"

"Why not indeed." Hunter smiled. "I'll tell you what. I'll grab us a bottle of champagne, and you go wait for me down by the lily pond." He reached out a hand and gave her right hip a gentle squeeze. "I'll be back in two shakes of a lamb's tail."

TWENTY-FIVE

"Miss Preston, no!" The waiter made a defensive flying leap in front of the champagne fountains, rattling the unsteady stack of glass down to its fragile foundation. "I'm so sorry, but there can be no underage drinking. Mr. Karp's orders."

Gabby scowled. *Why do they even invite me to these things?* She'd been so relieved to attend the party on her own—Viola was sick in bed with a cold—but they were treating her like she belonged at the kiddie table. "Margo Sterling is underage," she pointed out. "And I just saw her guzzle down about four glasses."

"Ah, w-well . . . I didn't see that . . . ," the waiter stammered. *Of course,* Gabby thought bitterly. As usual, there was one rule for Margo Sterling and one rule for everybody else. Margo had just waltzed into the studio one day, practically on a *whim,* and just because she happened to be in the right place with the right look at the right time, everyone was treating her as if she were God's gift to the motion picture industry.

"In the meantime, Miss Preston, something else to drink?" the waiter said brightly. "A Shirley Temple, perhaps?"

Gabby's eyes narrowed dangerously. "Do not even *talk* to me," she hissed, "about that bitch."

Storming away from the stunned waiter, Gabby opened the gold locket she was wearing on a chain around her neck. Inside, there was just enough room for two green pills. She'd been meaning to save them—the last time she'd gone to get her prescription renewed, Dr. Lipkin had threatened to cut her off when he saw how quickly she was going through them. But God knew she needed something to help her tolerate this miserable party, and she could always convince Viola to get some more from one of those "vitamin doctors" with the dirty offices downtown. She tipped back her head and quickly swallowed the pills down her dry throat.

If only Jimmy hadn't gone out to Palm Springs for the week. She'd asked him if she could tag along, but he hadn't seemed to think that was such a great idea. "No, Gabby," he'd said, fixing her with a strange, hard look. "And don't try to telephone me either. Just let me have this time to myself, and when I get back, maybe I'll be able to look at you again." *Poor Jimmy*, Gabby thought, and sighed. She'd expected Jimmy would be the teeniest bit annoyed with her for making sure Margo would catch him red-handed at the Chateau that night, although if you thought about it—and she was sure Jimmy would—Gabby had really done him a favor. Margo would've found out about Jimmy sooner or later; wasn't it better for everyone to know how she'd react before it was too late? Whereas when Gabby had begun to notice that Jimmy paid a little more attention to the boys in the chorus than the girls, it hadn't changed her feelings for him one little bit. She'd seen that sort of thing a million times, and it was usually just a phase. Boys like Jimmy all wound up with girls eventually; they had to, if they wanted to be stars. But they had to be the *right* girls, and Margo Sterling was all wrong. Jimmy knew that now, and that was enough for Gabby, whether she got him for herself or not.

Besides, Gabby thought, she knew the real reason Jimmy was so upset. The Tully Toynbee picture had finished shooting the same week as *The Nine Days' Queen*. Where was *their* party? Why wasn't it Gabby swanning around on Leo Karp's arm while Dane Forrest and Hunter Payne hung on her every word?

Well, it will be, Gabby thought. Anybody could get lucky once. Luck didn't make you a star; talent did. And this time next year, when her vaudeville picture was finished, they'd all see who the real talent at Olympus was.

Gabby gave a little shiver of excitement. *An American Girl.* It was a perfect title. She could hardly wait to see the finished script. She had so many ideas for it: things that had happened to her in real life, little details that would make the whole thing seem so much more real. Honestly, she should talk to Harry Gordon about them. He'd probably be grateful to her. Hell, he might even give her a screenwriting credit!

There was no time like the present, Gabby decided. She'd go and talk to Harry right now. Viola was always saying that networking was the whole point of these big Hollywood parties. Excitedly, she scanned the room. Harry had been slobbering over that Amanda Farraday all night, but right now he was standing next to the ice sculpture on the buffet, looking bored by a bunch of old accountant types in unfashionable suits. Amanda was nowhere to be seen. *Probably off with some other guy*, Gabby thought with a derisive snort, *showing him her "talent."*

Well, she'd save him. Steal him away from those dullsville squares and talk about artistic things. *He'll be so grateful.* "Harry!" she called. "Over here!"

He turned eagerly at the sound of his name, obviously glad to have an excuse to get away from the Bore Brigade. "Oh, Gabby," he said, walking over. "It's you."

"Well, of course, silly, who else would it be?" Gabby turned the full beam of her dimpled smile on him. "I figured someone ought to rescue you. Whatever those men had to say, it must have been awfully gloomy."

Harry smiled sheepishly. "Box-office projections. Enough to depress anyone."

"Oh, but you won't have to worry about that!" Gabby gushed. "*The Nine Days' Queen* is going to be a hit! How could it not be? It's been the talk of the town for months! And of course," she said slyly, "people are just dying to get a glimpse of Margo Sterling. How did you like working with her?"

"Me?" Harry looked uncomfortable. "Oh, she was all right, I guess. A little stiff, maybe."

Gabby felt an inward gleam of pleasure. "Well, that won't make any difference. Not with a script as brilliant as yours. I mean, you could probably just hire someone to sit in the theater and read the screenplay out loud like it was a shopping list, and the audience would be enthralled."

That was laying it on a little thick, even for her, but Harry didn't seem to blink an eye. "Do you really think so?"

Typical, Gabby thought. *Writers say they're insecure, but deep down they all think they're God.* "Oh, of course," she said eagerly. "But your biggest triumph is still to come."

"Oh?" Harry looked intrigued.

"*An American Girl!*" Gabby exclaimed. "Our vaudeville picture! Now, I know writers don't always like to talk about their work while it's in progress, but honestly, Harry, I'm so excited about it that I can't sleep at night." That, at least, was perfectly true. The blue pills had stopped working long ago. She needed to take at least five or six now to even drift off, and then it took practically an entire bottle of the green ones to get her back up again. It was much easier to just stay awake most of the time. "I have so many ideas, Harry." The words rushed out. "So many stories you can use. Things that happened to me, things I've heard about backstage, things hardly anybody even knows about except for me." She hugged herself. "For example, I thought maybe the main character should have an older sister, who's her best friend in the world. And she's in the act at first, but then she runs off with this magician and leaves the main character all alone, and that's when she really starts to feel the pressure to make it, for both of them. And then another time, she thinks she's booked into the Palace Theater in New York and she's finally hit the big time, but then it turns out the operator got the telegram wrong and it's actually the Palace Theater in *Newark.* And then later she's booked into another theater, but when she gets there, it's not a legitimate theater at all, but a hoochie-coochie parlor, so she—"

Harry held up his hands. "All right, all right, Gabby, just . . . just back up a minute, okay?"

"Sure," Gabby said quickly. "I mean, they're only suggestions.

Just some things I was thinking about. Obviously, if you've already finished the script—"

"It isn't that." Harry suddenly looked grave. "It's just that . . . well . . ."

Gabby felt something tighten in her chest. "What?"

"Just that we, well . . ." Harry looked down at the carpet. "We've decided to go in a different direction with *An American Girl*," he said finally. "It seemed like there was a surplus of musicals already set for next year, so the studio thought, and well, *I* thought it might work better as a . . . a drama."

"Great!" Gabby said brightly. "I'd love to do a drama! Although you really should consider sticking in a song or two, if you can. Not for me, you understand. But having a hit record from a film really helps out at the box office."

"I don't doubt you'd be fine in a drama, Gabby," Harry said. "But for this, well, the script has changed so much, we all thought it would be better for everyone to move forward with another actress in the role."

Gabby felt as though Harry had dumped a gallon of gasoline over her head and then, very apologetically, flicked over the lighted match. "I thought . . . *An American Girl* was based on *me*," she said, her voice cracking.

Harry looked at her mournfully. "I'm sorry to have to tell you like this, Gabby. But it's nothing personal, honestly. It's all my fault. A failure of imagination. When I sat down to write with the idea of you . . . well . . ." Harry shook his head. "I just couldn't connect. But when I started to think of Amanda—"

"*Amanda?*"

Harry nodded. "Somehow, when I imagined Amanda in the role, it all came together."

It was like being under a spell, Gabby thought. As though some evil witch had waved a magic wand over her, replacing all the warmth in her body with something hard and cold. "I'll just bet."

Harry raised an eyebrow. "I'm not sure I'm following you."

Gabby snorted. "You're not exactly the first man Amanda Farraday has 'come together' with, and I highly doubt you'll be the last."

Now Harry looked angry. "*What?*"

"The casting couch," Gabby said coolly. "Surely a wordsmith such as yourself is familiar with the term."

"You have no idea what you are talking about," Harry said, his voice low.

"You're right," Gabby said. "I don't know that it was a couch. It could have been a bed. Or the backseat of a car. Or even the floor."

"*How dare you!*" Harry's black eyes looked as though they could burn a hole right through her skin. "How dare you cast these kinds of aspersions on my character? Or Amanda's! You don't know the first thing about her!"

"Neither do you!" Gabby cried. "What do you really know about Amanda? What has she told you about her past? You think she's some kind of blushing flower? For God's sake, Harry, she used to work for Olive Moore!"

"Who the *hell* is Olive Moore?"

God! Could Harry really be that naïve? "Let's just say she's a woman who's bought herself a pretty fancy house 'helping out' girls like Amanda."

Harry's face went scarlet as he lurched toward her. Gabby felt her heart pounding. For a moment, she thought he actually might hit her. "No," he said, shaking his head. He took a step back. "No more. I'm not going to listen to any more of this. You're upset, that's all. I understand. You're going to go away, I'm going to have another drink, and we're both going to act like this conversation never happened. Do you understand?"

"But—"

"Do you understand?"

Gabby did. And maybe that would have been the end of it. If only Harry had turned the other way. If only he hadn't run directly into Hunter Payne, who was on his way outside with a bottle of champagne. And if only Hunter Payne hadn't chosen that moment to clap Olympus's newly anointed boy genius on the back and whisper into his ear, all jolly-jolly, man to man: "I see you've got Ginger tonight, Gordon. Guess we must be paying you writers a lot more than I thought."

"Harry! There you are!" Amanda called as she floated toward him on the terrace, enjoying the unaccustomed swish of her lacy fishtail gown along the smooth stone. She was glad she hadn't chickened out on wearing the pink. *It's nice to be dressed up like a princess for a change,* she thought happily. *And it was even nicer of Harry to think of it.* "I've been looking everywhere for you. Where have you been?" Playfully, she wrapped her arms around him from behind, nuzzling her face against the soft, sweet-smelling skin at the nape of his neck.

He wriggled from her embrace. "Maybe I should ask you the same thing," he said in a tone of quiet fury.

"What are you talking about? I just went to the powder room."

"For over half an hour?"

"It takes at least half an hour to walk anywhere in this house," Amanda retorted. Sometimes Harry's possessiveness was endearing, but this was not one of those times. "And then I stopped to chat for a few minutes with some friends."

"Friends of Amanda's," Harry asked in that same strange tone, "or friends of Ginger's?"

Amanda's jaw dropped. She felt as though a giant vacuum hose had sucked all the oxygen out of the room. She couldn't speak. She couldn't even breathe.

Her panicked silence was all the proof Harry needed. "So it's true."

"Harry, no!" The air rushed back into Amanda's lungs with painful force. "It's not . . . it's not what you think. I can explain."

"Don't."

So this is what it's like to be shot, Amanda thought. First the bullet, so swift and sudden you scarcely knew what had happened, then the slow, spreading stain of blood, and with it the knowledge that in some terrifying few minutes, "you" as you knew yourself would cease to be. "Please—"

"Stay away from me." He jerked from her grasp. "I can't even look at you. I don't even know who you are."

"Harry—"

"Leave me alone." He backed away from her slowly, as though she were a wild animal on the loose. "Whatever your name is, just leave me alone."

"Amanda," she choked toward his retreating form. "My name is Amanda."

And Amanda was going to be sick.

TWENTY-SIX

"Hello, Mr. Swan." Margo stood at the edge of the lily pond as the regal creature drifted toward her. "Are you sleeping? Are you asleep?" She leaned over the water, reaching out a hand to gently stroke the soft feathers of his neck. The swan let out a horrible, high-pitched squawk. Margo pulled her fingers away from its gnashing beak just in time and giggled. "Whoops! Guess not."

I should really drink champagne more often, she thought, still giggling. It made everything—and everyone—so much *nicer.* Just look at Hunter Payne. At the studio, people talked about him as if he were a cross between Ebenezer Scrooge and Genghis Khan, but at the party, with champagne flowing, he was just about the nicest man she'd ever met. He'd be here any minute now. They'd have some more nice champagne, and go for a nice walk, and have a nice talk. He could be a nice friend for her. It would be nice to feel that someone was looking out for her. Someone powerful. Almost the way a father might do—the way *her* father was supposed to do, until he'd proven woefully inadequate for the job.

And wouldn't it just kill all the small-minded snobs in Pasadena, the Gambles and the Winthrops and her own parents, when they found out how wrong they'd been, that no one less than a Payne of the New York Paynes saw no reason why a nice girl couldn't also be an actress.

"Hey," Margo leaned back over the water toward the reproachful swan. "I'm sorry I woke you up. That wasn't very nice."

Suddenly, she felt the sudden pressure of a hand on her shoulder. Margo let out a little scream. "Hunter!" she squealed. "You scared me half to death."

But it wasn't Hunter Payne behind her.

"Dane!" Margo cried. "What are you doing sneaking up on me like that?"

"I'm sorry. I didn't mean to startle you."

"Startle me? I could have fallen in the lake! And what are you doing here anyway?"

Dane stepped out of the shadows, his tense face very pale in the moonlight. "I came to get you."

"What?" Margo shook her head. "What are you *talking* about?"

Dane took her by the shoulders. "Margo, you have to listen to me," he said urgently. "You shouldn't be here like this. Hunter Payne is not a man you should be with."

"And why should I believe you?"

His face darkened. "Believe me, Margo. I need you to come with me. And if you won't come quietly"—he took a deep breath—"then I'll have to carry you."

"What?" Margo staggered back from him. "Absolutely not!"

"All right. You give me no choice." Dane took a step forward and with a single swoop of his arms heaved her off her unsteady feet and over his shoulder like a very expensively dressed sack of potatoes.

"What do you think you're doing?" Margo screeched, kicking her feet and pounding his shoulders with her fists. "Have you lost your *mind?*"

"On the contrary, I feel saner than I have in years," Dane said calmly as he carried her off into the night. "This is something I should have done long ago."

Gabby Preston ran.

Past the ice sculptures and the champagne fountains, down the steps of the ivy-covered terrace, across the open-air dance floor, and out into the darkness.

Because Gabby Preston was about to cry. And she was damned if any of them were going to see her.

She saw the shimmer of the lily pond on the horizon, the glowing white heads of the swans cresting into view. Almost like an illustration from one of the storybooks her sister Frankie used to read to her when she was a little girl. *Seems as good a place for a cry as any,* Gabby thought, as long as she could resist the urge to throw herself in. *Not that anyone would care.* Margo hated her. Jimmy hated her. Now Harry hated her too, probably most of all. The only person who might miss her even a little was Viola, and that was mostly because without Gabby to pay for the house and the car and the food and the clothes, her mother might actually have to get a real job.

But I won't do it, Gabby told herself. *I won't give any of them the satisfaction.*

There was something on the ground beside the lily pond. In the darkness, it looked like a crumpled heap of fabric, as though the wind had carried a tablecloth away.

It wasn't until she got much closer that she realized it wasn't a tablecloth at all.

"Amanda?" Gabby whispered. "Is that you?"

Very slowly, the girl turned her head toward Gabby. Her face was deadly white, sooty streaks of mascara running down from her bloodshot eyes. Her nose looked swollen, and when Gabby glanced over at the pond, she saw fresh globules of vomit still floating on the water. "Gabby," Amanda croaked.

"Are you all right?" Gabby asked cautiously.

Amanda didn't answer in words. Instead, she made a keening noise, like a wounded animal.

Tentatively, Gabby put her hand on Amanda's bare shoulder, half expecting her to push it away. "What happened?" she asked, although she was pretty sure she already knew. "What's wrong?"

"Hrrrree."

"Amanda, I can't understand you."

"Harry." Amanda hiccupped. "He . . . he found something out about me. Something . . ." She made that horrible noise again, a sound so pure and hopeless in its sorrow it sent shivers down Gabby's spine. "Something *bad*." She crossed her arms over her chest, rocking back and forth in a tortured lament.

Gabby felt afraid. If Amanda was this unhinged, there was no telling what she'd do next. Desperately, she tried to think of something soothing to say. "He told me about the movie," she said finally.

"The movie," Amanda repeated dully.

"Yes," Gabby said, forcing a note of brightness into her voice. "And I'm sure everything will be all right. Even if you two aren't . . . together, if the studio still wants you—"

"I don't care about the stupid movie!" Amanda's scream was terrifying, a primal wail of fury and pain. "I never cared about the movie! I only ever wanted him. The only reason I wanted any of this was for him. And now he's gone."

She began to weep. The horrible, wrenching sobs of someone who felt utterly alone in the world. Gabby had cried like that the morning she woke up and her sister Frankie was gone. The morning she decided she was never going to cry again.

Images of Frankie suddenly burst into Gabby's mind: Frankie, sitting on the train, reciting aloud from one of the big thick books that only she could read; Frankie, patiently untangling Gabby's unkempt curls with Viola's ivory comb; Frankie, wiping the sweat from Gabby's forehead when she caught the fever in Buffalo and they had to cancel three weeks' worth of bookings.

And suddenly, the images of Frankie seemed to melt into Amanda, that night in the powder room at the Cocoanut Grove. Amanda, paying off the attendant with more money than most people made in a week; Amanda, smoothing out Gabby's mussed hair and washing her smeary face with a damp warm towel; Amanda, draping her beautiful fur stole over Gabby's dress to hide the stains.

Gabby Preston had never felt so ashamed in her entire life.

She put her arms around the weeping girl as carefully as if she were a dainty china doll. "Come on," Gabby said gently. "Let's get you cleaned up. And then I'll take you home."

TWENTY-SEVEN

Margo's mouth was dry. Her head throbbed, as though some tiny blacksmith were using her forehead for an anvil. With great effort, she opened her eyes, squinting in pain from the blinding glare of the morning light bouncing off the windshield. *Windshield?* she thought groggily. *Am I still dreaming?*

Gingerly, she eased her throbbing head out the window of the unfamiliar car. She was sitting in the middle of an empty parking lot. At its edge, next to a deserted highway, stood a tall sign spelling out GAS FOOD LODGING in faded neon.

Before she could put this information into any kind of understandable context, Dane Forrest appeared. Dressed in a rough work shirt and flannel trousers, his dark hair slicked back with nothing but water, he was almost unrecognizable at first.

"Good," he said briskly. "You're awake."

Margo was finding it very difficult to speak. Her tongue felt thick and unwieldy, as though someone had removed it from her mouth and replaced it with a dry sponge. "I . . . I don't feel very well," she managed finally, before falling back against the seat.

Dane gave a little snort of laughter. "It's called a hangover, Margo."

"No." She shook her head, wincing at the resultant thudding of her brain against her skull. "That can't be it. A hangover couldn't possibly be this bad."

"Don't worry. You won't die; you'll just wish you would." Through the open window, he handed her a paper bag containing a roll and a steaming paper cup of coffee. "Here. Breakfast. Eat up. You'll feel better soon."

Margo was suddenly starving. "Where are we?" she asked between bites.

"Just north of Santa Barbara," Dane said offhandedly. "I think it's called the Red Mountain Roadside Motel, but I'm not sure. These places all look the same."

"Santa Barbara!" Margo jerked upright in her seat. "But that's hours away!"

"Really only about two," Dane said calmly. "I was going to explain everything on the way, but you passed out about three seconds after I got you in the car."

"Got me in the car? More like you kidnapped me," Margo snapped, the events of the night before rushing back to her. "I would never have believed you were capable of something so ungentlemanly. And poor Mr. Payne! He must have been worried to death!"

"Margo, cut the crap." Dane spoke in a low voice, his face very close to hers. "This isn't a movie, do you understand?

You don't know Hunter Payne. You don't know what he's capable of."

"And why should I believe you?"

"Because it's the truth."

"Well, that's a first!" Margo shouted. "You've never been honest with me about anything in your life!"

"I know," Dane sighed. "But that's all over now. I'll tell you anything you want to know."

His acquiescence disarmed her. "Why . . . why did you bring me here?"

Dane looked her straight in the eye. "Because I thought it was time for you to finally have some answers. Here." He handed over a parcel wrapped in a length of wrinkled brown paper. "Some clothes," he explained. "I bought them off the innkeeper's wife." Margo unwrapped the package and held up a dress, its calico fabric left faded and thin by numerous washings. It smelled like soap. "Not quite as stylish as you're used to," Dane said, "but it's clean. And believe me, where we're going, you don't want to show up in an evening gown."

As soon as Margo had changed, they pulled out of the parking lot and back onto the open highway past the Santa Ynez Mountains, watching in silence as the craggy hills of Southern California slowly gave way to the verdant lushness of the north. Through the open window, the perfume of flowering trees mingled deliciously with the sharp, salty smell of the sea. She whispered to herself, "It's beautiful."

"Yes." Margo hadn't expected Dane to hear her. "It was important it be someplace beautiful."

At last, they pulled off the highway onto a long country road leading up to a large, Spanish-style mansion tucked away behind a set of elaborate wrought iron gates. A small sign said EDENS GROVE SANATORIUM. A guard opened the gates for them as they approached, and they drove up the gravel driveway to the house, where an older man in a light summer suit awaited them on the stone steps. At his side was a plump, sturdy-looking woman in a nurse's apron and starched white cap.

Dane bounded out of the car, hand outstretched. "Dr. Allenby."

"Mr. Forrest," said the man, shaking Dane's hand warmly. "Always a pleasure."

"Thank you so much for allowing us to come on such short notice."

The doctor nodded cordially. "Of course. Anytime."

"And . . . how are things?" Dane asked. His voice had an anxious edge.

"Oh, I'd say pretty steady," Dr. Allenby replied carefully. "Nothing I'd call a major setback. Still, the progress has been quite a bit slower than I'd like."

"Is there nothing you can do to speed things up?"

The doctor sighed. "Mr. Forrest, it's as I've always said. In a case like this, the healing process is vastly influenced by the patient's mental state. The physical recovery is almost beside the point. She has to *want* to get better."

She. An involuntary shudder jolted through Margo's body. There was only one person in the whole world that "she" could be.

"And does she? How would you characterize her mental state?"

The doctor sighed again. "Let's just say she has her good days and her bad days." He smiled. "Just like anyone, I suppose. But why don't you see for yourself?" He tilted his head at the nurse by his side. "Nurse Morisco will take you."

"Thank you, that's very kind."

"Of course." Dr. Allenby headed back toward the entrance of the house. "I'll be in my office if you have any questions."

"This way, please," said the nurse with a brisk nod. Obediently, Dane and Margo followed her down the steps and around the side of the building. "She's out on the lawn today, getting some fresh air. I'm afraid it was a rather difficult night."

Dane stiffened. "How so?"

The nurse's eyes flickered toward Margo. "She got hold of one of those picture magazines—"

"*What?*" The color drained from Dane's face. "We *specifically* said . . . I mean . . . how could you let this *happen?*"

"It seems one of the younger nurses left it lying around by accident. She's been reprimanded, of course," Nurse Morisco added quickly. "It won't happen again. She's been given a sedative, so she's calm now, although she may seem a little more disoriented than usual. Still, I wouldn't say or do anything that might upset her." The nurse cast a long, meaningful glance in Margo's direction. "You must be Miss Sterling," she said.

"Margo, please."

"Mr. Forrest didn't mention you were coming."

"No." Margo forced out a nervous little chuckle. "Nor to me."

"It's very important that Margo be here," Dane said firmly. "Very important indeed."

Nurse Morisco pressed her lips together in obvious disapproval. "In that case, Mr. Forrest, I suppose you know best."

They were behind the mansion now, walking across an expansive green lawn. They passed a small vegetable garden being

316

carefully tilled by a handful of patients in green gardening aprons. A pair of nurses hovered nearby. A few other patients sat at a small grouping of easels, frowning over their boxes of watercolors with quiet concentration, the deliberative slowness of their movements adding to the feeling of eerie calm. *It's almost like being underwater,* Margo thought.

Nurse Morisco pointed across the lawn to a wicker wheelchair, positioned to face the sea. "That's her. She's been a bit agitated lately, so please try to keep your voices and your movements very calm. I'll be right over here if you need me."

Dane gave Margo's hand a squeeze. "Ready?"

She squeezed his in return. "As ready as I'll ever be."

And calmly—*very* calmly—they walked across the lawn to meet Diana Chesterfield.

TWENTY-EIGHT

Dane knelt on the grass in front of the motionless figure in the wheelchair, leaning forward to press a gentle kiss against her forehead. "My darling. How are you?"

Peering into the face of her idol for the first time, Margo felt a strange chill. It wasn't just because of the wheelchair, or the unsettling silence of their surrounding—although in all the years she had imagined meeting Diana, it had never been in circumstances quite like this. *There's something missing,* Margo thought.

She was suddenly reminded of a Shirley Temple doll Doris used to have. With its deep dimples, bouncy yellow ringlets, and adorably chubby cheeks, it was a perfect replica of the beloved child star, and yet there was something about the doll's blank, unmoving stare that Margo had always found deeply creepy.

That's how Diana looks, Margo thought. All the right features were there—the slanted blue eyes, the famous Chesterfield cheekbones—but something essential seemed to have
been drained out of them. Sitting stiffly in the chair, staring
glassily ahead, she looked like a doll. *A Diana Chesterfield doll.*

She was wearing a dressing gown of apricot silk over a set of
blue Mandarin pajamas, the frog clasp left open at the throat.
A pair of sunglasses was lying neglected in her lap, one of the
earpieces splayed open crookedly, like a broken wing. Her voice
was as strangely hollow as her expression as she slowly lifted a
hand to point at Margo. "Is this the new stand-in?"

"No, darling, this is Margo. Go on." He gave Margo a nudge.
"Say hello."

Margo took a step toward Diana, reflexively dropping into a
little half curtsey. She felt like a fool, but it seemed as if some
kind of subservient gesture was expected. "I'm so happy to meet
you," she said. "Dane has told me so much about you."

"She's much too tall, Ernie," Diana said. "They'll never get
the angles right."

Ernie? Margo thought, glancing back at Dane. *Does she even
know who he is?*

Dane, however, seemed unconcerned at being called the
wrong name. "No, darling, I told you. Margo isn't the stand-in.
She's my friend."

She was still staring at Margo with that same glassy gaze.
"And you're going to bed with her."

"Diana, please," Dane said firmly. "Be a good girl."

"I don't mind, you know." Her eyes were awash with tears. It
was the first hint of emotion she had shown since she'd laid
eyes on them, and its transformative effect was startling. *There*

319

she is, Margo thought. A melancholy goddess, gazing luminously up at Dane, exactly as she had done in picture after picture. "I never mind. I just want my darling to be happy."

"Then get well," Dane said quietly. "And come home. That would make me happy."

Diana let out a staccato cackle, her eyes glazing over as the color left her face. She was once again an empty shell. "They haven't sent me my script yet, you know."

Dane sighed. "I know."

"Well, can't you see that they do? How on earth am I supposed to prepare if I can't see my lines? They'll be terribly cross with me, and that won't do. Not at this stage." Diana twisted the silk sash of her robe worriedly around her fingers. "It must have been stolen." She pointed at Margo again. "*She* stole it, didn't she?"

Gently, Dane folded his hand over her accusatory finger. "No, darling, you're mistaken. Margo didn't steal anything."

"*Stop lying!*" Diana shrieked. "Don't *lie!*"

Nurse Morisco swooped to her side, grabbing Diana's flailing hands in her own. "Now, now, honey," said the nurse, holding Diana's arms firmly down against the chair. "This lady doesn't have anything of yours. Do you understand? This lady is Mr. Forrest's friend, and you must be kind to her, or he won't be able to come and see you anymore. Do you understand?" Diana shook her head. The nurse grabbed her chin and stared directly into her eyes with calm but undeniable force. "Do you understand?"

Diana inclined her head in the tiniest of nods. "Good." Nurse Morisco turned to Dane and Margo. "I'm afraid she's tired. I'd better take her back to her room."

"Of course," Dane said. "Whatever you think is best." He knelt before the wheelchair once again, gazing up into Diana's face. With his hair mussed, he looked like a small boy at his mother's feet. "I'll come back and see you as soon as I can, I promise."

"It's so bright, Ernie," Diana replied. "Can't you tell them to turn down the lights?"

Dane picked up her sunglasses, which had fallen from her lap onto the grass. He turned them over in his hands, examining them as though they were some strange artifact from a distant land, before he carefully placed them over her eyes.

"Thank you, Ernie." Diana smiled. "You always know how to fix everything."

With a brisk nod of farewell, Nurse Morisco wheeled her patient toward the house. Dane watched them until they had turned the corner, then rose to his feet and stood with his back to Margo, facing the sea.

Margo watched the gentle rise and fall of his shuddering shoulders with a kind of anguished awe. She had never seen a grown man cry before. She longed to comfort him, but it seemed somehow like a terrible intrusion. Like making love in another woman's bed.

Awkwardly, she reached into the pocket of the faded calico dress, eager for something to do with her hands, and felt something soft. It was a square of white cloth, clean and folded and smelling of lavender.

A handkerchief. Margo smiled. *Just like he's always given me.*

Silently, she held it out to him. They stood for a long time, and when at last his shoulders stopped trembling, she brushed his arm, just so he'd know she was there.

Absently, he reached for her hand. "She was pregnant, you know."

"Oh." What else could she possibly say? "I see."

"She couldn't have it. The studio wouldn't let her. She was at the height of her career, in the middle of her busiest year yet. And what's more, she was unmarried. Every contract player at Olympus, no matter how big or small, has a strict morality clause in their contract. Standard policy. Ever since the Hays Code went into effect."

Margo nodded. The office of Will Hays, the president of the Motion Picture Association of America, acted as Hollywood's all-powerful, if self-appointed, censor, policing every picture a studio released for any hint of what it deemed "immoral" content, a monitoring that all too often carried over into the public—and sometimes private—lives of its stars. "I know. It's something Mr. Karp is very keen on pointing out."

Dane gave a rueful laugh. "They're almost never enforced, of course. I mean, no adultery, premarital sex, excessive drinking, homosexuality . . ." He shook his head. "There wouldn't be an actor still working in Hollywood. Mostly, the studios just use them to intimidate people into doing as they're told. But for a star to have a child out of wedlock . . . well, that's different. Much harder to hide. And if it ever got out, there wouldn't be a theater in America willing to show her pictures. Her career would be over for good."

"That's horrible," Margo said.

"It's just how it is." Dane gave his eyes a final, matter-of-fact wipe. "And look, she's hardly the first actress to find herself in that kind of trouble. There are ways to handle it. Nobody's going to buy the old this-here-baby-I-just-happened-to-adopt story anymore, not after that stunt Loretta Young pulled with Gable. But there's a clinic just south of Santa Barbara, not too far from here. Safe, discreet, expensive. The sensible girls go up there on a Friday and make a weekend of it." He smiled sadly. "But Diana never was a particularly sensible girl."

"You mean she wanted to have it?" Margo asked, wide-eyed.

Dane shook his head. "I don't know. I don't know what she wanted. I'd been away on location for a few days. We were supposed to have dinner the night I came back. I went over to the house to pick her up and found her lying in a pool of blood at the bottom of the stairs." A choke of a sob crept back into Dane's throat. "I still don't know what happened. I don't know if she fell, or if she did it on purpose . . . if she was trying to get rid of it herself, or even . . ." He shook his head again, as if to defend against the horrible thought.

"So what did you do?" Margo asked.

"What do you think I did? I called Larry Julius. He was on the scene in five minutes flat. Private ambulance and everything. After all, we couldn't run the risk of information this juicy falling into the hands of the wrong paramedic." He barked out a bitter laugh.

"Oh, Dane." She didn't know what else to say.

"I didn't know she was pregnant until they told me at the hospital. She lost the baby, obviously. Fractured her ankle and one of her wrists." Dane sighed. "But the real problem was with her head."

"You don't mean . . . brain damage?"

"Nothing that wasn't damaged already. The first few days in the hospital, she wouldn't speak. And then when she started talking, she couldn't stop. Raving for hours about people who were out to get her, seeing things that weren't there. She was convinced the studio had put some kind of radio in her head so they could listen in on her conversations, maybe even read her mind. Don't think I didn't see a little lightbulb go on over Larry Julius's head when she came out with that one."

"The doctor called it a full psychotic break," Dane continued, "so we brought her up here. And since then, it's been pretty much the same. Sometimes she seems fine, other times . . . well . . ." He shook his head. "I'm glad today wasn't one of those times."

"You mean today was a *good* day?"

"Today was a happy medium."

Margo shut her eyes, struggling to take in everything Dane had just said. "But I still don't understand," she said. "Why all the secrecy? Why not just tell the press the truth from the beginning?"

"The press? Are you *serious?*"

"Well, not the whole truth, obviously," Margo amended. "But why not say Diana's recuperating from an accident, that she's not well—"

"Because *The Nine Days' Queen* was already in production!" Dane shouted. "Because the studio had two million dollars riding on her snapping out of it. And in the beginning, we all thought she might. Later, when it became clear that wasn't going to happen . . ." He looked over his shoulder, at the empty spot on the grass where Diana had sat. "That's when Larry Julius had the idea to gin up the mystery angle."

"But why?"

Dane gave her a sorrowful smile. "Because he found you, Margo."

"*Me?*"

"Diana's replacement. If he could keep up the public's interest in Diana, he could keep interest going in you. Either you became a moneymaking property in your own right, or the stage is set for Diana's magnificent comeback, the likes of which has not been seen since the resurrection of Christ. He could save the movie. He could protect the studio."

Diana's replacement. So it was true. She heard Leo Karp's voice in her head: "If Diana were here, what would we do with you?" Diana Chesterfield had been her idol, her inspiration, the woman she had dreamed of becoming one day. Well, that day was here. And the woman she'd adored was the one who could take it all away. Should Diana recover, they would never be the glamorous best friends of Margo's girlish daydreams, shopping and going on double dates and having glitzy adventures all around town. *They'd make us destroy each other,* Margo thought, *or be destroyed.*

Dane was staring bleakly out at the ocean. "If only she'd *told* me," he said. "If only I'd known. I could have helped her. I would have done anything for her. I would have talked to the studio, given her money, *anything. . . .*"

"Why didn't you *marry* her?" It was crazy to be furious at the man she'd been pining over for months for failing to make an honest woman of her greatest rival, but her rage on Diana's behalf, at the terrible turn of fortune that had bound their fates together, knew no bounds.

"Marry her?" Dane looked as though she had just placed a loaded gun against his temple. "*Marry her?*"

"It would have been the decent thing to do," Margo insisted. "The *right* thing. It would have fixed everything. She could have had the baby; you could have gone on with your lives—"

"It wasn't my baby."

"She could have—" Margo stopped midsentence, looking at Dane with her mouth agape. "What? What did you say?"

"It wasn't my baby. And I couldn't marry Diana, even if, God help me, I wanted to." Dane began to laugh, a horrible, anguished laugh that racked his body. "You see, Margo, Diana Chesterfield was never my lover. Diana Chesterfield is my *sister*."

TWENTY-NINE

Margo felt her legs give way. The ground came up to meet her, and she gripped the grass tightly with both hands, as though it were the last thing tethering her to the earth. "Your sister," she repeated dully. "Diana Chesterfield is your sister."

Dane nodded grimly. His face was deathly pale. "Yes."

"But you were in love." Margo felt a balloon expanding rapidly inside her chest. "You were her . . . her . . ." The balloon popped. "Who *are you*?"

"Margo, let me explain."

"What kind of sick, *twisted*—"

"Margo, please! You can't scream here!"

A flock of nurses were already barreling toward them, white-aproned and ready for action. Dane caught her hand tightly before she had a chance to protest, and together they walked quickly to the farthest end of the lawn, where a grove of trees surrounded a small artificial brook. Beside the brook was a limestone bench with a well-worn seat.

"Sit down," Dane said.

"No, thank you."

"Please." Dane's eyes were clear and sad. "The story you're about to hear is extremely difficult for me to tell. When I have finished, you will be one of only three people in the world who knows it, and one of them is currently babbling in the loony bin. And so I would appreciate it if you would stop looking at me like I'm some kind of monster."

His hands were shaking. *He's terrified*, Margo thought. No matter who Dane was, or what he had done, her heart went out to him.

"I'm listening," she said quietly.

Dane took a deep, ragged breath. "You know, I've imagined telling you this story many times. Now that you're here, I don't even know where to start."

"Why don't you start at the beginning?"

"Fair enough." He took another deep breath. "I don't know if I ever told you this, but I was born on a farm."

"So was Diana," Margo said. "Owen told me at the stables."

"Well, that would make sense, wouldn't it?" Dane said drily. "Our father was a small-time farmer. My mother was a mail-order bride, of sorts. Came from Sweden with her parents when she was a kid, wound up in Missouri. Her parents died of diphtheria, and she couldn't pay the taxes on their farm, so she answered an ad my father placed in the *Kansas City Star*." He smiled. "She looked just like Diana. When she sent my father her picture, he could hardly believe his luck."

Margo smiled. "Did she tell you that?"

"She never told me anything. The old lady who came over from the neighboring farm to deliver me forgot to wash her hands first. Childbed fever, they called it. My mother was dead within the week."

"Oh, Dane. How awful." It was a ludicrously inadequate choice of words.

"Diana—her name was Dinah then—was four. But from that moment on, I was her baby, and she was my second mother."

"And your father?"

"My father went from being a man who liked his liquor to being the town drunk. At least, that's what Diana said; I never knew him any different. It was Prohibition, so he brewed his own whiskey from his corn. Drank his own crop, and then some. The farm had been in the family since the Homestead Act. Then poof, it was gone." Dane flashed a bitter grin. "We beat the foreclosures of 'twenty-nine by at least five years. The Cudahys were always pioneers."

"Cudahy?"

"The family name," Dane said. "You are speaking to Ernest Woodrow Cudahy, originally of Hillsboro, Kansas."

Ernie, Margo thought suddenly. "Diana called you Ernie."

"Always. She was never crazy about the name Dane. She thought it sounded too made-up, too fake. Do you?"

Margo shrugged. "I don't know. I guess I'm used to it now."

"I'd be careful about that if I were you," Dane said darkly. "A person can get awfully used to fake things around here. Anyway," he continued, "after the farm debacle, Pa thought we might see how things treated us out west."

"And you wound up in Los Angeles," Margo finished.

"Right. We stayed in rented accommodations—and by that,

I mean it was a flophouse. The drunks across the way gave Diana such a hard time she was afraid to go to sleep. She found work from time to time cleaning houses, and I would go along with her, and knock on all the doors in the neighborhood until we found someone who would give me a couple of dimes to do some little odd job. But any money we earned, Pa would drink right up. So eventually, we just started to spend it on ourselves. We'd go to the movies, or spend a whole day's wages on candy. Once Diana got a seventy-five-cent tip from a house she was cleaning and she spent it all on a single lipstick. I can still see it. It came in a beautiful gold case with a little mirror inside. The way she carried on when she brought it home, you'd have thought it was a rope of diamonds." He smiled at the memory.

"Anyway, we'd been out here for almost a year when Pa disappeared. Went out to the bar one night and never came back. A week later a man from the city morgue showed up to ask if we could come identify his body."

"You must have been devastated."

"You know, it was almost a relief. It was just the two of us then, the way it should have been, with no one to get in our way. It certainly changed things for Diana. She was seventeen, and she was so beautiful." Dane looked off into the distance, as though the young Diana had just materialized before him. "There was a woman named Olive Moore . . ."

Olive Moore. The name sounded strangely familiar, as if Margo had heard it in a dream. "Who is Olive Moore?"

"Someone Diana once knew. It doesn't matter," Dane said. "The point is that there's always a way for a beautiful girl to make money in Hollywood. Eventually, she heard through the grapevine about a job as a singer at a nightclub on the Sunset

330

Strip, and from there, an Olympus scout saw her and brought her in for a screen test. They signed her up as a contract player, twenty dollars a week. To us, it might as well have been a million. And after she'd built up a bit of a reputation with a few small roles, she figured this picture business was such a cinch, even her useless baby brother might as well get in on the racket." He shook his head. "Somehow, she got me a screen test, although she didn't tell anyone I was her brother; she wanted them to think she was recommending me on talent."

"And no one suspected?"

"Why should they? Nobody knew us. She'd changed her name by then. She's so fair, like our mother. I'm dark, like Pa. I'm younger, of course, but I was always big, so we look about the same age. She tested with me. Some early version of that same scene you and I did."

"Lord Gregory—"

"And good old Lady Olivia." He sighed. "We had a good laugh about it afterward, having to play this ridiculous love scene. But obviously, I hoped for the best. Ha. Be careful what you wish for . . ."

"Because you just might get it," Margo finished.

"The unofficial motto of this town," Dane said. "Next thing you know, we're in Leo Karp's office, where he tells us he wants me to star opposite Diana in her new picture."

"*An Affair of the Heart.*" It was one of Margo's favorite films. She and Doris had seen it four times in the theater.

"'Just look at you two!'" Dane imitated Mr. Karp's gushing tone. "'So natural together! Like you've known each other all your lives!'" He shook his head in disgust. "If ever there was a time to come clean, that was it. But I don't have to tell you

331

how persuasive Leo Karp can be." He gave Margo a meaningful look. "Besides, we figured he'd kick us both to the curb. And after where we'd come from, what we'd been through . . . Never be poor, Margo. Poverty does terrible things to you. You'll do anything, literally *anything*, not to go back."

He shook his head sadly. "Diana was awfully clever about it, though. Whenever there was a love scene in the script—and believe me, when we first started shooting, there were a lot of them—Diana would say to the director, 'Darling, wouldn't it be so much sexier if we just leave it all to the imagination?' The Hays Office never had a stauncher advocate than my sister on that picture." Dane laughed. "It was a box-office smash. Diana was nominated for an Academy Award."

"America's Most Stylish Sweethearts," Margo said, quoting the caption from the *Picture Palace* cover that had graced her bedroom wall a lifetime ago.

"You got it. We were contracted for three more pictures together. A screwball comedy, a musical, and a historical epic. All romances." Dane looked stricken. "But Diana was making three thousand dollars a week and I was making close to that. Three thousand dollars a week. Three times as much as our father had ever made in a year.

"We might have been able to deal with it, if it hadn't been for Larry Julius and the press office. Remember, none of them knew the truth. Diana and I were costars, we were always out together, so why shouldn't we be having a torrid romance? So now, not only were we supposed to act like lovers on-screen, we were supposed to keep it up offscreen as well. The box office went through the roof. Diana bought a mansion in the

Hollywood Hills. I bought a stable full of horses and a garage full of cars. I had everything I'd ever dreamed of. And all I had to do was spend my life pretending to be passionately in love with my own sister. Can you believe it?"

Margo winced. The whole thing was so craven, so cynical, and yet, after everything she'd learned of Hollywood, of the charade she'd been ordered to act out with Jimmy, so *plausible.* "Every word."

"I suggested staging an elaborate breakup. Letting a photographer catch me coming out of a hotel with another girl. But Diana was no dummy. The studio had invested millions of dollars in marketing us lovebirds to the unwashed masses. If she was ever going to break out of the gilded cage, it was going to have to be on the wing of someone not even Leo Karp would dare to question."

"Hunter Payne," Margo whispered.

"Things got serious fast," Dane said. "Diana came to see me just a few days before . . . before she was hurt. Her eyes were shining; she was dancing around the living room like a little kid. 'He's going to marry me, Ernie,' she kept saying. 'He *has* to.' I didn't realize it at the time, I was so stupid. But it was because she was pregnant."

"Then what went wrong?"

"He's already married," Dane said flatly. "It wasn't like Diana to be so naïve, but desperate people believe what they want to believe. All I know is when I went back to her house to pack up some of her things, I found two telegrams from New York. The first was dated just two days before the accident."

"And what did it say?"

"'Get rid of it.'"

Margo felt the color drain from her face. "No," she whispered.

Dane's face was hard. "He's succinct, you have to give him that."

"And the second telegram?" Margo whispered.

"Even shorter: 'Or else.' It was wrapped around a money order for a thousand dollars."

"And you think that was the last straw?" Margo asked.

Dane nodded. "Diana could deal with a man being callous, even cruel. But to enclose payment, as if for . . . *services rendered*"—he spat the words hatefully—"would have been too much to bear. It would have brought back a lot of painful memories, of a time when there was nothing she wouldn't do for money. And it would have seemed to her that nothing had really changed. That no matter where she lived or what car she drove or what kind of clothes she wore, to a man like Hunter Payne she still was nothing but a little whore. She should have killed him."

"But instead, she tried to kill herself."

Dane turned to her. His gaze was so intense Margo nearly looked away, but she forced herself to meet his eyes steadily. "So now you know. And believe me, I won't blame you if you decide you want nothing more to do with me. But at least you know why I went so crazy when I saw you with Hunter Payne."

"Because of what he did to Diana."

"Because he doesn't deserve you," Dane said simply. "Because you're different, Margo. You don't have that emptiness at your core, that terrible need that eats away at you until there's nothing left. I had it. Diana has it. Everybody in this whole damn town has it. But not you. You don't need anything. You're a

334

whole person, Margo. A *real* person." He looked up at her, with a gaze that pierced her heart. "And I couldn't bear the thought of lying to you anymore."

Margo's heart was pounding. She felt as though a dam inside her had burst. "You're wrong," she whispered. "I need things."

"You do?" Dane was very close to her now. "What do you need?"

Margo closed her eyes. There were so many ways to respond to that question, so many answers that would all be equally true.

But for now, Margo Sterling gave Dane Forrest the only one she knew he wanted to hear.

"You."

THIRTY

It was one of those nights in Hollywood, the kind that made gossip columnists and newspapermen and the announcers on newsreels say, "It was one of those nights in Hollywood."

Searchlights combed the sky. Camera flashbulbs popped. The marquee of Grauman's Chinese Theater was ablaze with light.

And up the crimson carpet paraded Hollywood's brightest stars.

Clark Gable. Carole Lombard. Joan Crawford and Bette Davis, ignoring each other, as usual. Spencer Tracy. Olivia de Havilland, gazing adoringly at Errol Flynn. Gabby Preston in white, beaming on the arm of Jimmy Molloy. Amanda Farraday close behind them, pale and wraithlike in darkest black. John Barrymore, a little unsteady on his feet. Marlene Dietrich in top hat and tails.

Roaring with excitement at every new arrival, the teeming crowd basked in the reflected glow of the blazing marquee:

MARGO STERLING DANE FORREST
IN
THE NINE DAYS' QUEEN

"What do you think, duchess?" Larry Julius asked as the gleaming limousine pulled up to the curb. He reached across the leather seat of the limousine to give her knee a squeeze. "Ready to face the lions?"

She'd been speaking to journalists since the crack of dawn. Rex Mandalay himself had seen to her hair and sewn her into her gown. Congratulatory flowers practically buried the new silk brocade living room set in the bungalow. There were so many telegrams from well-wishers and social climbers littering the front step that she'd almost missed the funny little envelope at the bottom of the stack.

It had no return address, no name, instead marked with a single initial, written in a swooping, unfamiliar hand:

$$\mathcal{M}.$$

There was no note, no hint of explanation. The envelope contained a single thing, a tiny miracle. Returned to her as if by magic.

Her little pearl pin.

Just who had hunted it down on that Pasadena lawn, who had seen to it that the pin was delivered to her today of all days, she couldn't begin to guess. All she knew was that it was clearly someone who cared about Margaret Frobisher very much.

She was wearing it now, pinned inside her dress. No one but her would know it was there, pressing against her heart.

"Are you ready, duchess?" Larry repeated.

She peered out the window at the scene before her. Her name, blazing in lights. Dane Forrest, poised in front of the huge carved doors like a groom awaiting his bride. The sea of anxious faces staring hungrily at the car, wanting to look at her, to touch her, to see if she was made of flesh and blood like them. If she was truly real. She narrowed her eyes, and for a moment, she almost thought she saw the blurry shapes of two young girls, rapt with need and wonder, forcing their way through the crowd.

"Yes, Larry. I'm ready." Her sphinxlike smile was vague and benevolent and not quite of this world. It was the smile of a star.

Larry Julius nodded to Arthur. "All right. This is it." The chauffeur opened the car door.

And Margo Sterling emerged into a blaze of light.

ACKNOWLEDGMENTS

This might be the best chance I'll ever have to quote the opening lines of the Academy Award acceptance speech I've been practicing since I was a child: "What a surprise! I really wasn't expecting this. I don't even have a speech prepared. And there are so many people to thank! I hope I won't leave anyone out!"

Thank you for indulging me. But there really are so many people to thank, and I really do hope I don't leave anyone out. First among equals (of which she has few) is my beloved agent and dear friend Rebecca Friedman, without whom none of this would have happened. And by "this," I mean everything. Gratitude beyond gratitude to my brilliant editor, Wendy Loggia, whose wisdom, insight, skill, and patience are truly wondrous to behold. And thanks to everybody at Delacorte Press, especially the lovely Krista Vitola.

Out in the movie colony, enormous thanks to Shari Smiley, Elizabeth Newman, Kerry Foster, and the incredible Alex Block, who is more than just one of the good guys—he's an inspiration. Thanks to my L.A. families, both biological and spiritual: Lauren Marks, Suzanne Marks, Tony Nino, Michael Nino, Ariel Shukert, and Jeff Wienir. Thanks to all the usual New York cast and crew, who know who they are, and to my parents, Marty and Aveva Shukert, who throughout my childhood never suggested that there were better ways to spend my time than staying up all night watching old movies—for example, sleeping.

And most of all, thanks to Ben Abramowitz, my favorite leading man.

ABOUT THE AUTHOR

Rachel Shukert is the author of *Everything Is Going to Be Great* and *Have You No Shame?* She has been fascinated by the Golden Age of Hollywood since she was a girl, when she used to stay up all night watching old movies and fall asleep the next day at school. Rachel grew up in Omaha, Nebraska, and graduated from New York University. She lives in New York City with her husband. Visit her at rachelshukert.com.